The Tears and Fears

of a

Childhood

A Novel- Based on a True Story

Written By **K. Belle Draper**

Library of Congress Cataloging-In-Publication Data
2004-092101
Draper, K. Belle
The Tears and Fears of a Childhood

ISBN 0-9752904-0-1

1. Authorship   2. Memoirs   3. Title

I am dedicating this book to my son, Robert Beney, who is one of the greatest sons who ever lived and a miracle in my life. I am so proud of his accomplishments and abilities. I regret that I did not have the 'blueprint' on childrearing, but I did better than my best. I would also like to dedicate this book to a very special person, Al Jessup who may have never known the impact he made on my life, but I am here today to let him know, I have never forgotten. His going beyond and getting involved gave someone life and a hope for a brighter tomorrow. He dared to take the risk, even when the odds were against him. You changed a life and made a difference. To my Canadian friend Marg Anderson, who kept the faith for me through life's journeys. Finally yet importantly, I would like to dedicate this book to Carrie and Lewis Lightbody, for your encouragement, your prayers and a friendship built on real love.

Copyright © 2003 by K. Belle Draper –Printed and bound in the United Stated of America. All rights reserved. No part of this book may be reproduced or transmitted in any form or by any means, electronic or mechanical including information storage and retrieval systems, or by photocopying, or recording without permission in writing from the author.
Published by Belle Enterprises – Pekin Illinois 61554
Printed by Capitol Impressions – Pekin, Illinois 61554
For ordering information Contact: *Belle Enterprises*
(309) 353-4768   *1011 Washington Street*
bellentrprzs@bitwisesystems.com   *Pekin, Illinois 61554*

Table of Contents

1	The Obscure Transgression	5
2	The Golden Oracle	9
3	Loves Remnant Lost	13
4	Forgotten Witness	25
5	The Rape of Dignity	33
6	Fugitives Journey	43
7	Temporary Refuge	57
8	At Hell's Gates	69
9	Nature's Blessing, Life's Torment	79
10	Torture and Affliction	86
11	Parental Slave Masters	92
12	Hidden Secret	104
13	Stay Away From Daddy	114
14	Your Highness, Queen Drusilla	128
15	Good Ol' Brutus	139
16	Traffic Court for Bonnie and Clyde	149

17	Nothing to Celebrate	164
18	The Uncommitted Detective	179
19	A Friend and A Gift	199
20	First Kiss	210
21	The Sting of a Lost Virtue	229
22	Winner of Her Trust	250
23	Escape to Freedom	262

1
Obscure Transgression

The leaves have weeks been gone, and the darkness of the sky reveals that winter is pushing its way toward Pekin, Illinois. The last V-shaped flights of the great Canadian Geese have left for the southern most States early this morning, as nature beckons them on into migration. There is a deafening silence. Nature prepares itself for the treacherous winter months ahead. The songbirds have left and the bright colors of the Midwest United States horticulturistic plumage is gracefully put to sleep, so that it might survive the flurry of the season's icy temperatures.

This same time of year, forty-six years ago, a child was born. She was second in line, another little girl, born December 2nd, 1957, in a city not far from Waukesha Wisconsin. The birth of another female child had not been wished for nor wanted, especially when it proved to be that this female child was not the anticipated male child, that would be born to attempt to cure the hellish marital relationship of a couple who had gotten married to "quick fix" an unplanned first pregnancy. Unsuccessful attempts at aborting the second pregnancy had failed. Stool softeners taken in excess were not the perfect answer to "getting rid of it" procedures.

Therefore, with the birth of this unwanted child, who of course would carry the weight of a failed marriage for what seemed a lifetime, came more darkness than even nature in the worst of storms could inflict. This little girl's mom had gotten herself pregnant the first time, by who really knows whom, she could be "his", though her features do not really reveal him. The first child had olive skin and dark curly hair. The dark eyes and facial features resembled her mom, but there was not much that resembled the man who took her, and her mother into his life and into his heart.

Her daddy was a tall handsome man, with features that could melt any woman to her knees. His smile was kind and reassuring and radiated to the female internal urges. The sparkle in his eyes enchanted the female retinue. No one could say "no" to him. Her daddy was a traveling salesman. Successful in trade, a failure in family measures by generative repercussion. The chauvinism charmed the weakest of sexes, and tantalized his competition.

The little girl's mother was running from a life of abuse, and her pregnancy would achieve its directive in freeing her from her incestuous family environment, placing her in the middle of one that was immature and neglectful. She was only sixteen, physically attractive and very much aware of her physical drives. She could intrigue the male gender from all age groups, in their latent sexual desires. "Love" to her meant the embrace and fatal attraction of sexual advancement. "Love" to her, was hearing of her own beauty from men who could satisfy their own interests at the expense of her confusion. 'Love' meant being needed by so many, a drive that did not let being now married, to a traveling salesman, keep her down.

The long lonely hours, tossed into a life as a homemaker and now, mother of two little girls, with a husband out on the road all the time was not the life she had dreamed it would be. This reality was not at all, what she had planned on when she left her childhood home. Her first-born daughter brought back the memories of what used to be, and the birth of her second daughter revealed the reality of what was now. In her mind, "before" had been better, living on the edge. The "now" was torture, as life's fantasies faded when reality stepped in. With her husband gone for days to weeks at a time, there was no one to tell her how beautiful she was. Responsibility replaced the "dating" games. Demands from two infants barely fourteen months apart, seemed more than her eighteen years of immaturity could take.

She knew that she could not turn to her own mixed up family for help, and she also knew that her husband's mother loathed her for "tricking her son into marrying her", or so seemed the opinion of her mother-in-law. Life on the other side became an unwanted burden. All she could do was reach out to the baby who came from the "before" time, and rock herself slowly into a deeper double post-partum depression.

The days her husband was home became the good times, though she could feel that "things were distant between them" even then. Times came when he'd go off for days on end, and she would not even get out of bed, except to put a dirty bottle of milk down in the crib of her second born, and pick up her first born, rocking her in her depressed embrace.

The little girl, who was second born, lived alone in her own world, waiting for the day when her daddy would be home. He would always pick her up in his strong embrace, and would spend precious moments with her when he came home. Even though unwanted at first, her daddy grew to cherish his time with her. She found laughter even in the stench of unchanged diapers, and filthy bed sheets in her crib, when her daddy was away. Daddy would clean her up, hold her and take her and her sister to grandma's home from time to time when he did venture home. Her mommy would attack the joy that her daddy gave her, when he was gone. "Her daddy loved her more than mommy", or so she was told. The more her daddy loved her, the more her mommy rejected her. It was a lot for a young child to understand. These were emotional words that came from a young woman, a mother of two, who was feeling very neglected by her husband.

Twenty months after her birth, the son "that daddy always wanted" was born. Her mommy sure, this would make her husband happy so he would spend more time at home with them. Wishful thinking takes wishful planning, but even with the greatest of plans, there seems to be a hole that drops out from the bottom of the best-laid plans. Unfortunately, this plan turned out to be no different. Daddy stayed home for a few more days, but eventually found the urge to go bury himself into his career once more. His career provided him an escape from the woman he married, and the responsibilities of being a full time father to now, three children. He did not have a great father figure in his 'growing up' years, and the present realities of his choices in life were overwhelming to him. His only way of dealing with reality was to run from it, as he did when he left his family home. Life was repeating itself all over again. His way to deal with it was to run from it, leaving his wife and children behind.

Between the increased post-partum depression, and her husbands' abandonment, leaving her stuck to care for the three children by herself, the little girls' mom went off the deep end. The messy house, three crying babies, dishes undone, her husband gone, and a whole lot of inexperience without so much as a helping and nurturing hand to guide her, she up and left home. Could anyone blame her? They did.

Three days after her departure, she decided to call "home." No answer. She called her mother-in-law's house. She found that her husband had not come home on the day she left, and told her mother-in-law "the children were by themselves and that she couldn't take it anymore." When asked, "Where she was?" The little girls' mommy hung up.

Grandma arrived to rescue her grandbabies. They were crying, the fridge was open; milk puddles on the floor, because the eldest little girl had attempted to play the roll her mommy once played. She wanted to take care of her brother and sister, by filling up the bottles and trying to feed them. She was only three and a half years old, almost four when her mommy left. Diapers were lying on the floor, dirtied by hours of neglect. Evidence of feeble attempts to put clean diapers on her siblings had failed. Both children were naked, hungry and afraid.

Grandma tried to hold back the tears, as she now surveyed her surroundings, repeatedly asking herself "where had she gone wrong?" "How could this happen?" "Where was her son?" There were no clean diapers or clothes for the children. The house in such disarray, made finding anything very difficult. Grandma was beside herself, she figured she needed to call in some help. She dialed her eldest daughter's telephone number.

The children's Aunt Darlene stood at the door of the apartment in disbelief when she arrived to help their grandmother. Words could not describe the predicament that now faced them. Here were her baby nieces and nephew, alone in a filthy home, with nothing to eat, without clean clothes and diapers, and without a parent to care for them. She too, wanted to join in with the crying children, but decided that the sooner they got the children out into safe, clean and loving surroundings, the better.

Diligently, both Grandma and Aunt Darlene worked together, each knowing what to do without exchanging a word between them. The stench and mess made them sick to their stomachs, but determination undermined the circumstances, and before long, each headed out the door carrying one child in an arm and a 'shared' child between them.

Once home at grandma's house, there were warm bubbly baths for the three children. Their dirty clothes were laundered with loving care and hung out to dry in the sunlight. Each child fed, the youngest fell fast asleep in Aunt Darlene's arms, while the second female child fell fast asleep in her grandma's arms. The eldest fell asleep at grandma's feet, waiting her turn for grandma's lap. The deep breathing of sleepy contentment filled the air. The last three days had been stressful and frightening for them. Grandma knew that there would be 'things she had to do.'

2

The Golden Oracle

Declared unto you this day: "The best interests and the well-being of the three minor children; Crystal Arial Joyce, Angela Belle Joyce, and Christopher Cheften Joyce, will be best met by the paternal grandmother, Nancy Ezra Joyce." "Supervised visitation is awarded to both parents, as arranged by the paternal grandmother of the children, and this court and the State of Wisconsin.

The children's grandmother, Nancy, was a very busy woman. She ran a gas station not too far from Waukesha Wisconsin, all the while trying to meet the needs of her newly acquired family and the needs of her customers. Relaxation was foreign to her vocabulary in life's day-to-day existence. Life had dealt her some pretty tough blows, but nothing as she said was "worth crying over spilt milk for." Life was tough, but not as tough as she was. Nancy would never let things get her down, instead, the more that came her way, the tougher she got. She was a survivor! She could have run for Mayor, but the days of yesteryear suppressed the feminine existence. Her time schedule for what already got placed upon her plate in life, kept the drive to casual conversation in and outside the walls of her homestead. Rebuttal filled the air when guests came to call. All said and done, they all knew that "grandma was right." "There's no changing a mind that is already made up." Most would succumb to her opinions and walk away. If not Mayor, perhaps she should have been a lawyer. Then again, women were not lawyers in them days. Nancy was not going to let life run her over. She had guts, more guts than many men she knew. She would do her best not to let circumstance stand in her way.

Grandma Nancy was a woman, left twice, by two different men, with children still at her skirt-tails. They up and disappeared leaving her to raise the children by herself. The second husband not only left her with an additional two children, but with a business to run. The filling (gas) station and garage came with all its responsibilities, and in them days, service was service. The filling station personnel pumped your gas, wiped your windshields and checked your oil. For all her hard work, the government stepped in and took the business out from under her a few years later, stating that "back taxes" had not been paid. She had paid what she owed during the time she ran the business, but somehow they had backtracked to the time when her husband ran it, and "forgot" to pay them. The children's grandmother believed to her dying day, that if she had not turned the business into a moneymaking business when her second husband left, the government would have never taken it away. She may have had to pay the back taxes, but she would have still had the business.

Being a woman in her times, there was no business grace. The feminine intelligence back then, rated pretty low in the eyes of the officials (male) who ran the government at that time. They knew she could not afford to pay all of the back taxes being demanded of her, and timing was everything at this point. It was their word against hers, and like Grandma said, "You need an army to take on a bunch of ruthless men in politics." Like vultures upon a little defenseless animal, and quite vulnerable on an open prairie, in which the dust storms in life had blown away all the brush that once was its hiding place, they moved in and sold the business right out from under her.

A woman could go into factories and provide for her family during the wars, while their men were on the front lines, but God help them if they owned a business during times of peace to provide for the same. Women would labor like men in the factories and then come home and do it all again, cooking and cleaning, while their men laid around the house, relaxing from a 'hard days work'. A woman could raise children while holding down a business when the wayward husband would take off, leaving not even as much as a simple goodbye. Yet they believed that a woman did not have what it took to stand for what she believed in, she would be thought a fool if she tried to stand up for what she believed in. Nor were women considered credit worthy, despite the many proven records of women, when it came to applying 'grace' to "circumstances beyond her control." A woman could divide a cent four ways if she had to, to provide for her family, and many times it was a woman who kept the books and accounts for her husband. It was a woman's words that cautioned him on "his balances"; so as to "not spend their last cent on foolishness." Yet banks gave the men all the credit for the credit-worthiness of the homestead.

The government stepped in and took everything from this child's grandmother to repay the back taxes they claimed her husband owed them when he left. They took all but her children, and she would fight and die for them if she had to. The government sold the gas station to a businessman who could barely keep it afloat. The filling station then became a car washing business by yet another male businessperson. Prosperity left when unfair justice stepped in. Grandma believed that the business failures of all those who tried to run a business thereafter, on that property was the curse for the greed of those who had taken her life support from her and her family. The children's grandmother believed until her dying day, that if she had been able to keep the business, she would have kept it alive to hand down to her grandchildren. In addition, many who knew her, believed this to be so.

****

    The gas station came with living accommodations in behind it, and that is where their grandma brought her grandchildren after rescuing them from the desertion by their parents. This too, was where the judge had said that he would allow the three children to be raised. Life seemed to turn around for the three children, or though it seemed for a while. They had their grandma, Aunt Darlene and many cousins to play with. Their daddy came to visit from time to time when he was home from his business trips. They did not get to see their mommy; she made no attempts to see them, being off in the world trying to find herself in her search for love.

    Chicken pox was shared by all three children at the same time, as daddy was called in to assist their grandma. Their daddy would count each pox with the homemade remedy grandma had made up to take the "ichies" away. The night of the fevers, the children were so happy to have daddy with them, they even tried to play with him from behind fever-stricken glassy eyes. Finally, sleep set in, as their daddy stroked their foreheads with cold wet cloths.

    Grandma Nancy would close the gas station on Sundays, and most times take the three children to Uncle Franks and Aunt Alice's for Sunday dinner. Their Aunt and Uncle lived on a farm. Aunt Alice made the best beef stew in the whole wide world. Uncle Frank would chew tobacco, and spit the juice into a spittoon, which brought amusement to the children. With each visit they made, he would move the spittoon further away; take aim and spit. The children cheered when he made it. Curiosity got the best of them as they urged Uncle Frank to 'let them try.'

Uncle Frank obliged by placing a bit into each willing child's mouth. The taste of the tobacco alone, turned the children green, and dinner was spoiled "by such foolishness" as their grandma called it. She scolded Uncle Frank, "Now look what you've gone and done!" "What sort of nonsense has come over you, on giving these children chewing tobacco?" "Are you out of your mind?" "If you ever do that again, you will have me to contend with." Uncle Frank knew better than to rise up against the children's grandma. From then on, every visit thereafter, Uncle Frank did all the chewing and spitting of the tobacco. Grandma told her grandchildren, "it was a nasty habit, and that spitting was not for little girls."

Easter and Christmas had a completely new meaning. The holidays were fun filled, as the relatives gathered to celebrate. New dresses were bought, with her warnings to "stay clean." Crystal and Angela felt like princesses in the frills of the lacey dresses. Crystal, the eldest granddaughter, with the motherly attitude even early on in life, made certain that Angela stayed clean. Christopher was too young to worry about 'getting dirty'. He spent most of the time sleeping. Toys were given to the children as well as new outfits, and the Santa Claus story shared with them.

The days of past were lost memories, as the days in their grandma's home filled them with joy. This was normal life, a life that would long be remembered by Crystal and Angela. The memories would linger for many years to come. Memories that would give them hope during the lives that were yet to come for them.

3

Loves' Remnant Lost

Crystal, Angela and Christopher were happy spending their young lives with their grandma. Grandma, though busy with customers much of the time, seemed to be able to juggle the business and the nurturing of her grandbabies all at the same time. Then again, Aunt Darlene was always there to step in and give a helping hand when Grandma's schedule got full.

Their daddy had begun to spend more and more time away on 'business trips' or so he called and told his mother. An inside guess would reveal later that he really could not take his mother's criticism in relationship to being a father and the "I told you this would happen if you married that woman." "I told you right out from the beginning that it would not work." "Now you've made your bed, and now you can sleep in it."

So run, daddy did. Spending as little time with his children as his journeys would allow him, leaving the children's grandma to 'cover' during his absences, which was most often. Their daddy could not bare the truth, nor stand up to it. Instead, like many men, turned on his heel and high-tailed it out the front door, leaving three very confused children behind. Their mommy had left them to pursue her own identity in life, and now too, their daddy was gone. All they had was Grandma, Aunt Darlene, Aunt Alice, Uncle Frank, and all the cousins, biding their time to "baby-sit." Everyone seemed to know the story behind them living with their grandma, and each time someone came, there were hushed conversations as eyes turned to look upon them.

Then came the day when all seemed to start-off right with grandma and her three grandchildren at her heels. Breakfast was over, early as usual. Crystal, Angela and Christopher were ushered into their play area after Grandma finished the breakfast dishes. The telephone rang just before she headed out the door to go open up the filling station for business. It was their daddy on the other end of the line. He was coming home and he had a surprise for everyone. Grandma frowned as concern grew inside her. She wanted to remind him of his long absence from his children, but just as she opened her mouth to speak, he hung up the telephone on the other end. A dial tone returned as grandma put down the receiver on the cradle.

Grandma went into the playroom and looked at her grandchildren. They were quietly playing together. She contemplated not telling them that their daddy was on his way to see them, but then in the end broke the news. Angela and Crystal giggled and jumped up and down with excitement. "Daddy's coming home, daddy's coming home!" They shouted with glee. Christopher watched as his sisters danced all around the playroom. He giggled, because they giggled. They hugged one another. The playroom came to life with some very excited little children. Daddy was coming home!

The rest of the day seemed too long. Lunchtime turned into daydream time, as children stared out the window, anxiously waiting for their daddy's car to pull into the driveway. From time to time, they turned to one another, and reminded the other "Daddy's coming home!" Squeals of delight would burst out, as they turned back to the window to watch for him. Grandma could not even contain them during naptime. The restlessness from their excitement left grandma no choice but to give up on the nap and let them stay up to watch for him.

By late afternoon, daddy's car finally pulled into the driveway. They all saw it at the same time and let out shouts of "Daddy!" "Daddy!" "Daddy!" They went running to the door with Grandma close at their heels. She opened the door and out they ran to him, giggling and squealing with bursts of joy to see their daddy! Just as they got to him, the shouts of joy ended; silence filled the air. A stranger was getting out of the passenger side of the car and coming around to their daddy's side. A stranger they did not know. She held out her arms to them, a smile on her face. They stood staring up at her. She began to approach them. Not sure, who or what she was, they backed up and hid behind Grandma, turning their expressions of inquiry up to their daddy.

Daddy knelt down and introduced the stranger as the "woman he was going to marry", and she was going to be their "new mommy." Crystal and Angela surveyed the stranger from a distance while hanging on to Grandmas' legs. The woman picked up their baby brother, Christopher, and held him in her arms. Crystal and Angela looked on, bewildered. Their daddy was now smiling at this woman in approval. The little girls stood and stared back in disapproval. That was their baby brother, and she was not their mommy.

Daddy came closer, reached down, picked Angela up, and was now walking over to where the woman stood holding her brother. "This is my youngest daughter, Angela." The woman looked at her and then back down at Christopher in her arms. Angela started to cry. Daddy gave her a big bear hug and set her back down next to her sister, Crystal. Crystal was then introduced to the woman as Daddy's eldest daughter. Tears began to fall down the little girls cheeks. Daddy looked at them and then turned and walked back over to the woman.

Grandma came to their rescue, as she swept up Crystal and Angela into her arms, giving their daddy a 'piece of her mind' as she headed back to the house. Daddy just ignored Grandma's lecture. He followed the trio to the house with Christopher in his arms, put him into his crib and walked back out the front door not offering a word of rebuttal. You could tell he was hurt from the look on his face. Grandma followed him, her words flying at him as he got in his car with the woman and drove off. Tears began to fall from the eyes of his children. Grandma had her arms full. Their hearts had been broken by their daddy's short visit. You might say, Grandma was not pleased with her son, nevertheless, she lifted each of his children into her arms and rocked them to sleep, one at a time. The nap that they had missed finally caught up with them in this moment of sadness.

Two weeks later, Daddy returned home, empty-handed. Grandma did not speak to him when he came in. Crystal and Angela clung to his pant legs the entire time. This was their daddy and he was finally home. His little girls had missed him so much, they could not let him out of their sight for fear he might leave them again. Their daddy played games with them all afternoon. There were many hugs and kisses from him for them and from them for him. He seemed a bit on the 'down' side, but both girls were just so happy to have him home to themselves, that nothing else mattered.

The telephone rang suddenly, bringing the joyous laughter into a deadening silence. There was an accident out on the highway. It was the woman on the other end, crying and begging their daddy to come and get her. Daddy decided that he had to go; now leaving Grandma put the children to bed for late naps. Tears fell from their little eyes, bringing back the sting of pain from familiar heart break as their daddy left their presence. When would he come back? They did not know. They cried themselves to sleep. Eventually, the soft steady breathing from three very sad children filled the quiet house. Grandma looked down at her sleeping grandchildren. What was life to bring them? She thought to herself. She was doing the best she knew how. Would her son ever be able to stand up to the plate as their father, or would these children be raised in her care? Questions seemed to come without answers just now. Nonetheless, she would take life as it presented itself to her and her three little grandbabies, doing the best job she knew how with what she had.

Suddenly the silence broke as the front door opened. Their daddy came through the door with his arm around the woman. The winter storm howled as gusts of wind followed him into the house. The children woke up with a start from loud sudden noises that now filled the room. Crystal and Angela sat up and stared at Daddy and the woman through sleepy eyes. Was this a bad dream, or had this woman invaded their life once again?

The woman was a mere child herself. Sixteen at the most. Their daddy was twenty-six. What was she doing back in Daddy's life, and now taking up space in theirs? The little girls looked at one another and laid back down in their beds and fell back to sleep. Their daddy wanted this woman in his life, and from the infrequent visits to see them, they rated somewhere near the bottom of his priorities now. They had grandma to look to their needs and give them the love they needed. Yet, somewhere off in their young hearts, they needed their daddy. He did not realize this. Sleep could drown out their sadness from life's stresses for now.

The girls woke to the calling of their names; Grandma requested their presence at the supper table. Getting out of bed, hand in hand, Crystal and Angela went to join Grandma at the dinner table. The smell of grandma's home cooking and freshly baked bread beckoned their appetites, as they followed the delicious aroma to the dining room. Grandma was the best cook; she put love and attention into everything she did. Mealtimes were happy times, these were the times when Crystal and Angela could sit down and talk and laugh with Grandma. Even though Grandma worked hard all day, she always had time for them, especially at the dinner table.

Just as the girls turned the corner to enter into the dining room, they both stopped, there, in their home was this woman again. This time, she was sitting next to their daddy holding onto his hand, watching as Crystal and Angela approached. Daddy smiled as he held out the other hand to his daughters. Looking at each other, Crystal and Angela went directly to their high chairs, ignoring his gesture of welcome. Daddy looked at them with disapproval in his eyes, scolding them for not coming "to see him." Their grandma came to the rescue, stepping into the room with a few words of 'wisdom' for him. Silence overtook the mealtime.

Crystal and Angela stared at the woman while chewing their food. Grandma's meals were always good; it was tonight's female table guest that made the dinner atmosphere tense. The woman had some bruises on her face and arms, and some stitches in her chin and forehead. She had been involved in a car accident while driving out on the highway in the winter storm. What she had gone out in the storm for was only for her to know. Their daddy was doting on her with attentiveness, like a mother ape to her baby. She had replaced them in his life; or was it that his mother could not attack him in her presence. The woman smiled at them when their daddy was around, but out of his presence, the looks she gave them were venomous. There was no doubt that she did not like them. Grandma became their "safe haven" from this woman's venomous stares. She could turn on the charm in the presence of their daddy, and turn it off just as quick when he left the room. Crystal and Angela looked at one another and then began eating again trying to ignore her. The woman let them know early on, that she did not like them and that she just wanted their daddy.

The children's grandmother took Aunt Darlene aside the next day after Daddy left with the woman and told her all about the previous day's events. Crystal and Angela listened from the playroom when they heard their daddy's name mentioned. Grandma was saying that their "daddy and the woman had fought over the way she responded toward his little girls the last time she had come with him to visit them." "Daddy had been on the right track when he had broken off the relationship then, but then this woman had gone and done a stupid thing like try to come make up with daddy in a blinding snow storm and got into a car accident." "The accident played on his heart and boom, she's back into his life and he's forgotten his children all over again." Their grandma was frustrated. She knew that "these children needed their fathers' love and attention" and that "he had his priorities all messed up." She was shaking her head. "I don't know that boy; I've done everything to give him the best, but he just doesn't realize it." "Kids, they don't listen." "He's a lot like his father, who up and left me with the children." "They think they know more than you do, when you've lived and they haven't yet lived life to know." Aunt Darlene just sat and listened, nodding her head in agreement from time to time. Crystal and Angela sat in the playroom, listening to their grandma vent. When all was said, and nothing more could be done, Aunt Darlene got up and hugged and kissed her mom, and left to go home.

****

  Their daddy and the woman went to live with Aunt Darlene. The woman was pregnant with another man's child, and their daddy did not like it. Daddy had been through this once before, and had decided that this would not happen again. Therefore, to prove her love for their daddy, she let him help her abort the unborn child in their bedroom at Aunt Darlene's home. Blood was everywhere on Aunt Darlene's guest bed. The woman ended up in the hospital, hiding the fact that they had intentionally aborted and killed the baby. This would be the fact that would prove to be a noose around Daddy's neck for years to come. They had not had the money to leave the State of Wisconsin for an abortion, so their inexperience almost cost the woman her life. She would hold it over their daddy for the rest of his life, as you will see in the chapters to come.
  Shortly after the abortion, their daddy convinced his mother, the children's grandma, to release custody of his children to him and his new wife. His new wife's name was Drusilla. He had married the woman who did not like his children. There was no court order made to change the custody, but Grandma felt that maybe her son was finally taking on some responsibility that had been a long time in coming. Afterall, there were two of them to meet the needs of his children, or so she prayed. They would not be far away, so she could keep her eye on them.
  The children moved back to the city not too far from Waukesha Wisconsin with their daddy and this "new mommy." Daddy spent a couple weeks at home getting to know his children, and then returned to his traveling sales position, leaving behind him, his three children with the

teenaged child he now called his wife. The woman who did not like his children or want to be tied down with them, which signified the beginning of a grave disaster.

Drusilla had had a very abusive upbringing herself, and had run away from home, working in hotels as a cleaning girl, or though most were led to believe. That is how she met their daddy. He was on one of his business trips and she cleaned his hotel room. She too, just like their mommy, needed to be in the arms of men in order to feel loved and wanted. Daddy, in all of his charms fell into her web of lustful desires, thinking, that not only was he gaining a female beauty, but one who would take on his responsibilities to his children. Assumption becomes the kiss of death. Their daddy was letting history repeat itself. There is really no difference between abuse and neglect, they both eventually come to the same end if left unchecked. They both batter the body; one inside, the other outside and they both batter the emotions, saying the same thing. "I don't love you and I don't want you", and love never enters in.

The children's visits to see their grandma became fewer and fewer, especially when daddy used the excuse that he was being transferred to a company not too far from a major University in Central Wisconsin. He painted a wonderful picture for his mother, saying that the money was good, the children would have everything they wanted and needed, and that they would come back for a visit with her every other weekend, or whenever he was home from his business trips. With that, Grandma gave them her blessing. The children did not know that this would be the last time in quite some time before they saw their grandma again.

Their daddy left for his trips for days and weeks on end. Drusilla hated it and became more and more restless with the pressures from added responsibilities of taking care of her husbands' three children. She had no free time to herself with three toddlers running around the house. His extended absences brought out much insecurity for Drusilla. She knew that she had met her husband in a hotel and now his trips were growing longer and she was wondering if he was having affairs. Her anger burned inside her. Her temper grew short and so came the abuse upon this man's children.

Crystal looked like her biological mother, bringing memories to her daddy of his first marriage, and Drusilla did not like competition of any kind. His first marriage was the cause for these children being in her life right now! Drusilla was very young and very immature and had grown up seeing violence as the way to deal with situations you could not control. Drusilla tied Crystal to her bed daily so that she was out of her sight. Crystal had a weak bladder and began wetting the bed. Drusilla put her in diapers and beat her if they were wet before she released and allowed Crystal to go to the bathroom. Crystal was only allowed to go to the bathroom four times a day.

Crystal could not get away. The ropes burned into her wrists if she tried to avoid being whipped with the belt in Drusilla's wicked hand. If Crystal cried out, Drusilla would get on top of her and choke her, leaving scratches from her long fingernails and bruises on her neck. Many times, Crystal lay motionless at the end of the beatings and chokings. Angela thought on many occasion that her sister was dead. Fear penetrated every bone in her body as she stood motionless trying to hear even a moan or a breath from her sister. Eventually, Crystal would come to, and start crying in silence, asking Angela to "untie her;" she had to "go potty." Angela was stuck between her loyalty and love for her sister, and being scared to death that if she untied Crystal against the wishes of their stepmother, she would get a beating in the same manner.

Nevertheless; there were occasions when her compassion for her sister, and not wanting to see her get beat up again, made her take her chances at untying her sister. A few times the attempt was successful. Crystal would quietly go to the bathroom, and then sneak back to bed. Angela had to tie her back up, this time leaving the knots loose. Drusilla eventually caught them in the act. Crystal got beat, and Angela was no longer allowed to enter into the room during the day.

Crystal's beatings grew worse and more frequent. Angela stood down the hall covering her ears and shaking from head to toe. What was to become of her sister Crystal at the hands of this Amazon? Tears flowed down her face and her body shook with fear far greater than she had ever felt. Frightened half to death…scared of the woman her daddy had brought home.

Crying out for her sister proved to be the wrong thing to do. Drusilla wanted to undo the bond between the two girls, so in order to do so, now turned her anger on Angela. At four years old, Drusilla had Angela washing dishes, and the crusty blackened oven. Drusilla used her "white glove inspection" method of teaching housework. Beatings would follow every task given, because they would not meet the satisfaction of Drusilla. At four years old and very new to housework, was not a consideration made by Drusilla. Perfection was the expectation, nothing less, nothing more. Angela, became a white little slave girl to the long finger-nailed venomous beauty her Daddy brought home for them to call "mommy."

Dishes that were not perfectly cleaned became blunt objects cracked over the top of Angela's head, or shoved into her gut, knocking her from the chair she stood on. Water spilled on the floor got Angela a swift kick in the butt, which made her fall from the chair to the floor on her face, her teeth penetrating her lips, the blood dripping down her chin as she attempted to stand back up. Drusilla would assist her to her feet by taking hold of Angela's hair bringing her back up to her feet. She would continue to look for and find dirty dishes, repeating the punishment for each one found. The battery of Angela, the slave child, became this Amazon's playground.

A dirty oven delivered a belt across Angela's backside while she bent over the oven door or another swift kick to her butt lodging her into the oven headfirst, smearing oven grease onto the side of her face as it traveled along the bottom of the oven. The job never done to Drusilla's perfection, because she would only allow Angela to use the dish soap on a dampened rag to clean the oven; while most homemakers were using Scrub pads and oven cleaner to complete the same task. Angela stayed up scrubbing the stubborn burnt on stains in the oven until very late into the night. Her body ached from the beatings as Drusilla finally released her to go to bed. On her way down the hall, Angela would hear Drusilla spraying the oven, and by morning, the oven was clean, as if by magic!

An unswept floor amounted to Angela being fed the dust and dirt from it's surface, as Drusilla ordered her to stick out her tongue as her head was smashed into the floor from corner to corner of the kitchen floor. The floor was to be scrubbed with a scrub brush and rag. Any puddles, provided a slippery surface for Drusilla to smash Angela's face into, yet another sickening reason for Angela to endure the battery upon her young body by the Amazon. For every chore given, there was an unfair time limit set. Unreasonable yes; but nonetheless enforced by Drusilla, her new mommy.

Vacuuming was a task that had to be done a certain way and if not excelled into perfection, the hose and metal end became a torture tool to use on Angela's body. Dazed in fear, she finished the task. Her knees shaking from the fear that Drusilla would never meet the standards set by her new "mommy." Sure enough, the beating and torture became a regular event, no matter what effort Angela gave the task. Drusilla loved to inflict pain upon her little stepdaughter. There was no one to intervene, and no one to say she could not abuse her stepchildren. The children she never really wanted, but had had dumped on her, when she married their daddy.

Drusilla too, had developed a potty schedule for Angela. Her dresses were tied tight by the Amazon, which made it difficult to breathe and being told that she could not go to the bathroom until Drusilla allow her to do so, complicated things even more. There were times when she had to go to the bathroom before her 'allowed' times, but when she informed her new mommy that she needed to go, the answer was always "no." The result, wet panties, giving Drusilla more reason to inflict her brutal punishment upon Angela. Urine on the floor meant that Drusilla would smack Angela to the floor and rub her face in it ordering her to "lick up the mess." Angela gagged and before she could vomit, Drusilla's hands were around her neck choking her so the puke would not come up.

Angela would have to stay in her wet panties all day while incurring verbal attacks from Drusilla. "You are a big baby, you wet your pants." "I'm telling your daddy…" The verbal attacks brought shame and sadness to her. Having to face her daddy, after Drusilla told him that she had wet her pants, would be devastating and shameful. Drusilla would leave out the part where she had not let Angela go to the bathroom when she had needed to. Her daddy would only see that it was her fault. Drusilla was mean and cruel. Tears would fall down Angela's face as she stifled her sobs, fearing repercussion for crying, it was not allowed.

Angela and daddy had always been very close and she feared that these reports of her behavior would cause her daddy to dislike her even more. This in fact proved to be Drusilla's intent. The false reports of his misbehaving little girls while he was gone on his business trips put a growing distance between them and him. Drusilla got the victory, and the abuse never stopped.

Christopher was too young to become this Amazon's slave and torture victim, and he was his dad's only son at this point. Christopher slept most of the time as if sedated. He was slow in development and motor skills. In his infancy, Drusilla did not find him a threat. He would be spared from the physical and emotional abuse at this point in life, too young to be her slave, and what would be the excuse for an infant having bruises?

"Daddy come home time", lost its thrill, as Drusilla would meet Daddy at the door with a whole dialogue of how bad his little girls had been in his absence. When he would ask where they were, she would tell them that "they had their dinner and baths and had been sent to bed early for their misbehavior." Most times, he no longer came to kiss them and say "goodnight" anymore. Crystal and Angela would listen from their beds to the conversation between their daddy and Drusilla, wishing that he would come to rescue them. However, he never came. Silent sobs and tears filled their dark bedroom. They were losing their daddy to this woman, who did not want them around. Sobs filled the dark room as both girls longed for the days when their daddy loved them. They would listen to his voice as it drew near just outside their door and then he'd pass without even opening their door as he retired into his own bedroom, tired from his journeys as the "traveling sales man." Silent cries of pain from broken hearts, from the loss of their daddy echoed in the darkness of their bedroom. Cries muffled by pillows for fear of retaliation if overheard.

Creaky floorboards kept Crystal and Angela at room's length from finding solace in one another. One-step out of bed, and Drusilla would plant Angela in the hallway for the entire night to stand in the corner just outside her bedroom. If fatigue took its toll in the wee hours of the morning, and if Angela fell to her knees, Drusilla would use the golden locks of this little girls' head to upright her back onto her feet in the corner. Angela's body would shake from her head to her toes, her heart racing with fear of her body giving into sleep. She would literally cling to the corner, wedging herself upright into the corner, to keep from falling down. Many times, she would pass out and wake up later, finding herself in her own bed. Fear would penetrate her body as the thought of perhaps she had slept walked and put herself to bed, or maybe her daddy had found her and placed her there without Drusilla's permission. Her heart pounded in fear as she awaited Drusilla's arrival to give her the permission to "get up and get dressed" came. She would surely be beaten again if Drusilla had not put her to bed.

Other mentionable abuses took place during and after the dinner hour. Crystal was a slow eater according to Drusilla's expectations. When the rest of the family had finished their meal leaving Crystal still eating, Drusilla would take what was left on Crystal's plate and force-feed her. Shoving the food and fork down Crystal's throat, causing Crystal to gag and vomit it back up. The vomit was then force-fed to her. Drusilla would pour the vomit and the rest of Crystal's dinner into a glass and manually pour it down Crystal's throat in front of Angela and Christopher. Drusilla would use her own two fingers to push the rest of the food down Crystal's throat, as her siblings watched in horror.

Tears flowed down Angela's face as she watched this brutality taken out on her sister. The scene made her sick, as she herself choked back her own vomit from having to be witness to the brutality her sister had to endure, time and time again at the meal table. The smell from her sisters' vomit had Angela holding her breath from across the table. Christopher just stared in fear and without speaking as Drusilla mutilated his oldest sister's throat and face in her obsession to "abuse these intruders of her freedom." Stunned silence from both Angela and Christopher fell as they watched in horror the repeated chokings and torture inflicted upon their sister by this Amazon "new mommy."

4

Forgotten Witness

The move to central Wisconsin took all parental accountability away from Drusilla, or so she thought. The summer months endorsed her abusive attacks upon Crystal and Angela, over and over again. No one knew, no one would suspect the abuse that went on in this house. The neighbors did not know that there was more than one male toddler living at 4922 Iyer Lane. Drusilla did not allow the girls out of the house, nor did she take them with her when she did errands, even though they were all under-aged. Therefore, no one knew that there were actually three small children living in the house.

September brought school for Crystal and Angela. Crystal started second grade and Angela began kindergarten. Angela had had to wait an extra year to begin school since her birthday fell in December. Drusilla took them on their first day, warning them that not a word was to be spoken about their home life, and if word did get back to her that they had opened their mouths, they would pay the consequences.

School proved to be a refuge for them. Getting out from under Drusilla and her torturous parenting tactics was like having to leave hell for heaven. An indescribable weight lifted from them for the time spent in school. There they were safe, sitting in their classrooms with other children their own age, teachers with smiles and warm greetings. Every school day was a day of being freed from the dungeon of torture. At days end, having to face going "home" brought the fears and the tears back. The order was to come straight home in ten minutes. They had to run the distance, hoping that they arrived on time or all hell would be their encounter when they came through the door. This did not give them time to have friends or to talk to anyone. No one was allowed to come home with the girls either, therefore, enabling Drusilla to contain her secret within the walls of the pale green house with white shutters.

Crystal wasn't even in school for a week when her second grade teacher had taken the class into the washrooms for their morning break. As each child finished their business, they were allowed to go play out on the playground. It came Crystals' turn to go potty. She entered the cubicle closing the door behind her. Lifting up her little dress, she attempted to undo the safety pins on the diaper Drusilla made her wear to school. Frustrated; she struggled with the safety pins. Her teacher overheard her grunts and asked if she was "alright." Just as a frightened voice responded, "Yes", the diaper fell to the floor. Crystal began to cry; frightened that Drusilla might find out that her teacher knew about the diapers.

Her teacher asked Crystal to unhook the latch on the stall door for her so she could "help her." Her teacher's voice was soft and gentle, surveying the little girl standing before her, with bruises all over her bottom and legs. Holding back the tears, Crystals' teacher gathered up the diaper from the floor, tidied Crystal's dress and headed for the school office with her. She stopped to ask another teacher to watch her class while she was away, and then turned back toward the office. Crystal cried all the way there, her teacher attempting to console her, through tears of her own.

Arriving at the front office, they headed for the Nurses Office. The door closed behind them as the school nurse began to inspect Crystal while conversing with her teacher. They asked Crystal questions. At first, Crystal was afraid to speak to them, remembering Drusilla's warnings, and then through tears and sobs, Crystal tried to describe how her "new mommy" was treating her. Her teacher and the nurse held back their own tears, trying to console this little girl from the trauma she was living through. They notified the Principal and Children's Services was contacted.

Crystal's teacher held her in her arms, rocking her back and forth, while waiting for Children's Services to arrive. Crystal was scared to death, in fear that Drusilla would be contacted next and that eventually she would be made to return home with Drusilla, be tied to her bed, and beat severely for telling on Drusilla. Drusilla never came. Instead, representatives from Children's Services arrived, gently asking questions and listening as Crystal described how her "new mommy" treated her. Moved deeply by what Crystal told them, she was led away to a car parked outside the school office.

A ride downtown to another office, more questions and body inspections, more people gathering around, more telephone calls and conversations, tuckered this little child out. Crystal felt lost. She was taken for an ice cream cone and gifted with a Teddy Bear to cuddle with.

She was given a clean pair of under panties with the promise of going to another home, not her own, after they visited the hospital first. It was getting dark outside by the time they got on their way to the hospital. Curled up now in the back seat of the car, she fell fast asleep. It was a light sleep, yet still, sleep. Crystal felt safe for the moment because she was out of Drusilla's reach.

The inside dome light came on when the door was opened. Crystals' eyes tried to focus as she tried to remember where she was. A somewhat familiar face stooped over her, and she was lifted out of the car and assisted to her feet. Two strangers waited outside, looking with curiosity at her. She felt isolated without her sister Angela, there with her.

A wheelchair met them at the entrance and they wheeled her to the children's ward. The lights were bright and uninviting to a little girl who had already had quite a day. All she wanted was her sister Angela to be there with her and to go to sleep. Tears welled up inside, as she gazed around her in these unfamiliar surroundings. Fear still played its toll on her, as she kept wondering whether Drusilla would show up to drag her home and beat her in retaliation for "telling their secret."

Surveying the faces around her, Crystal did not know whom she could trust. Everyone was friendly, or though it seemed to her. From experience, she knew that even Drusilla herself could turn on and off the "friendly" as quick as you could snap your fingers. Crystal had not known what trust was, since leaving the safe environment of her grandma's home. Where was her grandma now? With their move to central Wisconsin, came daddy's alienation from his mother, which meant that it had been quite awhile since the children had seen their grandmother. A completely new feeling of hurt welled up inside her. Tears again began to flow down her swollen face.

The nurses obtained the attending physicians permission to put Crystal to bed, and then she was wheeled down the corridor toward what was to be her room for quite some time. The bed was cold, the room dark. Only the occasional footsteps of a nurse walking by outside her room were heard. She felt alone. Cuddling up to her new Teddy Bear, she silently cried in his ears until sleep over took her. Her steady breathing broken by the occasional rushing intake of air from all the crying she had done that day. Then finally, a steady deep sleep that took her into the afternoon of the following day fell upon her.

After many x-rays and examinations from attending physicians, it was discovered that Crystal had a broken collarbone, rope burns around her wrists, much bruising and health and emotional issues that needed medical attention and a lot of tender loving care. She spent about a month or so in the hospital having tests and being counseled by attending physicians. It was her time to heal from both the physical and emotional scars that had been inflicted upon her by Drusilla. In the hospital was better than being home with Drusilla. Her nightmares were replaced with restful nights of sleep. Crystal was eventually able to hold down food, after all the damage Drusilla had caused to her throat from her force feedings. She could finally eat without the fear of getting sick and having to drink her own vomit. The hospital did not put time limits on her eating habits. She could eat as slowly as her heart desired.

The doctors and nurses fell in love with Crystal. She was shy and spoke in a small soft voice. The bruises left her complexion and were replaced with the prettiest olive colored skin. A smile replaced the tears from all the pain of the abuse she had had to live through. The hospital released Crystal into the custody of the State of Wisconsin. She had now become a Ward of the Court.

Crystal was placed into a foster home in the city, but that only lasted a few days. She still feared that Drusilla would find her and come to get her, so the State decided to move her to a location that would convince Crystal that she was going to be safe. The agent came and got her, taking her out into the countryside to live with an older "foster" couple. She missed most of her second grade year, which gave her time to adjust to a normal lifestyle of countryside and home cooked country meals, from a foster couple who administered some real tender loving care while she was living with them. Crystal started third grade at a country schoolhouse. Up until then, she had not gotten to go home to visit and had not seen her sister Angela.

****

Meanwhile, on the first day that the school intervened on Crystal's behalf, Drusilla was contacted by the school and by the Police Department. Her daddy was not yet home from his business trip and knew nothing. After their questioning of Drusilla, she was released to go back home. Upon arriving home, she immediately called Angela into the livingroom and threatened her with bodily injury if she told anyone of her life at home. Drusilla fed her answers to questions that the school and intervening authorities might be asking her stepdaughter. Angela was made to rehearse the answers over and over again. Then Drusilla told her that she was to return to school the following day and "cry because her sister was taken away, and they were hurting her new mommy, and that she wanted to live with her new mommy." Threats of bodily injury and never seeing her sister Crystal again, followed if she did not do this. She would also be taken away and would never be able to see her daddy again if she did not do as she was told. Drusilla did not have to ask Angela twice. The fear Drusilla had already instilled in her stepdaughter was constant reminder that what Drusilla wanted, Drusilla would get. Drusilla was desperate to "save her own soul." What once was her secret was becoming public knowledge. She would not go down without a fight.

Not being able to ever see her sister and daddy again if she did not follow Drusilla's orders, sent fear all the way into her bones. Angela was scared. She gave it her best performance the following day at school, when sure enough; she was called out of her classroom and questioned by the school authorities. They looked her over and asked her how she had gotten some of her bruises. "I fell off my bike." She lied, as Drusilla had instructed. Angela did not even have a bike. Her legs and body shook as she answered their questions. She did not want them to take her away where no one could ever find her. She still loved her daddy and she wanted to be able to see him.

Daddy came home early from his business trip. Drusilla had so many excuses for the whys and how's of Crystal had gotten her bruises and why the school found her in diapers. According to Drusilla, Crystal had been peeing her pants on a regular basis, and the diapers were to prevent her from wetting herself. Their daddy was mad. An argument followed. Neither would take blame for what had happened. Each had reason why they "didn't need this happening to them." Primarily pride stood in the way of reason. The "how dare you's" flew back and forth, each trying desperately to blame the other. Either giving an inch or accepting responsibility. Both worrying more about what was to happen to them, than what was going to happen to his little girl and possibly the other two children.

Angela hid her head in her pillow sobbing for the loss of her sister. The bed on the other side of the room lay empty. Her only friend and confidant, was gone; taken away from her. Crystal had shared this hellish life with her, and now she had no one to give her strength to endure the hell Drusilla inflicted on her. The only one who brought any comfort to her at night was gone. Gone...gone...gone... The sobs came so hard that it was difficult muffling the sounds in her pillow. Drusilla and her daddy were arguing so loud that her sobs down the hall went unnoticed. Her chest felt as if it would burst. She was broken hearted; all she wanted to die was to die. The pain was unbearable. No one heard, no one cared. Crystal was gone, not coming back.

It was her fault. Angela should have protected her, or so she felt now. Crystal needed her, and she needed Crystal. "I want my sister back," she sobbed into her pillow. Angela could no longer look at the empty bed across the room. The pain of heartache made her turn her head away. She did not want to be here. She wanted to be with her sister. Where was she? Where had they taken her? Why couldn't she go with? She sobbed throughout the night, until sleep fell upon her. Her body lay limp in the cool darkness. The room coldly lay still...

Crystal became a forgotten topic. It seemed as if they had forgotten all about her. After all, Angela's daddy was carrying on with his business trips, as if it was just another day. The only difference seemed to be the growing distance between himself and Drusilla, in which now gave her all the more reason to increase her abuse on Angela. When there were marks on Angela, Drusilla would not send her to school. Instead, she would call the school and state that Angela was sick in her "fake" friendliest voice. The school would not investigate, even when the record of being out of school grew almost daily.

With the distance placed by the turn of events in Drusilla and Angela's daddy's life, Drusilla decided to see an "old friend" while her husband was out of town on his business trips. Angela was caught getting out of bed one night to go to the bathroom. Drusilla landed her in her bed so fast; Angela did not know what had attacked her. The noise in the next room had awakened Angela. Knowing that her daddy was not home she had gotten out of bed to see what was causing the noise and she also had to go to the bathroom. Drusilla was in bed with someone, not her daddy. When she saw them, fear shot through her, especially when she realized that Drusilla had seen her staring at them. Drusilla jumped up out of bed, grabbed Angela, and threw her into her room. Angela hit the wall and bounced onto the floor off her bed. Drusilla then grabbed her up and threw her into her bed, with a whispered growl, "stay here; I will deal with you later." The door slammed as Drusilla left. Angela's head and body hurt. Drusilla would keep her promise of revenge, there was no doubt.

From that day on, when her daddy was on a business trip, Angela was sent out into the late hours of the night to the ice skating rink at the bottom of the hill in the park. She was not allowed to come home until Drusilla came to get her. The temperatures would be freezing. It sent shivers into Angela's bones. The quad-bladed, strap-on, metal skates on her shoes quickly froze her feet. A few couples remained on the ice, trying to coax Angela to go home. It was late. It was probably past her bedtime. Her family would be worried many said. She did not answer them. She skated in circles around the couples ignoring their questions and inquiries. She dared not go home without Drusilla's permission. She stared up the hill at her home. A strange car was parked in the driveway. She knew that this man must be over again visiting her stepmother.

One night, the hours went by until no one was left on the skating rink. Even the skating rink lights had been shut off a few hours before. The darkness embraced her little body and the howling wind sent stabbing pain from frost bitten extremities through her. Angela could barely move. Falling to her knees, she began to dig a hole in the snow. The snow was hard. Her fingers were numb and bleeding. Taking off her skates, she slowly began to dig. Every now and then, she would glance across the street and up the hill to her home to see if Drusilla was coming for her. The house was dark. The strangers' car still parked in the driveway. The silence of darkness embraced her. Car headlights would pass by the park without hesitation. Then the darkness would return, as Angela continued to dig. The hole had gotten big enough for her to crawl into. She was tired, very cold, and hungry. Curled up, her whole body shivering and shaking, she fell asleep.

It was just about dusk when Angela was awakened by a blunt blow to the head. Her coat collar was being used to yank her up onto her feet. Her feet were frozen, and she could no longer feel them. Down on her face she fell. Drusilla kicked her in the side, over and over again, as if she was a sack of discarded potatoes. Angela was ordered to stand to her feet.

She tried to rise, but there was no feeling in her feet or legs. Even her hands were numb. She just laid there gasping for air. Her body was stiff. Her lips frozen together. The skin on her face raw from the cold. Breathing was difficult, her mouth was sealed shut by ice between her lips and mucous had coated the back of her throat and sinuses. Drusilla grabbed Angela up by her coat and literally dragged her up the hill and into the house.

Taking off Angela's clothes, Drusilla threw her onto her bed. The numbness eventually began to wear off and a burning hot pain torched her entire body. Angela felt like she was suffocating. Her lips were still tightly together and the tears were falling, causing her nose to plug up. Angela struggled for her life, trying to breathe. She was slowly suffocating. Her lips tore apart, blood trickled down her throat. Gasping for air, she lay in the dark coughing a dry raspy cough. Her head pounding, as if it would explode. Her heart throbbing in its cavity working to get the frozen blood in her veins thawed out. Her body was on fire as it thawed in the darkness. She felt like she had been tossed into a fiery furnace. So much pain, she could not go to sleep. It was her fault. If she had not gotten out of bed to see what was going on in her daddy's room many months ago, she would have never had to go out to the ice rink, night after cold night. Angela was only six years old. Too young to die…or was she?

5

The Rape of Dignity

Crystal had begun coming home for "trial visits" to the "family home." Angela and Christopher were kept away from her, as if she had leprosy. They could only stare at her from a distance, as if she was a new stranger in their home. It was sad for Angela, because she could not even talk to Crystal in the darkness of their bedroom. Crystal was always being sent to bed earlier than Angela was, and had fallen fast asleep by the time Angela's weary little body came into the dark room to go to bed. She lay in the darkness, staring at the silhouette of her sleeping sister. How long would she be visiting them this time? Where did Crystal go when she left their home? Who was taking care of her when she was gone? Did Crystal miss her as much as she missed Crystal? Where did she go to school?

So much on the mind of such a little girl. Stress rocked Angela into a deep sleep, only to bring on the new daylight with still a heaviness of fatigue. A new day, same old repetition of household chores too complicated, yet well accomplished, by this seven year old, to a greater degree than some grown housewives themselves. Of course, the fear of being beat to a pulp put the fright of perfection into the application of the tasks forced upon this little girl.

With repetition of chores imposed upon Angela, brought repetition of the beatings Drusilla dealt out. The severity pretty much depended upon the mood swings of the Amazon. Drusilla herself, Angela's wicked stepmother, made the stepmother of Cinderella seem like a fairy princess and even more delightfully charming. If P.M.S. was to blame, Drusilla had it every day of her life with her husband's children. She did not want his children, yet, she did want him.

Crystal's little visits home became more and more frequent, yet still, Angela couldn't get near enough to her big sister to find out everything she needed to know about where she lived, and what it was like living in another home where she wasn't being beat up every day. Moreover, could Angela go with her next time she left? Drusilla kept them far apart. No questions could be asked, no answers shared between them. All she could do was stare at the silhouette of her sister in the bed across the room, and then turn back toward the wall before Drusilla caught her "out of the assigned sleeping position."

Crystal seemed to be in her own little world. Drusilla let her spend time outside playing with the neighborhood children across the street. Something new, Drusilla had never let Crystal do before the State had taken her away and placed her in foster care. Angela would glance with envy out the living room window as she vacuumed the rug. Longing to know what it was like to "play" with other kids. Angela would sigh, turn from the window and tears would fill up her eyes. When she was with Grandma, Angela had her sister and brother and all her cousins to play with before they moved here, but now, she had no one. No one was allowed to play with her. She had chores to do all day and night long, every day. Loneliness momentarily overtook her, as she dusted the furniture and wiped dirty marks off the wall. Big tears began to roll down her face as Angela thought about the happier times with Grandma.

Wham! Angela's body flew across the room from the blow to her head! Drusilla had caught her with tears in her eyes! A "bad attitude" was not allowed! There was no defense required, just the assumption that Angela was mad at having to do chores. Drusilla must have had her own judge and jury on guard in her head, because if there were tears, there was never a good reason. Crying and tears were against the laws of Drusilla. For Angela to exist in the same world Drusilla did was against the law. Who then, would do the housework, if not for Angela? A question perhaps, never ventured by the Amazon. Angela was slave and property for the Amazons' boxing mania. As long as Drusilla was getting away with abusing her stepdaughter, she would continue to mercilessly.

The demand was to "get up!" Dazed, Angela climbed to her feet facing the Amazon who had just knocked her to the floor with the unexpected blow. Another blow met her head as she attempted to upright herself after the first blow. Drusilla tried to explain that it was all for "looking like she was now feeling sorry for herself." Down Angela went again, only to be raised up by her ear. Sharp pain ripped through the side of her face from the neck up. Mumps did not hurt this bad. Angela reached for the side of her face and her arm was punched away from her face. Drusilla pulled tighter on Angela's ear. Angela felt a stinging pain and felt a pop, some burning sensation and finally Drusilla let go. The pain did not leave, and her ear felt hot. It seemed as though it were plugged. Angela stood with her arms at her side. There was no defense allowed. No answering back. Angela stood with her mouth closed tight, while the Amazon poked her long fingernail into her lips emphasizing each word she spoke. Angela did not move, she barely even took a breath. She was dazed. Grey shadows filled the room. She could do all she could to keep from giving into the feeling of passing out.

The command was to "put a smile on her face", before Drusilla counted to three, or she would suffer further consequence. With quivering lips, Angela forced the corners of her mouth up, hoping with all her might that it would meet the approval of the Amazon. It didn't of course, and wham! A fist to her gut knocked the wind out of her lungs! The air exited her lungs with such percussion that made it feel like no air would ever return again. Angela gasped for air and fell to her knees. Her head was being yanked up by her hair, as the expectation was that she rise to her feet again without fail! How dare her little body react to the brutal infliction upon it! Drusilla wanted to use Angela to take her frustrations out on.

Angela's legs felt like jello, as she tried desperately to stand. Drusilla imitated Angela's feeble attempt at rising to her feet in mockery. Angela held back the tears and pretended not to take notice, but deep inside the mockery cut like a knife. Drusilla continued to make faces at Angela, mocking her attempts to keep from crying. The Amazon spit in her face, and told her to "get out of her sight."

"Getting out of her stepmother's sight meant going to another room in the house and working. The bathroom still needed cleaning as it was on the list of Angela's chores that needed doing every day. Angela bent over the toilet bowl with a rag and some cleanser powder, trying to muffle the sobs from the pain coming from her ear, and the heartache being inflicted upon her by this awful stepmother her daddy had married. In the distance, Angela heard the livingroom door open, and the cheerful voice of her big sister coming in for lunch. Drusilla slammed the door behind Crystal. Waiting...the house grew quiet. Then Drusilla told Crystal to get up to the table. More silence fell in the house as Crystal ate lunch. Then Angela heard it. The sound of a slap and a crying out from her sister! "Don't eat like that!" snarled Drusilla. This was the first time in a long time of visits made by Crystal, that Drusilla had actually hit her. When Crystal cried out, her cries were followed by more slaps. Crystal's chair flew backwards and thud...chair and child fell onto the floor.

Drusilla lost all control. She kicked, punched, pulled Crystal up, and threw her back onto the floor. Crystal kept on crying out, and the Amazon kept on beating her up.

"I'm not going to have any government agency telling me what I can and can't do to you idiots!" Drusilla yelled with a vengeance. She had gone mad! Angela cried in fright and in sympathy for her sister. They would really take Crystal away this time. This could not be happening. Angela trembled in fear, listening…hoping for the Amazon to stop beating up her sister. She shut her eyes and put her hands over her ears, wishing that it would stop. Tears streamed down her face. Snot dripped from her nose, this was too much. First, she had gotten beat up, now it was Crystal's turn. Would Drusilla ever stop?

Just then, the telephone rang. Drusilla answered it as if she had been having a wonderful day. Her voice was pleasant, and at times, she laughed as if everything was so happy and going just great. Hanging up the telephone, she turned into the vicious monster she had been before the call came in. Crystal was dragged down the hall and thrown into her bed. Thud! There wasn't a sound, except for Drusilla heading out of the room and back up the hall again. Angela diligently worked on the bathroom, hoping with all of her might that Drusilla wouldn't make her, her next victim. Footsteps came back down the hall and Drusilla walked into the bathroom, putting Angela on notice; "You've got five minutes to get this room finished 'spotlessly', or else." Angela shook as she responded with an obedient "yes mom."

The bathroom was cleaned and Angela was told to take a nap. Drusilla was going grocery shopping. Threats were given to them all, as always, before she left anywhere. "Do NOT get out of your beds, or I will beat the crap out of you both when I get back!" Drusilla's warning penetrated the conscience clear to the soul. Both girls nodded, turned and faced their independent walls as Drusilla left their rooms and headed back up the hall and out the front door.

The family car was heard leaving the driveway, heading down the hill and off to the store. Crystal and Angela were not allowed to face each other. They had been instructed to remain turned away from one another facing opposite walls very early on, in this hellish place called "home with their new mommy."

A small voice broke the silence…"Crystal…Crystal…are you okay?"

"Yes, she should have never hit me…I'm going to tell my foster mom…she's going to be in trouble."

"I miss you when you leave here." "I want to go with you next time you leave." "She is really mean to me now that you are gone." "She says that I can't talk to you." "She says that you're a stranger." "She says that they'll take me away, and I'll never get to see Daddy if I tell anyone, she beats me up." "I'm scared of her." "I cry for you at every night." "I want you to come back home." Tears rolled down Angela's face as she tried to convey to her sister, the pain her sister's departure made on her life. Sniffles followed the tears. "Can't you stay home, please…or just take me with?" "I don't like it here."

"I don't want to come home." "The other people are nice to me."

"But I miss you…I need you Crystal…You're my sister", Angela begged, tears running down her little face.

"Just go to sleep before she gets home." Crystal tried to sooth Angela's pain.

"I don't want to go to sleep; I want to talk to you."

"But we'll get in trouble if she sneaks in on us and finds us talking", whispered Crystal in rebuttal.

Tears continued to flow down Angela's face. She felt the agony of the break up that the distance from having her sister living in one home, and herself in this one brought. She knew that Crystal was right, that they would "get into trouble" if Drusilla caught them talking to one another, but there had been so much distance between them since Crystal left. Angela did not want to be here, she wanted to go where her sister got to go. A foster home, sounded so much better than what this home was to them.

The room was dark when the girls awoke. Drusilla had not come home. Sleep had brought them to roll over facing one another. Realizing that they were not in the "approved" direction in bed when they awoke, they both rolled back over to face opposite walls. Lying there, they listened for the familiar sound of Drusilla's car pulling into the driveway. Hours went by or though it seemed. Suddenly the front door opened. Both Crystal and Angela felt their bodies stiffen, as they listened for the command to "get up."

Footsteps were coming down the hall. Their bedroom light was turned on. "Hey girls!" It was daddy! They both jumped out of bed and into the arms of their daddy! "Mommy had a baby!" Both little girls stopped their squeals of joy and their jumping up and down. Daddy noticed the bruising on Crystal and asked her where it had come from.

"Mommy did it", Crystal replied.

Daddy just glanced at Crystal with a bit of a concerned look and did not comment further. "You two have a new baby brother, what do you think about that?" Their Daddy seemed excited. His excitement passed itself on to his little girls. They were excited because Daddy was excited. If it made their daddy happy, it made them happy. They had not had time alone with their daddy since before this woman came into their lives. This was like the good ol' times. Daddy was with them. Hugging, kissing and spending precious time with them. There was no threat of Drusilla cutting in and separating this happy event. She was in the hospital with the new baby, and they were here having a wonderful time, climbing all over him. Laughter filled the air. The pains from the earlier beating by their stepmother only hurt when he tickled them, but they didn't complain. Drusilla would be home, Daddy would be sure to confront her if they told him, and then when he left on his business trip, there would be more hell to pay. Then again, where did he think the bruising came from?

It was Mother's day, May 11th, 1964. Dennis entered this world. Daddy seemed excited. A second son, … perhaps…

They would go see him tomorrow, because Daddy would be taking them to the hospital. Right now though, they had him all to themselves. Daddy was nice to them. He let them laugh and play with him. There was no Drusilla to interfere, telling them to work or to get to bed. Daddy even let them watch TV with him. He cooked them dinner, washed their faces and said their prayers with them as he tucked them into bed. This would be a night that they would never forget. Not because Drusilla brought a child into the world, but because it was the one rare moment in time that normal happy life returned for the three children. The first time in a long time, daddy paid attention to them.

Crystal returned to her foster home and daddy got a "friend" to stay with Angela and Christopher. Daddy returned to the hospital to visit Drusilla and the new baby. It was dark, and Angela and Christopher had been put to bed before their daddy left. Angela had just fallen asleep when she felt someone touch her. Her covers were being pulled up as a hand touched her leg. She did not breathe. This was not her daddy. The hand very carefully was placed between her legs and now a stinging sensation brought her entirely to her senses. This man was touching her "tinkler" as Grandma had called it. She tried to roll away from him, but he tightened his grip on her tummy and arm with his other hand. She tried to yell out, but he placed his elbow down hard on her chest, pushing the wind out of her so she couldn't breathe in to get air to yell out. Panic-stricken fear went through her little body as he continued to stick his finger up inside her little body. It hurt. What was he doing? Tears fell down her cheeks onto her pillow.

Just as he entered the room, the man left her room. Daddy had arrived back home. Angela felt sick. Her body shook in the dark. The stinging pain between her legs in her private parts wouldn't go away. She felt dirty and ashamed. She feared the man, but more so her stepmother if she found out. Daddy was sure to get mad at her too, if he found out. Tears streamed down her face like little waterfalls upon her pillow. She couldn't go back to sleep. Fear kept her up throughout the night. A chill inside that wouldn't leave her, made her body tremble beneath the covers.

The next day, Daddy took Angela and Christopher to the hospital to visit Drusilla and the new baby, Dennis. The three children had to stand outside on the ground and look up to a window above to see their stepmother and her son. The nurses beckoned them in to come see, but Drusilla said that she would rather have her "other" children remain outside.

As quick as they had been ushered to the hospital to "see their new brother", they were whisked home again, but not before Daddy stopped and picked up some McDonalds for them to eat when they arrived home. Cheerful dinner chatter filled the air. This table had never had the joyful sounds of children enjoying a meal at dinnertime. Laughter filled the air, as French fries became boats and cars. The children were just about finished eating when Angela heard Daddy call the same man from the night before, over to baby-sit them again. Panic rose up inside of her. Angela did not like that man, and began to cry when her daddy left them with him. She could not tell her daddy why, only that she did not want her daddy to leave. She continued to cry as she watched her daddy drive away, to go back up to the hospital.

Night fell and Daddy was still not home. The man had put Christopher to bed much earlier. Angela wanted to avoid this man, but everywhere she went, he went. It came time to get her PJ's on and she wanted to do it by herself, but the man wouldn't let her. He had to try to help. She pushed him away, so he stood there and watched. When finished getting her pajamas on, she brushed her teeth and got into bed. The light was turned out, but she could still feel him standing there in the dark watching her. Angela wrapped the covers tightly around her body. She moved as close to the wall as she could, hoping he would leave her alone tonight.

Suddenly, she felt him getting into bed with her as if she had made room for him. Angela clung to the covers, as she felt his hands begin pulling at them to loosen them from around her. She fought. Her mouth was covered with his big hand. She tried to breathe, but to no avail. She felt herself beginning to get dizzy. The room was spinning as she felt a stinging sensation from between her legs. The man let go of her mouth, and was now holding her down with his arm. Angela wanted to cry. She wanted to scream, but no one would hear her. Helplessly, she just laid in the dark with this monster raping what dignity she had left. Her body stiffened from the pain and the fear. She was petrified. She could not fight him off her, he was too big. Not as tall as her daddy, but heavier in size.

Somewhere off in the distance of her fainting mind, she heard a car pull up. The man on top of her quickly left his perch upon her, and was heard tidying himself as he made his way to the bathroom. The front door opened, and her daddy called out the man's name. The toilet was heard being flushed, water was run, and a friendly greeting greeted her daddy in the hallway, from the mouth of the monster that had just hurt his daughter.

Angela lay in the dark, dizziness engulfed her. The room was spinning. Sweat poured from her forehead. She got out of bed and headed toward the bathroom. She was going to be sick. Daddy saw her from down the hall, as did the man who had come to baby-sit. All she wanted to do was throw up. Daddy asked if she was all right, as he headed toward her. The man quickly said his goodbyes, and left out the front door before daddy got to her.

Angela was shaking. She was pale. Sweat poured from her temples, and her body was drenched in it. Her body stiffened when her daddy touched her. Fear sent more shivers through her. Daddy cast it off as a fever. Angela could not tell him the truth, he would certainly be angry with her. It was her secret for a lifetime.

The new baby arrived home, bringing reassurances that this man would never be coming back to "baby-sit." Drusilla was wrapped up in her little bundle of joy. Crystal, Angela and Christopher became part of the walls. They were there, but no longer any part of the "family." Christopher spent a lot of time in his bedroom. Angela had her chores to do, and Crystal came home for short visits and then left again.

Drusilla worked on Daddy to get him to pay more attention to her and their new bundle of joy. Her latest addition of abuse for Angela came when Drusilla could no longer send her out into the cold nights, as summer was now upon them. Daylight grew longer; there were more people in the park to notice a little girl wandering around without parental supervision. Daddy would be on his business trips and Drusilla would take Angela downstairs to the basement to jump a few hurdles, made out of Styrofoam inserts from boxes Daddy brought home from his work. The track was set up throughout the basement, and Angela was ordered to jump each one continuously, and not to stop until Drusilla said she could.

Angela was all legs and arms and coordination was definitely not her better talents. Clumsy, really spelled out her physical composition, as well, Angela had no self-esteem. She would run, and fall over the hurdles. Drusilla would pick her up and literally pull Angela up over each Styrofoam block by her hair. This occurred night after night, time after time. Angela never did master the hurdles. The hurdles broke into pieces as she fell over them, nearly breaking her neck and other bones in her body. Drusilla made her continue, at times chasing her around the basement and kicking her in the butt when Angela didn't get over the hurdle. This happened most every time she was sent down to the basement to "jump hurdles." Angela was not only bruised from her clumsiness, but also from Drusilla's deliberate abuse.

There was even a time when Angela had to go to the bathroom and Drusilla decided not to let her go. Angela's bowels moved uncontrollably. Her pants filled up. Drusilla beat her up and then made Angela continue jumping the hurdles. The feces worked its way out the leggings of

Angela's panties and down on the floor it fell. Drusilla took advantage of this opportunity to rub Angela's face into it, going from one piece to the next. Angela gagged and struggled to get away. The feces got into her mouth as she choked back the vomit. Drusilla finally let Angela up and then made her continue jumping the hurdles with the feces on her face and in her hair.

The tears fell as Angela attempted each hurdle. The smell sickened her stomach. Hours later, Drusilla came down to the basement to get her. Daddy would soon be home and Drusilla didn't want daddy to know what she had done to Angela. Giving her a scrub brush, she ordered Angela to "clean the mess up off of the basement floor spotlessly" and "then meet her upstairs to take a bath." It had been the first bath since her daddy had left. Drusilla would always wait until the day of Daddy's return before bathing his children.

Daddy came home and Drusilla told him that Angela had "crapped her pants." She left out the "why" part. Daddy looked at Angela in disgust. Once again, Drusilla had succeeded in turning Daddy away from her. His love for Angela was growing weak. His love for this woman and her child (Dennis) was growing greater. Angela was losing Daddy's love. Drusilla made sure of it.

6

Fugitives Journey

Arriving home from school just about a year after Dennis' birth, Angela noticed packed boxes all over the house. The rooms seemed empty, as she gazed around in bewilderment. Drusilla came into the room. "Mind your own damned business, you little bitch!" It was a welcome home greeting never experienced by most children after a long day at school.

Quickly Angela looked down at her feet while taking her coat off. She was not about to remain curious while being accused of being nosey by an extremely abusive step-parent.. Her intentions of surveying her surroundings had been pure curiosity, but apparently, once again, she had broken one of Drusilla's laws. Sure enough, before Angela could look back up at Drusilla, Drusilla had caught her by her arm, and was dragging her down the hallway toward her bedroom. The attack had caught Angela off guard, so the trip down the hallway was primarily one in "flight", as she bounced on and off her knees, her body hitting the wall as it swung back and forth with each step her six foot tall, two inched Amazon stepmother took.

The twin beds in the room were standing up against the wall with the mattresses next to them. Everything had been packed in moving boxes. Her expression of curiosity was met by the glare of anger from Drusilla's face, and boom! Angela's little body landed inside the closet, headfirst! She was dazed, and her head and neck hurt instantly. The door slammed behind her. She did not move.

The darkness engulfed her little body. Angela felt dizzy. Even in the blackness of the closet, the room seemed to be spinning. She closed her eyes very tightly as she reached up to feel the lump on her head. Crying was not allowed, and it was better that she stick to the rules. Any noise from her "little prison" would send in her Amazon stepmother with more "brutal attacks" on her little body. Very quietly, Angela sank into the corner of the closet, resting her head against the wall and eventually drifted off to sleep.

An hour went by, or was it moments? Inside her "holding cell", Angela could not really estimate how long she had slept. There were noises and voices coming from somewhere off in the distance. Whom would they belong? What are they doing out there? Quietly, she changed positions, moving her body closer to the closed closet door. Angela wanted to hear what was going on.

"We'll pack the truck later, for now; we'll keep it in the parking lot at the shopping center, so they won't see it when they get here." "Close the drapes; we'll meet them out at the driveway." "If they want to come in, we'll just explain that we are having the wood floors polished in the morning." "They won't come in, they never do." "We can sit on the step as if we are enjoying the evening talking out there, they won't suspect a thing." "Mike said that he would help out when we got there." "We'll stay with him for awhile until the situation cools down." "Honey, you got the maps in the truck?"

There was a mumbled response, as the sound of a car pulling up into the driveway was heard outside. Her sister was home for a visit!

"She's here already!" "Quick, let's get out there and meet them, don't let them come in." Footsteps ran to the front door and down the walk to the driveway.

Muffled voices, a laugh or two echoed through the walls of the little prison where Angela sat straining her ears to here more. Nothing could be made out clearly, just her daddy's charm, and Drusilla's fake laughter, and then the front door to the house opened and closed behind the footsteps that now ventured in. Crystal was telling her daddy something as they walked in the door, and then all of a sudden there was silence.

"What happened to the furniture daddy?"

"Well honey, daddy wants you to stay home with us from now on, so we are going to move to where you can stay home with us."

A long silence followed Daddy's answer to his daughter. "Why are you crying?"

"I want to go back to my other home." "I like living where I live now." Sobs were coming from ten-year-old little Crystal.

Angela closed her eyes, knowing that Crystal's comment and sobbing would not be well received. Drusilla started to yell something in response to Crystals' remark, when suddenly a soft voice from daddy interrupted. "It will be nice where we are going, and you will like it there." "We're going to start a new life somewhere else, so we can all be a family again." "Honey, we love you and want you to live with us."

Daddy's charm turned on once again. This time he was wooing his daughter into believing that by moving, the whole world would change for them. He was a great salesman; had fed his family for years on making others believe they needed something, and that by changing one thing in life, life could be changed all together. Even Angela, from her little dark closet cell bought into his words, and leaned back with a sigh of relief. Excitement began to build in her little body. The words "together as a family" stuck right out front. "Family, family, family…It's going to be nice", she spoke into the darkness. The happy thought began to drown out the growls of her empty little tummy. Suppertime had long since passed, and this would be yet another night without a meal in Angela's young life, but the joy of what daddy had just said to her sister Crystal made it all seem so much better.

Angela lay down on the floor of the closet. The stresses of the day put her into a deep sleep. It was chilly in her little "holding cell", but curled up tightly with the ray of hope for a 'better tomorrow' brought warmth within her little body. Angela had new dreams to tuck into that hope created by her daddy's words and instilled in her tonight.

****

Bang! Bang! Bang! Bang! Screech! Came noises from outside her closet prison. What were they doing out there; Angela thought sitting up with a start and moving over closer to the closet door. She was barely breathing; didn't want to miss a single sound. The wood floor outside the closet echoed as the room was emptied of all of its furniture. Footsteps came in and went out. She sat motionless, not wanting to breathe in case someone heard her inside the closet. What if someone heard her and opened the doors, then she'd be in trouble with her stepmother. Then again, if Drusilla heard her make a sound, she'd know that she was awake and she'd be on top of her, beating her up again. Her body trembled in the cool air as she laid back down, very quietly.

As abruptly as the noises had awoken her, the noises in the room outside her closet cell seemed to move off into other parts of the house. Angela laid still in her surroundings, listening for voices in conversation, but could not understand the muffled voices. Her head still hurt from the bump she had received when Drusilla threw her into the closet. Rolling over on her side and lifting her knees to her chest in the fetal position made her feel warm and safe.

Sleep had once again taken over her body, when suddenly; the door of the closet flew open. It was dark in the room. Why weren't they turning on any lights? An arm reached down, grabbed her, and led her up the hall and out the front door. Was this all a dream? The brisk morning air hit Angela's face, and her eyes opened wide as she was pushed into the back seat of the car. She wanted to sit up to try to collect her senses, but a stiff whack to the side of her head, indicated that that unsolicited movement was not allowed. Angela was forced to lie down on the back seat of the car; a blanket was being thrown over her head and body. Thinking that there must be some mistake about the blanket being over her head, she pulled the cover down to her shoulders, only to feel a fist slam into her cheek. The blanket was thrown back over her head. The pain from the blow to her cheek added itself to the pain on top of her head and the tears were difficult to hold back. The tears fell down her cheeks beneath the blanket as Angela choked back the sobs that wanted so dearly to come out. The words of 'promise' spoken by her daddy the evening before dissipated into the darkness beneath that blanket. If this was the 'family' he promised, she did not want it, nor like it.

Angela closed her eyes in surrender to the unknown. Sleep seemed to be the only answer to the pain, confusion, and the heartache. Life was only a day at a time. Each new day brought more challenges than this eight-year-old little girl really wanted, or needed. However, there seemed to be no one who would come and "make things better" for the children.

****

Streaks of light filtered through the little holes in the blanket that covered her face. The car was moving. Sounds of sleeping children came from the back of the station wagon. Angela lay motionless; in fear of the consequence, that even one muscle flicker might get her. Pretending to sleep, she laid as if dead. Her tummy was empty, and the motion of the car was not helping. Nausea threatened to present itself as vomit on the back seat of the car. She swallowed hard each time, and then tried thinking about something else besides the pain in her stomach. Her mind went to the sleeping sounds coming from the back of the station wagon. Was it Crystal and Christopher? Did they come too? Were their heads covered up just as hers was?

A sound from the front seat brought Angela's attention to the crying of a baby. Dennis had just awakened and was making it known that he was hungry and needed changing. Drusilla tried to console him from the drivers' seat, but to no avail. Her child had never gone without, and today was not to be different. His cries of hunger pierced the ears of all inside the car. It was annoying, especially when the rest of the children had gone without dinner the night before, and Dennis hadn't. Yet Drusilla didn't care for any of the other children's hunger pangs, just the hunger pangs of her poor child that cried out up in the front seat next to her.

From beneath the blanket, Angela could hear the car beep a couple of times and then the window being rolled down. Drusilla was asking someone if they could pull over at the next filling station, Dennis needed to be fed and changed. He had just turned two, and when Dennis wanted something, Drusilla made sure he got it.

The voice outside the car was their daddy's voice in response. "Well, yeah, …I guess so. Are the other kids awake?"

Without even looking to check, Drusilla replied, "No, but Dennis is crying and needs to be fed and changed now."

Affirmation to stop for a break, between the two, ended the road trip for now, as they pulled into the next service station. Their stepmother took Dennis from the car and voices were heard moving away, seeming to drift off in the distance and then disappear.

Christopher woke up and sitting up, he reached over and woke up Crystal. Crystal sat up as he pointed out the window toward the restaurant that set just behind the filling station. "Daddy and mommy went in that place", he said.

Crystal reached over the seat to Angela and told her to look out the window. Very cautiously, Angela lifted her head and sat up part way; just enough to peek out the window. She did not want to be caught by Drusilla; one, for sitting up and two, for uncovering her head. The bruise on her face still hurt bringing back memory of when she thought she would take the blanket off her head earlier that morning. They were at a Truck Stop. Daddy and Drusilla had gone in with Dennis to eat breakfast, leaving the three older children in the car.

The mouths of the three children watered as they thought about the food their parents might now be eating. Tears welled up in their eyes when they thought about the fact that they had been left behind. Knowing that they would be in trouble if seen sitting up, Crystal, Angela and Christopher laid back down in the positions that they had been left in when their parents left the car. Their sad voices reassuring one another of the injustices that had been done to them now and in the past. Dennis was treated the best; a whole lot different than any of them had been treated. This had not gone unnoticed by the three. It was a fact, no one could deny. Their daddy and Drusilla had had many arguments regarding this issue, but Drusilla always won, and their daddy always walked away. Dennis was "her baby."

Just when all seemed to quiet down, and the children ran out of words to describe their situation, the back of the station wagon opened and Crystal and Christopher were asked to "get out." Drusilla made them sit on the tailgate of the car, as she reached into the ice chest and handed them bread with butter. "There would not be any drinks, because they didn't want to make a lot of stops."

Angela was next. The back door of the car came open, the blanket was taken down off her face, and buttered bread was tossed at her, as if she were a dog. Sitting up, Angela hungrily ate the buttered bread, licking the butter that got on her fingers, as if not to waste even a smidgen. Each bite seemed to be inhaled as if it had been days since she had eaten, instead of just the two meals that she had missed. Her tummy dissolved every thankful bite. She wanted and needed more, but dared not make the request.

The car doors were closed and the three children were made to lay back down with blankets over their heads once again. Unusual, yes. However, not disputed. The children lay motionless, listening to the sounds that surrounded them. Dennis was up front with Drusilla playing with toys in the front seat. A neighbor had brought over toys and candy as going away gifts for all of the children when she had observed their daddy and Drusilla packing the U-Haul truck. The neighbor had said that "since she had gotten to know Crystal, as she had been over to play with their daughter, she wanted to give the children something as going away gifts." Their daddy had thanked her and given the gifts to Drusilla, thinking that she would distribute them to the children. The gifts and candy went to

Dennis; the other children did not get any of them. Crystal, Angela and Christopher lay listening to the "privileged" noises Dennis was making from the front seat.

Twice, Daddy and their stepmother left the car while the three stayed behind in the car that day. Crystal had to "go potty" by the second stop, and was not' going to let "no" be her answer. She left the car, as Angela and Christopher laid quietly, hoping that their sister would return to the car before Drusilla and their daddy returned. The tailgate of the car opened. Christopher and Angela lay motionless, except for the pounding of their hearts. Angela's body was shaking in fear of what might happen if daddy and Drusilla caught Crystal outside of the car. Had their parents returned, or had Crystal opened the tailgate of the car up?

A body flew into the rear of the car and dove underneath the blankets. It was Crystal! She had made it back before their parents came. Angela's heart pounded wildly! Relief from the anxiety of not knowing if her sister would return to the car in time! She would hope that her pounding heart would settle before her parents returned. The uncontrollable shaking of her body from nerves would give away their secret, that her sister had left the car. Knowing Drusilla as well as the children all did by now, she would not let an inquiry rest, and the obligation of explanation would be forthcoming, or it would be beat out of them. Taking deep breaths and slowly expelling the air, calmed the nervous tension Angela now felt. It was just about gone by the time Daddy and Drusilla returned to the car.

The front car door opened. Christopher got asked to join his daddy in the U-Haul truck, while Crystal and Angela were told that they could sit in the back seat, but they were to sit on their hands. No speaking to one another and they were not allowed to look out the side windows. They were to face straight ahead and look out the front window from the back seat, almost if they were not to be seen by people traveling by their vehicle.

The little girls' behinds grew tired, but neither moved a muscle. Their little hands were numb and their wrists ached. Tears streamed down Crystal's face, while Angela sat expressionless. Tears on her husbands' children always rubbed Drusilla the wrong way, and sure enough, this time was not going to be any different. Crystal was right within reach of the

Amazon's hand and it flew into her face! Slap! The hit came directly from the front seat. Crystal's head hit the back seat. She let out a cry.

Angela closed her eyes, not knowing where this would end. Slap! Came the second hit from the front seat, landing directly into Crystals' face. The car swerved a bit as Drusilla attempted to land a third hit. Crystal had the imprints of Drusilla's hand on her face. Would this ever end?

Angela held back the tears from the hurt that penetrated her heart for her sister Crystal. Sitting helpless next to her sister while the Amazon smacked her, there was nothing that could be done. Angela held her breath; fear gripped her insides. All too often, she too had received similar treatment from this woman. The children were defenseless. No one to protect them, not even their daddy.

****

Darkness surrounded the car as the dome light came on when the door opened. The ice chest was brought out from the rear of the station wagon, and peanut butter was spread on bread. One sandwich for each of the three children to eat for supper, and no drinks to wash it down with. The children ate the sandwiches as they watched the trio, Daddy, Drusilla and Dennis head off to go into the restaurant. They were thirsty, and the peanut butter did not help quench the thirst. Slowly they finished the last bite, swallowing hard, hoping to keep it down, so it would not come up for an encore swallow. Barely able to speak, tears fell from each face, wondering if their parents and their half brother would be getting something to drink.

Angela and Christopher had to go "potty", so Crystal became to 'look-out' for them. Each took their turns relieving themselves at the far side of the car. Drusilla and their daddy always parked out away from traffic, so no one would notice the three children left in the car. For Christopher, going to the bathroom outside came easier than it did for his two sisters. Angela's heart pounded as she went through all that a young girl in a pair of pants must go through to 'complete the task.' First making sure that no one was looking, and then to squat down…primitive, yes. But what child is ever restricted from responding to the call of nature? Most parents cannot wait until their children are able to successfully respond to the call on their own. With Drusilla, it was a way to make their daddy think that they were slow learners and had not achieved the simple task of being potty trained. Making them wait for her command and instruction gave her 'authority' and control over them. Their daddy never caught on to Drusilla's method of operation.

Once back in the car, the children sat in silence. Sweet victory when you are not caught. They watched people come and go from the restaurant. It was rare for anyone to park near them, and if the occasion did arise, the truck would always be parked between their car and the next one. On one or two occasions when there were no extra outer parking spaces, the three children would be ordered to 'assume the position'. This meant, blankets over the head and lay still. Dreading the consequences of not following the orders, the children did as they were told.

Daddy and Drusilla returned to the car. Drusilla brought out the children's toothbrushes and led them to the backside of the service station. Each child took turns brushing their teeth and trying to drink even the slightest of a swallow of water from their cupped hands. It was not much, but it did taste good. Faces were washed and hands were cleaned up, then all were marched back to the car, each being once again required to lie down.

Traveling further into the night, the truck and station wagon finally pulled into a parking lot. Daddy went in somewhere and then came out to the car, giving Drusilla a key to a room. The car was moved slowly into a parking space, and then her door opened and the dome light came on. Crystal was brought forward to the front seat and told to "lie down." Angela stayed where she was in the back seat and Christopher remained in the back of the station wagon. Each was wished a goodnight's rest and the blankets were pulled back up over their heads. Daddy, Drusilla and Dennis left them and the silence of the darkness filled their ears. Crystal asked Angela if she "knew where they were at?" "No", came the response.

"Wait awhile, and then I'll sit up and see."

They laid in silence, listening. From time to time, a car could be heard pulling up, maybe some voices, and then the deafening peace of the night would embrace them. It was quite a while before Crystal sat up to survey their surroundings. "Angela, quick...look where we are."

Cautiously Angela sat up. In front of them was a building with many doors. Curtains on the windows. The one story type of building. Dim lights broke the darkness and lit up the walkway. Not a soul in sight, except for an occasional glimpse of a man over in the brighter part of the building that read "office." From time to time, an occasional silhouette of a person behind a closed curtain would catch their eyes, but mostly the emptiness of being left on the outside, all alone filled their thoughts.

Crystal looked at Angela, and Angela back at Crystal. Christopher started to cry, saying he was afraid. Both girls tried to comfort him, without leaving their assigned positions. Words of reassurance were whispered to him, encouraging him to be brave, and that they would all be here together. "It's okay; nothing's going to happen to us out here." "The doors are locked", Angela pointed out to him.

His tears and muffled sobs eventually turned into the steady breathing of a sleeping child. The girls could not have asked for more. The coolness of the night crept into the car, and all they had to do now was to block out the fact that their little bodies were shivering, so that they could get some sleep. No one strong to keep them from harm. No one to tuck them in. No one cared. Not even their daddy who seemed to be in his own little family, with his wife and her son.

****

Two days later and several hundred miles traveled, an early morning rising brought them to yet another Truck Stop out in the desert. Crystal, Angela and Christopher could barely move. They were stiff all over. The combination of sleeping in the car and having to sit on their hands when they were allowed to sit up really was not enough exercise to keep their young muscles in shape. The lack of water did not help either. Standing up out of the car and walking around had pretty much been forbidden most of the trip, except of course the 'permitted' few occasions they were allowed to go to the bathroom to brush their teeth. The children grew more and more tired as the trip progressed. They spent more time sleeping now than they did staying awake. Drusilla seemed to enjoy the quiet, and to her, their fatigue did not bring on any warning signs.

Dennis played and slept up in the front seat next to her, and left the car whenever she did. His play time didn't' seem to make any more difference to the three children in the back of the car. They knew what they knew and they couldn't change a thing. At this moment in time, it really didn't bother them any more. He was her child and they were just the "extra baggage", that happened to be packed along with.

This was just another day of traveling until they arrived at their first rest stop. The tailgate was let down on the car, and the children were allowed to sit out on it, while their daddy, his wife and her son went into the restaurant to eat. The three hung their legs down, swinging them back and forth, while glancing around at their surroundings. Being able to sit out on the tailgate and move their legs exercise the atrophied muscles. This was the best treat they had had since the trip began. Each of the three children ate butter bread, as they began to talk, laugh, and giggle together. The sight of their first cactus brought laughter. They imitated the "one arm salute", and laughter again filled the air. Some man approached them and asked if they wanted some soda. The three children shook their heads no. It is not that they did not want the soda; it was that they were not allowed to talk to strangers, or accept anything from strangers. The man laid down the bottle of soda on the ground next to the car and walked away. The three children looked at the bottles of soda and back at the restaurant. Had their parents seen what the man had just done? Their mouths were awfully dry, but Drusilla's rules were rules. The bottle of soda sat on the ground by their car for quite some time. The children kept looking at the bottles and reassuring themselves verbally between one another that they had made the right choice in not accepting the soda from the "stranger", yet all were very thirsty, nonetheless. Heavy stressed out sighs filled the morning air. Their heads turned away from the bottles that sat on the ground next to the car, their feet kicking back and forth, but now with a more forceful blow each time.

Suddenly something caught their eyes. It was moving very slowly across the parking lot and coming closer to them. Curiosity got the best of them and they just had to go see what it was. It was coming closer, but they could not wait so down jumped Christopher off the back of the tailgate, running up to the creepy-crawly hairy thing. He came running back laughing and shaking at the same time. "It's a big spider! It's a big spider, I know it is!" His sisters squealed and goose pimples rose on their arms, just to think that a spider could be that big!

It was Angela who followed him back to see for herself this great big spider thing. Crystal cautioned both that their parents could see them from the restaurant window, and they'd both be in trouble if they did. Neither child heeded the warning as they ran up to the spider and back again. Angela came back shaking like a leave on a windy fall day. "You should see it, you should come see it!" She excitedly told her sister. This was the most exciting thing the children had ever seen, and they were having fun, eventually forgetting that Drusilla had warned them to stay sitting on the tailgate of the car. Crystal kept cautioning both to return to the car before…too late. Drusilla and Daddy were on their way out of the restaurant and they had witnessed both Angela and Christopher leaving the tailgate.

"Angela and Christopher!" Crystal saw Drusilla's face. Anger burned through the stare of disapproval.

Angela and Christopher tried to explain about the hairy spider, when Daddy's look suddenly changed to terror. That hairy spider is a tarantula and you could have been bitten! The three children were asked to get into the car, and then their daddy went to get the gas station attendant to do away with the spider. The same guy who had offered them the soda earlier, responded to Daddy's request.

The tarantula was directed away from the family's car and the guy started up a conversation with their daddy. He told Daddy of his attempt to give the children a soda each, but they turned him and the soda down. Their daddy turned on the charm, thanked the guy for the soda, and goodbyes were said.

Returning to the car, daddy tried to explain the reasons for the children not to go up to any more spiders like that or things they do not know what they are. Those spiders can jump far and bite hard. Angela and Christopher promised never to do it again. Daddy then handed each a bottle of soda that the kind man had left for them. They began to drink the first real drink that they had had in awhile. It tasted so good! Their daddy returned to the truck with Christopher, and Drusilla climbed into the seat of the station wagon. She had barely pulled onto the road when she turned to Crystal and asked for her bottle of soda. Crystal reluctantly, but obediently handed Drusilla her bottle of soda. Drusilla opened the car window and tossed it up and over out the window. Looking in the rearview mirror at Angela the same request was given. Angela had had a few more swallows than Crystal had had, so when the order came she too, handed Drusilla her bottle. Like Crystal's bottle, Angela's bottle crashed to the pavement on the side of the road.

Tears welled up in the girls eyes. They were thirsty, frustrated and hurt. Drusilla's excuse once again was that she did not want to have to make any unnecessary stops. Order was given for them to sit on their hands, and like every time before, they obediently followed it.

The U-Haul truck overheated and another had to be brought out to replace it. Daddy was steamed, but once again, they were on their journey again. Daddy had asked that Angela be allowed to ride with him this time. After a brief hesitancy on Drusilla's part, she gave in; but not before, she had warned Angela that she was not to talk to daddy.

In the cab of the truck, Daddy offered Angela some candy, but Drusilla had already warned her about that too. Angela rejected the candy, making up some excuse and turned her head to the window as the tears began to fall. She really wanted to have some candy. Afterall it had been given to the children by the concerned neighbor, but Drusilla was in control now. No meant no and even daddy was not allowed to break her rules.

Daddy wanted to sing songs with Angela. Through sniffles, she joined in. The weight of the journey seemed to have been lifted, as the joy caught on. Daddy and Angela had not sung together since Grandma's house. It felt so good. So very good. Bringing back the good times from before Drusilla walked into their lives. Would daddy and Angela ever be close again? Questions that would just have to be put on hold for now. They were caught up in the moment. Johnny Cash was Daddy's favorite singer, and her daddy had taught her his favorite songs. This was yet another cherishable moment in this young girls' life. A rare gem of an occasion to be exact.

"Daddy, where are we going?" questioned Angela.

"California, honey." Daddy answered.

"California...what's in California?" her little inquiring mind wanted to know.

"Somewhere we can start all over." "Somewhere we can live, and your sister can live with us, and no one will know where we are."

"Why don't we want anyone to know where we are?"

"So we won't be bothered anymore." "You know what?"

"What?"

"You ask too many questions."

"Mmm...I just wanted to know." "Does Crystal get to go back to her other home?" "She wants to go there you know."

"She does, does she?"

"Yeah..." pause..."but I don't want her to leave me again."

"Me either...and we're making sure it won't happen again." We get to start all over again."

Silence fell captive to the turning of their thinking gears. Angela was trying to understand what her daddy had meant when he said, "to start all over again." Then again, she had wanted to talk about Drusilla to him for quite some time, and her ongoing fears of losing him as her daddy and friend, but then again, she didn't' know if she could trust him anymore. So much had happened. He always seemed to believe Drusilla.

"You've gotten quiet...what you thinking about?" her daddy inquired.

"Something...but it doesn't matter...I love you daddy."

"I love you too, sunshine." "Things will get better, you'll see."

The trip in daddy's U-Haul truck ended rather abruptly, when Drusilla, for the first time in the journey, decided to pull to the side of the truck and motion daddy to pull over. Daddy obediently did so; thinking that there was some kind of emergency, and Angela was taken off the truck by Drusilla. Christopher took her place on board with daddy and the "show was on the road" again.

Angela sat on her hands in the back seat of the station wagon, pondering over her discussion with her daddy. "Things will get better, you'll see," kept being rehearsed repeatedly in her mind. Angela wanted to see this come true. So much so, that she would set her heart upon it.

The snapping of fingers in her face brought her back to her senses. Drusilla was demanding to know what the conversation with her daddy had been all about. Angela answered cleverly, "we talked about a song", and then left it at that.

One more day, just one more day. California...why California?

7

Temporary Refuge

"Sit up, you idiots!" came the order from the front seat. "I want you to all listen carefully to every word I'm saying to you." "If you don't do exactly what I tell you to do, I'll beat the crap out of you ...do I make myself clear?"

"Yes", came the robotic responses from the children seated in the back seat.

"Now, we're just about to your grandparents home where we will be living for a while." "You are to do as I say, nothing has changed." "I am your mother." "You are not allowed to have treats or food or TV without my permission." "You are not to do what they tell you to do; I am the boss of you." "You guys are not to go anywhere with them, or do anything they ask, unless you check with me first." "You don't answer any questions they ask." "You don't talk about me." "Do I make myself clear?" Drusilla hissed the orders from the front seat as they pulled into a driveway.

"Yes", the children echoed in obedient response.

Two people came out of the house to greet them with smiles on their faces. Smiles that drew the attention of all three children from inside of the car. 'Grandparents.' Grandparents the children had never met before. They were motioning for the children to come out of the car, but the three did not move. They looked toward the direction of Drusilla waiting for her approval for them to leave the car. None came. All she wanted to do was to impress them with her baby, Dennis. The three children sat motionless just watching and waiting for Drusilla to give the approval to get out of the car. Inside, their little bodies they wanted to run into the arms of these kind people who were their grandparents. Nevertheless, they knew all too well, the "threatened consequence" that hung over their heads. So here they sat, perfectly still not responding to the welcoming gestures from their grandparents.

Finally, Daddy came to the rescue after jumping down out of the truck. "Come on kids, let me introduce you to my dad and his wife; your grandparents."

The three children responded, "Mommy doesn't want us leaving the car until she says we can." Ignoring their answer, he lifted each one out, one at a time, introducing them as he did. "This is Crystal, my oldest daughter." Granddad smiled so wide that you could feel the hug that came with it.

"Hello Crystal, you're beautiful."

"This one here, dad, is Angela." "She's my Blondie."

Granddad knelt down and gave Angela a big squeeze. "You are a pretty one, aren't you?" His hug was genuine, something she had not felt in a long, long time. She leaned into him, never wanting the hug to end. Feeling the tears well up inside her, she turned her head and walked away. She choked back the tears for she knew the consequences for them. Granddad was taken a-back a bit when she walked away from his squeeze, but daddy came to the rescue when he introduced Christopher.

"And here dad is my tiger, Christopher." "My first born son."

Both girls were surprised that their daddy even remembered Christopher being his first-born son. As of late, Dennis seemed to be their daddy's central focus and both Angela and Crystal were the comforters and encouragers in Christopher's life now. Christopher turned to his daddy for a hug, but it was met with daddy walking away toward Drusilla and Dennis. Instead, Granddad reached down and gave Christopher a great big teddy bear hug. Even the part about Angela's nickname being Blondie, brought a sense of false hope that maybe Daddy was remembering that she was "his special little girl" once upon a time? Daddy had not used that name for Angela for a long time. Drusilla had taken his pride for her away, by lying to him about Angela's behavior, giving excuse as to why she had to discipline Angela all the time.

The children were invited to come in for some fresh baked cookies and cold pop. It had been a long trip and Granddad's wife had taken the time to prepare such a wonderful home-warming snack. Just as the invitation to have the pop and cookies was given, Drusilla interjected with the fact that the car and truck had to be unloaded and that she wanted the children to help unpack some of the things from the car and truck before they did anything further.

Opposition from Granddad's wife, Eden, met Drusilla's interjection. "Things can wait and then Mark (Granddad) will help his son unpack the truck and bring any necessary things in." "It's been a long ride for the children and they need a snack, and then they should be able to go run and play and stretch out a bit." Granddad and his wife would not take 'no' for an answer, no more than would Drusilla. Therefore, Granddad and Eden joined the children in unpacking the truck and car when Drusilla insisted that the children do it. Drusilla was mad, fuming even! They were undermining her authority over the children, or so she figured and complained profusely to their daddy. An argument ensued, and Drusilla and their daddy went out behind the house to talk while Granddad and his wife quickly helped the children unpack. When they got finished, the children were seated down on the front step to the house, and a plate of cookies and a can of pop for each child was brought out. Immediately there were echoes of 'no thank yous" from fear of the repercussion they'd receive from Drusilla if they accepted.

Granddad and his wife encouraged the children to accept the treat, but the refusal was eventually read through. Daddy was called out by Granddad, and after a few harsh words between the two, Daddy turned and encouraged the children to accept. Joy filled their hearts, until Drusilla came out to see what was going on. The anger on her face would have stopped a herd of charging buffalo. The children swallowed the mouthful of cookies and pop. Barely a movement had passed; fear struck, Angela started…"Daddy said we could."

"You fucken brats!" "I told you that you would get beat if you accepted food without my permission!" "Get in that fucken house!" Drusilla sneered through her teeth in a low voice. From afar, it looked like a smile, up close the look made the children's bones tremble. All three stood up, leaving the plate of cookies and their pop on the step and turned to go into the house. Their grandparents who had been talking to their daddy out by the truck noticed the entourage moving into the house and asked; "what's wrong?"

Drusilla put on the fake smile and cheerfully responded, "Nothing was wrong, she was merely taking the children in to the house to get them cleaned up."

The children were pushed to the back bedroom where they were going to be staying. Angela felt a foot kicked between her legs, which in turn, dropped her to her knees. The pain felt as if her insides were coming out, but she struggled back up on her feet to stand before Drusilla. Her body shook from the pain. Christopher was crying for lack of being allowed to finish his cookies and pop. Tears streamed down Crystal's face. She had never wanted to come on this trip. Terror struck her. This was not going to be a better home and family as daddy had promised. Drusilla had just moved out of the jurisdiction of the State of Wisconsin, now she could do anything she wanted. Crystal wanted to go back. Back to her foster home in Wisconsin, where there was a couple who really cared about her and loved her, and treated her wonderful.

"I told you fucken brats that if you accepted anything from anyone without my permission I would beat the crap out of you, and I meant it!" Drusilla growled, her long fingernail piercing the lip of her victim, which once again, Angela seemed to be her target. Drusilla grabbed for Angela's neck and began squeezing it tight. Angela couldn't cry out. Gasped breaths of air came as Angela struggled to breathe. She fell to her knees, choking from the stronghold Drusilla had on her neck. Crystal and Christopher watched in horror. Crystal began to cry.

"Let her go, let her go, let her go!" Crystal was terrified that her stepmother would kill her sister.

Drusilla let go of Angela's neck, only to grab a hold of Crystal's neck. "You bitch!" "You're the reason we're here!" "You think you can tell everyone about me!" "You think you can tell me what to do…well (slap!) (slap!) "I've got news for you!"…"They're not going to find me or you here!" (slap!) (slap!)

Just then, the front screen door opened. Drusilla kicked the bedroom door closed with her foot so that whoever had just walked in would not see what she was doing to the children. She was breathing deeply, as she angrily pointed a warning finger at the three of them. "You pull any more crap with me, and I'll kill you all!" "Now get your PJ's on and get into the beds." "Do not come out of this room or I'll give you what you had coming from the start."

All three children began to dress themselves in the bedroom. Drusilla left the room, closing the door behind her. Crystal and Angela were shaking uncontrollably. Christopher was still crying silently from not being able to finish his cookies and from seeing his sisters being choked. They quickly got into the beds that had been made up for them, as they had been told to do and turned their faces to the walls, as was customary orders by Drusilla.

Angela's throat ached and it was difficult swallowing, but she dared not cry. The imprint of Drusilla's hand decorated the face of her sister, Crystal. Christopher just couldn't get past the fact that he hadn't been allowed to finish the cookies and pop. He was hungry. He wanted the cookies and pop.

The room was silent. The sun shone into the window. It was only late afternoon when they were sent to bed. Voices from outside their bedroom door became the concentrated object of Crystal and Angela. Christopher had since cried himself to sleep. The trip had tired them all, but how much more sleep could they possibly need?

A question was asked somewhere down the hall by Eden, as to the particular likes and dislikes of the children when it came to eating meals.

"The children will eat anything that is set before them", was Drusilla's response.

"What will they want for dinner tonight?" questioned Granddad's wife.

"Nothing, I've put them to bed." "They were tired." "The trip must have tuckered them out." "However, Dennis will be eating with us tonight." "I will feed him from my plate." "May I help you make dinner?" Drusilla attempted to redirect the focus from the children onto herself.

"Well...yes...but the children should have really had something to eat before they went to bed, don't you think?" came the concerned response from Granddad's wife.

"No...no, not really." "They were tired, and they won't be eating until morning," countered Drusilla's rebuttal.

Silence filled the house, except for the banging of pots and pans. Eventually the sound of a table being set, and then the voices of daddy and Granddad entering the house from outside, filled the room.

"Where's the kids?" their daddy inquired.

"They're in bed", responded Drusilla.

"Why?" asked Daddy.

"They were tired after I gave them a bath and cleaned them up."

"For a nap, right?"

"No, for the night." "They were tired after the long trip."

Footsteps were heard coming down the hall. It was daddy. The door to their bedroom opened. Not one child moved. Drusilla was close behind him and they knew it. He kissed each one good night. They wanted to respond, but dared not move. Drusilla was there in the room with him, watching every move they made. The dread of doing anything that would upset her made them lay so still, they hardly even breathed.

When Daddy got to Crystal, he kind of paused, reached down and kissed her gently, not saying a word about the marks on her face. He knew, he just had to know that they were the handprints from being hit by Drusilla.

The door closed behind them. There were a few angry muffled whispers, but then the sounds of retreating footsteps back to the kitchen. Voices of merriment filled the hallway from the dining room as if the children had been forgotten.

****

The bright California sunshine shone in the window of the children's bedroom. One by one, it beckoned their response to rise and shine. The yawns and the stretching of their little bodies filled the room. A peaceful silence filled with the melodious songs of the birds chirping outside their window. The occasional buzz of a bee or fly hitting the screen that now separated them from the outside. The smells of bacon crept into their room from beneath the bedroom door, churning the hunger pangs in their bellies. Quietly they whispered their insights of what possibilities the day ahead held for them. They still faced the walls that their tiny beds embraced.

A sigh or two, and then the emptiness. Had hope been long forgotten, and now only replaced with the fear of their stepmother? They really could not see past the threat of Drusilla coming in to release them from the invisible "holding cell" of their beds.

The door opened as the hair on their heads rose in response from the fear of the unknown intruder. What would Drusilla do next? They waited. Someone had come into their room, and a gentle hand lay on Angela's shoulder beckoning for her to "wake up and come to breakfast." Fear gripped Angela, as she realized that this was not Drusilla, but instead, Granddad's wife, Eden. She wished that she could follow this woman to the breakfast table, but if she valued her life, Angela would remain pretending to be asleep. The gentle touch of this woman was a welcome feeling. A drawing of the inner spirit. Reality brought her back. If Drusilla caught this woman in their room, there would be a confrontation. Fear returned, as Angela tried to ignore the hand on her shoulder. Really, if this woman knew what was good for her and good for the children, she would leave before Drusilla woke up.

Eden moved over to Crystal's bed and just as she placed her hand on Crystal's shoulder to try to wake her, she noticed the bruising on her face. She caught her breath as the children heard the voice of Drusilla at the door.

"What do you think you are doing in here?" she inquired angrily.

"I was just getting the children up so that they could eat their breakfast." "They didn't get dinner last night, so I knew they would be hungry this morning." Came Eden's response.

"I'm the one who gets these children up, not you", barked Drusilla.

"This is my house and Mark asked me to make breakfast for his grandchildren." "I did, and now we don't want it getting cold." "They've got to be hungry, seeing that they missed their dinner last night." "You were sleeping, so we felt we could wake them up to feed them." Eden shrugged as she tried to explain the normal logic for waking up the children.

Just then, the children's daddy came to the door and asked, "what was going on?"

Drusilla pointed out that she "didn't want the children up until she got up." "I will feed them when I get up."

Granddad arrived in the doorway. He had heard just about enough..."This is my house, and Eden will be feeding my grandchildren right now." "End of discussion." The order was direct. Drusilla wanted to continue the argument, but she backed down. Granddad was no match for her. She had better quit while she was ahead. She did not want to be thoroughly seen through. The children were ushered into the dining room by their granddad, and each allowed to pick the chair they wanted to sit in. In Granddad's house, there were no assignments. His grandchildren got to choose. He respected them, and they were beginning to respect him.

Drusilla glared at them from her place at the table. Confusion and fear filled their little bodies. They were on thin ice and they knew it. For now, they had a "defense" in place by way of their Granddad, but it would only be a matter of time before they would be alone again with her. The thought made their hearts pound and their bodies shake. The food was warm and delicious, but fear choked them with each bite. Eden was aware of their reactions, but said not a word about it. Instead, she offered other items on the menu, until each tummy was filled. They had not eaten that well in a long, long time. They wanted to push more in, like there was no tomorrow, but shrunken bellies only let so much in.

The children each asked to "be excused from the table", to return to the room to get dressed. There really had been no baths the night before, so the smell of small bodies needing bathing filled the air. The children hoped that they wouldn't be followed into the room by Drusilla, but hope was off the menu most of their young lives, at this point. Drusilla came in and closed the door behind her. Just as she was about to mutter some angry phrase to them, the door opened unexpectedly, and a voice threatened her from behind, "Don't you dare!" "Don't you dare touch them!" "I was the one who got them up, and if you have something to say, say it to me!" Granddad was glaring at the Amazon. He was angry! He had figured Drusilla out.

"Mind your own fucken business!" "These are my children, and I will do with them what I want to…get out of here!" She yelled back at him.

Granddad ignored her language and continued, "This is my house, these are my grandchildren, and you will not abuse them under my roof." "You want to pick on someone, pick on me, I'm more your size." "I guarantee you, I'll take you down!" Granddad deserved a hero's welcome, but the children stood motionless. Drusilla could see a reaction a mile away, and the children were not in the position to offer a 'bias' now.

Daddy came into the room. Seeing the anger on his father's face, made him think twice on whose side to take. Quickly he took Drusilla by the arm and led her out of the children's room without speaking a word.

The children stood bewildered, afraid and confused. This had never happened to them before. Nevertheless, since Drusilla was only a room away, they still felt the fear of making one wrong move. Granddad gave them each a big hug, concern echoed each squeeze. They could not say anything, and just in case Drusilla was listening or could see them, they could not return the hug, though they wanted to so badly. Granddad was becoming their friend. Trust was new to them, not something they could give out freely. It had to be earned.

The children dressed themselves and cleaned up their room by making the beds and folding up their PJ's. Eden said that they didn't have to do it anymore, but the children knew that Drusilla wanted it that way, and as long as she continued to be a threat to their lives, they would continue to follow her wishes. Eden told them that "she liked cleaning up rooms for children", but the children had an ingrained order saying that they would be doing it themselves for as long as they lived, as long as Drusilla was around.

"Go out back and play; see what Granddad bought for you guys." Eden encouraged.

Cautiously, the children headed out the house and into the backyard. Granddad had gotten them a swing-set. They looked in amazement, smiles beamed from their faces. Running over to the swing-set the girls grabbed the swings and Christopher climbed the ladder to the slide. Just as they began enjoying their gift, Drusilla opened her bedroom window. "What the hell do you guys think that you are doing out there?" She growled.

"We were told to play," was Angela's answer to her stepmother.

Crystal and Christopher stopped playing and stared at the woman who was at this point hanging her head out the window, so they could see her face. Their bodies began to tremble.

"What did I tell you all the other day?"

"..N-n-o-t-t-t-a," the children replied in unison.

"That's right, so what the hell do you think you are all doing out there?" "Did I tell you to go play?"

"…N-n-o-o-o…"

"Then why the hell are you out there?" Drusilla unjustly inquired.

The children looked at one another and then back at the window. Tears began to fall. They were confused. Who to follow…whom not to. Wanting to have fun…this woman not letting them. Their legs shook in fear, knowing that they were going to have to pay for this, too.

"Get your asses in this house right now!" Drusilla's voice echoed throughout the backyard.

All three children 'double-timed it' into the house. Drusilla met them at her bedroom door. The first blow caught Angela off guard.

Dazed, she stood back up, only to be knocked down by Drusilla's fist. Crystal began to move backwards up the hallway in an attempt to get away. She wanted to run away, head back to Wisconsin. To the safety of her foster home. Christopher began to cry. His little legs started shaking as he bellowed, "I'm sorry mommy, I'm sorry mommy, I'm sorry mommy." "I won't do it again," He said hoping to save his soul and himself from bodily injury.

All the commotion had caught the attention of Granddad who had been out in the front yard of the house. The screen door slammed behind him as he hurried to rescue his grandchildren from their abusive stepmother. The three children were led down the hall away from Drusilla, and ushered over to his wife to care for them. He then returned to her bedroom and a bitter argument broke out between their stepmother and their granddad. The children sat very still at the feet of granddad's wife, listening to their granddad's words to their stepmother. Granddad was going to get the last say in his house; he was not backing down when it came to his grandchildren's safety.

Eventually, Granddad returned to the livingroom. Sitting down in his chair, his breathing deep from the episode down the hall, he shook his head in disbelief. "How long have you children had to put up with that Amazon?"

There was no response from the children. They looked at one another with eyes of caution, knowing full well, any response to their granddad's question would cost them dearly. They stared blankly back up at him, and then at the TV set he had just turned on for them. All three blocked out all reality of life, if just for this moment, as they stared at the program on TV. Drusilla had not let them watch TV. This was a new privilege, granted by their granddad, scorned by their stepmother.

****

Things were a bit better while they lived in their granddad's home. They knew that he would come to protect them, and both he and his wife kept an eye out for any negative reaction from Drusilla toward them. Eden stayed home with the children when granddad was at work, and she was his eyes and ears while he was away. Granddad wanted his grandchildren to have a good life. This began to build a more positive hope for tomorrow for their young lives.

Granddad had offered their daddy a job at his hardware store. Daddy and Granddad worked together day in and day out. They came home laughing and talking of the day's past-times. The children listened intently and were allowed to interject questions and comments in Granddad's house. Laughter was allowed also. Dinnertime conversations filled his home with cheer, for all except Drusilla. She did a whole lot more sulking and trying to pull daddy away from his father. Drusilla would call their daddy into the back bedroom, voices were heard and then more times than not, an argument would break out. Drusilla did not like living under Granddad's roof. She felt he didn't like her and her son, Dennis. Granddad was always looking at her with disapproval. He would not let her say anything to the three children. They wouldn't let her son run around the house in diapers, he had to be dressed. She laid endless accusations directed at Daddy's father, hoping Daddy would stand against his dad. She wanted to leave, to move out, so they could be a family again. By themselves...

Daddy tried to convince Drusilla that "it would only be for a few more months, until they could get out on their own."

"Stand up to your dad, and make him give me back control of our kids!" She demanded.

"No!" "Just leave well enough alone!" "We can't afford to be out on our own yet." "There's no money yet." "We don't need my father and his wife telling anyone about you mistreating the children, he's threatened to do so, you know." "So no!" "I won't tell him to give you back control of the kids." "Just bear with this for a while longer, I've got my own plans on when we will be moving out." "Right now, they are looking for us in Wisconsin." "Here, there is no trace of us." "Sit tight."

"I can't stand it here!" "Maybe Dennis and I should go back to my mom's place to live." "Then I don't have to worry about you and your kids any more, or the fact that your dad wants to turn me in for child abuse!"

"I said we are staying here!" Daddy was mad. Life was complicated, but nothing he didn't have a part in. You make your bed, you will sleep in it, or so his father warned.

Granddad chuckled to himself, as the children sat on the edge of their seats listening to the conversation down the hall. Drusilla sounded like a wounded animal, trying to get her way, but she wasn't succeeding. No one was feeling sorry for her. Drusilla was used to getting her own way every time and being told a definite "no" this time set the course for disaster. She became a ticking time bomb. They all knew that it was only a matter of time before she blew, and they would become the objects of her blame. Revenge hung over them like a plague waiting to pounce upon them, the first chance she got.

8

At Hell's Gates

Granddad had left the house early in the morning and Eden and gone with him to help him in their Hardware Store in Del Monte. Daddy had said that he was not feeling good and that he would be staying home. With the closing of the front door and both on their way to the Hardware Store for the day, Drusilla came into the children's room.

"Get up you lazy lard bucket brats, we're moving," she said with an air of victorious celebration. The children were confused by her words. This was the first time anyone said anything about them moving. Where was their grandparents? Eden normally came in to get them up, ever since Granddad had chewed out Drusilla. Why was Drusilla in their bedroom getting them up? Where was Eden this morning? Where were they moving to, and why didn't Granddad know. Why wasn't he here?

The children realizing that perhaps Granddad and Eden were gone and they were left alone with their stepmother, they had better respond quickly to her orders. They got dressed in their old clothes. The stress of times past leaped into their souls one by one, and deep sighs filled the air. They really didn't' want to be leaving the safe environment of Granddad's protective care and home, but robotically each did what Drusilla commanded.

The joy-filled words of Drusilla's freedom echoed throughout the house as suitcases were packed and taken into the car. Their small beds were taken apart and loaded into the rental truck. Each child had tears streaming down their faces. They did not want to go anywhere with Drusilla and were sensing what life would become once they left the safety of Granddad's home. Sensing the expressions of sadness, Drusilla responded slyly, "It's just you and me kiddies…just you and me." "We'll see who's in charge now." Her eyebrow rose, and the wicked smile of her own satisfaction became apparent to Crystal, Angela and Christopher. Revenge would be sweet for Drusilla, this moment had been a long time in coming; but for the three children, it would now be a struggle for survival. What they had already had to endure in Wisconsin, and in their journey to California, and by the look on Drusilla's face, they were assured that things were not going to be for the better.

Drusilla was a physically beautiful woman, but within her tall, thin shapely body, manifested a driving force of wicked brutality toward these children, so strong that no one could question her intent. Manipulation and control seemed to be her lifetime goals. She could snap into the most dreadful human being on the face of this earth in one moment, and then at the sound of a telephone ringing, or a knock at the front door from a concerned neighbor who had overheard the cries of the children, Drusilla could appear as being the sweetest person, so convincing, that no one would suspect that she was as horrible as she was. Hollywood could have used her expertise to train actors, but constant contact would eventually let them know that it this was not just an act, it was for real. Almost as if, she had a split personality.

Even their daddy worshipped the ground she walked on, despite the fact that he had long since caught on that she hated his children and was quite abusive to them. Drusilla was out of control, and both were now partners in crime. He had taken his family out of the State of Wisconsin to flee from further investigation of his wife's parenting skills and his accountability. What was it that made their daddy side with this woman, instead of coming to the aid and defense of his own flesh and blood? Is lust for a woman more powerful than love for your child? This question would be asked repeatedly throughout the course of their growing-up years. The answer repeatedly and apparently, was "yes."

The front door was locked behind them, and the children sat in the car watching as their daddy embraced Drusilla. She was a wild animal finally set free from the cage that had limited her from pouncing and devouring his children. The two of them exchanged silent glances, not a word spoken as they climbed into their separate vehicles. Daddy drove the rental truck, Drusilla the station wagon. The children stared blankly ahead, not moving a muscle. The station wagon followed the rental truck to a storage garage. All three children were ordered out of the car to assist their Daddy in loading boxes from the storage unit to the truck as Daddy and Drusilla carried the bigger items together. Then they all got into the car and assumed their familiar positions in the car, as daddy led the way to their 'new' home.

The trip in the car did not last long, just a short jot around unfamiliar neighborhoods, and then they pulled into the driveway of the ugliest old beat down house on the block. The gray speckled tiles siding it resembled the inside feelings of the children in the back seat. The roof had missing shingles. Peeling paint embraced the broken windows. Weeds grew like giants in the yard surrounding it's dilapidated structure. Eucalyptus tree branches and leaves littered the broken asphalt driveway. The old detached garage looked as if it would fall down with the first gust of a big wind. The children looked with disbelief, not uttering a word between them. It was creepy, even scary looking.

Daddy said, "Well guys, what do you think of your new home", braking the silence of their shock? "We can fix it up."

The children could not answer. They slowly got out of the car, still mesmerized by the scenery around them. Daddy was not pleased with their reaction, but tried to be encouraging anyway. "Go see the great big backyard, it's huge!" "Big enough for a farm."

The children went running to the back of the house, stopping suddenly when they got to the corner of the house. There in front of them laid a huge field of tall giant weeds, and an old dilapidated shed. The children stood with tears coming down their faces. It was ugly. It didn't look like a 'new' home. They turned back to look at the house from the backyard. Heavy sighs came from the children's mouths, indicating the let down feeling within them. Looking back in the direction of their daddy and Drusilla, they slowly headed back to the driveway. They did not like it. Angela kicked at the eucalyptus seeds on the driveway. Their heads bent down, they had seen all they needed or wanted to see as they headed back to their parents.

Suddenly a noise caught their attention, and all three ran over to the old rusted wire fence that separated their yard from the neighbors' yard. There were horses next door! What a sight! Finally something exciting to lift their spirits. "Daddy, Daddy…come see!" "Horses Daddy!" "It's horses!" All three shouted together.

Daddy was at their side. "See guys, I told you, you'd like it here." "As soon as we get this mess cleaned up, we'll get some horses too." "Maybe even some other animals too." "We can have our own farm."

"I want to have a bunny", Crystal acquisitioned matter-of-factly.

"I want to have a horse of my own", Angela requested.

"Okay…I think you can have them, but first we need to get this place cleaned up." "You guys are going to have to help Daddy if you want him to get you them."

"Daddy, can I have a dog?" It was Christopher's turn.

"Sure, now lets go get the truck unpacked, and start cleaning this place up."

The children were ecstatic. They had never dreamed of living on a farm, but the excitement of their daddy saying that they could have something of their very own, made them jump for joy. Right now, all three children would have walked to the ends of the earth for anyone, just from the promise of being able to own something of their own. All three children wanted to help fix up the house and yards just to be able to receive the pets they asked for. They ran back onto the driveway to help unload the truck.

Their daddy unlocked the door to the house, and each child stepped inside. The feeling of dejavu' entered their souls as they walked into the house. The house was a total mess! The walls had holes in them, bloodstains and dirt lay all over the floor. Old and new spider webs embraced the corners of the room or just hung freely from the ceiling. Dirt everywhere! Rocks from thrown through now broken windows, fragments of splintered glass scattered all over, resting amidst the calamity and mess on the floors. The coolness of the early spring breeze blew in through the broken windows. The three children shook from the chill that ran up their spines. It was the realization that they were the ones who would be used to clean up the mess.

The suitcases the children were carrying were set down one at a time as they took in the scenery around them. Angela was first to move into the hallway with sincere curiosity. Christopher followed her example. There were bedrooms and a bathroom. The toilet was rusted and very, very dirty. Decaying human feces lay at the waterless bottom pit with the flight of flies buzzing around laying eggs amidst their larva that was feasting off the toilet contents. Both children gagged at the sight and the morbid smell that penetrated their surroundings. "Eeeewwweeuuu...!" retreating back into the livingroom where they had started out. "Oh Daddy, it's stinky in the bathroom...Somebody did a dump and didn't flush it." "They must of run out of water or something." "And flies are eating it...yek!"

Drusilla entered the house with a bucket and some rags. There was cleaner and a scrub brush too. Angela felt the hair on the back of her neck stand on end. Something let her know that she was Drusilla's contestant.

The pipes rattled when they were turned on in the kitchen. A burst of water sprayed into the bucket as Drusilla poured in disinfectant cleaner. Steam drifted from the hot water as it filled the bucket. The bucket was then carried into one of the back bedrooms. Drusilla did not even have to ask Angela to follow her, this was Angela's job and she knew it. The 'scrub and clean' person from the very beginning of their daddy's marriage to Drusilla. Angela knew that Drusilla would not get her hands wet for any kind of work, and that is why she had such long fingernails. Drusilla pointed out the dirty walls, a measure that really did not need doing this time around. The walls were filthy, and nothing was clean. Drusilla also pointed out the windowsills, the closet, its drawers and the filthy floor. "You know what to do, now get busy!" "I want it all spotless!"

The water was hot, very hot. The steam off the water and now the scrub brush burned her hands. It ran down her arm and into the front of Angela's shirt. She stood on the chair Drusilla had conveniently provided for her. Each squared off section of the wall was thoroughly scrubbed and then wiped off with the rag. Her hands burned with each entry into the hot water, but she knew better than to complain. Angela continued scrubbing and wiping repeatedly. The cost or consequence for disobedience was too big and extremely painful, and Angela knew it. Drusilla had full reign of her life now, and the nightmare had returned.

Sounds of someone else scrubbing something somewhere down the hall, with sounds of furniture being brought into the house echoed through her mind. Streaks were not allowed, so she chased them with her rag. Wiping and re-wiping each area until it was nearly bone dry. The windowsills had thick dust and dirt, dead and alive spiders on them. Angela chased them with her rag until she caught them and squished them. The rag was rinsed out and the sill cleaned to perfection. Drusilla was known for her 'white glove' inspection from previous experience gained in their Wisconsin home. This time would be no different, Angela was certain. Drusilla had let them know that she would regain control one day, and this day had arrived. The children walked on eggshells now.

Suddenly the chair was pulled out from under her feet. Angela's face hit the wall on the way down to the floor! Blood trickled down from her lip as she picked herself from off of the floor to face her attacker. Drusilla stood with her hands on her hips glaring at her. "What kind of job is this?" "What are these streaks?" "Have you forgotten how to clean?" Drusilla grabbed the bucket of water and went into the bathroom to fill it again. Pipes were heard groaning, screeching and shaking from the bathtub. Water sputtered as it poured into the bucket. Water was being dumped back out and then the bucket got filled up again. The steaming bucket was brought back into the room as Angela moved the chair back to the corner where she had first began the task, and started scrubbing the walls again.

It was difficult trying to get the streaks out of the dirty stained-up walls. As the water ran to the section below the section she was working on, more streaks appeared. The walls had not been painted or washed in many years. The porous cement walls were not going to release the years of dirty neglect. Nonetheless, Angela continued to work on them, hoping with all her heart that they would get clean enough to meet Drusilla's inspection. However, the stubborn stains brought torment and agony to a hopeless situation.

"Smack!" "Why the hell aren't you done with these walls and this room by now?"

Angela's face kissed the wall again. Her body dropped off the chair. She was shaking, not only from the fear of surprise, but from the fear that now was the time, Drusilla was getting revenge for all the days they spent at Granddads' where she was not allowed to touch them.

Drusilla grabbed Angela by the hair and pulled her up to her feet. Angela's legs felt like jello beneath her, yet dared not to give in to the feeling of crumbling to the floor. She did not want to be lifted up by her hair again, nor give Drusilla further reason to carry out a more brutal attack on her. "You've got just ten more minutes before I come back in here." "If the job is not finished, you'll taste the belt you've missed for quite sometime. There's no Granddad to 'protect' you now!" Drusilla wryly smiled, pleased with her new freedom. The room would never meet her expectation of clean, and she knew it. Part of the torture was having her stepchild have to wait to get beat up.

Angela shook, as she raced to get the job completed before her stepmother returned to the room, before the ten-minute time limit was up. How could she get done in that short period of time when perfection was expected. Her body shook so badly now that it was quite difficult to even do the job correctly. Her heart beat hard in its cavity as fear gripped her. Two more walls, a whole closet for the second time, the whole floor…shoe drawers…how…how…how. Tears flowed down her face, blinding her with their salty presence in her eyes. Her shoulder sleeves became the handkerchief she needed so dearly as she wiped her nose and eyes off on them.

Quietly sobbing, knowing full well that Drusilla would be back with every intention of using the belt on her. Ten minutes was unjust…no one could achieve perfection of this room in that time, let alone any time limit. Not all the scrubbing and repeated clean water buckets could ever clean this room to Drusilla's perfection. The walls needed sanding and new paint. The framework needed scraping, sanding, and new paint. The wood floors needed stripping and new varnish. The threat of being beat up had nothing to do with how the job was done. Drusilla didn't need a reason to beat her stepdaughter up. The pain of unfairness tore apart the heart and mind of this little girl.

A whipping sound and a sting of pain embraced Angela's waist. Her body fell off the chair again. She was on her hands and knees, as Drusilla repeatedly brought the belt down on her body. There was no specific target. Drusilla swung the belt up and down, up and down, up and down. Angela's head, back, legs, bottom and arms suffered the attack from her stepmother.

"You little bitch!" "I'm going to show you who is in charge. "I told you to obey me at your grandparents, and I meant it!" "You fucken little bitch!" "You didn't listen to me, did you?" "You got the sympathy of those poor old people, but now you're going to pay!" "Who's in charge now?" "I'm asking you…who's in charge!"

"You are…you are…!" sobbed Angela.

"You're damn right I'm in charge, and I'm going to show you just how much I am in charge!" With every word spoken, the belt landed on Angela. Drusilla didn't stop swinging it. She had gone berserk! Angela was on her side leaning against the corner walls like a small defenseless animal trying to survive. The blood dribbled down her chin and onto the front of her shirt; she was open prey for her wicked stepmother's attack.

"Hey, what's going on in here?" Daddy had entered the room.

"I caught her playing around in here instead of working." "It was the second time." Drusilla had her excuses (lies) down pat.

"Angela didn't respond, it would cost her more inflicted brutality from this Amazon. Daddy looked at her and said, "I thought you wanted a horse?" "Well if you don't help clean the house and yard, you won't get to have one." "Now get busy young lady, and do what you were told to do." Daddy and her stepmother left the room. Angela could not defend herself. The way Drusilla put it to him; she was nothing but a disappointment to him.

Angela rose up from her knees, shaking from the pain and with a stronger fear of Drusilla. Daddy did not know the truth, and now he did not like her anymore. She was 'bad' in his sight and Drusilla was determined to make sure she painted the picture that way. Angela hurt all over. Welts swelled up on her legs, arms, across her back and hips, on her face and neck. She looked a mess. Her hair stuck to the sweat that poured from her head and brows. With her hand, she attempted to brush it back out of her face. Every movement brought severe pain. However, nothing was more painful than losing her daddy's love. He had not died, but Drusilla had successfully turned him from her, or so she felt.

The bucket had tipped over on the floor during her beating and there was dirty warm water everywhere. Tears fell as she tried to hold back the sobs of helplessness. She wiped up the mess, the pains from her beating beginning to ache as her muscles stiffened. She just had to finish the job before Drusilla came back in. Angela used the front of her shirt to wipe her tears from her eyes, it didn't seem to help. Water was all over her. The smell of pine cleaner in her shirt, gave her the understanding of why wiping her eyes with her shirt made her eyes burn even more. Angela just had to see what she was doing. Attempting to reach behind her for the dry part of her shirt brought further realization of the swollen welts on her back. The added pain made it difficult to pull on the dry part of her shirt to dry her eyes, but she did it anyway. She just had to wipe the sting from her eyes so she could see what she was doing.

Angela finally got the murky water cleaned up from the floor. It was cold and dirty. Angela took the bucket to the bathroom and dumped it into the bathtub. She was filling the bucket back up with clean water when, pow! Her head hit the wall. She lost her balance and fell into the tub.

"What the hell do you think you are doing in here?!" "You're not done with the room yet." "Did I say you could come out?" The glaring eyes of Drusilla penetrated Angela's senses.

Meekly she tried to respond, "The water was dirty, and I-I needed some clean water so I could finish it." "The bucket got dumped…"

"And whose fault is that?" "Since when do you make choices for yourself?" "I'm the one who makes choices for you, and not the other way around, do you hear me?"

"Y-y-e-s-s-s…" Angela stammered cautiously. She was still hanging half in and half out of the bathtub, and could not move to get up.

Drusilla did not have any problem yanking her out of the position she was in. Angela's arm just about came out of its socket as Drusilla brought her up by her arm. "Get up and get into that room!" "Don't come out until I say that the job is finished, do you hear me?"

"Y-y-e-s-s…Angela's shaky voice responded as she headed obediently back into the room.

She stood in the doorway of the room waiting for Drusilla to bring her the bucket of clean water. Angela listened as the hot water pipes shook and screeched. Her body ached. She wanted to sit down, even lay down, but knew better. The pain made her dizzy as her vision became fuzzy with dark shadows, everywhere she looked. Nausea filled her. Angela tried walking around the room to keep from passing out. She looked at her hands, raw from the water, and bloody from her beating.

Sure enough, the water was blistering hot. It stung her hands; nonetheless, Angela reached in and took the scrub brush and began scrubbing every nook and cranny with vigor and diligence. The strong smell of pine cleaner filled the air. The newness of clean in this room brought forth hopefulness for this old ugly house. The pain from her little body cried out for mercy, only to be ignored by the fear of Drusilla catching her not working. In this home, there was no mercy as long as Drusilla ran it. The taunting fear of the return of Drusilla brought forth the determination and perseverance this little girl needed to continue in her endeavors to please her wicked stepmother.

The smell of food being brought into the house gave birth to once ignored hunger pangs in her belly. She continued to work while envisioning sitting down with her family for a meal when she completed the job. Hurriedly she worked, finally coming to the last corner of the floor by the doorway leading out into the hallway. She sat down in the doorway and waited for Drusilla's return to inspect the job. Her mouth watered as she thought about the food that might be on the dining room table. She could hear the rest of the family enjoying the meal in the other room.

"Angela, I don't hear you scrubbing any more," came the inquiry of Drusilla's voice from the room where everyone was eating.

"I am finished with the room" Angela responded.

"Are you sure?" The question was more in warning, than inquiry.

Angela looked around the room, trying desperately to reassure herself that it was Drusilla qualified, and replied back, "Yes…I'm sure."

With that, Drusilla's footsteps approached. Angela's body stiffened. Second thoughts of doubt ran through her mind. Was it really going to meet Drusilla's approval?

She stood up as Drusilla rounded the corner into the hallway. Glancing around the room, and then back out toward Drusilla, and then stepped aside to let her stepmother into the room to inspect it. Drusilla walked around the room, checking everything. She opened the windows and the shoe drawers. Walking out of the room, she told Angela to "wait there"; she "would be back."

Thinking that Drusilla had gone to get her some dinner, Angela sat down on the floor in anticipation. Her tummy growled. She had already missed two meals today. She was ready to eat, hunger burned inside her belly and her mouth watered.

Drusilla returned, but as she entered the room, Angela's face dropped. Instead of dinner, Drusilla carried blankets. Her stepmother threw them down on the floor and instructed Angela that 'it was bedtime.' "No dinner tonight for you, you don't deserve it" Drusilla stated a-matter-of-factly with that sly smile of mockery on her face. The head of this little girl hung sadly down, as she tried to make a bed for herself from the blankets that now lay upon the damp floor. Drusilla left the room, closing the door behind her. Tears began to well up and flow down her cheeks as she laid in the big empty room with the evening sunlight streaming down upon her. She was hungry, hurting, and rejected. Granddad did not know where they were. He could no longer stand in the gap for her now. Angela cried herself softly to sleep.

9

Nature's Blessing, Life's Torment

The morning sunshine shone brightly through her window. Outside the birds were singing songs of joy. Angela tried to sit up to get a better view of her surroundings. She was stiff all over. Bruises and welts covered her body. Her muscles ached, bringing back to reality the episodes of the previous day.

She laid back down trying to drown out the beauty of the sunlit morning. Maybe if she fell back to sleep, the next time she awoke, she would find out that this was all just a bad nightmare. Angela covered her head up with the blankets thinking that the darkness beneath them would put her back to sleep, but the songs of the birds outside her window made her uncover her head to listen.

The songs sounded happy and cheerful. Every now and then, the fluttering of little wings passing by her window entertained her as she laid back listening and enjoying nature's morning melodies. The warmth of the sun coming in through the bedroom window upon her little body brought her comfort from the pain. The sadness within her soul began to fade with every cheerful chirp from the joy-filled songs of the birds outside her window. The peaceful gift from nature embraced even the deepest of hurts, making Angela wish that this moment would never end.

The sky was dusty blue, with a cottony fluff of a cloud passing by now and then. The call of a crow penetrating the songs of the sparrows enhanced the beauty of natures' freedoms. Angela laid back listening and watching. Her soul was at rest. The physical and emotional pain seemed to dissipate as the scenery unfolded all around her.

The house lay silent, except for the slight sounds of snoring and heavy breathing somewhere off down the hall. She lay peacefully still, not wanting anyone to awake, to spoil her interlude with nature. She longed for the same freedoms being exposed by this morning's ensemble. Unable to obtain it for the moment, she accepted this mornings' grace as it momentarily presented itself.

****

    Her bedroom door opened without even a sound. Angela was still mesmerized by the scenery outside her window; that she hadn't noticed the woman standing over her. Suddenly, the blankets were caught up from beneath her body and the immediate pain from muscle stiffness and that of being rolled over onto the hard floor, brought her back to the reality of what was now her wretched life.

    "You can get up now." "I've got another project for you." The sly almost mocking expression displayed on Drusilla's face, brought chills to Angela's spine.

    Angela jumped up quickly to her feet, her body shaking from the sudden fear that now pierced her insides; following Drusilla across the hall to the bathroom. The sight of the bathroom made Angela remember that it had been a great while since she had gone. The urge from a full bladder was not what she needed now, especially not compounded with the fear of the Amazon that now stood by her side.

    There on the floor stood the bucket of water with pine cleaner in it. Drusilla was pointing out all the dirty fixtures and standards, along with the walls, the floor, the window and sill. "One half hour, babe, and I'll be back." "If it's not finished by then, you know the consequences."

    Looking around, Angela watched as Drusilla left the room, and she then got started. Maybe, just maybe, she could meet the deadline. Natures' introduction to her morning made her feel somewhat positive and she would give it her best shot. First, she needed to relieve herself.

    The toilet had been flushed from its ugly contents of what was in it the day before, but the residue of the mess still clung to the sides. The musty odor of the dirty commode lingered in the air. Carefully, Angela squatted over the toilet. The relief felt so good. The stream seemed endless. Her bladder had been so very full. Relieving themselves was a privilege, or so Drusilla had led Crystal and Angela to believe. This time she had not even asked permission, figuring she was already in the bathroom, she would take the opportunity.

    It was the wrong decision. Drusilla was upon her before she even finished going. Bam! She found herself stuck between the wall and the toilet, her urine still running out of her. Angela was stuck there, as the fisted blows kept coming to her head and face. "What the hell do you think you are doing?" Drusilla angrily inquired.

Angela was dazed, upset, scared and very hurt, all at the same time. She could barely answer. "I…I," she gave up. The pee trickled on the floor between her legs. She was in a dirty, stinky puddle, and stuck between the toilet and the wall. The smell made her gag. She could not throw up, for there was nothing in her stomach to throw up. A high-pitched 'zinging' noise penetrated inside her head after all the fisted blows Drusilla had connected to the side and front of her head. With each blow to the side of her head, the other side of it hit the wall, and with each blow to her face, her neck flew back and the back of her head it the wall.

Drusilla left her stuck between the toilet and the wall, and walked out of the room. Angela rested her head against her arm. The room seemed to grow darker each time she opened her eyes. She struggle to keep her eyes open, as the high pitch noise in her head grew. Angela felt herself growing weaker, she could not move. The feeling of faint grew stronger as each moment passed by. She tried to fight the feeling of her weakening body. She didn't want to die, really, she didn't.

Some time had gone by when Angela felt a hand upon her shoulder. Her body jumped with a start. Fear gripped her as she opened up her eyes trying to focus on the person standing over her. She attempted to remember where she was, while at the same time trying to figure out what it was that she was doing, or supposed to be doing and how she had gotten there. Her head was spinning. Fear gripped her when she realized that it was Drusilla standing over her. By instinct, Angela tried to rise to her feet. Nothing happened. She was still stuck between the toilet and the wall and feeling very weak. Her memory came back to her as to how she had gotten here.

Drusilla reached down toward Angela, as Angela retracted in fright, thinking that Drusilla was going to beat her up again. Afterall, how long had she been sitting there since Drusilla had left the room, and had she returned the "half hour" later to find Angela still sitting stuck in the corner? Instead, Drusilla lifted her out of the tight corner and was now pulling her dirty wet pants up for her.

Angela was wet and filthy. She smelled badly. The urine she had sat in, the dried sweat from working the day before, the murky water, and all else that was on the sides of the toilet and on the floor added to the stench and stains on her clothes. She needed a bath very badly. Instead, Drusilla led her out of the bathroom, down the hall, through the livingroom, down the steps of the dining room and back up steps into the kitchen. Sitting Angela down on the floor of the kitchen, she handed her a bowl full of oatmeal. Angela's hands were very dirty, but her stomach ached for food. Gulping down the hot cereal without even a pause to chew it, she ate it like a hungry animal as Drusilla stood watch.

Finishing the cereal, she was handed a glass of water to wash the oatmeal down. Angela gulped it down. She ached all over, but did not complain. Drusilla then told her to "return to the bathroom and finish cleaning it"; she would "be in, in half an hour to inspect it."

Angela walked stiffly to the bathroom. She was still dizzy, but her energy was returning moment by moment as her belly digested the food. Bending over the now cold bucket of cleaning water, she began to wash the walls. She hurt all over, and to apply pressure brought jolts of pain throughout her body. Still, she worked diligently without giving up. The clean walls smelled better than she did. Her hands worked on and on as she struggled to apply muscle power to the stubborn stains on the walls and fixtures. The water in her bucket was filthy but she dare not empty it. Drusilla would beat her for doing so, if she did.

"Mommy...mommy..." she called.

"What is it?" Drusilla responded.

"I need some clean water, please."

"I'll be right there." Footsteps approached.

Angela began to shake, even though she had been the one to beckon her, Drusilla did frighten all life out of her.

The bucket was dumped out and refilled with hot water, the pine-cleaner added and then the bucket handed back to her, without so much as a word spoken between them. Drusilla headed back up the hallway and into the livingroom to continue watching her soaps on TV. Angela worked diligently to complete the task.

The walls cleaned up well, she moved on to finish the standards and fixtures. The bathtub and sink revealed salvageable capabilities. New life came back as their glazed enamel surfaces began to shine. Not so with the toilet. It had been years since being cleaned and sanitized. The dirty stains inside did not want to give in to the elbow grease Angela gave it. She scrubbed and scrubbed the stains. All she had was a dirty old rag and the water from her bucket. She better than her best, growing weary from the effort she put into trying to get it cleaned. Finally, she gave up and decided to move onto the floor.

The mess at the side of the toilet brought back the fear of the earlier event. Quickly, she cleaned it up. The smell turned her stomach, but she worked on. By the time Angela had finished cleaning from around the toilet, the water desperately needed changing again. She called out to her stepmother and asked for the water to be changed.

"I'm busy', was the response. "Go on and do the rest of the floor, and then I'll be in."

Angela, very slowly, went back to her bucket of dirty water. She really did not want to stick her hands back into the filthy water, but did it anyway. Foot square, by foot square she worked on. The tiles did not appear any cleaner to her, but obediently she continued until she reached the doorway. The room reeked of urine and filth, missed with soured pine cleaner. It was stomach churning.

"I'm finished" she called out.

Footsteps responded this time. Angela knew that the room would not get a clean bill of health from Drusilla. The dirty water had not really cleaned the floor. The smell in the bathroom was so bad, that it indicated that urine and dirt had just been wiped all over the floor. Drusilla had not come to empty her bucket and given her clean water to do the floor, so what she had cleaned up from the side of the toilet, was now all over the floor. Angela's body began to shake vigorously as Drusilla took the bucket from her. The bucket was filled back up and then she inspected the job. The walls seemed to meet her satisfaction, as did the window and sill. The bathtub and sink got the mark of satisfaction, but when Drusilla got to the toilet, she pointed out the dirty stains in it.

"I tried to get those out, but they won't come off with just my rag" was Angela's response.

"They'll come off, jut a little more elbow grease, that's all it takes", came Drusilla's rebuttal.

Angela didn't respond. She knew the consequences if she did in this case. Drusilla was always right, no matter what. Therefore, she'd try again, hoping with all her might that they did come off. If not, there were more consequences to pay.

Drusilla left the room once more. Angela was not hit this time. Unusual, yes. Nevertheless, she would work diligently on the toilet once more. Her hands felt raw from being in the water bucket for two days straight. They were bleeding where the skin had been broken open from yesterday's beating. The cleaner stung as her hands became more and more chapped with each entry into the water. Angela did not stop. She worked with all her might to get the stains out of the toilet bowl. Sweat poured down her face as tears of defeat fell down her cheeks. The toilet bowl stains would not surrender to her efforts, or the primitive methods available for her to clean it out. She knew that Drusilla would not be pleased with her imperfections. Giving up on the toilet, she moved on to the floor. Scraping the cracks and crevices with what little she had for fingernails and with the edges of the scrub brush, she worked to prepare a spotless floor presentation for Drusilla. The clean water helped to bring somewhat of a shimmer to the old floor tiles. The filth smells form before were dissipating as fresh clean pine cleaner water was used to clean the floor tiles. Angela felt better as she surveyed her surroundings. If you didn't look into the toilet bowl, you could say that you were looking at a clean bathroom. The project had taken her more than the allotted half hour limit, yet Drusilla had not come to impose it. Why? Who knows. Angela was not going to insist upon it.

"Mommy...I'm done."

"Be right there." Came Drusilla's reply.

Angela waited with a feeling of satisfaction. She wanted to please Drusilla if she could; then maybe, she would not treat Angela so badly. Drusilla came to the doorway, eyeing Angela's workmanship. Looking intently on finding an imperfection in the project, but nothing could be pointed out. Nothing of course, until she opened the lid of the toilet and peered in. Drusilla was not happy. Once again, Angela found herself on her knees in front of the toilet with scrub brush in one hand and a rag in her other hand. Nothing else. She continued to scrub the toilet until the bristles of the scrub brush wore down, and the rag began to fall apart. Still, the stubborn stains remained. She had sores on her fingers and knuckles from all her efforts. Hour by hour went by, and the stains would not give in. At dinnertime, Drusilla came to inspect the job. It did not meet her approval and Angela went without dinner. At bedtime, Drusilla came to inspect the job again, and still it did not meet her approval. This time, Angela was ushered off to bed in her filthy, dirty, smelly clothes. She was so stressed out, she really didn't' care. It felt so good to lie down upon the blankets in her bedroom. There was no insomnia for this little girl. She was fast asleep within the first few minutes.

10

Torture and Affliction

Twelve days later, the clean up in the house revealed almost livable conditions. Angela had been assigned to the daily scrubbing of a room or two, as she worked her way through the house. The torment of Drusilla's attacks, frequency and severity depended on the mood she was in at the time she administered the brutality to her husbands' children.

As each room was cleaned to perfection, daddy followed through with paint. Daddy had stolen lumber, paneling, paint, screens and aluminum framing, housewares and many supplies from Granddad's Hardware Store, before that final moving day. Granddad had let their daddy do the ordering of inventory for his Hardware Store, and while ordering for Granddad's store, ordered extra for the home he was moving into. Granddad trusted his son and was not aware his son was stealing from the business. The children's daddy would store the extra inventory in the storage unit, until now, when he needed it to fix up the house. Daddy had bragged that it was the least his father owed him for abandoning his mother, sister and himself many years ago.

Granddad didn't catch on to the theft until after his son and his family had moved out of their home, and then the invoices began coming in. The inventory on the invoices from the suppliers could not be accounted for at Granddad's Hardware Store. Even after their daddy left his father's home and the opportunity to work with his dad, he would call the suppliers for things like window glass for his house and more paint. They would ship it to 7171 Wallowing Avenue, in Balding Park, California, using his dad's good credit and good name. Silly thing, their daddy did not want his dad to know where they moved to, but the invoices were sent to his dad's Hardware Store, and that is how Granddad found out where the children were living. The invoices also let him know what items had been shipped to his son. Granddad called up his son and the two had a major falling out. Granddad wanted his son to pay on the invoices.

In response, their daddy changed his phone number to unlisted and no one answered the door when Granddad came to settle the accounts. The children were not allowed to go outside when their Granddad came calling. They would see his car drive slowly by from time to time, but they were not allowed near the man that once supplied them a refuge and safe haven. Their parents told them that he was a crazy man. To them, he was a nice crazy man. One who had protected them from Drusilla.

The children would just stare as Granddad drove by. Sadness filled their hearts as they watched him leave. They wanted to go with Granddad, but didn't dare move. Every time they would see his car, so would Drusilla. She would call them all into the house to do chores inside the house. Once or twice Angela would see Granddad's car while outside and contemplated making a run for it. Nevertheless, Drusilla could out run her. She also did not know if Granddad would protect her if she did get to his car. A million 'what-ifs' crossed her mind, all landing on the torment of torture when Drusilla caught up with her. The fear of Drusilla made her freeze in her tracks as she stood standing and watching, as her Granddad drove by.

A chill ran up her spine, as she pretended to be looking down at her feet as if to not acknowledge his presence. Frustrated from the confusion of indecisiveness, she began sweeping the driveway with a mighty vigor. The tears started flowing down her face as the feeling of being stuck into a life without hope taunted her heartstrings. Anger burned within her! She swept harder and faster until she was exhausted and out of breath from putting her 'all' into a somewhat mediocre task, she bent over gasping for air. Her sleeves became the handkerchief for her eyes and nose. Angela wanted to cry out, actually, scream! Maybe it would have made her feel better, but thinking twice about the outcome of doing so, chose not to. Drusilla would strongly and physically object to any kind of outburst.

"Excuse me, but are you all right?"

Startled, Angela looked up to see where the strange but friendly voice was coming from. The neighbor woman with the horses next door was now standing a few short feet from her. Angela dried her eyes and tried to smile a reassuring smile. "Y-y-e-ss, I...I...guess I am, I just have something in my eye." She lied. Angela knew that if Drusilla was watching, and caught her in the presence of a stranger, she would be in big trouble.

"May I help?" questioned the woman.

"Uh…n-n-nooo…I think I got it out, I'll be okay, really." Angela responded quickly, taking a nervous look toward the house to see if Drusilla had witnessed the exchange of conversation.

The neighbor spoke on, introducing herself as "Verna". Her husband, "Wilbert", and two daughters, "Aaron" and "Betty." It sounded like a wonderful family, and like this woman was a great mom. Her introductions of her family members had deep seeded tones of love and admiration, something that Angela longed for in a mom. Nevertheless, a fence and heredity separated her from having either a mom or a family.

Angela smiled rather sheepishly, hoping that this woman would go away from her quickly, because Drusilla would never approve of Angela speaking to anyone, let alone someone making conversation with her. She kept glancing toward the house to see if Drusilla was looking. For this woman to get the message to go away; Angela began sweeping the last bit that was left of the driveway, and was not responding to any inquiries being made by the woman. Eventually, the woman looked over toward her home and headed in the direction of her house. Angela didn't want to appear rude, actually she liked having the lady talk to her. However, Drusilla would not approve.

"Angela, would you come in this house," it was Drusilla's voice.

Angela dropped the broom and quickly headed into the house. Drusilla met her in the doorway, indicating that she had seen what transpired out on the driveway.

"I can't even trust you to go out there to sweep a driveway, and you've gotten the neighbor feeling sorry for you."

"N-no", Angela replied trying to defend herself from the accusation. "She just came up to me."

"You were crying…what were you crying about?" Drusilla's question seemed to have a know-it-all approach.

"Nothing…I…um…just got something in my eye and it was making it water." Angela was terrible at lying. Drusilla could see right through it. It took a liar to point out a lie.

"You were crying and I would like to know why right now!"

"I guess I was sad," Angela responded looking down at her feet.

Drusilla was not going to let this one go by. "Sad about what?" She pushed.

"I...I...don't know, just feeling sad." Angela didn't care if Drusilla could tell that this was another lie, she was not about to give up the truth.

"Well, maybe you need something worth being sad about." "Get in here and close the door and drop your drawers!"

Angela began to shake as Drusilla went to get the belt out of her room. Tears of hurt and frustration filled Angela's soul. Damned if she told the truth and damned if she didn't. Drusilla would beat her for nothing.

"Bend over and grab your ankles!"

Obediently Angela assumed the position she had held so many times before. One!...Two!...Three!...Four!...Five!...Six!...Seven!...the sting on her bottom and back of her legs just added to her hurt and frustration.

Drusilla finished the beating and told Angela to pull up her pants. "I don't want you to go near that driveway." "Get out front and pull those weeds, I want them out by the roots!"

Angela was pushed out the front door after hitching up her pants. There in front of her stood weeds taller than she was. A whole front yard of them, reaching from the house to the street. Angela stood looking at them, when suddenly Drusilla's fingers were leading her by the ear to the furthest point out. "Start here." She ordered as she pushed Angela to her knees.

Angela stood to her feet and then bent over, wrapped her hands around the base of the first tall weed. The ground was hard and it didn't budge. She grunted while pulling it with all her might. It still didn't budge. Drusilla stood watching from the front porch and began to mock her. She bent over and pretended to pull at a weed and grunt aloud with all her might. She looked ridiculous, as she made funny faces in mockery. Angela was embarrassed, as she grabbed the week with anger building inside of her. The weed let loose from the ground, springing Angela backward into the tall weeks behind her. Drusilla laughed hysterically at the sight.

Tears fell down Angela's face but not for self-pity. Anger grew within her as Drusilla continued to mock her. . Her anger at her stepmother's mockery made the adrenalin flow, which gave her more strength than she knew she had. Weeds surrendered and broke up out of the hard clay dirt as Angela tugged them out by the roots. Eventually

Drusilla gave up the charades on the front porch and went into the house to get Angela's brother Christopher out front to start pulling weeds from the other end of the yard. Then Crystal was led out into the front yard by Drusilla and assigned the area over by the driveway, to work forward from that direction. With her three little white slaves diligently at work with the threat of bodily abuse if they stopped working, Drusilla went inside the house to watch her soaps. The children were not allowed to talk to one another; just another rule of Drusilla's', reinforced by placing them at opposite ends of the large front yard.

    Each child struggled; whispered grunts were shared all around as they tugged at the tall weeds. They worked in the hot sunlight in the mid of day in an early summer season. It was getting warmer out as bees buzzed around their heads, looking for the little white and yellow blossoms produced by these tall giant weeds. The children ignored the presence of the bees as they worked diligently into the late afternoon hot sun.

    Crystal was called inside to prepare dinner. Christopher went in to get a drink and to entertain their half brother Dennis. Angela drearily continued on attacking these tall giants, wishing for even a glass of water, but none was offered. Quitting before Drusilla gave permission guaranteed a severe consequence. On into the late evening she worked as if they had forgotten her out there. Her hands were filled with numerous blisters and the first layer of blisters had long since opened seeping clear fluid out of them revealing the tender soft tissue under layer. Even then, other blisters had formed on top of the old ones and burst in the tender skin, now oozing of bloody serum. The sting of pain had turned into an aching of muscle and tendon distress. She couldn't open her hands up wide, they stayed in a half crescent position. Almost arthritic.

    Angela had missed lunch, and had not been offered or given any drinks all day. Her mouth was dry from the dry summer air. Yet she worked on. Many weeds lay dying on the ground, but there were millions more in the big yard and field that surrounded their house. She had to keep going.

    "Angela!" Drusilla was calling her from the front porch. She tried to stand up straight, but couldn't. Her body was stiff from being stooped over all day beyond fatigue. It was painful to walk as she made her way to the front porch through all the weeds.

    "Coming."

"Why are you walking like that for?" mocked Drusilla.

"I can't stand up, it hurts," replied Angela.

"Well maybe a swift kick to the butt will help." Drusilla laughed unsympathetically, as she said it.

Angela tried with all her might to stand up straight. The pain made her involuntarily yell out, whereas, Drusilla used it to her own benefit to inflict more pain.

"If you can't stand up straight, you won't be able to sit down at the dinner table, so maybe, you should just go and get your PJ's on and get to bed."

"No!" Angela burst out. She had worked hard all day and was famished. Water was her greatest need, but food came in at a close second. She straightened up and walked right for Drusilla, ignoring the shooting pain charging out from her spine. Drusilla smiled to herself.

Angela went to the washroom on Drusilla's approval, washed her face and hands and got up to the table where everyone else was just about finished with their meal. Angela ate her pancakes and drank the water that was now placed in front of her. She wanted more, but knew better than to ask for it. Excusing herself from the table, she was instructed to "get to bed."

Going to bed sounded great to her. Gladly. She ached all over and could not wait to get into her bed. She had dirt stains on her body from the dust and dirt being blown into the sweat that had poured from her pores in the hot sun, but this didn't worry her. All she wanted to do was lay down and close her eyes. Her sheets felt great. All she had was a top sheet to cover herself with. The cool air of the night breezes blew through her window. She drew the sheet up around her neck and rolled over to face the wall. The customary position approved by Drusilla. Silence filled the room, rocking her to sleep in solitude.

11

Parental Slave Masters

The summer months progressed slowly by. The sun burned down upon Angela's back. Her muscles ached less and less as the days of hard laboring turned into weeks, and the weeks turned into months of the summer season. When her house chores were finished, she was sent out into the hot sun to pull weeds. Weeds that grew taller than she was. Weeds that stubbornly clung to the dried up clay soil, like a cemented tethered pole. Nevertheless, determination on her part made each eventually release and lay dying on the ground behind her.

Sweat poured from her body until the dry gasping of her breath was heard amongst the tall weeds. Angela worked on. Drusilla made her wear long sleeved shirts and jeans that only added to her body heat. In the morning hours, and the late afternoon hours she could venture toward the shade of the tall weeds, but a high noon, closely before and shortly after, the sun was at its' highest and hottest and there was no shade to lean into. Regardless, Angela worked on, never knowing if or when her stepmother was keeping watch, ready to pounce in if she detected even so much as a hesitation or break in her work.

Determined to receive Drusilla's acceptance, Angela worked steadily hoping to complete a large enough section to meet the approval needed to be allowed to have a lunch break, which would include a glass of water. There were many times, lunch never got served. Angela would transfer her anger from a missed meal, into the strength needed to pull these tall giants from their rooted foundation. The added motivation brought each wee to its permanent death. The dry clay soil flew from the twisted roots, stirring up the dusty earth beneath.

By sundown, every muscle, tendon and every last bit of strength had been drained from her. Her head pounded from dehydration of her thin little body. She was nauseated and her heart beat quickly. Still clinging to the next weed in line for its final degradation, she pulled. Her lips cracked and the dry dust from the dirt beneath her feet had been stirred up constantly and breathed into her small lungs. The grit of dirt in her mouth and teeth and within the membranes of her nasal passages and throat made it difficult to swallow.

A light came on and the front door opened. Drusilla called to her from the porch. Angela stood up slowly and turned toward the house in response to the call. She hoped she had met Drusilla's requirements so that she could finally have a glass of water. Drusilla surveyed the covered territory of the day's diligent efforts. Drusilla smiled a cunning smile, and then led Angela into the house by the back of the neck. She was told to take off her dirty clothes at the door and was then led in her underwear up to the table to eat. The rest of the family had already long since eaten and left the table. Pancakes were stacked upon the plate in front of Angela, and along side her plate was a wonderful glass of water. She reached out for the glass of water, taking it to her lips and gulping its contents down. It tasted and felt so good. The glass of water was gone before the thirst was quenched. Angela stared at the stack of pancakes on her plate. There was only a small amount of syrup poured on them, which had already been absorbed by the top pancake. They, like her, had needed a bigger drink.

Angela was thirstier than she was hungry. Slowly, she cut a wedge off the edge of one of the cakey pancakes on her plate. Placing it in her mouth, she knew that Drusilla would expect them all to be eaten. She chewed and chewed, hoping that this would bring some saliva into her mouth, but her body didn't have enough moisture in it to perform this task. She was dehydrated, and in a dehydrated little body, there are no reserves of liquid. Angela just about choked to death on swallowing her first bite.

Christopher came in from being out back with his daddy. Angela whispered to him to get her a drink of water. He looked toward the door leading up into the livingroom and took the glass from his sister to go fill it. Retreating to the backyard, she heard the garden hose turn on and the water running. She hoped that Drusilla had not heard it. Shaking a bit, she made some noise on her plate with her fork as if to indicate that she was eating.

Christopher came back into the house, quickly gave her another glass of water and proceeded on through the door into the livingroom. Angela drank the water down, sucking on the last drop of the upturned glass. The cool water ran down her dry throat soothing it as it went down, filling her belly. She was hungry, but her unsuccessful attempts at swallowing the dry pancakes without enough syrup to wash them down, brought in the reality, that there would be no food in her belly tonight. She stuffed them into her panties and under her arms as she made her way into the kitchen to place her dishes on the counter, and then proceeded to walk passed Drusilla who was sitting in the darkened livingroom watching TV.

"Get your PJ's on," came the instructions from Drusilla's mouth as Angela walked by her. Drusilla was 'glued' to the TV, as if hypnotized by the movie that was on the set.

"Okay" came Angela's response, as a sigh of relief blew through her lips. Quickly she walked to her room. Once there, she took off her panties and the pancakes fell to the floor. Opening a shoe drawer and sliding it all the way out, she stuffed the pancakes underneath it. Angela put her PJ's on and went into the livingroom to ask Drusilla if she "could brush her teeth and use the toilet."

"Yes, but you've got five minutes" was her response.

Running back into her room, she opened the drawer up wide, taking the pancakes into the bathroom and threw them into the toilet one by one, sat down and relieved her full bladder. Flushing the toilet, she watched as the water level climbed. Holding her breath, hoping that it would not overflow, she watched. Her heartbeat sped up from fear the toilet would overflow, when a gurgling sound was heard, and the water retreated down the porcelain threshold. She let out such a sign of relief, the sound itself startled her. What if Drusilla had heard?

Angela was a bunch of nerves. She walked over to the sink to brush her teeth. As she reached for her toothbrush, she heard Drusilla get up from the couch and was now approaching the bathroom. A commercial had come on and she needed to supervise the actions of her stepdaughter. Earnestly, she brushed her teeth. Swishing the water around her mouth, she spit the contents out. She needed a drink but knew Drusilla's rule. She must ask permission for the "extras" in life. Slowly she turned toward Drusilla and asked for a drink of water.

"No, you just had one at the dinner table." End of subject.

Angela walked across the hall and into her bedroom with Drusilla close at her heals. She peeled down the sheet on her bed and climbed in. Angela said her goodnights to her stepmother and was just about ready to roll over and face the wall as per Drusilla's permissible sleeping position for her, when suddenly she grabbed the sheet off Angela's bed and took it with her.

"You won't be needing this tonight, it's warm enough in here." Drusilla walked over to the windows and opened them all the way up.

Being satisfied with the condition she left things in, Drusilla turned on her heel and headed back down the hall to the livingroom. Her movie had come back on.

    Angela lay in the dark room; the cool night air blew upon her. Her skin twinged as she felt goosebumps rise in response. She did not just need the sheet for warmth; it was something that surrounded her at night to bring her comfort. Tonight, it had been taken. With it, what warmth and comfort they had brought to her. She was exposed to the night and its uncomforting coolness. She curled up facing the wall, her knees tucked up under her chin, with her arms embracing them. In her little nighty, she felt naked. Drusilla would not let her wear panties to bed, so the sleeveless nighty was all she had covering her. Open now, to the elements. The cross air from both the open windows played on her senses as the chill inside of her grew. Though exhausted from the long hard days' labor, she could not find the comfort that would bring the sleep she so desperately needed. Her body shivered in the blackness of the night.

****

    The house was dark and not a sound could be heard. All had gone to bed. Angela was still awake and laid curled up, shivering from the cool exposure. She was tired, yet could not find the peace and comfort she needed so desperately to relax so that sleep could take over. She closed her eyes tightly, longing for her body to give in to the sleep she inextricably needed. Tears of weariness filled her eyes, journeying to the mattress beneath. She did not have a pillow to cry into. Drusilla had long since deprived her of that privilege. She had been awake most of the night, and now, the feeling of a full bladder. The two glasses of water she had had at dinner ran right through her, being that there was no food to absorb into, as she had thrown her pancakes down the toilet. The rule was that none of Daddy's children were allowed out of bed until Drusilla granted them her permission. Angela could not wait until morning, and she definitely was not going to call out to her stepmother at this hour to ask to relieve herself.

    Quietly, she sat up in bed, a spring or two squeaked. She sat listening to see if there would be a response from the other end of the house. Drusilla had great hearing, antenna like, or so it seemed. The children knew that you could not say or do anything without Drusilla finding out. She always seemed to know, and then an exaggerated interpretation brought a brutal reaction.

Everything in the house remained still, so Angela stood up on the floor at the side of her bed, ever so carefully, hoping that there would be no sounds from the floor beneath her feet. One-step…two-steps…three, she held her breath as she took each step toward the bathroom. Pausing on occasion to listen, if a board squeaked under her feet. The journey to the bathroom seemed endless tonight, though it was just across the hall from her bedroom. The sweat poured from her body, making the air around her feel cooler than it was.

Once in the bathroom she sat down on the porcelain throne and slowly began to relieve herself. The trickle echoed in the silence of the quiet house. She tried to stop it, but the urge of relief was overpowering, and continued on. Finally, the stream ended and a few drips later, Angela stood up letting her nighty fall back down to her knees. She didn't want to use toilet paper, as it was evidence that could be used against her or her sister Crystal if Drusilla found it. Drip-drying was the answer and bore no evidence against them.

She headed back to her room without flushing the toilet so as not to wake up Drusilla. This way, indication could be that Dennis had gotten up during the night to go potty, and no one would know the difference. Angela climbed back into bed, assuming the required position facing the wall, curled back up and smiled to herself. She had just defied the reality of the unjust charge over her life. She had gone to the bathroom without getting permission. It was a small victory and a sense of satisfaction and bravery to her soul. It felt good to be back in bed. What most children would take for granted of being able to go to the bathroom without having to ask permission, this little girl considered a privilege.

Angela placed her arms into her nighty and tucking her knees back up to her chest, she fell asleep. To Angela there was always a solution to the small problems. Believing this, kept her alive.

****

Footsteps were heard coming up the hallway toward her bedroom. She was awfully tired from being awake most of the night. However, the threat of being caught with her arms inside her nighty and her knees tucked up under it, brought Angela to sudden awareness of the morning and the misery she faced if Drusilla found out that she had gone to the bathroom without permission. Unwrapping herself like the hatching of a new born chick from an egg in 'fast forward' she lay motionless, still facing the wall waiting for the command from Drusilla to "get up."

Drusilla did not come to her room, but proceeded on to the bathroom. Angela held her breath, listening for any indication that Drusilla might have in knowing that she had gotten up during the night. The toilet flushed and Drusilla was heard relieving herself. The toilet flushed again, and the shower was heard being turned on. Angela sighed a sigh of relief, as her aching muscles were felt relaxing beneath her nighty. She always stiffened from the fear Drusilla's presence caused every time she came near her.

Angela decided to go back to sleep while Drusilla took her shower. She would need all the strength she could muster to get through the day. She needed sleep, and even if it were just long enough to last the duration of Drusilla's shower; every little bit could only help.

****

It was late morning when Angela felt a nudge on her shoulder. Startled, she rolled over to find Crystal looking down at her.

"Come on, get up" her sister instructed.

"Hey, what are you doing in here?" quizzed Angela, amazed at her sister's presence in her bedroom. They were not allowed to talk to each other normally, and especially not allowed in one another's rooms. Angela sat up puzzled and petrified all at the same time.

"Drusilla called and said to get you guys up." "Now get dressed." "She wants all the chores done before she gets back home." "You get to have some breakfast too, when your chores get finished." "So hurry up." Crystal was just fourteen months older than Angela, but when given the role as mommy to play, did a better job than any mommy Angela had ever had.

'Breakfast.' A welcomed word to Angela, and Drusilla was not home to deny her the right to a morning meal. She wanted breakfast. Her tummy growled with a vengeance. She had not eaten a good meal in quite some time. Angela got dressed in a hurry and did her chores. She wanted breakfast and the ability to sit at the same table as her brother and sister and to eat a meal, what a privilege. This was a treat. Excitement filled her soul as she diligently completed every chore assigned to her. Even though Drusilla was not there, she knew that Drusilla would still inspect her every effort, so she gave it her all, just a little more hurriedly this morning. Cleaning her bedroom was a breeze. No sheet to pull up and make neat. Her nighty folded and placed in her top drawer. Then applied the dust mop to her wood floor, and moved on to the bathroom. Drusilla had taken a shower, so out with the scouring powder and the rag. Then a dry towel to shine the faucet and tub. Moving onto clean the toilet brought the memory of her little trip to the toilet without permission. She smiled to herself yet felt a shiver go up her spine. She could have been caught and suffered a beating for her actions. The mirrors were polished and shining and the sink was washed out. Taking the rag and bucket, she wiped up the floor leaving a sparkling clean bathroom behind her as she headed down the hall, dust mopping the wood floor in the remaining two bedrooms in that end of the house. The boys' room was always a mess, and today was no different. She made their little beds and put their toys away, wishing that toys had been included in the plans for her young life. Their closet doors were closed and she dust mopped their floor. Heading out to the livingroom, she picked up the area rug and sat it on the front porch. Moving the furniture to mop under it, and then returning it to their assigned places, she went out to the front porch and shook the rug. Bringing it back into the house, she put it in its place and turned on the vacuum to vacuum it. The dusting followed and then on to the dining room. It had a tiled floor and the backside of the fireplace. She wiped the legs of the dining room chairs and vacuumed the floor. Taking the rag and a bucket, she wiped up the floor and headed up the steps into the kitchen. Setting the bucket on the kitchen floor, she headed out the door to go feed and water the dogs and outside animals. This was many chores for one little girl, but a 'routine' established long ago, one that had to meet the ideals of a perfectionist, her stepmother.

Breakfast was the traditional bowl of oatmeal, but today it tasted wonderful. The children spoke not a word to one another, as Drusilla forbade it. Still, being in one another's presence for the first time in quite awhile brought a peace. Especially since Drusilla wasn't sitting across from them and staring at them. The fear of Drusilla lessened in her absence, but never really left them, because they knew that she could return at any time and sneak up on them like a wild cat. For now, they would enjoy the peacefulness of her absence.

The children ate hungrily, glancing up on occasion, casting smiles of reassurance, that they had all made it thus far, and that each was aware that their lives had become a constant torment. Not a word was spoken between them. They never knew when Drusilla would walk in unannounced. Eye contact was the only communication between them as they finished their breakfasts.

Crystal was last to finish, so without a word, Angela walked over to her sister, picked up her bowl and poured some in Christopher's bowl and some in her own, and then handed the bowl back to Crystal. They all finished Crystal's breakfast together. They weren't about to let Crystal get beat up for being last finished at the table, Angela would make sure of that.

Getting up from the table, Crystal instructed Angela that Drusilla wanted her to continue to pull weeks in the front yard, and then quickly added a thank you for helping her at the table. Angela smiled at her sister and headed out the front door, just in time to see Drusilla pulling into the driveway. Fear turned up its ugly head with a vengeance within her. Just to see her stepmother, brought panic throughout her little body.

There were no friendly greetings from either. Drusilla got out of the car and headed for the front door of the house, as Angela headed for the last corner of weeds in the front yard. Angela was just about finished with the front yard, but there lay a whole field in the back yard and she was sure Drusilla would assign them to her when she finished here. Her hands were callused and her arms and legs had muscles most children never develop at that early of an age, and sometimes not even into adulthood.

Angela worked bent over, grabbing each weed by its trunk, just above the hard clay earth and pulled with all her might. With each tug on the stubborn giant, Angela vented her frustrations from her childhood of injustices that had been brought on by her daddy's marriage to the Amazon. The fear of that woman ripped at her insides and in return, there was no mercy for these forbidden plants called weeds. By the end of each long day, her body lay weary, but the weeds lay dying. A trade-off given for the lifestyle granted to this little girl.

By mid-afternoon, the last weed was pulled in the front yard. Angela walked down the driveway to the garage to get the rake. There was a good feeling welling up inside of her. A sense of accomplishment as she carried the rake back to the front yard to clean up the dying giants. Pulling the rake filled with weeds toward her she piled them high. She would pick them up, put them into metal trashcans, drag the cans out to the far corner of the backfield, and dump them. The front yard gave way to a promise for a better-groomed future. All it needed now was a tilling, some grass seed and water.

"Mommy…I'm finished with the front yard."

"Who says?" Should Angela have expected anything positive from her stepmother today?

"Come and see, I know you'll like it." Well, Angela was trying to change the tone of her stepmother, despite Drusilla's first remark that would send the wind out of anyone's sails.

"I'll look at it later, now start weeding at the side of the house in the backyard." Drusilla was wrapped up in her TV show and was not going to be pulled away from it to "come see" for anyone. Especially, not for her little stepdaughter-slave-girl whom she loathed.

Drusilla's response was unexpected and sucked the pride of accomplishment right out of Angela. If Daddy were home, would she be able to take a break from pulling weeds, and would he come look? Afterall, she had worked for days, mostly by herself without food, water, rest, or any appreciation from anyone. She really did not know her daddy these days, so really didn't know how he'd react. For the longest time he seemed totally compelled to taking Drusilla's side against his children, so from her standpoint, she had no one to turn to for comfort and encouragement.

Her daddy had taken a job with an airplane tire manufacturer. He was at work and not here to view her finished product anyway. Would he have been pleased with her work and granted her the time off for good behavior? There was hardly a chance. That would mean that he would have to stand up to Drusilla. Angela knew the answer to her question without him even being there. Daddy always did what Drusilla wanted. She bent down to grab hold of the first weed in line for her attack. A whole field of weeds awaited her attack, enough to fill up her entire lifetime.

From the window above her, she could hear her sister Crystal fixing lunch, as she pulled the weeds below. Would there be enough servings to include her? Even if she didn't get a break, surely she would be given lunch. Her mouth watered in anticipation while she continued pulling the weeds. The sun was hot as it was just after twelve noon. The beaded sweat poured down her face. She did not stop pulling the weeds. Obedience led her forward in the task. If Drusilla were to glance out the window, Angela would want her to see her working diligently. Lunch was an earned privilege and she didn't want to miss out today.

Suddenly a pitcher of cold water poured out on Angela's head. Relentless laughter filled the air. It humored Drusilla to "cool off" Angela in this manner. Angela gasped in surprise as she jumped in unexpected fright from the shock caused by what Drusilla had just done to her. Cold water dumped onto a hot body was a very shocking experience, and truthfully, not one relished by Angela at the moment. Tears came to her eyes as she looked up in disbelief of what Drusilla had just done to her. "Why did you do that?" Angela inquired.

"Drusilla didn't like Angela's response and came back with, "Maybe you should just come in and go to bed." "Cry babies with bad attitudes need their sleep," she mocked.

Angela was hungry, but yes, after the night that she had had last night, she could use some sleep. She would consider it the 'break' she didn't get earlier. No food, just sweet, sweet sleep. As she entered the house, she tried to look as if Drusilla had just given her another injustice. If Drusilla felt that Angela desired to go to bed, then the opposite would happen. She would be out working in the hot sun all day without food, water or rest.

The warmth of the afternoon air filled her bedroom. Her mattress felt good as she laid down upon it. Rolling over to face the wall, Drusilla was heard closing her bedroom door. This rest had been intended for punishment, but Angela was thankful for it. She fell to sleep in no time. A peaceful rest fell upon her taking her into the world of dreams. The only place she knew that she could relive the happy time of her life. The time before Drusilla came into their lives. The times when Grandma had filled the shoes of 'mommy' to them. Grandma had been nice to them all the time. With Grandma, there was lots of love and hugs to go around. With

Grandma, she could ask you to do something for her, and when you got finished, she would give you a hug or a cookie. Grandma loved her.

****

Somewhere off in the distance a voice was calling her. She didn't really want to respond to it. The comfort of sleep embraced her not wanting to be disturbed. Lazily she hung on to sleep, ignoring that all too familiar voice calling her as it drew nearer. The voice let her know that her sleep would soon end, bringing her to her senses.

Her door opened and immediately the invasion of her territory brought her wide-awake. She opened her eyes, trying to focus on the woman's figure that stood above her.

"Why aren't you responding to my calls?" Drusilla's hands were on her hips.

"I…I…was sleeping."

"Well get up to the table, it's time to eat."

Eat…she was awake now. Two good acquisitions back to back in one day. She was two for two. Sleep, and now eat…it had been a long time since the invitation had been extended to her to join them at the dinner table. Savory smells of cooked meat penetrated her nasal passages. Her mouth watered and her tummy growl with anticipation. Getting up from her mattress, she followed Drusilla into the dining room expecting to see her siblings seated around the table. Rounding the corner, only Daddy sat at the table. Crystal and Christopher had finished their dinners already and had left the table. Crystal was doing the dishes and Christopher was entertaining Dennis in their bedroom.

Daddy had a big steak on his plate; Drusilla sat sipping her coffee, while in front of Angela stood a tall stack of pancakes. She was hungry nonetheless, and tonight, thirst didn't stand in the way of indulging into these dry specimens. There was a glass of watered-down dry powdered milk (sour chalk) to wash down each bite full.

"You did a nice job out front kiddo," Came a compliment from her daddy's mouth.

She was shocked but responded, "Mmm…thank you." Angela looked up at Drusilla to see what boundaries for communication with her daddy was going to be allowed. From the look on Drusilla's face, she had already said enough to her daddy, so she would now close her mouth from that point on.

Angela was glad for her daddy's approval, even if it came by way of just a small sentence. It had been quite awhile since any approval of any kind came from him on her behalf. Drusilla had not even said a word of approval, but that was typical and customary coming from her. If nothing was said, it met her approval. If it didn't, you'd hear about it and feel the consequence. She would get physical about jobs that did not meet her approval, and there were times, just because she was in a bad mood (which was most of the time), Angela would get beat, just because Drusilla felt like beating her up. It was the way of life and she had become accustomed to it.

Finishing her dinner of pancakes, she asked to be "excused."

"Sure," came daddy's answer, "but first, why don't you clean this T-bone off for me."

Angela looked at Drusilla for her approval, and then hungrily sat back down gnawing what meat remnants she could get off the bone. Meat was not something the three children were allowed to have. It was 'expensive' to have them eating meat, or so they were told by Drusilla. Both daddy and Drusilla worked, yet nothing new would be bought for the children, and nothing nutritious given to them to eat.

Angela left the table with a smile on her face. She had finally been rewarded for all the effort she put into working in the front yard. She was ready to face the backyard the next day. When work becomes a reality of life, instead of fighting the reality, you learn to accept the reality, and that is just what this little girl was doing. Tonight, she would put her PJ's on and jump into bed for more sleep. There would be no hard feelings from her tonight. You might say that she was privileged today. There was a sense of happiness as she was given the approval to go to the bathroom before going to bed for the night. The lights turned out, one by one and in the stillness of the night, tucked her arms and legs into her nighty and fell fast asleep.

12

Hidden Secret

"Come on, get up and put this dress on!"

Angela sat up in bed, still dreary from the hard work she had done all day and into the late night hours of yesterday. She had been pulling weeds out in the backyard. It had seemed as though her parents had forgotten that she was out in the night. The lights in the house had been turned off, and yet it was expected of her to work on. Only Drusilla gave the order to quit and retire to bed, but that order did not come until some time after the midnight hour, when a light came on in the house and she was called into the house. With those types of hours, this morning came sooner than expected.

"I am taking you three children to school this morning, and I want you to repeat after me." "Angela Meyers."

Angela looked at her stepmother inquisitively. "Angela Mey...errrs." The name did not feel right, and she wasn't used to it. That was not her real name.

"Meyers!" "M-E-Y-E-R-S!" Drusilla spelled it out for her.

"Meyers." Angela echoed. She was confused but did not ask questions. Instead, she put on the dress Drusilla handed to her. It was an old dress, maybe one of Crystals', or from some second hand store. She was sure she had never worn it or seen it before. Drusilla was inspecting Angela, when she decided that Angela needed a bath. The dirt stains on her arms and legs showed. It had been many weeks since Angela had had a bath. Drusilla lifted off the dress and dragged Angela across the hall to the bathroom. Angela was showered, dried off and sent back to her room to re-dress. The dress hung on her little body. Ankle socks and saddle shoes adorned her long narrow little feet. They were Crystals shoes from the previous year, and a bit snug at that. Crystal may have been first-born daughter, but she was not as tall, nor was her feet as long as Angela's. Angela had long narrow feet. Feet that her daddy had told her, she would grow into one day.

Angela cleaned her room and obediently went to "get up to the table" as Drusilla had instructed. Oatmeal swam in the watered down powder milk. She ate hungrily and without hesitation. Upon finishing,

Drusilla ordered her to brush her teeth and wash her hands and face. Drusilla seemed nervous. Who was starting their first day of school... the children or their stepmother?

Crystal and Christopher were ushered through the same routines somewhere off down the hall. Christopher kept asking Drusilla questions. He was nervous and a bit on the crabby side this morning. A spanking was Drusilla's answer to his moody crying. With each swat applied, his sisters froze, hoping that Drusilla could control her temper, and become more understanding to their brother's first-school-day jitters.

Eventually they were on their way out the door and each child filed single order to the car, not speaking a word to one another. They took their assigned seating positions in the back seat, as Dennis and their stepmother hopped in the front seat. She drove them down and around some neighborhoods, all the while attempting to show them the way home from school. "Your new school is Peach Wood Elementary." Drusilla informed them from the front seat. The children just looked at all the unfamiliar surroundings hoping that they would get the 'going-home' directions right.

Drusilla parked the car and ushered the children out. She had a friendly disposition today, and made the children thing that they were her pride and joy. Just before reaching the OFFICE door, she turned to them and muttered warning between her clenched teeth. "I will do all the talking, you guys, don't say a word."

"Okay," the three children replied in unison. They were confused, yet obedience took precedence to their understanding of what was going on. They followed Drusilla at her heels into the office.

Drusilla was smiling and speaking with an air of false pride as she introduced 'her three little children'. They were "new to the area and neighborhood," and she'd "like to enroll them." She carried on about how "well mannered and behaved her children" were. "Angela excels in the classroom, she's a smart one." Drusilla's charades were taken as believable by the office staff.

"Do you have their records from their last school of record?" The woman behind the counter asked.

Drusilla became quite nervous, but within a brief moment replied, "I've let their last school know where we've moved to and they said that they were forwarding their records after we got them signed up."

The woman listened and then took a moment to respond. "Well, we will sign them up today, but when you receive the records, please bring them in as soon as you get them." "We've got to have them on file."

"Oh sure, I'll do just that." Drusilla had been let off the hook. Her nervousness turned to fake friendliness. She jumped at every question answering it before the children could answer.

"Which one of you girls is Crystal?" The woman on the other side of the counter asked as she bent down smiling at the girls.

"I…" Drusilla quickly took Crystal by the arm and brought her forward to the woman. "This is Crystal."

"Hi Crystal," came the friendly greeting from the woman. "So you are in the fourth grade, I understand."

Crystal looked at Drusilla, who of course answered the woman for her. "That's what I put down on the paperwork in front of you."

Taken back by Drusilla's response, the staff member began filling in the application. Crystal had been warned not to communicate, so she stood solemn with her hands at her side.

Next came Angela's turn. "I know that you are Angela, because there is no other little girl in front of me…how are you doing?" A warm smile embraced the question.

Angela looked up at Drusilla, waiting for her to answer for her. "You're fine, aren't you?" Drusilla said to her with a cool smile of warning.

Angela nodded her head and said "yes."

The woman finished filling out Angela's application for registration giving her reassuring glances from time to time, as if to say, "Everything will be alright."

"Last but not least little guy…how are you doing this morning?" "You look at bit concerned, but we've got some pretty fun teachers here at our school and lots of things for you to play with." The woman smiled a reassuring smile as she spoke. Her words gentle and kind. This was a bit of a tough day for Christopher. He was only in kindergarten. Up until now, he had done pretty well on holding back his tears, but when she spoke to him, the tears began to fall. Both girls looked with concern at their brother, and then up in Drusilla's face. Her expression indicated very clearly that she was not pleased with his performance. If looks could kill, Christopher would have died at this moment.

The friendly woman continued to fill out his registration sheet. Christopher tried hard not to look up at Drusilla, all the while trying to wipe his tears on his sleeve. His sisters looked down at their feet, holding back their own tears on behalf of their brother. What would Drusilla do to him when she got him back home? Fear ran up their spines as they wished that their brother would be able to stop crying.

The friendly woman offered Christopher a handkerchief. He took it and wiped his face. She came around the counter, leaned down, and gave him a big hug. Taking him by his hand, she led all three children to their classrooms.

As Crystal arrived at her classroom door, Drusilla knelt as if to hug her. Wrapping her arms around Crystal, she whispered warning in her ear; "Don't talk to anyone about anything, and your last name is Meyers...remember that." Letting go, Crystal nodded in obedience and shyly entered the classroom. Her new teacher and the Office woman exchanged a few words, and Crystal was introduced to her peers in the classroom. Her teacher walked her to her assigned seat and with a smile, welcomed her.

Christopher wanted Angela to come to his classroom with him, so the next stop was his classroom. A very nice teacher met them at the door. Smiling, she held out her hand to him and he slowly, was led into his new classroom, wiping the tears from his eyes as he went. The other children stared as he entered. A little boy was called over by the teacher. Introductions were of the boys were made to one another, and the teacher asked the other child to "show Christopher all the toys." Putting an arm around Christopher's shoulder, his newly found friend led him back to a corner where a group of children played. Looking back briefly, Christopher waved to his sister. Angela waved and nodded to him and now it was her turn to be taken to her new classroom.

The woman looked down at her with a smile. She offered her hand to Angela. Angela looked up at Drusilla, and Drusilla's eyes gave warning. Tucking her hand down around her back, Angela avoided the woman's reaching hand. She wanted to take the woman's hand, but seeing the look on Drusilla's face, reminder her that there "was no getting close to anyone, allowed." The woman ignored Angela's rejection as they arrived at her classroom. Drusilla knelt down next to her stepdaughter and applied the same warning embrace she had done with Crystal. Angela was not to talk to anyone, nor was she to forget that her last name was Meyers. Drusilla let go and stood up. By this time Angela was peering into her new classroom. All eyes were upon her. Stares of survey from her soon to be peers penetrated her being. The children just stared. There were no welcoming smiles, except by the teacher as she now approached the trio. Introducing herself, she then turned to the class and introduced Angela.

The feeling of rejection came over Angela. She was dressed differently than the rest of her peers. Most of the girls had pants on, or short skirts and knee socks. Here Angela stood, swimming in the big dress she had on that went half down her calves, nearly touching the bobby socks. The saddle shoes were scuffed up from the previous owner, her sister, Crystal. Whispers and occasional giggles met her ears as some of her peers compared their attire to hers. She held back the tears and faced the blackboard once seated in her assigned spot. She did all she could to drown out the snickers and jabs of mockery as she concentrated on what the teacher was teaching at the front of the classroom.

Recess, was a lonely experience for Angela. She tried to approach a few girls from her class, but they just laughed at her and walked away. "Granny dress, granny dress...look at those weird shoes." "She's got little bobby-socks on too." "She hasn't grown up to wear knee socks." Laughter penetrated Angela's ears and into her little body, cutting to her soul. She had to wear what Drusilla made her wear. This was Drusilla's way of making sure she had no friends to tell her secrets to. No friends to confide in. Tears fell as she looked down at her feet, trying to close out the taunting mockery being delivered by her own peers. They did not understand that it was not her choice to wear such clothes. She lived in a home, where she was not to get close to anyone. There were too many secrets to uncover, all of which Drusilla intended to keep disclosed within the parameters of their home. What good parent would want their children to be abused by other children? Drusilla did not care. She had her reasons why her husband's children did not need to be liked or accepted by anyone. This way, there was a guarantee of keeping her secret, a secret.

Angela looked out to the playground searching for the familiar faces of her siblings, hoping to find them there. Where were they and what were they doing now? She later found out that the older kids had recess at a different time and her brother had his own play yard connected to his own classroom. She was very much on her own. Angela stared at the ground, kicking a pebble that had worked itself free from the asphalt blacktop. Tears began to flow down her cheeks; there was no making new friends, if no one liked what she wore. She wanted the bell to ring so she could go back to the classroom and hide her hurt feelings inside her schoolwork, the 'safe haven' of this situation. Drusilla did not have to worry about Angela talking to anyone; no one would talk to her.

Deep within her studies and assignments, the lunch bell rang. Reaching into her desk for her lunch, she joined the rest of the children in the cafeteria. A noisy group at that. Each seemed to already be paired off, or sitting in their own group. As she entered, it was as if she was invisible. No one noticed her as she stood glancing around the room for a place to sit and eat her lunch. She finally found an open spot at a table with some other children and went to sit down. Right away, whispering started, and then the tone picked up as laughter filled her surroundings. A bold young child came up to her and asked her, "Why do you wear such funny clothes?" Laughter followed.

Angela choked up and could not give an answer. She held back the tears as she looked inside her lunch box. There a peanut butter sandwich sat. A thermos of water to wash it down with. Too bad the water could not wash away the hurt and tears, the result of her peers' mockery toward her. The pain gripped her. Stuffing her mouth with the dry peanut butter sandwich, and trying to drink the water by the gulp-full did end up causing her to choke. Angela began coughing and spewing involuntarily, all over the table in front of her, which only brought more laughter and painful mockery out of the mouths of the children around her. "You are weird and disgusting!" One little boy said as he left the table followed by an entourage of children as they headed out to the playground.

Other children got up and left her still coughing and trying to clear her throat. Suddenly someone came up from behind her and lifted her arms up above her head. On last big cough and the bite of peanut butter sandwich flew from her throat, and Angela could breathe again. Tears flowed down as she cried. Choking on the sandwich and not being able to breathe had put a fright into her. The last words of the children, as they left the table, cut into her feelings deeply. The lunchroom volunteer put her arm around Angela, telling her softly, that she would be all right. "Would you like me to call your mommy?"

"No!" Angela shot back with a start. Just the mention of someone having to contact Drusilla, sent fear straight through her to the bone. Instead of comfort, Drusilla would be angry with her, and she would probably be beat up for "making someone feel sorry for her." Angela knew Drusilla's regimented reaction to just about every scenario. She did not want Drusilla contacted, nor did she want to go home. Drusilla would send her out to the field of weeds to work…no…no…"I will be all right." "I don't want you to call my mommy." With that, the lunchroom volunteer and Angela cleaned her spot at the table, and Angela headed out the door to the blacktop. There were children everywhere. Walking pass the tether pole ball game the children there just stared at her. One child began chanting "Granny dress, granny dress," and all the rest in line joined in. Some little boy threw the ball out at her head. It stopped just before hitting her head, as it rebounded back to him, the tethered ball tied to the pole. The children laughed.

Angela was just about to walk away, when a kind teacher instructed the children to "stop the name calling." Taking Angela by the hand and placing her right into the middle of the tetherball court. "This is Angela, she's new." "It would be nice of you all to invite her play with you."

There stood Angela, right smack dab in the center of the tetherball court facing her opponent. The little guy let the ball swing toward her, still taken back from the teachers' instructions to let her play. Angela reached up and slapped the ball back. It flew over the head of the little boy on the other side of the court. She slapped it again and again, as it came around and around. The little boy stood bewildered. He did not even get a chance to return or block her plays. Angela put all her frustrations out on the ball, and had won that game in a split second.

The next child in line stepped onto the court. The child swung one hit…jumping up, Angela smacked the ball with all her might. The ball flew around the pole again and again. The other child tried to block it, to no avail. Angela gave the ball a few more smacks and it wrapped around the pole tightly, indicating that the game was over, and it was the next person's turn. She had won two games and was on to playing another. Angela smiled at her next opponent. One, two, three, four, five…they all left the court and returned to the end of the line. She may have not been fashionable in the attire she wore, but she was good at the sport of tetherball. The children were amazed at this girl in the "granny-clad" dress. They stood watching her as she defeated the next opponent. The teacher who had involuntarily placed Angela onto the court, smiled to herself. Angela was having fun. The teacher had found a way for the children to look beyond the outside of a child who dressed differently than they did, to find something within the child they could accept. Angela was having fun. The first fun she had had in a long time. The teacher became a hero that day.

The children let Angela play tetherball with them; despite the fact that they still thought she dressed weird. They even fought over her, as to who could have Angela on their team. Angela was graced with sports agility, and it made her a winner. Not just a friend, she became a real winner. She put all of her frustrations into the sports she played, an outlet for pent-up anger.

****

The children were not allowed to dawdle home. Though the school was quite a distance from their home, Drusilla wanted them home in ten minutes. When school let out, the children would be seen dashing out of their classrooms and running to the crosswalk, nervously waiting to be escorted across the street, and then the race to beat Drusilla's clock began as they raced through the neighborhoods, rounding the corner out of breath as they made the last trek of the journey home. Classmates would call out to them, but they were not allowed to stop and talk. Drusilla was counting the seconds and minutes. A late arrival would mean the belt. Many times she was still not home when they arrived, but she'd make up some story about seeing them get home late, and the belt would swing against their backsides.

Once home, they would get dressed into their work clothes, and get started on their afternoon chores. There were pets to feed, a re-dusting of the wood floors, windows to wash, and the sidewalks to sweep. She would then start pulling weeds once more until supper was called. Though she had homework to do, Drusilla did not think it more important than the chores being done. Many days, Angela had to return to school and make up some story about why she did not do the homework. Then she would get a beating if she didn't get straight "A's." To Drusilla, homework was schoolwork that did not get finished in the classroom, and if Angela had homework, she must have messed around in the classroom and not gotten it done. More reason to beat her stepdaughter up.

Drusilla began driving bus for the School District. An amazing career for a fleeing child abuse fugitive, but what the School District did not know, would not hurt them. She would build her credibility before the records caught up to her. She had a job that would possibly convince social services that she could not possibly be a child abuser, right? Wrong!

Supper was called when Drusilla or their daddy arrived home. If the chores were not finished, they went without. Then again, if Drusilla was in a bad mood, the chances for a lost meal increased. She really did not have to have a good reason, if she didn't want Angela having a meal, Drusilla would conjure up some feeble excuse or accusation to justify the denial of the meal and, or the cause for brutally beating her up with the belt or her fist.

California rain has a chill to it that soaks through a person, right to the bone. It is not like the humid rains that fall in the Midwest. Instead, it has a frigid unwelcoming embrace and makes pulling weeds in the backfield, a near impossibility. The mud would squeeze up between her toes of her shoeless feet. Angela would slip and slide as she fought to pull the tall giant tares up from their sticky clay foundation. She would be covered in mud by the time Drusilla called her in for bed those nights.

Being too muddy to come into the house as she was, Drusilla would take the garden hose with its frigid cold water and squirt Angela down from head to toe. She would have to stand there shaking from the chill that encompassed her body, while Drusilla washed her down. Angela was not allowed to react or to move away from the direct spray coming from the garden hose, or Drusilla would demand that she 'stand still.'

Next Angela would be instructed to take off all of her clothes. She did as Drusilla told her to. She stood naked in the darkness of the backyard, while Drusilla continued to hose her down, making the water go directly into Angela's ears, nose and mouth. At times, she could not breathe because Drusilla held the hose right in her face for a long time. Angela would instinctively turn her head gasping for air, only to get the garden hose smacked into her face. Drusilla even found pleasure in sticking the hose up Angela's crotch, as she was told to bend over and wash her dirty legs off with her hands. Being given a small kitchen towel to dry off with, Angela was then led naked through the house in front of her family naked.

    Arriving in her room, Drusilla instructed her to "get dressed for bed." The frail little nighty did not stop the chill in her body. She shook as she laid down on her mattress. There were no covers given to her to crawl in under. Her hair was wet, which added to her discomfort. Angela laid in the dark shivering and shaking, wishing for a blanket. She was tired, but the chill kept her awake long passed the hour her family retired for the night. Cold and exhausted, Angela got up. The house was still. The bottom sheet that hugged her mattress was the only resource she could turn to for comfort. Angela wanted some sleep and some warmth. If this was the only way she could get it, it was worth the risk. Against the wishes of her stepmother, she burrowed beneath the bottom sheet bringing the much-needed sleep to her weary, shaking body.

13

Stay Away From Daddy!

Day after day, week after week, month after long month, Angela labored through the field of weeds behind their house. Come rain or shine, the treacherous task trudged on. From the time she got home from school to the time she was allowed to go to bed, with very little breaks in between, if any. Entire weekends were spent working on pulling up the weeds that plagued their two-acre lot.

As Angela cleared the ground of its unforgiving giant tares, new ones sprang up from the fallen seed on the broken ground, making the task an endless progress. Like the painting of the Golden Gate Bridge in San Francisco; It is said that by the time the painters go from one end to the other, the end where they first started needed painting again. Her hands were callused and the muscles in her arms and back made strong. As her strength grew so did her tolerance to her environment. Raw lambsquarter leaves became nutrients to her hungry body. The sweet suckling flowers from the honey suckle clover became a real treat. Missed meals no longer meant a total deprivation for her. She found other means to meet the demands of her hunger. A kumquat tree and a nectarine tree behind the garage provided fruit in due season, and supplied her with a diet sufficient to carry on in her day-to-day work.

One day, she heard the roar of an unfamiliar engine, followed by a sputtering, and then silence. Peering around the corner of the shed, she saw her daddy sitting in the seat of an old rusty red farmer's tractor. It had a couple rear-claw-like attachments and another with round discs, setting off to the side of the tractor. How amazing! Her daddy was trying to get it started. He was versatile in the mechanics of things, and determination would bring this old tractor to life. He had repaired his own automobiles and mowers and this contraption would eventually surrender to his expertise, Angela was sure, as she peered around the corner. Seeing Drusilla leaving the house to join her daddy in the backyard, Angela returned to the area she was working in this bright Saturday morning. Standing around and watching Daddy was not permitted. So back to work she went before Drusilla noticed her. There was now some new hope that laid in her future. Perhaps, the endless job of pulling weeds would be over soon as Daddy got the tractor working and toppled each weed as he drove over them. The mechanical method would soon be replacing her manual method. Her heart leaped for joy with the thought of being freed from this 'slave labor.'

The steady roar of the tractor motor brought her out of the daydream mode and back into reality. Daddy was test-driving the tractor all over the yard. It was trial and error on choosing the right attachment for the job. Daddy was no farmer. He tried the different attachments until he found one that would topple the giant weeds and turn up the soil the best. He drove around to the front yard. The clay earth did not allow the claw attachment to dig in. It was not heavy enough to dig into the surface of the hard clay land. All the children were called out front to sit on top of the attachment for weight, and only then, did it sink into the dried earth. The children rode around and around the yard. This was great fun! They cheered as they rode. Well, they did until Drusilla came out of the house. The look on her face was that of disapproval. There was to be no fun in this family, ever! Walking up to their daddy and getting him to stop the tractor, a small argument ensued. Afterward, Crystal and Christopher were able to continue their ride on the tractor, while Angela was sent back to the backyard to pull weeds. Silence, except for the noise of the tractor dominated the air. The children sat quietly on the back attachment not making a sound, for fear, Drusilla might think they were having fun, and put an end to their ride.

The steel disc succeeded the claw, as the large clumps were consumed from the front and sent out the back of the attachment as broken bits of clay. The children, including Angela now, were given garden rakes to rake up all the little weeds and the rocks from the broken earth. The front yard lay like an earthen blanket of dry ash but not for long. Daddy had gone to a farmer's home and got some stinky cow manure for just this occasion. The assignment was to fill up the wheelbarrow and spread the manure all over the front yard by using the rakes. The children worked diligently as queen Drusilla watched from her throne on the front porch, flinging out commandments at the children's' every movement. As they worked in the front yard, Daddy rode the tractor into the backyard and then out to the field to break up the ground. Daddy had a new toy, and today, he would find every project he could use it on. The tractor did the work while he rode around on it.

Once finished with the front yard, Crystal was sent into the house to make the noonday meal and Christopher was sent inside to keep Dennis company. Angela was sent back out into the backyard to begin raking up the weeds, the tractor was digging up. Lining up the rocks along the shed and raking the weeds out from the clumps of dirt were the driving orders coming from Drusilla.

"Angela," her daddy called to her.

Looking up she responded, "Coming."

Arriving at her daddy's side, he instructed her to "get on the back of the steel disc attachment."

Obediently she climbed on board on top of the bricks he had set there for weight when Crystal and Christopher got off. The ride was fun. Angela watched the dirt rise and fall with the turning of the discs. The weeds were conquered and cut beneath its sharp discs. Victory, sweet victory. Do not stop until this whole yard is completely emptied of every weed, Angela thought to herself. Literally, she did not want to spend even one moment more pulling one more weed. It had been months since she started the project out front, and if she didn't have to bend over a moment longer for another weed, the opportunity would come too soon. The backyard looked more promising with each passing tour.

Suddenly a strong vice-grip like hand grasped her arm and yanked her off the tractor's attachment and onto the ground beside the tractor. Drusilla had a way of showing up unexpected and making her brutal presence known. She was not happy. Angela stared up at her in surprise, like that of a mouse just taken as prey by a hungry hawk. Angela jumped up to her feet facing Drusilla, as her daddy realized that his daughter was no longer in tow.

He shut off the tractor, questioned Drusilla as to her intentions, and stated his desires. A small argument followed the confrontation, and then Angela was sent to get her rake and return to cultivating the soil like she had been instructed before her daddy had asked her to be the 'weight' on the back of the tractor attachment. Her daddy followed Drusilla into the house for lunch. Tears of frustration fell down her face as Angela vigorously worked on the clumps of soil, separating the rocks and weeds out from them. She realized that she had missed out on lunch because she had obeyed her daddy. It did not make sense, but nothing in the last many years of her young life made any sense to her. Anger burned inside of her as the tears fell down her cheeks.

The dining room window faced the backyard, so she had to keep her back to the window, for fear that Drusilla would see her tears. Tears were not acceptable to Drusilla and Angela knew it. Hunger and thirst competed with the anger that now welled up inside her. Foot by foot the job was completed. The sun was blistery hot and beat down upon her, the feelings of anger turned to frustrated energy needed to accomplish the job given her.

After eating his lunch, Daddy returned to his tractor. He gave his daughter a quick hug as he passed her. "You're doing a good job...looks good."

Quietly Angela tried to tell him that she was "very hungry and thirsty", but that was met with "Mom said you ate earlier." She shook her head 'no' and looked down at her feet. He could see the disappointment in her, but only turned back around on the seat of his tractor and started it up. Crystal and Christopher were brought out of the house and used once more as the 'added weight' their daddy needed for the attachments to handle the job. Angela was told to continue cultivating the dirt.

Day turned into night, as daddy drove in from the field. Crystal was instructed to make dinner, and Christopher was told to "go play with Dennis." They walked passed Angela as if she did not exist. She had a lot of work ahead of her; a whole two acres to be exact, so until she was called into the house and released from the job, she'd continue on. Daddy put his tractor into the garage and headed into the house. The songs of the summertime crickets echoed in the dark night. The light coming from the rear of the house faded as it crept out into the darkness toward her. Still, Angela worked on without hesitation. Lights shone from the rooms within the house as nighttime drew on. The people within its walls were about their own business as if Angela did not exist.

With each small section finished, Angela moved back further into the night. She could not see exactly what she was doing, but the habitual endeavor of the daytime hours, brought about the confidence that she could even accomplish the task in her sleep. Hunger burned within her gut. Glancing up toward the dining room window, she saw Crystal and Christopher sitting down and eating at opposite ends of the dining room table. Assumptions told her that her daddy, Drusilla and Dennis were eating in the livingroom while watching television. Here she was, out in the dark once more, going without, why? She did not know. What she did know is that she was hungry. Angela stared through the window watching as her siblings ate, not saying a word to one another or even looking up at one another. They had Drusilla's laws of the table down pat.

Angela needed to eat. She needed food. She was hungry. Dropping to her knees, she felt around for the familiar texture of lambsquarters and clover. In the darkness, she could not tell the mustard weed from the lambsquarters and with all the dirt dug up, the clover was scarce. The upturned dirt ended her search for her food supply. Tears began to fall as she sobbed out in the darkness. A beetle crawled over her hand and made her jump. Shaking her hand vigorously, a cool shiver crawled up her spine. A change in climate, perhaps. The tears eventually stopped and she wiped her nose on her sleeve. She could not be caught throwing herself a pity party out there, Drusilla would never understand.

Angela rose from her knees, using the rake to steady herself, her hands embracing its long heavy handle, she continued in silence. She could not really see what she was doing, but continued to work on into the night, forcing back tears for the feeling of abandonment and for the hunger and fatigue that now embraced her body. Looking up she could see that her brother and sister had finished their dinners and had left the table. Crystal was at the kitchen window washing dishes and Christopher was gone from sight. Only the remnants of cooked supper aromas still lingered in the air from the houses that surrounded their property.

The lights inside her house were being shut off one by one as the hours passed on by. Darkness now embraced her body. Fatigue from the long day slowly weighed her down, as she knelt in the dirt that lay in weedy clumps all around her. She wanted to give in to the feeling of sleep, when suddenly she heard the back screen door slam!

Adrenalin shot up her spine, as it seemed to lift her to her feet almost immediately. A dark figure was coming toward her. It was Drusilla's silhouette. Pretending to be working Angela waited for what laid in store from her stepmother. Surely, this Amazon would not criticize her performance of the job. It was too dark out to see if it was good or bad. Nothing could be seen.

"Now you, get over here." Drusilla growled at her stepdaughter.

Obediently, Angela moved toward her, the hair standing up in fear of what this woman was going to do to her.

"You ever pull that crap with your dad again, after I told you to stay off the tractor, you'll be spending the night out here." "Do I make myself clear?"

Angela was confused, but nevertheless, answered Drusilla with a sheepish, "Y-yes." She dare not disobey her daddy and she dare not disobey Drusilla. So how was she going to meet this order?" It was bedtime, and all she wanted to do was to crawl into bed.

Tomorrow was Sunday and she would have to figure out a way to endorse Drusilla's new law. For now, Angela needed and wanted some sleep. She had missed two meals that day and though the hunger burned in her belly, sleep was more inviting.

In the darkness of her room, she undressed for bed. Laying down on her mattress, she felt her tense muscles begin to relax. It felt so good. Morning would be here all too soon and she was sure that there would be more hours spent working out in the field. Rolling over to the wall in the approved position, she fell fast to sleep.

****

The morning sunlight brightened her room as the sparrow sang outside her window. The warmth of the early morning sunshine brought life to the new day, as the incense of the eucalyptus tress spirited her senses. Their clean, fresh medicinal aromas opened her lungs wider to the fresh air that filtered into her room through her window screens. The house was still. These morning moments brought with them the peace, joy and hope she so badly needed. Nature embraced her as she lay gazing around at her surroundings. The sky was blue, the puffs of clouds moved gently through the heavens above her home. The flutter of wings from the sparrows blending in with their chirping of song brought gaiety to this moment in time.

It was a beautiful morning! Angela just had to look out her window. Sitting up slowly, listening to the stillness of the house around her she glanced out into the backyard. The fresh scent of newly turned up earth smelled sensational this morning. Birds flocked to the ground picking up the beetles and worms the morning dew had brought up to its surface. The sight was sensational! Angela watched as the birds busied themselves with their morning harvest of food. It was a remarkable sight. One to treasure, as just one of those times when life "seemed better – if just for this moment."

Suddenly, the morning cheer was broken, as footsteps were heard approaching Angela's bedroom. Quickly she lay down, twisting to assume the approved position. Her heart pounding. Sweat beaded on her forehead and the room seemed to grow warmer and warmer as the footsteps approached closer and closer.

"Get up, it's chore time." Drusilla was in the sarcastic throttle this morning.

Angela rolled back over and sat up. The cheerfulness of the day began to fade away, as 'home-life' reality set in. Life was one command after another. There were no "good mornings" with Drusilla around. Just "chore-time", all the time. Angela did not have to be told twice. Her life was one big chore day after another.

Angela wasn't making a real effort to accomplish the task of getting dressed too quickly this morning, so when Drusilla got finished with her morning pee, she came back into Angela's room and ripped her nighty off of her. It tore as it was lifted off her, and Drusilla threw it on the floor. Then quite violently set about dressing her stepdaughter in her panties. They were pulled up into her crotch, and when Angela tried to adjust them, Drusilla just repeated the process and pulled them up and in with a vengeance, picking her up off the floor and slamming her down again. Angela got up and did not dare to reach in and adjust the severe wedgey. The painful discomfort brought tears to her eyes, which in turn, brought Drusilla's hand across her face.

"You want to cry, well I'll give you something to cry about you little bitch!" SLAP! SLAP! "How's that?" Angela's pants were pulled up into her crack now joining her undies in the discomfort. Then came her shirt. It was pulled over her head, smearing the blood from her nose in streaks down the front of it. She held back her tears as best she could.

"Now for your bad attitude... You can go without breakfast."

"No mommy, no." The sobs came from Angela's mouth as she begged to be granted the meal. "Please mommy...please...I'm so hungry." "I need something to eat...I do."

"You should have thought about that before you got in your bad mood!" Drusilla responded matter-of-factly, trying to convince herself the punishment fit the purpose.

A voice from behind Drusilla interrupted the whole affair. "No, I really think that Angela does need something to eat." "It might make her feel better." "Afterall, she missed her meals yesterday." It was Daddy coming to her rescue.

"Are you undermining my authority with my daughter?" "You weren't here when she was giving me a hard time dressing her." Drusilla tried to defend her best interests.

"I'm quite sure with a meal in her; Angela will be more cooperative for you." "Now, let her eat her breakfast." Angela stared in disbelief that her daddy was coming to her defense. This had not happened before, but she welcomed what help he could give. Then again, his assistance now would prove to be reason for Drusilla to turn against her later on.

"Get your ass up to the table then," Drusilla did not like to admit defeat.

Obediently Angela pushed passed Drusilla in an effort to do what she was told to do. Suddenly she found herself down on her knees. Drusilla had given her a swift kick, her foot landing right between Angela's legs, as she passed by her stepmother, and down she went. The pain from her crotch ached. Angela was hurting bad. She could not get up by herself, so Drusilla kicked her again while she was down. Angela let out a cry of pain, which in turn brought her daddy back to the scene.

"What the hell are you doing to her?" Daddy was mad.

"The little bitch gave me a dirty look after you left, and I was showing her just how much I liked it." Drusilla lied to him. Angela knew better than to express any kind of look when Drusilla was in one of her moods.

Daddy picked up his little girl from the floor. She could barely stand. The tears ran down her face. "Say you are sorry to mommy."

How could she? She had not done anything wrong, or to her. She would never ever consider doing anything wrong. Drusilla scared the living daylights out of her. Life was like walking on eggshells, fearing to do anything wrong at any time. Angela feared for her life around Drusilla. Why would she ever do anything wrong? Nevertheless, saying she was sorry for something she did not do, was the easy way out, and the quickest way to the breakfast table. "I'm sorry."

Daddy smiled down at her and led her to the table. Drusilla was not thrilled and Angela knew that this was not going to be the last of the antics surrounding this episode. She would have to watch her back and be extra alert and perfect in behavior.

Sure enough, Drusilla's antics began the moment Angela sat down at the table to eat. Drusilla poured bacon grease from Daddy's cooked bacon on top of Angela's pancakes and followed it with watered down dry milk. A disgusting and stomach turning mess. The tears welled up into her eyes as Drusilla ordered her to start eating. An insidious smile of satisfaction and victory swept over the face of the Amazon who now sat directly across the table from Angela.

Angela fought back the tears and began to cut the soggy pancakes. The grease had turned to waxy lard-like chunks in the watery milk substance. She was hungry and did not want to lose her breakfast, even if it meant choking down this mess. It tasted awful, and continued to come back up for an instant replay, but she choked the feeling down. Maybe it was good that she was very hungry. The less time it spent in Angela's mouth the better. She barely chewed it before swallowing each bite. Her tears and now snot, dripped into her plate. Eating the mess beat losing out on another meal.

Daddy pretended not to notice as he ate his eggs, bacon and toast. The other children were served their pancakes normally with diluted syrup. Drusilla stared at Angela with a wry smile of mockery from across the table, not speaking a word. Her face spoke volumes on the victory of the vengeance she was feeling. Angela would continue to regret ever having her daddy come to her defense, and Drusilla was letting her know it. This was going to be yet another, very long day.

Getting up from the table, still swallowing hard to hold back her breakfast; Angela placed her dishes into the kitchen sink. She proceeded into the back rooms to get her chores started. Right away, Drusilla was on her tail.

"I'd like you to start by cleaning the bathroom." Dragging Angela into the bathroom, she shoved her head into the toilet bowl, pointing out the dirt, then pushed her down to her knees and dragged her across the floor using her face like a mop, 'showing her all the dirt.' Picking her up she shoved Angela's face into the sink and reached down around the faucet and pointed out the spot of calcium that was just on the underside of the faucet. There was a ring around the bathtub and Drusilla wanted Angela to 'have a closer look', shoved her into the tub, and drove her head into the side of the tub.

"Fifteen minutes." "That's it." "Just fifteen minutes and I will be back to inspect this room." "If it is not done, you will be beat, I promise!"

Angela hurriedly got the cleaning rag and the cleanser and began to clean the bathroom spotlessly. She did not want to get beat today. She was not feeling well, especially not after having to eat what was served to her for breakfast. As a matter-of-fact, she never wanted to be beat. Drusilla was in a mood of vengeance, and the beating would be extreme, Angela was sure of it. Drusilla was out for blood this morning, and Angela was her target.

The bathroom fixtures shined. The walls and the floor were like new. Angela was just wiping up the last square in front of the door when Drusilla returned. Walking right passed her and onto the freshly scrubbed floor, Drusilla began her inspection. She got down on her hands and knees, looking around the toilet bowl and around the base of the tub, behind the door and in the bathroom closet, scraping the corners hoping to come up with so much as a speck of dirt, but Angela had known better. She had cleaned it spotlessly. Drusilla was not happy, as Angela watched the disappointment on her stepmothers face growing more vivid, because she could not find dirt, something to give her that 'reason' to beat up her step daughter. Drusilla got up from her knees, giving Angela the impression that the job was finished and approved. Drusilla turned, opened up the window and the screen and found the dirt she was looking for. She called Angela over to have a closer look. Angela brought in her rag, and just as she went to wipe off the sill, Drusilla punched her head from behind. Angela's mouth hit the frame and her teeth went through her lip. Blood ran down her chin and down her throat. Another slug to the back of her head and a kick to her butt brought Angela to the floor. She lay dazed.

Drusilla continued to kick her in the ribs, her thighs and shins. Angela tried to protect herself when each blow came, but the six-foot-two Amazon was all over her. Drusilla was a vulture in to kill her prey. Angela could not move or breathe. She was gasping for air. Drusilla had a smirk on her face, like that of an evil Cheshire cat. One that said that she wanted Angela dead. Was Angela going to die? She felt like it at this moment. The room grew dimmer and dimmer. Darkness filled her senses as she fought to breathe through all the pain. She passed out.

****

Angela awoke. Dried blood held part of her lips closed. Her face was stiff, both from the bruising and from the crusty dried blood that had bled from her open wounds, Drusilla had inflicted upon her. Angela's' hair was tangled and dried blood coated the strands that hung from around the wounds on her face and scalp. She ached all over and still had difficulty taking in air. Her rib cage hurt and she could not move without the aching surges of pain embracing her body. Still, as Angela looked around, she knew that it would be Drusilla's expectation of her to clean up the splattered bloodstains and mess that now covered the once clean surfaces of the bathroom.

Glancing over at the door, it had been closed and the latch locked. How long had she been there, and where was her family? The house lay quiet, the brightness of the daylight let her know that it was still daytime. Slowly Angela sat up. The pain from her injuries was bad. She hurt all over, and by not being able to take in a deep breath made her feel all the more dizzier.

Dried bloody splatters were on the floors and walls. Even the window above her gave trace of the violent attack she had suffered. Reaching for her cleaning rag, she found that it had dried, indicating that she had been out for quite some time. She needed to wet it in order to be able to clean up the dried bloody mess. Drusilla would be back all too soon, and before she could order Angela to clean up the mess, it would be best that Angela clean it up before Drusilla returned with the family. Angela had to please the Amazon, her life counted on it.

Rising slowly to her knees, she felt the stabbing pain of muscles that didn't want to move or to be moved. Still she had to get the mess cleaned up. There was no time for a pity party, nor time to survey the damage that had been done to her. There would be no doctoring of the wounds, in this family, 'you got what you deserved.' Angela would clean up all the evidence before Drusilla returned. This was the first time

Angela remembered ever passing out from her beatings. She really didn't know how long afterward, Drusilla continued to beat her, but the damage done to her body indicated that it may have been quite awhile before Drusilla realized that her stepdaughter wasn't moving any more. The bloodstains were dried up and not really easy to clean up. Nothing short of spotless would ever meet Drusilla's white glove inspection.

Angela worked very, very slowly. The pain made it difficult to move or to apply any type of pressure. The pain made her nauseated and the mutilation of her body and head sent her world spinning around her. The feeling of passing out was a constant option of giving up and giving into reality. Angela fought the feeling. If she gave up, she would die, or so she felt. She would persevere, endure and struggle to fight the feeling. The thought of death and the unknown was not yet anything she wanted to give in to. If she lived, she could continue to hope that one day, 'things would change for the better.' Choosing to die would make this misery permanent.

After cleaning up the blood from the floor, window frame and wall, Angela glanced around for any unseen splatters that Drusilla would be sure to find in her inspection. As she surveyed her surroundings, she happened to look at her reflection in the mirror. It was Drusilla's law that Angela was not allowed to look into any mirror in the house, but the sight of herself in the mirror caught her by surprise. She looked back into the mirror and tears welled up in her eyes. Her lips were fat and split. Black and blue and purple. Slight bruising blemished her cheekbones. The dried blood fell from her nose and the corners of her mouth, stained and scabbed onto her face and teeth. Her nose was swollen so that the tears that now spilled down her cheeks would not allow the mucous to flow from it. She felt like she was going to suffocate. Angela didn't recognize her own reflection in the mirror. The swelling on her face made her look like a deformed monster. It was horrible!

Turning on the water in the bathroom sink she painfully bent down to wash her face. The cool water felt so good, but her head ached with the pressure of bending down. Splashing the water carefully onto her face, so as not to make a mess in the sink she tried to clean up. Dried blood let loose as it mixed with the water. Quietly she stuck her head into the sink to get the dried blood out from the strands of her hair. The pain was constant and unbearable. Lumps all over her skull, made it difficult to clean her hair. The bloodstained water ran down her arms and into the drain. The smell of iron or metal rose to her face. Patches of her hair had been pulled out by handfuls by the Amazon. Oozing yellow-red liquid from her scalp. The sting of soap in the open wounds brought more pain and discomfort to Angela's physical duress.

Not wanting to get blood on the bath towels, Angela took her shirt off and used the back of it to dry off with, and then put it back on. Lifting her arms above her head brought unbearable surges of pain and agony and she would cry out; nevertheless, she had to get her shirt back on. Drusilla would return soon, she was sure. Angela quickly cleaned up the bathroom sink and searched the floor for any left over evidence of the trauma she had suffered. Nothing, except that which was evident on her face, body and head. Drusilla's bathroom was immaculate.

The closed door meant that she was to remain in the bathroom until such time Drusilla freed her from it. Sitting down on the closed toilet lid, she waited for Drusilla's return. The house outside the bathroom door seemed very quiet for this time of day. Angela stood up and looked out the window to see if everyone might be out in the backyard. Daddy's tractor stood still and deserted. No one was to be seen anywhere. The neighbors' horses stood grazing the field, swooshing their long tails in the summer evening breeze. Everything else around seemed to be very deserted. Where had they gone? Did Drusilla think she had killed Angela and left her for dead?

Sitting on the toilet seat was hard and uncomfortable, so Angela got down off it and sat on the floor and leaned up against the wall. She was tired. Very much alive, but extremely tired. She had been put through more than any child her age should have ever been put through. Sleep overtook her and gave to her a moments peace.

Angela had not been asleep long when noises were heard down the hall. Her family was returning home from somewhere. Dennis and Christopher were laughing and Daddy was saying something about having to go put his tractor away in the garage. Angela opened her eyes. It was the night hour, and the shadows of a setting sun embraced her surroundings. Next was Drusilla's turn to come free her stepdaughter from captivity.

The bathroom door was unlocked from the outside and in walked Drusilla. Her eyes met Angela's inquisitive stares. Yes, Angela was alive but badly mutilated. Quite content with herself and what she had done to her stepdaughter, Drusilla surveyed the bathroom as she smiled to herself and ordered Angela to "get to bed."

"Now maybe, you'll stay away from your Daddy; right?" It was a question, Drusilla expected Angela to answer.

Angela didn't even have to think of the right answer. "Yes." She was too tired to even think, could barely move, let alone think about ever disobeying the woman who had earlier tried to kill her.

14
Your Highness, Queen Drusilla

By now, all the yards were planted with grass seed, the garden with vegetable seeds, and the "off limit" warning from entering the garden given to the children. Drusilla had to find alternative chores for Angela to do inside. The majority of Angela's chores had been 'outside' chores, and Drusilla did not want her stepdaughter near the garden.

Now limited, she started out with assigning Angela some spring-cleaning that included white washing the walls, doors, closets, ceilings and scrubbing the hardwood floors. Once all that was finished, Angela would be moved into doing all the kitchen appliances, shelve units, the walls, ceiling and floor in the kitchen. Her hands became raw from having her hands in water with harsh detergents without the use of gloves. Her fingernails were already soft without calcium in her diet, and this constant introduction to detergent water was not helping. Her nails became like cellophane and began peeling past the quick. The spring-cleaning lasted a couple months.

A teacher at school had thought that she had a nail-biting problem and might even suck on her hands. Angela could not tell her the truth. Therefore, the teacher continued to think wrong and accused her of being immature. Nothing like bringing a child's already low self-esteem a bit lower, especially when the remarks about her sucking her fingers and biting her nails happened in front of Angela's peers.

Angela was in her first year of Junior High School. The school was directly across the street from her house. Wallowing Wood Junior High School included grades six through eight. Eleven years old, tall, skinny, clumsy and unsure of herself, Angela was sent to school with the expectation of getting straight 'A's, and yet, not allowed to work on homework at home, nor do any studying, guaranteeing that with every report card there would come a beating. Expectation was that schoolwork was schoolwork, not homework. If it was not done in school, it meant she was goofing off in class. They never bothered to check it out with the teachers, or if they had, the rule was never changed. Angela could not defend herself, letting them know that the teachers did give homework for the specific purpose of studying and preparing for tests, because if she did, she would be called a liar by Drusilla and get punched in the mouth. No one came to her defense.

Drusilla would start swinging the belt across her behind and legs for anything less than an 'A', and then when her daddy came home, she had to hear 'what a disgrace she was to him, in not applying herself.' Angela had tried so hard to ace everything given in school, but really needed the opportunity to do homework so that she could excel and get 'A's. Teachers counted points against her if the homework was not done. She would even try to rush through her morning chores and sneak doing it, so that her grades wouldn't be downgraded by not doing it. The job was half-assed and by rushing through it, she really did not get it done right, nor did she learn anything from it. Because she could not go to a library and do research, the "project-type" homework received 'F's. Then of course her grades would drop and she was guaranteed a beating. She had lost in life before even leaving the gate, Drusilla made sure of it.

Compounded with the stresses to perform with the utmost perfection academically, Drusilla and her daddy sent Angela to school in skirts, saddle shoes and bobby socks while the rest of the female peer group at school were wearing mini skirts and nylons, or pants. To make matters worse for her stepdaughter, she was also cutting Angela's hair within an inch and a half of her scalp, while the other girls at school had long hair. The teasing and harassment from her peer group was more than she could handle. Nevertheless, handle it she did. She had no choice, Drusilla fed off making her stepdaughter the laughing stock of school. No one would approach Angela to get to know her, and therefore the family secrets remained secret. Angela looked like a boy in long dresses and skirts, wearing bobby socks when nylons were the fashion trend for her generation. Embarrassment plagued her scholastic years. People constantly judged others by their looks and not by what was inside. If anyone had taken the time to get to know Angela from the inside out, they would have found an intelligent, yet shy and scared little girl. She was a girl who was creative and talented, but not given the chance to venture outside of the corporal laws and restrictions imposed upon her by a brutal stepmother.

Angela did not have any friends to speak of. The teachers even sat her at the back of the class and kind of ignored her. When her hand would go up to answer a question, someone else was granted the ability to give the answer. They would look right passed her, which made her not want to participate. She was in her own world, a world that no one else wanted to venture into. They thought that she was weird and they even thought that she enjoyed dressing the way she did; they never took her aside to 'ask'. It might have been an awakening for them and an opportunity to find out that something was going on in this girl's life that should not have been going on. Perhaps an opportunity to give a child life and protection? No one ever tried to "become involved" or tried to investigate as to why one child among many would dress so differently.

    At recess time, Drusilla had Angela would out to the school fence in front of their house across the street. Drusilla wanted to make sure that during recess, her stepdaughter had no opportunity to talk to anyone. Drusilla did not want to go through what she went through in Wisconsin with Children and Family Services, and this way she could make sure. Teachers were not asking questions, and her daughter was not volunteering information. The school officials would think that Angela was a loner, and she would be unfairly documented as being one. It is amazing that assumptions can be diagnosed and written as facts, when in essence they are not. In the classroom and during class time the teacher taught. Out at recess, Angela was at the fence in view of her stepmother, obeying her commands. Without friends, no one knew what was going on in their home.

    After school, Angela had five minutes from the time that the last bell rang to let school out to get home. If she did not meet this time limit, she would be beat and punches would fly. It did not matter if the teacher held the class in after school; Angela would be battered for being late. There was no leniency or excuse in Drusilla's book. To her, there was no legitimate excuse for breaking one of her rules. Many times another child would act up in class or the teacher would have to finish giving out the instructions for homework and the class would be held in afterward. Tears welling up in Angela's eyes and teachers thinking that this was immaturity on her part. They never asked why. Had they; she probably would have admitted to them that her parents expected her home in five minutes from the last bell. Would this knowledge have provided perhaps some sort of leniency toward Angela, or would the teachers have become concerned enough to become involved to investigate further the terror in this girl's eyes when she was not let out of the classroom on time to meet her parental curfew? Would this information of the lifetime nightmare have helped it to end? There are no guarantees in life, like there were no 'anti-child abuse' tactics or training for teachers available. "Don't get involved." "Close your eyes; you are there only to teach."

Arriving home from school Angela had chores to do. The grass in the yards was plush and firm and Daddy had started to restore the shed. Angela was asked to be his assistant. Daddy and Drusilla discussed Angela helping him and Drusilla finally gave in. Angela was taken aside and warned that she was there to help him, but not to talk to him. Angela learned how to build, wire, paint, saw, measure, cut wood, nail and design interiors. Her daddy was a good teacher, not demanding, just patient and understanding. Though she wouldn't talk to him except to reply to his inquiry for some item, she felt they still started once again to build a good rapport.

Daddy preferred Angela's help to any he had received from Crystal, Christopher or Drusilla. She was quick and efficient, caught on quickly and very dependable. She made few mistakes and when they happened, she was quick to recover, corrected them and the job got finished. She worked well beside her daddy, and by the time the project was nearing an end, her Daddy didn't even have to describe what tool he was asking for or needed, she was there handing it to him. Daddy was pleased. The shed looked great at completion. They stood back admiring all their days of hard work. Inside, Angela beamed with happiness and pride. She felt accomplishment, and better yet, her daddy was proud of the job she did. She had been a big help to him. She was his little helper.

The next project was the chicken coup, and then they needed a barn built for the horse that was arriving soon. Her daddy was taking wooden pallets from his place of work and bringing them home to build up his little farm. Angela knew how to tear a wooden pallet apart for the wood needed for the many projects Daddy had. The fence separating the backyard from the front yard grew to be three pallets high, for privacy. It was nine feet high, to keep the family secrets in and the normal life out. The garden was surrounded by one-pallet-high fencing. It was a huge garden; it took up almost one third of the back two-acre yard. Daddy's garage shop was the final project. Restoring the dilapidated garage and putting in a workshop. Angela worked by his side the whole time. They had become a team.

As the building projects were completed, Daddy bought "Golden Nugget", a Shetland pony for Dennis. She was gorgeous, but not to be touched by the other children, except for Angela, she got the opportunity to clean the stall, feed her, brush her, and clean her hooves. Dennis got to ride her after Angela did the care taking of Golden Nugget. Dennis had been given Golden Nugget as a gift. He didn't have to take care of her, he just got the luxury of riding her and enjoying the other aspects of owning a pony. Daddy filled the chicken coup up with hens and purchased one rooster. Bantam Reds roamed the yard during the day and nested in the chicken coup Angela and Daddy had built for them. Angela also got the opportunity to clean, water and feed them. Added to this fine array of animals, were two sheep. "Bonnie and Clyde." What is a farm without ducks? Laurel and Hardy joined the entourage, as did a whole hutch full of rabbits. One would think that this would bring some meat to the family table. No, it did not. Drusilla, Daddy and Dennis enjoyed the homegrown table meat, but the other children still feasted on pancakes and oatmeal. Drusilla and Angela's daddy sold the meat to people at their places of work and to various butcher shops. Daddy's children did not get to benefit, except on rare occasion.

Angela was to find out at 'harvest season' the value of pets. When her daddy said that they would have a farm, little did she know that it meant that her pets would become future meals on tables, and that she would have to participate in their "dressing." Since she was not allowed to have any friends from school or anywhere else, and because there was no real love from her family, she took an active interest in the lives of the farm animals. They seemed to know her woes and took an added interest in her. She could imitate them and they would come running. They would let her pet them as she talked about her problems to them while releasing the pent up frustration from the abuse she was going through. There was no one else she could talk to. To any by-passer hearing her talk to her pets might think it odd, but these animals brought her the inward peace that she needed so badly. Her farm pets seemed to respond in a way that made her feel like they cared for her. With them, she would be all right.

Angela loved animals and they acted as if they loved her. They would run to her when she came outside. She had friends in them. They were happy to see her. Wherever she went they followed, bringing with them happiness this life had failed to bring up until now. They were a comfort, and seemed to bring a bit of balance, where once only hate and grief plagued her life; and now there was this simple happiness that tipped the scale of defeat up to that possibility of hope. Not everything in her life was misery anymore.

The farm animals did not have this rapport with any other family member. To the rest of the family, they were just outside animals, being raised for meat and conversation pieces for the neighbors and to their friends at work. When any other family member would try to approach anyone of the farm animals, they would run from them. Angela was the only one that they would come to and allow to pet or touch them. It is as if they sensed that she needed their presence and attention. It was amazing to see by others, this close relationship between Angela and the farm animals. Drusilla also noticed.

****

Drusilla decided that she wanted to raise German Shepherds. Not just from U.S. Kennels, but purebred Imports. They were huge with pure European bloodlines. Champion bred. They were Drusilla's dogs, but once again, yet another responsibility for Angela to take on. A large fenced in portion of the yard was designated just for them. Angela was to clean up the feces in the large dog pen, put down straw, brush the dogs, scrub out the water buckets twice per day, every day, and to feed them twice per day, every day. The dogs were about as big as she was, but very strong. The only time Drusilla came out to admire her dogs was when she had friends over, or she was selling their pups. She acted as if she had worked so hard to keep them healthy, when in fact, that if it had not been for Angela, the dogs would have starved or thirsted to death, had matted fur, and the pen would have been maggot infested. Owning a pet, does not make you a good pet owner. There is a whole lot of work involved, and 'work' was foreign to Drusilla. She didn't want to break a nail, and because she had stepchildren for slaves, they could work and she would take all the credit.

Because these Shepherds were used for breeding, there were times that the bitches suffered from mastitis during the times when they were feeding their pups. The bitches had to be placed on antibiotics, and Angela got the wonderful job of bottle-feeding the pups. An added task to her already full schedule of chores to be done before and after school. The new pups brought in plenty of cash for Drusilla and her daddy. The pups were sent to the army, or Police dog training facilities, or sold directly to private homes. The smaller pups were sent to the "Seeing Eye Dog training facilities. Angela was never given a cent for the chores she did to maintain and care for Drusilla's dogs.

A few cats found their way onto the farm and were immediately accepted as one of the family pets. They did their own multiplying and seemed to lead quite independent lives. Daddy added to the farm each year. Turkeys came in one year and new chicks and rabbits were a constant replenishment.

The manure from the farm animals kept the vegetable garden fertilized. There were many varieties of manure as Angela cleaned the horse stalls, chicken coup, dog kennel and yard droppings from the sheep and ducks. When Angela went out to clean up the stalls for the neighbors, she was paid but had to surrender her hard worked-for earnings over to Drusilla who stood with her hand out the minute Angela walked through the back door. She had brought the horse manure home from cleaning the neighbors' stalls and dumped it into the garden. Most of the vegetables were taken off the farm and sold to people or given to people at her parents' places of work. Angela was the one who weeded the garden and took care of it, yet rarely got the opportunity to taste from it. She never got a dime or allowance from all the time she spent tending the garden and making sure not even a weed grew in the midst of the vegetables. The only way Angela got to taste the vegetables, was to go out and eat them off the plants while she weeded the garden. To most, it might have been know as stealing, but when Drusilla refused Angela a meal, the garden is where she would head. While the children ate mediocre meals high in starch, their parent's and their stepmother's son would indulge themselves in fresh veggies and freshly cooked farm meat. "Dressed and cooked to perfection." Then they would sell the abundance for profit without feeding daddy's hungry children any.

There were weeds to pull in the garden and more to conquer out in the backfield. There was work enough to keep Angela busy for a lifetime, while her parent's got to enjoy the benefits of her hard labors. She had no toys, no friends, and no love given to her. Nothing to stand in her way or to keep her from working. Drusilla was only satisfied when she had

Angela busy at work and that was all the time. The only work that Drusilla knew was driving a school bus. It convinced everyone that she could get along with kids. Other people's kids and not the ones she had to live with. All other times, she sat watching T.V, reading a book or being slave master to her husband's three children. The kind of job that does not get your hands dirty or make you break a nail.

****

Daddy hammered the last steep nail into the back fence and picked up his tools from off the ground. The farm was finished. Everything had its own place and the animals seemed to enjoy their surroundings. Daddy called an end to work for the day and told Angela to "go get cleaned up."

Obediently she ran into the shed to wash up. It was unusual to be allowed to end a day of work when it was still light out, but nonetheless, she was excited to get the break. What was daddy going to let her do now? She cleaned up quickly and headed back out the door wiping her wet hands on her pants as she went looking for her daddy. Drusilla met her at the back gate that stood between the house and the garage.

"What the hell do you think you are doing out here?" Drusilla came out of nowhere.

"I was looking for Daddy," she responded.

"Why?" Came inquisition from Drusilla.

"He told me to get cleaned up and I thought that he wanted to do something with me afterward."

"Like what?' Drusilla was not relenting.

Angela really did not know how to answer Drusilla, because she really did not know why her daddy had asked her to clean up. Shrugging her shoulders and looking down at her feet, she fearfully walked passed Drusilla. Of course, Drusilla had to take this opportunity to give Angela an unexpected shove to the back of her head which made Angela stumble a bit. Angela kept on walking toward the shed. Drusilla was on her heels stalking her every move, demanding an explanation when Daddy walked out the back door of the house.

"We are finished out here and I decided to give her the rest of the day off." "She's been a great help to me, and we both deserve the break to sit back and enjoy the scenery.

Drusilla shunned his explanation, giving her stepdaughter the look of murder, and turned on her heel and headed into the house. Daddy handed Angela an ice cream bar and asked her to join him on the front porch. Angela stared at the ice cream bar in disbelief. It had been years since she had tasted ice cream. A glowing smile came to her face as she stared up into her tall daddy's eyes. Daddy smiled back in approval and offered her his hand. Her heart was pounding as she cautiously took his big hand. Drusilla would be watching from somewhere, she was sure, and the price for getting "close" to her daddy could cost her, her life. Nevertheless, having her hand in her daddy's for the first time in years felt so good. She had missed it.

The porch was shady and felt cool and wonderful to sit down on the steps and relax. Daddy sat in his chair and they both ate their ice cream bars without a word between them. Five minutes had not even lapsed before Drusilla made her entrance out onto the front porch. That lurking oppression invading the peaceful tranquility of the moment filled the air around them. A severe intrusion on the nerves to say the least, as she took her chair on her side of the front porch. A few cars drove by as the wind gently blew on the geraniums in the front gardens. The ice cream seemed to stick in Angela's throat as she tried to swallow. Tension growing from Drusilla's presence made swallowing difficult. Somehow this privilege of a break was not going to be one of enjoyment. The ice cream did not taste as great as it had when she was first handed it. Drusilla's presence could take any appetite away.

"Hey kid." It started. Drusilla was now reminding Angela of who had control in this family.

Angela turned to face Drusilla. "What?"

"I'd like you to rub my feet."

Angela looked down at her stepmothers filthy dirty bare feet and then back up at her in disbelief. "What?" This type of order was new to her and it caught her by surprise.

"You heard me, I want my feet rubbed." "You've got nothing else better to do, and I want you to rub my feet." Drusilla was sneering at her stepdaughter. There were no breaks for her stepdaughter; she would make sure of that.

Timidly; Angela picked herself up off the porch step, sat down on the cement at her stepmother's feet, taking one of Drusilla's dirty feet into her hands, and began to rub it. This was a tall order for this girl. How to rub the feet of the one who has spent years tormenting your everyday life. A kindness so undeserving, yet Angela massaged the dirty bare foot.

About an hour passed before Drusilla took the foot away from Angela and laid her other one in her lap to be massaged. Angela's hands were sweaty and the dirty from Drusilla's feet transferred onto her hands. When the feet were done, Drusilla ordered her to massage her calves and thighs up to her shorts. Angela worked without complaint; fear outweighed the inconvenience and injustice. As evening set in Crystal came out and asked Drusilla what she wanted her to cook for dinner. Instructions were given her and she returned inside the house. Angela was now being asked to go wash her hands and get Drusilla's brush. Her next job was to brush Drusilla's hair. Angela did as she was told. The brush went through Drusilla's hair over and over and over again endlessly, until finally, Drusilla got up and went inside. Angela was tired. So much for a day off. Angela thought she might take a bit of a break before Drusilla got back and moved over to the step to sit, just as her daddy asked her to rub his feet. Drusilla had started a parental tradition. Angela looked up at her daddy in disbelief, yet went over to him, sat down at his feet and began to rub his feet. Daddy had cleaned up some from being out in the fields earlier so his feet weren't too bad. He was pleased with her efforts and complimented her.

Dinner was called and Daddy and Angela responded. Angela went to the bathroom to wash her hands before sitting down to eat. Returning to the table, Drusilla asked her where she had been.

"Washing my hands," came her response.

"What for?"

"They smelled bad and they were dirty." Her daddy chuckled at the comment, but Drusilla did not.

"Next time, there will be no dinner for you if you are not up at the table with the rest of the family when asked to do so." "Do I make myself clear?"

Daddy winked at his daughter. Drusilla glared at her. Angela understood both languages.

"Yes." Angela looked down at her plate. There again were pancakes stacked high while Drusilla and Daddy got steak, potatoes and salad. Drusilla shared her dinner with her son. Crystal and Christopher had spaghetti in front of them. Angela felt tears well up in her eyes, but held them back. Each mouth full seemed too difficult to swallow like the injustice that caused the hurt inside of her. Oatmeal and pancakes seemed to be the only diet 'approved by Drusilla' for her. Even Crystal and Christopher go to have spaghetti from time to time, and Crystal was allowed to finish up what Drusilla and their daddy didn't eat. Angela's head began to throb. The stress was making her sick. This didn't turn out to be the day that she thought it might be. Getting a break in life was not written in the books for her. Drusilla made her feel so useless in life. It would be a long time before she took her daddy up on having a break again. Especially since Drusilla had a way of making even ice cream, taste bad.

15

Good Ol' Brutus

Before Drusilla left for work, she would get the children up out of bed; make sure they had started on their chores and then leave with Dennis in tow, dropping him off at his elementary school after she did her first route. Dennis was pretty much kept separate from the rest of the children, except when Drusilla needed Christopher to entertain him. Drusilla had a completely different upbringing for Dennis. He was her baby. She moved him up the ranks of inheritance by default. The other children would be out of the picture, while she pranced him in front of her husband. Dennis was treated like royalty and he grew to know it.

The rest of the children had their individual chores to do and once up and dressed they'd begin doing their chores. No breakfasts until the chores were completed. Christopher had his room to clean and the garbage to take out. Crystal had the kitchen to clean, breakfast to make, dusting to do and of course, tidy up her room. Angela put her nighty away, smoothed the sheet on her bed, cleaned the bathroom, vacuumed the house, dust mopped all the wood floors, and then head out the back door to do the outside chores. The dogs pen was cleaned up, their water buckets cleaned and refilled with fresh water, the horse stall cleaned, food dumped into the trough, Golden Nuggets water bucket cleaned out and fresh water poured in. The chicken coup was raked up and clean straw laid down and the food trays filled, clean fresh water in the dispensers and then Angela would head out into the yard in search of sheep and duck droppings. The pond for the ducks was cleaned out and filled with fresh water; the sheep were given clean water and some food to supplement their grass grazing.

By the time Angela was finished with her chores, a sweat poured from her body. Most times, she did not have time to eat any breakfast. Picking up her books, she would fly out the door and head for school just before the tardy bell rang. She smelled like the barnyard. Drusilla did not allow regular showers or baths for Angela, so it wasn't uncommon for children to cruelly comment on the way she smelled. Holding back the tears, she would stare into her textbook. It wasn't her fault. She did not want to smell or look the way she did. It was Drusilla's way of making sure she did not have to worry about Angela finding any friends to possibly confide in.

Physical Education class added to the line of peer insults, when all the girls in her class were wearing beginner bras, Angela wasn't even allowed to wear a bra. It wasn't that she had anything anyway, but neither did the majority of her classmates. A bra at that age was part of the acceptable fashion trends and expected by her peer group. When Angela tried to approach the subject of getting a bra, Drusilla laughed at her and mocked her flat chest. "You don't have anything anyway, why would you want a bra?" She would laugh.

Angela looked down with shame upon her flat chest. The girls at school called her a boy. The same chest if she could cover it with a lacey bra would stop all of the peer harassment. However, Drusilla did not understand, or if she did, she wasn't letting on. She herself had nothing to brag about. Drusilla refused to buy Angela a bra and that was that, she'd go to school and her peers would have a 'field day' making nasty remarks that would somehow later infiltrate the locker room of her male peers. It was almost as if Drusilla was happy that the vicious teasing of her peer group compounded the torment in Angela's life. If Drusilla had any heart, she would have sent Angela to school in the manner that the other parents sent their children to school. Dressed acceptably to her peers. Drusilla was not known for her kindness or understanding ways when it came to her husband's children; especially not when it came to Angela.

Angela would return home at lunchtime to re-water all the animals and to hear about what chores Drusilla felt she had not accomplished to her liking. Discipline would be administered and the loss of the noonday meal would be included in with the beating. Angela was sent back to school right as the first warning bell sounded, which meant that Drusilla had given her five minutes to get to school, go to her locker, and then get to class. If she was late and the school called to tell Drusilla, Angela would get another beating when she returned home that afternoon.

After school, Angela would get out of class, rush to her locker, and then rush home in five minutes. Any tardiness on arriving home guaranteed a beating. After arriving home, she would take off her school clothes and get into her work clothes. Once again, she would go through the same chore ritual she'd make every morning. Although she was not allowed to do homework, she would open up her books at any free opportunity and try to sneak doing it. Her heart pounded as she tried to concentrate on what she was doing, all the while listening for approaching footsteps coming down the hallway. In the darkness of her room at night, after everyone had gone to bed she would try to see the writing on the pages to study for a test, or she would wake up in the early morning hours and try doing it. She could not give it her best, because though no one was awake in the house, there was no peace and quiet. Her nerves tensed with each distant noise as she listened for approaching footsteps that might catch her up doing her homework. Angela was not allowed to give her schoolwork entirely what she could, and knew by not doing the homework; her grades would not meet her parental expectations, let alone her own expectations. She would have given her eyeteeth to be able to concentrate souly on her studies, instead of having to spend out working on the farm. Her daddy would not be pleased with her; Drusilla knew that there was no way Angela could achieve a 4.0 grade point status without giving her stepdaughter time to study every night. Yet, continued to deny Angela the access and ability to study.

****

Spring turned to another summer, and summer to another autumn. Each passing year, Angela gave what she was allowed to, to her education, but she was being stretched beyond her limits. This was her last year at Wallowing Wood Junior High School. Grade 8 became a reality, yet nothing had changed since grade six. The workload at home increased, her parent's academic expectation remained at the 4.0 GPA, she was still being sent to school in a crew cut hairstyle, wearing long skirts, bobby socks and saddle shoes. Her friends remained the farm animals, accepting her for who she was, and giving her the 'time of day.' Angela would find solace in the fields as she bent over to pull up weeds that had returned from the seed left from the previous plants, year after year. When her chores were all done, and Drusilla could not find anything else for her to do, Angela was sent out to the backfields. This was her life. Instead of looking at it as an injustice, Angela now saw it as a safe haven. The backfield was far enough away from Drusilla to feel halfway comfortable. With the children about her feet clucking and scratching at the dirt beneath, Angela was able to find a moment's peace and tranquility.

Dennis' Shetland pony would neigh from over on the other side of the fence. Angela would talk to the animals and they would seem to talk to her in their own ways. She would bring a large handful of long grass over to the fence to feed to Golden Nugget, giving her a hug in the process. Drusilla saw that Angela was finding happiness, as she would watch Angela and the animals in the distance. Almost over night, the hens were restricted from going out into the backfields, and every time Drusilla caught Angela petting one of the animals, she would send Angela to another part of the field. The garden was the only place none of the animals was allowed, so quite often, Angela would get sent there. This was okay with her during harvest time, but not so good when the seedlings were yet young. During harvest time, a feast of fresh garden veggies lay before her. When Drusilla was not looking, Angela would shove a cherry tomato into her mouth. The bell peppers tasted great off the bush. The beefsteak tomatoes were huge and juicy as she hid the one she was eating beneath the pile of weeds, broke off juicy pieces, and shoved them into her mouth. The string beans were fresh as she snapped them from their vines. Summer and early autumn were the best times of year, and the only time of year, Angela would get nourishment from eating vegetables.

Late autumn, after Daddy and Drusilla sold the harvest to the people at work, the garden lay destitute. The rainwater made it muddy as Angela sunk in it while cleaning out the dead vines and plants. The sky now dark with rain clouds and the land grey with sleep, daddy took all the rabbits to a butcher and sold them. Then he would boil water in the big grey pots and grab his hatchet. Angela knew that it was harvest time for most of her pet chickens and ducks. Tears streamed down her cheeks as she watched her daddy catch and kill each one. They would run around without their heads and then drop helplessly to the ground, heart still beating. It was Angela's job to take them by their feet and dunk them into the boiling hot water. As she brought them up out of the hot water, she was to rip out their feathers. She cried in silence as she worked. Suppressing the hate for the ones who were making her do this to her 'friends'.

Horrified she worked in obedience and in silence, praying that her innocent friends would forgive her. Their bodies still warm in her hands. The pain that they must be going through felt inside of her, guilt stricken with being made to contribute to their death. Her tears dripped into the blood stained water, as she realized that this was the last time they would be together. She hated herself for having to do this to them. It was awful and yet another sad day in her terrible life.

Daddy saw her tears and began to mock her. He told her that she was stupid to be so attached to the 'birdbrains'. He tried to hand her the hatchet to make her do the killing of the last hen. She cried aloud now and shook her head "no." "Please don't make me, please don't make me." "They are my pets." She cried out, sobbing. Her daddy shook his head in disgust and walked away to go finish off the last hen himself. Angela closed her eyes, as she heard the hen struggling to break free from her daddy. Whack! The hatchet fell down. A scuffle of feathers was heard and then the familiar thud of a dead friend.

This part of being her daddy's right hand helper killed her from within. Daddy tried to explain that this was how farmers survived and fed their families. Angela could not even think of eating her 'friends.' Her parents sold most of the 'dressed chickens to acquaintances at their places of work, and the few that remained, the family ate in front of Angela. Somehow, her diet of pancakes and oatmeal tasted better these days.

Angela spent time mourning the loss of her feathered friends as she raked out their coup and brushed down each nest. The few lucky ones that now remained, huddled in their egg laying nests, and seemed to be mourning the loss of their coup-mates themselves, not knowing their own futures. Egg production went down, and now her daddy was not letting the hens out of the coup. Angela cleaned the coup with tears streaming down her face. Reaching up, she would pet the few that remained. They would coo at her as if they understood. She would lift each one up looking for eggs and give each one a special hug.

Brutus was the survivor of the roosters. He was big, beautiful and a very proud bird. Quite dominant by character and everyone knew it. Angela was the only one he would let near himself, except of course for the hens also. He was known to chase and viciously peck anyone else that would venture near him or his hens. His bite was brutal. He would bite down and turn his head, ripping into the skin of anyone other than Angela. When his hens disappeared after being butchered, Brutus seemed to get meaner. The family noticed a change in him, and now they were very afraid of him. Angela had not really noticed, because Brutus had always been nice to her. She considered him her protector. Even Drusilla feared him and he knew it. Drusilla paid less visits to the backyard, and most of her commands were yelled out the closed screen door, blocking any attack Brutus could come up with.

One day Drusilla decided she wanted to wash clothes, before opening the backdoor she looked both ways, making sure the coast was clear and then made a victorious leap and run from the back door into the shed to do the laundry, slamming the door behind her. A shrilled scream sounded from inside the shed as Angela approached the corner of the shed. "Angela!" "Get this fucking bird out of here NOW!" Drusilla was up on top of the washer; Brutus flapping his wings and flying up and down trying to attack her.

Angela opened up the shed door and grabbed up Brutus carrying him out into the yard away from Drusilla. She took him into the chicken coup and closed the door trying to save him from any retaliation Drusilla might offer. Drusilla was MAD! Brutus would be in deep trouble if he continued his attack upon her. Closing but not locking the door to the chicken coup, Angela proceeded out to the horse stalls to clean them. It wasn't long before Angela heard the familiar shrilled scream from Drusilla.

"Angela, come and get this fucking bird, now!" "I am going to kill him!" "I am going to kill him!" Drusilla was threatening and extremely angry.

Angela raced over to her rooster. Brutus was mad! He would not let Angela near him. Drusilla was hitting him. She grabbed Angela. It was the wrong thing to do. Brutus bit Drusilla repeatedly on her legs and ankles. Brutus was only protecting Angela. Drusilla ran to the shed and slammed the door to get away from him. Brutus attacked the door of the shed over and over again. Angela was finally able to calm him down and picking him up, returned him to the coup and just as she went to lock the door, Drusilla shoved her out of the way and opened the door. She had an ax in her hands. Angela looked at the ax and then at Brutus, and then at Drusilla. Hell's fire burned in her eyes. "Get that fucking bird and hold him, I am going to kill him!" Drusilla ordered. Angela loved Brutus, and there was no way she was going to hang on to Brutus while Drusilla put an ax in his back and killed him.

"I said, hold him, or you will get it too!" Drusilla had gone mad.

Angela started shaking and crying out, "no mommy, please, no. No! Mommy no!" she sobbed.

Drusilla struck Angela across the face and Brutus flew out of Angela's arms at Drusilla. Drusilla swung the ax in the air missing Brutus. He figured out that he'd better turn and run, this woman now meant business. Drusilla was wildly chopping the ax down through the air as she gave chase. There was no way that this rooster would live.

Angela watched in horror, sobbing and crying out, begging her stepmother to stop, but to no avail. The woman had gone mad and would not quit until Brutus was dead. Brutus ran for his life with the maniac Amazon quickly on him, chopping through the air, narrowly missing him. It was not until Drusilla cornered him against the back fence and drove in the deathly blow to his back. He let out a squawk and attempted to get away, blood flowing out into his feathers, flapping his wings as he rose in the air trying to get passed Drusilla. Nevertheless, the ax caught him again. Brutus was down, mortally wounded but not dead. He lay helpless, still trying to move out of Drusilla's range, but Drusilla picked him up and placed him wounded on the butcher stump, and continued to drive the ax into his mutilated body over and over again. He was dead, but she didn't stop. Her stepmother was making sure that vengeance was her victory.

Angela bent over and threw up at the sight. Her body shook with fear. Tears ran down her face as she sobbed for her hero, Brutus. "Stop it, stop it, stop it! She screamed in horror at her stepmother. Drusilla kept chopping as if he wasn't dead enough for her. He was limp and his blood had splattered everywhere. The ax was covered in Brutus' blood. Drusilla was splattered with his blood. His body jumped with each blow falling to pieces as the Amazon chopped him to bits with each deadly blow.

Finally, Drusilla gave up. She lowered the ax, looked down at the bird and then over in Angela's direction. Angela was sobbing. She had dropped to her knees her face in the dirt.

"Shut up or you'll be next!" Drusilla warned her. She growled at Angela like an angry animal.

Angela rose up to her feet trying desperately to control her sobs. Her body shook so bad from the fear that gripped her inner being now. Drusilla was capable of killing, and had just threatened her. Drusilla walked up to her with the ax still in her hand. Angela could not breathe. She stopped in front of Angela, a strange smile came to her lips, and then she dropped the ax at her feet. "You ever train another bird to attack me, and you'll get the same Brutus just got." "Now, go bury your bird." Drusilla walked away.

Angela looked down at the bloody ax that now lay at her feet. Tears welled up in her eyes as she then looked over to her dead pet. Slowly she turned toward the shed to get a shovel and a box. Holding back the sobs, she walked to the shed. Drusilla did not want her crying, she had made it quite clear.

Drusilla was in the shed taking off her bloody clothes and tossing them into the washer. She then began washing the blood off her skin in the laundry tubs. Angela came in to get the shovel. Fear crawled up her spine as she passed by Drusilla on her way into the back of the shed.

"Make sure the hole is deep. I do not want any wild animal digging it up. If they do, I will feed the bird to you raw." A morbid threat from a morbid mind. Since when did Drusilla care if a wild animal ate the mutilated body of the bird she just killed? Could it be that she did not want someone else digging up the evidence from the moment she went mad?

Angela did not comment or give answer. She took the shovel from its hanger and headed out the back door of the shed. Walking passed her dead pet, his body in bloody pieces; she found a place of solace to bury him. Tears streamed down her face as the shovel broke the clay beneath its sharp edge. Angela could hear the back door of the house close shut, as Drusilla went inside. Alone out in the late evening hour she mourned the death of her friend, as she diligently dug his deep grave and final resting place. She cried to herself as she worked into the night. Her body ached from the heartbreak of losing the only friend who had ever come to fight for her to defend her best interest.

The hole was about four feet deep when she knew that she would now have to go get her mutilated pet. She sobbed as she walked back toward his body. She fell to her knees as she looked at her dear friend, covered in blood and laying in so many pieces. Terror ripped through her when she realized that the Amazon who on so many occasions had beaten her mercilessly was the one responsible for this horrific scene. Her hands stroking his cut up little body, crying out from the pain of heartbreak and from intense fear. Carefully she lifted every piece of his bloodied body. As some pieces fell to the ground, she cried even harder. Walking over to the freshly dug grave, she laid his body to rest. "I love you Brutus," she sobbed. She walked back to the butcher stump, picked up the rest of the pieces of Brutus, and placed them into the grave. She sobbed as she laid the last piece to rest in the dark cold grave she had coated with newspaper. Covering her friend with the remaining newspaper pages, she told him goodbye. The tears flowed freely now, as her bloody fingers dug into the loose dirt beneath her. She had to put the dirt over him and she really didn't want to. Handful, by small handful she tossed in the dirt on top of him, crying out, "Oh Brutus, Oh Brutus, why?" "I'm so sorry." "I love you." She stood to let the shovel do the digging and tossing now. She wished she could die and lay still right beside him; perhaps the pain would go away.

Angela was surrounded by the darkness of the night sky when the last shovel full was patted down upon his grave. She felt lost and lonely, and at this point had no desire of returning to the house. She sat down by Brutus' grave, rocking back and forth and back and forth, and back and forth, wishing this was just a bad nightmare, knowing otherwise. The pain pounded inside her chest. Angela wanted to understand the purpose of life. Why live? The feeling of hopelessness filled her entire body.

****

Angela had been at the graveside of Brutus for quite some time, when she finally rose to her feet. The pain had gone and was now replaced with a strange numbness. Her tears had dried up and for some reason she could dry no more. Blankly, she stared toward the direction of the grave and walked toward the barn in an almost hypnotic state of mind.

She gave Golden Nugget a big hug, and then proceeded to the chicken coup. There she went in and sat down in the straw holding her head in her hands. She was in shock. Stunned. Dead on the inside. Here, in the chicken coup, she found refuge.

Looking up toward her house, she noticed that all the light had been shut off. Another night of being left outside and forgotten. Still, being here with the chickens felt so much better than being in there, with the woman who had murdered her pet earlier in the evening. She laid her head back on the straw and tried to go to sleep. Angela felt numb all over.

The cool night air blew freely in through the chicken wire. She felt nothing. An empty feeling inside. Closing her eyes brought back pictures of the brutal murder of her pet. She opened her eyes. Angela could not sleep. She stared up into the starry sky of the heavens. Counting stars, she attempted to block out the dreadful memory of what Drusilla had done to her pet.

Two hens flew down from there nests and joined her on the ground. They nestled up to her as she stroked their feathers, over and over, and over again. A dog barked in the silent distance. Nature comforted her aching heart. Solace to a wretched child.

16

Traffic Court for Bonnie and Clyde

In the days that followed Brutus' violent death, Angela became very introverted. She barely talked to anyone, whether at home or at school. She felt tired much of the time and experienced a loss of appetite. Still, she accomplished her chores at home and did her schoolwork at school. She kept her distance from Drusilla and made very little eye contact with her. Angela would busy herself in areas that she knew Drusilla would approve of, which would keep her at a distance from her. Angela's pain had turned to anger and hate toward her stepmother; the woman who had shown her nothing but hate and rejection and brutally battered her often. Angela had spent a lifetime trying to get this woman to love and accept her, but this woman had had it in for her from the first day she had come into her Daddy's life.

Angela would make herself scarce by going out into the field and pulling weeds when dinnertime would come around. This way, Angela would not have to eat, sitting across from the Amazon. The once joyful, bubbly child was truly seeing life for what it was; painful and wretched. Pulling weeds out in the field, the clay hard and unforgiving soil became the source for her pent up anger. As the weeds came out, the roots bringing with them huge clumps of dried clay she would hurl them over her shoulder, the feeling of tension being released with each bunch hurled. Angela had so much hurt and anger within her that this job was no longer a chore; it was an outlet for her. Looking over at the gravesite of her dearly beloved murdered pet, tears would well up in her eyes. The pain would not loose its grip on her heart and soul. Reaching down she took two twigs and made a marker for his grave. Walking over to it, she pushed the marker into the dirt on top of the grave and pulled weeds from around it.

Silently she walked back from the area in which she had been working and continued pulling weeds. The wind blew in through the weeds as her body stiffened from the cool evening air. Angela wasn't really cold, just feeling dead on the inside. A relentless submission to the life she now lived. It was getting late when she finally straightened up and slowly headed to the back yard to do her chores for the night. The horse was put into her clean stall and the chickens herded into their coup for the evening. The dogs' water was freshened and then she turned to get the sheep tied up.

Looking around her, Angela could not find them. She ran around the entire backyard and out into the field looking and calling for them. Fear crawled up her spine. Where were they? Had they gotten out of the yard somehow? She ran to the gate and out into the front yard calling to them. Still, no familiar bleating response. The door of the house opened and Drusilla walked out onto the porch. "What is going on?"

"I-I can't find the sheep." Angela stammered. This was the first time the two had spoken to one another since that bloody day, and had it not been for this direct inquiry, this conversation would not have happened.

"What the hell do you mean you don't know where the sheep are?" "Where could they go?" "Get your ass out back and look for them!"

Obediently, Angela returned to the backyard. She called and called. Retracing her earlier steps in search for 'Bonnie and Clyde'. It was as if they had just vanished, and of course, it was her fault. She could not find them anywhere. Her heart began to pound. What had happened to them? Drusilla would surely use this opportunity to beat her up if the sheep were not found, and found quickly.

Angela shook with fear as she checked all of the fences and bushes along their back property. Suddenly she heard Clyde. Following the bahing of his bleating response to her, she found him in her neighbors' yard. How had they gotten themselves in there? She called to them, and reached through the bushes to them. Trying to encourage them to return home the same way they had gotten through.

Both sheep ran to greet her, but could not get back over the fence. Angela tried to find the spot that had gotten them into his yard, but to no avail. Therefore, she went around to the neighbors' house and led them both safely home. They seemed happy to be back. Their dinner was waiting in the box. She tied them up and gave them each a joyful hug. Angela was thankful to have them back home, just like the parent of a wayward child who had returned home. She hugged them and stood back watching as they began to eat their dinner. A smile turned up the corners of her mouth, as a sparkle of joy and thanksgiving penetrated her broken heart. She wouldn't get a beating for losing the sheep tonight. Before going into the house, Angela gave the farm a quick glance to make sure she hadn't forgotten anything. Everything and everyone seemed to be in its and their place, 'tucked in for the night'. She closed the door behind her, and walked through the livingroom passed Drusilla who was watching T.V. Angela mumbled her goodnights as she headed for her room.

"You find the sheep?" Questioned Drusilla still staring at the T.V.

"Yes, they were in the neighbors' yard."

"What neighbors' yard?" Drusilla's voice raised a few octaves, but her eyes never left the T.V. screen.

"The old man's yard, down the property line."

"How did they get there?"

"I really don't know." Angela answered her stepmother hoping that she wouldn't press the issue.

"Then go find out, I would like to know."

Of course, she would, Angela thought sarcastically to herself. Anything to make her life miserable. It was late and very dark outside. How was she to see in the dark? Why couldn't the matter be investigated in the morning when it was light out? Going out now didn't make much sense, but then again, nothing ever made sense so why try to figure it out? Drusilla got what she wanted when she wanted it. Pretty much, she wanted Angela out of the house.

Angela returned to the backyard and walked over to where the old man and them shared the property line. Feeling her way along the fence line, she couldn't really come up with a legitimate answer for Drusilla. There were no holes or low areas vivid enough to identify that that was exactly where the sheep had gotten through, or over. Eventually Angela gave up the search and ventured out into the darkness of the backyard, located some leftover pallets that her daddy had brought home from work and dragged them over to the old mans' fence section of their property and made a make-shift fence, in front of the old mans' fence, to keep Bonnie and Clyde away from it. This way there would be a double reassurance that the sheep would not get back over, or go through the fence again. It might have been a short cut to solving the mystery of how they got into the old man's yard, but that did not matter. Angela could have spent the whole night outside looking for the answer and never come up with it. This way, there would be no way they could ever get back in.

Problem solved, and matter settled, she returned indoors. Sweat beaded from her forehead. The pallets are heavy for any man, let alone a growing young girl. She now explained to Drusilla what she had done to prevent any further trespass of their sheep. Sarcastically Drusilla asked if "all that was necessary?"

"Yes, I feel that it is." "We really don't know how they got in his yard, but this will make sure that they won't get back in."

"I'd still like to know how they got through."

Angela did not argue. She wanted to go to bed. Daddy wasn't home from work yet, and Drusilla seemed kind of agitated by his absence. The sooner she climbed into bed, the sooner she could get away from Drusilla.

"Goodnight," Drusilla conceded, when she finally figured out that her stepdaughter had taken the only recourse given the present circumstances.

"Night," came the grateful response from Angela. She did not need an engraved invitation. Getting Drusilla's permission to go to bed sent her quickly down the hall into her bedroom. She was undressed and wearing her nighty, with lights out in five minutes. Sleep came quickly.

****

Angela was in a deep sleep, when suddenly she felt herself being pulled out of bed by her hair. The pain of it being ripped out of her skull brought her to an abrupt awakening. Startled, she looked up at the angry eyes of Drusilla. "Get your ass out of bed and get the oven cleaned!" Demanded Drusilla from between clenched teeth.

Angela instinctively responded by heading bewildered to the kitchen. She only wished this was a nightmare, because then she could wake up from it and it wouldn't be reality. She could roll over and go back to sleep and forget it ever happened, right? Wrong! Unfortunately, this was not a dream; Drusilla had gotten her up at two in the morning to clean the kitchen oven. A wet rag was handed to her and some dish soap squeezed onto it. Angela was trying desperately to get her wits about her; her brain had been turned in to sleep and was now being forced into instant awareness. A rude awakening one might say.

Angela looked into the oven, it was filthy. Food had been baked on to the sides, bottom and top and Crystal had not cleaned it in some time. Why hadn't the food been wiped up when the spills happened? That of course would have been too easy, and then this oven wouldn't be this messy, and Angela wouldn't be up at two in the morning cleaning it.

Drusilla shoved Angela halfway into the oven and demanded that she get it cleaned in half an hour or she would get her ass kicked. Angela was still trying to wake up as she began scrubbing the oven with just the soapy rag Drusilla had handed to her. They both knew that the oven would not be cleaned in half an hour with just a soapy rag. It was hopeless to expect that a soapy dishrag could clean a dirty grease-baked-on oven in just a half an hour. Angela was going to get beat up tonight and they both knew it.

Why was Drusilla so mad tonight? Where was their daddy anyway? Why wasn't he home? Was he at work, or was he out with someone as Drusilla constantly accused him? Angela was Drusilla's hostage and the person that she was always choosing to take her aggression out on. Angela was once her daddy's favorite child, and recently their relationship that Drusilla had spent years destroying was now starting to rekindle, in a way that Drusilla was starting to feel a bit insecure again. Angela had been warned about becoming reattached to her daddy. Now she would pay again for Drusilla's insecurities.

One half hour later, and to the minute, Drusilla came into the kitchen swinging the belt across Angela's back as she knelt in the oven. The sting of pain pierced her spine. Over and over again the belt whipped into her back and sides. Angela knew better than to move away from Drusilla, or to start crying. It would only make matters worse. She closed her eyes and held her breath as each blow landed on her body. Drusilla stopped swinging the belt and grabbed her by her ear and stood her to her feet.

"You fucken bitch!" "You make me sick!" Drusilla spit in her face. "Now get your ass to bed!"

Angela shook from head to toe and wobbled back to her bedroom, wiping Drusilla's spit from her face. The welts on her back burned as she slowly laid down on her bed. She was still dazed and bewildered. Her ear ached from being pulled so hard. Finding a comfortable way to lay her head on her pillow in the 'approved position' was difficult. It hurt bad. Angela felt weak. She tried to get to back to sleep, but that too was difficult. Having been yanked out of bed while sleeping, made her restless. Her body couldn't stop shaking. Fear made it impossible.

It was not until she saw the headlights from her daddy's car pulling into the driveway and reflecting off her bedroom walls, that she started feeling safer. She heard his key being turned in the lock and the front door open. Then as he closed it behind him, the mad woman came to life.

"You fucken no good, cheating slob!" "I called your work tonight and they told me that you weren't there!" "So where have you been?" Drusilla was on him.

"You don't know what you are talking about, lower your voice, the children are sleeping!" Daddy warned.

"I'll lower it when I get some truthful answers from you, you pig!" Drusilla was shrieking.

"Let's take this discussion in the back room." Daddy seemed calm.

Angela heard their footsteps head toward the back room, as Drusilla continued with her accusations of him cheating on her. The argument lasted into the late night hours. Angela tried to shut it out, but the sound of Drusilla's voice kept her wide-awake with fear. Threats flew back and forth as well as accusations from both of her parents.

Eventually the tone dropped and then silence came. Lights were shut off in the house, and Angela laid awake in the darkness of her bedroom. Taking in a deep breath and slowly blowing it out, she now felt that maybe it might be safe enough for her to get some sleep. Afterall, her daddy was home. She closed her eyes and drifted into a light sleep, one that would still allow her to be aware of all the noises around her.

****

Angela was really tired the next morning, and very stiff from her beating last night. When Drusilla gave the order to 'get up', it was tough for her to respond with the expected 'quickness' Drusilla desired. Nonetheless, Angela gave it better than her best shot. Drusilla and her daddy were not speaking to one another, which brought about an atmosphere that 'could be cut with a knife'. Angela walked as if she was walking on thin ice, in and around Drusilla. Her chores were completed as per Drusilla's white glove specifications and then she sat down at the table to eat her oatmeal. Drusilla did not join them at the table this morning.

Instead, she went out into the backyard. Silence echoed around the breakfast table as each member of the household finished their meal.

Angela was just about finished eating when she heard a loud crack, come from the backyard. Rising to their feet, the family glanced out the window. Drusilla had just torn down the fence that Angela had built the night before to prevent Bonnie and Clyde from jumping over or getting into the old man's yard. Tears welled up in Angela's eyes as she witnessed Drusilla tearing down the project that had taken her over an hour to accomplish in the dark. Daddy looked at Angela with an inquiring look. "How did that get there?" He asked.

"I had to build it because Bonnie and Clyde got into the neighbor's yard last night. I couldn't find how they got into his yard, so I built the fence so they couldn't do it again, and now she's tearing it down." Angela explained through her tears. They both stood watching as Drusilla broke it into pieces through her temper tantrum. Angela felt defeated once more.

Daddy noticed the hurt in his daughters' face and reassuringly told her that "he would check it out today, and do what he could to fix it so that the sheep wouldn't go back over the fence." He then gave her a squeeze and guided her back to the table to finish her breakfast.

Drusilla came into the house. She was out of breath and gasping for air as she gave Angela the order, "Now get your ass out there and clean up that mess." "Find out how the sheep are getting over the old fence and fix it!"

Angela looked at her daddy, who didn't say a word. "Okay" came her response. She then proceeded to eat her breakfast.

"I said NOW!" Drusilla grabbed Angela's arm, led her to the back door, and shoved her down the back steps. Angela landed outside on her hands and knees on the back sidewalk leading to the shed. She was hurt, but got up and limped over to the fence she had built last night. Pieces of the fence were strewn around as if a tornado had hit it. Drusilla couldn't have just broken the pallets apart from one another so they could be used again, instead she had taken her anger out on the pallets and broken them in pieces so they couldn't be used for anything but firewood.

Angela went to the shed to get the ax to finish tearing up the pallets for firewood. Drusilla had made a big project out of a small one. Seeing the ax brought a shiver up her spine. This was the tool that Drusilla had used to kill her pet rooster. It had been cleaned up, but nonetheless, the brutal murder of Brutus was significant to this tool now being held by Angela. A shiver crawled up her spine as she tried to block out this fact. Angela chopped up the pallets to fireplace sized wood pieces and stacked them with the firewood up against the shed. The small slivered pieces got placed into the kindling box, and Angela was now ready to investigate the "how" part of their sheep trespass into the old man's yard.

The bushes were tall and thick at this portion of the fence. Angela had to penetrate them in order to check the wire fence beneath the heavy bush that embraced it. Everywhere she looked, the fence seemed to be fine. Only one area concerned her and that was where area dipped down at the top. Could this be where they had climbed over? Can sheep climb? Wouldn't someone notice? Wouldn't the fence be crushed beneath the weight of their heavy bodies as they climbed over? There was no evidence on how they entered his yard. Regardless, she would go let Drusilla know of her observations and assumptions.

Angela went into the house to look for Drusilla to give her the findings. Both her parents were nowhere to be seen. The entrance to the den that led into their bedroom was locked. She could hear her parents inside.

"Um...I found out how I think the sheep might be getting over the fence into that old man's yard," she said through the locked louvered door.

"Get the hell out of here!" came Drusilla's command.

Angela went back outside, shaking from the fear that Drusilla's response put into her. Her answer had been totally unexpected to say the least and threatening sounding as well. She did not know what Drusilla wanted her to do to the fence to resolve the issue, and as long as there was no direction given, Angela proceeded to check on all the animals' welfare before she headed out into the backfield to pull weeds. This was her refuge; the furthest point away from Drusilla she could get. Bent over, she tugged and yanked on each weed until they surrendered to her.

It was mid-afternoon before Drusilla and her daddy surfaced from the house. They seemed to be all lovey-dovey now. Drusilla went into the shed to do laundry and Daddy got out the mower. Angela bent over to continue the job she was doing. The bees buzzed around her and the whinnying of the neighbors' horses came from behind her. There was a sense of peace as she worked in sections pulling out weeds. Out in the field there was some distance between her and the wretched chaos of life with Drusilla.

"Angela," her name was being called.

Standing up she responded, "Coming." She ran from the backfield into the backyard, closing the gate behind her and met up with Drusilla and her daddy.

"Where are the sheep?"

Glancing around the yard and back up at them she answered, "I don't know."

"Then you better get your butt going and find them!" Drusilla kicked Angela in the butt as she turned to go. Angela had not expected the physical contact and dropped to her knees when Drusilla's foot struck her. Pain climbed through her spine, but she scrambled to her feet and ran over toward the old man's fence in search of Bonnie and Clyde.

Just as they arrived, she heard the bleating answer to her calls to them. Looking over the fence, she could see that the old man had them tied to the tree in the center of his yard. She would have to go ask him for them. Running passed her parents she called out to them that she had found them and that she had to go get them.

"Where?" they called out after her.

"In the old mans' yard again," came Angela's breathless response.

Arriving at the old mans' gate to his house, she called out for him. The old man came out of his house pointing a finger at her, anger in his voice. "Now I'm fed up with them getting into my yard here." "I will not give them to you, you hear." "I have called the police and they are on their way."

Angela was bewildered. The police? Last night had been the first time they had gotten into his yard, and there had been no other times before that, so what was this old man talking about? Tears began to flow down her cheeks. She would really be in trouble now. She not only had the police to answer to for her family's sheep, but she would have to answer to Drusilla for the sheep getting into the old mans' yard and now for him calling the police on her.

Frightened, she headed back home. Her legs shook, and it was difficult breathing. She would surely be mutilated for this. Her daddy and Drusilla were waiting on the front porch for her return. Seeing that she did not have the sheep with her, Drusilla began the interrogation. "Where the hell are the sheep?" She inquired.

"The man won't let me have them," Angela tried to explain between the sobs that were now coming out of her mouth uncontrollably.

"What the hell do you mean he won't let you have the sheep?" "Get your ass back there and get them!" growled Drusilla angrily.

Angela was not allowed to argue or give rebuttal, or to even explain. She headed back over to the old man's house crying all the way. Fear took hold of her, her body shook as she headed back. Drusilla was not the only one she feared at this point. The mean old man who would not return the sheep to her, was adding to her trepidation. Tears streamed down her sweaty face as she arrived back at his front fence once more. In most normal situations, a parent would not send the child over to resolve any adult issues, but Angela's 'family' situation was not normal and this was just another reflection of the abnormality of it.

The old man saw her standing outside his fence and told her to "go back home," he had not "changed his mind."

"My mommy said that I had to get our sheep," she cried out to him.

"I don't care what your mommy said; I'm not giving them back to you." "They are in my yard, and when the police get here, they will be taking them with them." The grumpy old man would not give in.

Angela stood sobbing in his driveway. Drusilla would beat her if she returned without them. She could not go home. Just as things looked like they could get no worse, a police cruiser pulled into the old man's driveway. The sight of the police cruiser arriving made her shake and cry even harder. As the officers approached her, in between sobs, she tried to explain to them that her mommy wanted her to bring the sheep home.

"Now hold on little girl, I need to explain a few things to the officers." "I don't want the sheep getting into my yard any more." "I am fed up with them eating my flowers and plants all the time." The old man lied, and Angela knew it. There was no "all the time" in this matter. This was only the second time.

"Calm down, and tell us your side of the story." The officers listened as the old man tried to relate to them his side of the story. He went on about how the "sheep were always getting into his yard and gardens and destroying his plants." He ended with, "they won't do anything about it when I've asked them to, so you'll have to take the sheep away from them."

Angela stared at the old man in disbelief, the tears still streaming down her face. The officer then looked at her and tried to explain the old man's viewpoint. Angela tried to tell the officer that the old man was lying, but the officer did not seem to hear her.

"Where do you live?" the officer asked her.

"Around the corner," she answered.

"Show us."

Angela led the officer to her house with their sheep in tow. Her parents got up from their chairs on the porch. Drusilla was not pleased; she was almost panicked by their presence. Now what had her stepdaughter done to her? Angela would pay for this, she was sure.

Daddy tried to joke with the officers to lighten the charge, and Drusilla tried to use all of her charms. In the end, the Humane Society picked up the sheep, and her parents received a ticket to appear in court. The neighbor had wanted to press charges but none materialized. The officers left.

Angela ran into the backyard, tears streaming down her face. Bonnie and Clyde were gone. She ran all the way out into the field and dropped to her knees crying for her sheep. How could they do this? The old man had lied. Her parents had not listened to her when she tried to tell them how she thought they were getting out. They were too busy in their bedroom when she had tried to bring it to their attention. If Drusilla had kept the fence up that Angela had built the night before, none of this would have happened! Anger and sorrow spilled out of her at the same time.

"Angela!" Drusilla called her from the back door.

Angela looked up and responded, "Coming!" Part of her wanted to ignore the call and the other part of her knew better. Getting up from her knees, she walked through the backyard and into the back door.

She was ushered into the house and told to drop her pants and grab a hold of her ankles. Drusilla would now beat her with the belt because the sheep had gotten into the old man's yard. Of course, Angela was at fault for this. Drusilla would never concur that anyone else had any responsibility to this occurrence, or any other thing for all that matters. If she could beat her stepdaughter for this, why should there be any real reason?

Twelve stinging welts later, Drusilla directed her to pull up her pants. "Do you think that you can keep all the animals in the backyard now?"

"Y-y-es," Angela answered Drusilla through clenched teeth while holding back the tears and sobs that wanted to come out from the pain from her beating.

"Now get your ass outside and do your chores!"

Angela ran out of the house. She hurt all over. It had not even been twenty-four hours since her last beating. She was tired, hurt and angry all at the same time. She wanted to scream out, but did not dare. Drusilla would be coming down on her in a split second. Instead, Angela ran hard, working with vigor and intent through each and every chore, completing them in record time, and then headed out to the backfield to take out all this anger, pain and confusion on the weeds. She tore them out one by one, throwing them as far as she could. They shot like missiles through the air.

The tantrum lasted until her body fell weak and breathless to the ground. The sun had set and night had fallen. She just laid there, staring up in to the sky. Tears still fell hours later. Closing her eyes, she was breathless and winded. Slowly she fell into a deep sleep.

****

A few weeks later, Drusilla beckoned the children to dress in their school clothes. They were paraded into the car, each taking their assigned traveling position. They were informed that they were going to court with Drusilla to respond to the ticket she had been given for the sheep. "I want you all to behave, and not to talk to anyone." Drusilla didn't have to ask twice. They were quite accustomed to the consequences for bad behavior.

The tour to the courthouse was one of the first times Drusilla had taken her husband's three children anywhere by car in quite some time. They watched the scenery go by with interest. They didn't know anything outside of the route to and from school. Once arriving at the courthouse, Drusilla parked the car and the children were paraded behind her as if she was a mother goose. They had been brought with her for display and to play on the Judge's good sense.

The door on the courtroom read "Traffic Court." Had their stepmother gotten a ticket for driving also? The children looked at one another, but dared not remark. They followed her into the courtroom. They were led to the front row on the left side of the courtroom. Not saying a word, they watched the proceedings, as people were called to the front to answer for their traffic violations. Angela found the courtroom fascinating and listened intently as each case was called and the response and verdict given.

Finally, the Judge reached for another folder and said: "People versus Bonnie and Clyde." The people seated in the courtroom broke out in laughter. Leaning over to the bailiff, the Judge asked if "this was a joke?" The bailiff shook his head. The Judge looked down at the paperwork in front of him and called "the party responding on behalf of Bonnie and Clyde please come forward."

Drusilla rose and walked forward. The children stood up as she stood in front of him. The Judge looked at the children and then back at Drusilla. "How do you plead?"

"Guilty, with explanation," she responded.

"Okay, let's hear it."

The courtroom burst into laughter once again as Drusilla tried to make light of the charges pending before her. The Judge hammered his gavel trying to bring order back into his courtroom, while holding back laughter himself.

Drusilla attempted to claim poverty, using her children as exhibits. She wanted him to know that they all missed the sheep very much and wanted them back home. "The sheep are the children's pets." Drusilla lied. The only one who really knew the sheep or tended to them was Angela. She was the only one that wanted the sheep back for sentimental reasons. Daddy and Drusilla wanted them back because they had purchased them and there was that monetary significance.

The Judge looked at the children once more and then back at Drusilla. "There will be a twenty five dollar fine, and once that is paid, you will have to pay the Humane Society their charges and fines to release the sheep back into your care." "Please make sure that the fence is secured so that Bonnie and Clyde will no longer be able to get into your neighbor's yard." "Do I make myself clear?" "The next time I will not be lenient."

"Maybe another farm outside the city limits will be better for them."
"Good day."

"Yes your honor, thank you." Drusilla went over to sign some papers and then left with the children trailing behind her. She wasn't thrilled with the outcome, because it was not her intent to get stuck paying any court costs, but Drusilla couldn't have everything her way in the real world. Reluctantly she paid the fine and then they went to the Humane Society and she paid their fines and fees before Bonnie and Clyde returned home. The fence was mended. This time her daddy did it and Drusilla did not tear it down. The sheep were brought home from the Humane Society. They bleated their contentment, as if to say that they were happy to be home. Angela gave them both big hugs and kissed them. Leading them into the backyard, she finally got to release them from the ropes that had tied around their necks. They ran over to their food tough sniffing it and began eating. They looked up and Angela as if to say "thanks."

Angela heard the old man's door slam shut and a tingle of fear ran up her spine. Nevertheless, she was happy to get her sheep back home. The fence had been fixed by her daddy, so they were here to stay, she would not have to worry about them getting into his yard again. Her worries with the sheep were over...or were they?

A few days later, Angela came outside to do her chores. She had gotten in the habit of looking for Bonnie and Clyde the moment she left the backyard. Today she did not see them, so instinctively she went around to the side of the shed to see if they were there. Bonnie was just beneath the bushes, lying on her side not moving. Clyde was on his belly, fighting to get up when he saw Angela approaching him. However, for some reason he couldn't rise up. Angela ran over to them and dropped to her knees. Bonnie did not move. Clyde laid his head in her lap. Thick saliva dripped from his mouth. His breathing, unsteady. Angela looked at the sheep in disbelief, and tried to cry out to get her parents' attention. She was too choked up. Nothing came out. Tears fell down her cheeks as she got up, laying Clyde's head down on the ground and ran to the house. She was sobbing too hard to get out what she wanted to say to her parents, when she found them. They sat looking at her bewildered, as she motioned them to follow her. Daddy got up from his chair and Drusilla followed at his heals. They followed Angela outside and over to the sheep.

"What happened?" Anxiety was rising in her daddy's voice.

Angela still could not speak. She just shook her head, stroking Clyde's curly coat. He was fighting to live as he lay dying next Bonnie, his dead mate. Drusilla ordered Angela to "get some water, quick!" Angela ran with everything she had in her to retrieve the bucket of water. When she returned they tried to get Clyde to drink the water, he would not do it. Clyde tried to fight to get away.

"Call the Humane Society; they will know what to do." "Someone has poisoned them." Daddy was sure of himself.

Just as Drusilla left to call them, a door closed on the other side of the fence. The old man had been out watching and listening to what was going on. Daddy and Angela looked at one another. They knew right away, that the old man had done this to their sheep.

Clyde was on his side now, still fighting for his life. Angela hugged him as death drew near him. Drusilla returned form making the call and told daddy that the humane Society was on their way. It seemed to take them a lifetime to arrive. Clyde finally lost his battle with death. Angela broke down and cried.

"Oh get the hell out of here!" Drusilla yelled at her.

Getting up, Angela ran away. The tears still falling as she made her way out to the backfield. She sat down on the big rock embracing herself with her arms, rocking back and forth, and crying in silence.

Angela was called for supper later that evening and was told that the Humane Society had confirmed that the sheep had been poisoned with arsenic poisoning. Looking down at her pancakes, she lost her appetite. Asking to "be excused", she headed out into the backyard to do her chores. The stillness of death hung in the air, and the empty sheep-feeding trough gave birth to the darkness of the grave memory.

17

Nothing to Celebrate

Crystal, Christopher and Angela despised the times when school would let out for holidays or summer vacations; because it meant that, they would have to be home with Drusilla, all day, every day. She worked for a School District driving a bus; so when school let out, she was also home. School being out for any amount of time was detrimental to their well-being.

The rest of their peers at school saw these breaks in education as something to look forward to. Many went on trips during school vacation time and came back with pictures and stories to tell of the experiences. Most other children used this time to relax, play and have fun inviting friends over. Because Crystal, Christopher and Angela were not allowed to make or have friends, they did not have anyone stopping by to invite them out. Where most of their peers anticipated that last minute to come before vacation began, these three children dreaded that moment. Vacation was a fear of the unknown. What would Drusilla be like this time? What chores did she have up her sleeve and on the 'little white slave' menu for them to do before returning after school break? What mood would she inflict on them while they anxiously awaited school to be back in session? The children never went anywhere nor did anything fun. Drusilla made sure that all they knew was home and the route to school, therefore if they ever had inclination on running away, they really wouldn't get very far, because they didn't know the area, even directly surrounding the location of their home.

Vacation time meant hard work, a lot of pain and agony, and hunger and thirst for Angela. Summer vacation was the longest and most treacherous time of her life. Every day was a fight to survive and Drusilla made sure of it. Somehow, she made it through summer after summer, but it wasn't easy. There is no word to describe how relieved she was when the first day of school arrived. School was a safe haven, even with all the mean peers who made fun of her day in and day out, because of how her stepmother sent her to school looking. Drusilla was a monster who tried to kill her many times, but the kids at school were just under informed and showed no compassion. Their words embedded themselves inside her, but she could accept them or excuse them. Angela knew that she was not stupid and ugly, so when the kids called her stupid and ugly, she shrugged it off. They did not know what she was living through at home and that dressing the way she was made to, wasn't done because she wanted it that way. What was painful, was knowing that Drusilla wanted her to be made fun of and to have no friends to confide in.

Christmas vacation was a farce in itself. While the rest of her classmates shared their excitement of the season, listing the many things on their wish lists and what they were going to do for Christmas, Angela sat hoping that Christmas would be called off so she would not have to spend the dreaded two weeks at home, all day, every day. The days when family meant joy and laughter left her life, when she and her sister and brother were taken out of Grandma's home and given to her daddy and stepmother. Since then, there had been no family or joy to speak of. There was never a Christmas for daddy's three children; Christmas day was a day just like all the rest. There were no presents for them. What their Grandmother had sent for them, Drusilla took to work and gave their gifts "to the needy children on her bus route." Drusilla would take out the knitted vests and afghans Grandma had sent them, take pictures of them wearing or holding them up, and then take them away and give them to other children. Many people at Drusilla's job thought she was a 'very nice' person, and that she had a knick for knitting. Drusilla didn't know what a knitting needle was, and yet took all the credit for all Grandma's hard work.

Dennis got to keep his gifts from Grandma, as well as whatever he wanted to keep of the other children's gifts, the rest would be boxed up and taken to work by Drusilla the next school day. No one knew that she would steal these gifts from her husband's children, leaving them without a Christmas. She had a bad reputation for covering up as if everything was "sugar and spice and everything nice." The State of Wisconsin knew the truth, as did the three children she resided with. Their Daddy and Drusilla got into a fight every year on Christmas day as she would spend money to make sure her son received a great Christmas, while his children went without. She would always use the excuse that his children were not good enough during the year, and didn't deserve anything. Somehow, their daddy would buy into the excuse or just give in to try to restore some sort of peace into their Christmas. In the meantime, envy and jealousy grew from the three children toward their half-brother.

Christopher had tears in his eyes as he watched Dennis receive much more than he had ever gotten in his life, year after year, and then Drusilla would have an excuse to send Christopher to bed. She had Christopher on Ritalin medication now and would give him much more than the prescription would call for. He would be fast to sleep before he knew it, or 'dazed' and in his own little world. Dennis played with his new toys all by himself throughout the Christmas day. If the other children came into his presence, he would point out his new toys to them. It was like pouring salt into an open wound, for the rest of the children. The children knew that it wasn't Dennis' fault he was spoiled. Drusilla was behind the whole set up. The other three children would look down at his new toys, and walk out of the room with tears in their eyes. If caught by Drusilla with tears in their eyes, they would get beat for having a bad attitude.

One of their homegrown turkeys (Angela's pets) would be served for Christmas dinner, as well as all the trimmings. Even Angela got to eat this unfamiliar food once per year. She wasn't used to eating it, nor as much as was given her on this occasion, but ate it nonetheless. She did not know when her next real meal would come again. Afterward, she returned to the backfield to pull weeds, and would get sick. The food was too rich for her pancake and oatmeal traditional appetite. Once she threw up, she was fine.

When school resumed after the Christmas holidays, Angela would be faced with her peers adding her about what she got for Christmas. At first, she would ignore their badgering questions, but then every teacher came up with the idea of going around the room asking every student to give an account of the fun Christmas vacation they had, and all the Christmas gifts they received. Fear welled up inside Angela couldn't ignore the voice of authority, and she wasn't allowed to talk about her family as it really was, so all she had left to do was to lie. When it came her turn to tell the class she felt embarrassed and ashamed. She had heard the lists that the other children gave, so she selected a few items from the other lists the children mentioned, and gave similar account as if that is what she too had done or received for Christmas. The lump in her throat choked her afterward. She had lied. Just more lies to protect Drusilla and her cruelty inflicted into Angela's life.

The three children's birthdays were not celebrated either. Dennis was the only one who had his birthday celebrated. The other three children had a difficult time remembering when theirs were because it was a day like all the rest. From time to time, a birthday card would be handed to them that came from their grandmother, and Drusilla had already taken out the money she had sent with it. Drusilla's excuse for taking the money out of their birthday cards was that the children had no use for it. They weren't allowed to have toys, and they weren't allowed to leave the property except to go to school. Her husbands' children hadn't been to the store in years and Drusilla wasn't into starting up bank accounts for them. By the way Drusilla treated Angela; maybe she would not live long enough to get any use from a savings account. Therefore, Drusilla kept all the money they got from relatives and neighbors. What she did with it, only she knows, because none of the three children got anything new; even their clothes were hand-me-downs. Christopher's clothes came as hand-me-downs from a friend of Drusilla's from work. When her son outgrew his clothes, Drusilla would be given them for Christopher. Crystal's clothes came from the Salvation Army. Angela would get Crystal's hand-me-downs, even though Angela was much thinner than Crystal and her feet much longer than Crystal's. The clothes would hang on Angela, and her toes pinched down to her foot. From their diets to their clothes, their daddy and Drusilla didn't have to come up with much financial support for them, yet they both worked. The property owner wasn't charging them much for their home and farm, and most of the work was being done by these three children, so their parents didn't have to hire it out. What the children could not do, their daddy did. The children were never taken to a doctor except for Christopher on two occasions. One; because of an asthma attack, and the second time, because the school thought he was educationally handicapped, there were times when he'd act out a bit violently and needed to be placed on Ritalin so he could apply himself better. The 'acting out violently' could not be from what he experienced or saw demonstrated by Drusilla in his family home during his most impressionable years and those that followed, could it? Heaven's no, something must be wrong with the kid. Let us just cover the effects of a harmful lifestyle with a prescription drug that could cause permanent brain damage in the end.

Drusilla would double and triple Christopher's medication without receiving a doctor's permission. She had worked in a nursing home and had administered drugs to patients before. She must have known what she was doing, right? Hardly. The job with the nursing home ended before it got started. She was fired. Drusilla even used Christopher's prescription on Crystal and Angela. It had a controlling affect, and Drusilla used it on them, quite often. Crystal and Angela would spit out the pills daily. It made them feel senseless, and numb. They did not like the feeling and as they got older, they knew that this drug was not doing them any favors. Every time they'd discover the pills in their food, or when Drusilla would make them take them directly, they'd put them in their cheek and spit them out when Drusilla turned her back. The doctor had not prescribed them for the girls, and their brother really did not need the pills either. All he needed was to get out of this environment and into one that was not violent, but instead, filled with love, and he would be fine. A pill could not cure what was wrong with him.

Drusilla caught on that the girls were not taking the medication she was illegally giving to them, so she began blenderizing the pills into powdered milk and water solution and force the girls to drink it. The feelings of numbness and stupidity would take them over. They would walk around in a daze. It wasn't until Angela started acting dopey around her daddy when she was supposed to be helping him repair the cars that she took the opportunity to inform him of Drusilla's antics with giving her and Crystal, Christopher's medication. It wasn't until he started yelling at her for making so many stupid mistakes that she blurted out that Drusilla was drugging her with Christopher's Ritalin. Her Daddy asked her how she knew, so she told him the whole story on how at first they were spitting out the pills and now Drusilla was making them drink them ground up in blenderized milk.

Angela's daddy stared at her in disbelief. The tears rolled down her face. He was without words, but eventually it must have all made sense to him because he headed for the back door of the house. An argument broke out between her daddy and Drusilla as he was trying to let her know that she had gone too far! In her own defense, Drusilla was trying to say that giving the girls the Ritalin was the only way she could find to get control of them. Angela's daddy didn't believe Drusilla for one moment. The argument grew heated and lasted for quite some time.

Her daddy came out to the driveway at the end of the argument. Angela was still feeling dopey, so he told her to go inside and to lay down for a nap. She didn't want to go inside where Drusilla was, and yet, she obeyed his instructions. She walked to the back door, looking back at her daddy to get his reassurance that it was okay, went inside to rest. Angela knew that the nap would bring her back to her senses, after the pills wore off, and until they did, she would take her dazed body to bed where they had less detrimental effect to her physical and mental condition.

The house was quiet. Almost on tiptoe, she crept down the hall to her bedroom. If Drusilla did not know she was there, perhaps things would turn out all right for her. Her bedroom window was just above where her daddy was working on his car, so she felt a sigh of relief as she laid down to rest. She felt guilty that she wasn't out there helping him, but the state of mind the Ritalin had put her in, made her useless to him. Her head was buzzing from the drug. Her senses unclear and numb. A feeling that couldn't be fought. A feeling that made her feel more insecure than she already had been in life. A feeling of cowardliness embraced her as she drifted off to sleep.

Angela had been asleep quite awhile before she felt a hand on her gently shaking her to get up. It was her daddy. She could hear his voice in the distance, but her body did not want to come to awareness. Angela felt extremely tired, limp and numb. The Ritalin was still in her system. Quite heavy dosages, which even her nap, had not worn off.

"Come on, let's go." "It's dinnertime." Daddy was still gently nudging her trying to get her awake.

Angela was still very groggy. How much Ritalin had Drusilla given her anyway? She took in some deep breaths trying to bring herself to her senses. Slowly she woke up, sat up, and took daddy's hand and followed him into the dining room for dinner.

"Are you all right?" Daddy sounded concerned as he led her to the table.

She nodded, feeling just a bit better as she took her place at the table. Looking down at her food, she noticed that she had spaghetti on her plate; the same food that everyone else had on theirs. Angela smiled at her daddy, as she began to realize that Drusilla was nowhere to be seen. She wondered where they might be, but at this moment, she really didn't care to find out. A feeling of comfort set inside her body. Drusilla was not here to torment her.

There was only one time that her daddy took into account Angela's birthday, and that was when she shared with him, that she would like to have a bicycle. Daddy hadn't seemed like he was listening at the time, so like every other topic of discussion, it got dropped. It had been ridiculous of her to ever imagine having a bike anyway, when Angela wasn't even allowed to have toys or dolls. In Angela's life, dreams or wishes did not come true as long as Drusilla was in charge.

A few weeks later, Angela was weeding the front geranium beds and her daddy walked up to her with a homemade unicycle. Angela looked at it and then at her daddy. Was he making her a bike and then didn't get it finished? Was this a joke? He was holding a seat on a bar, with one wheel, and two attached pedals protruding from it. No handlebars and a second wheel attached to a frame. She started laughing at it, thinking he was joking with her. Angela's daddy laughed with her, until he realized that she thought he was joking around and hadn't completed putting her bike together.

"No honey, this here is called a unicycle." "It's like a bicycle, but only has one wheel." He placed it on the ground and tried to show her how it worked, but could not keep his balance, and was no pro at it himself. Sending her across the street, he told her that she could hang onto the school fence to keep her balance, and then one-day get good enough to let go. Angela hung onto the school's fence for dear life as she sat up on the unicycle. She had no point of balance and coordination was not her prodigy in life. She felt like an ape hanging from the fence her arms outstretched trying to stay up on the seat. Her daddy sat across the street at home on the front porch laughing at her feeble attempts to ride the unicycle. Eventually Drusilla joined him on the front porch and now both laughed and gave out orders of advise on how to ride it, neither person knowing how, or able to ride a unicycle themselves.

There teasing and outbursts brought out some of the neighbors to watch and tease her, also. Angela was too embarrassed to continue and was going to cross the street to go back home, when Drusilla's unwelcome voice rang out.

"No, no…now get back over there and get on that thing and ride it."

Tears welled up in Angela's eyes as she obediently returned to the other side of the street to try to ride the unicycle, hanging onto the school fence for dear life. Her arm pits ached from being stretched so far out of their sockets when the unicycle would go one way and her arms still hanging in the opposite direction, fingers white-knuckled. Her fingers were scratched up and dirty from the fences' imperfections. Placing the seat between her legs after falling off it, she would try again and again. Eventually the seat gave out and twisted sideways from her last fall. She tried to straighten it, but now it was too loose and dropped down on the pole. It was too short for her, so she headed home.

Many onlookers had left in sympathy for her, while some stayed watching. "Now didn't I say to keep your butt over there?" It was Drusilla's obnoxious objection to her return home.

"It's broken and now I can't use it."

"What do you mean it is broken?" Your daddy just made that for you, and I think you broke it on purpose, you ungrateful kid." Drusilla was doing a fine job on letting the neighbors know how terrible she was without realizing it. Her words hung heavy in the air and in Angela's mind. With that last remark from the Amazon, the rest of the neighbors left. Angela looked down at her feet as she crossed the street to return home. Her daddy got up from his chair on the front porch and met her on the driveway to have a better look at the broken cycle. Angela really did not want him to fix it for her. She did not like it anyway. Following her daddy to the garage, she took a chance at asking him if he wouldn't fix it. She did not like it and she did not want it. Her arms hurt from hanging on the fence, and she showed him the cuts on her dirty hands. Her daddy looked up at her as though he was going to say something and then back down at the seat on the unicycle. He fixed it in silence, and then shoved it into her side when he was finished. "Get back over there and ride it!" "It's no different than riding a bike!"

Angela took the unicycle and headed back to the sidewalk across the street. She cried quietly to herself as she tried with everything in her to ride it. Tears streamed down her face, her arms ached, her hands stung and the frustration grew. Daddy and Drusilla just sat on the front porch reading the newspaper, and from time to time looked up to make some kind of rude comment of ridicule. Their words penetrated an already battered heart, and still, Angela could not ride the unicycle. She desperately was trying to teach herself because it might give her some fun in life, and then again, it might even make her daddy happy and proud of her. For now, she was just their idiot kid making an ass of herself out in public as she gripped onto the school fence trying to balance on the unicycle.

The sun was setting in the west and the cool evening breeze gently blew by as she continued to try to ride the unicycle. Her daddy and Drusilla left their perches on the front porch to go inside the house. They left her all alone out there by herself to learn how to ride this on-wheeled contraption the inventor called a unicycle. Angela hated it. She had asked for a bike, and when most children ask their parents for bikes, they get bikes. Two wheels are safer than one wheel. Parents love to see their children happy. This unicycle was the counterfeit of what Angela had asked for, mastering it would not be a possibility given her clumsiness and the lack of parental assistance or support and encouragement. Being forced into something takes the fun and pleasure out of it, and it becomes a chore. Angela could not wait until they called her home. That call would be her only ticket to put an end to this misery and hopefully, she'd never have to ride it again. She preferred pulling weeds and doing chores to riding it. There was no one helping her to learn, and when you are forced to make mistakes out in the eye of the public, the embarrassment sucks out every bit of the esteem that might have been there. No, the unicycle was not a gift. It was just another instrument of torment to her.

It would be wishful thinking to say that Drusilla and her daddy put the unicycle away forever once she did get called back home after that first time. However, they didn't. Every time they had nothing better for Angela to do, they would send her out to make a complete fool of herself. Drusilla enjoyed seeing her stepdaughter tormented. Sending Angela out in public to make a fool out of herself became a favorite past time for Drusilla. Just one more way to make sure that Angela knew who was in control.

****

When the unicycle wore out, Angela never did master it, nonetheless, she was sent out to try for over a year. The next venture of exercise imposed on Angela was that she would have to go around the fence into the schoolyard and run the track, where Drusilla could sit on the front porch and watch, or see her while she sat in the livingroom watching TV. Rule was, that Angela had to run it, not walk it and continue on until Drusilla called her to come home. This challenge was a bit more fun, until an hour or so passed by, and all her endurance left her and there was no more catching a breath. It was all gone. Dehydrated and out of breath, there were many times that she had to stop, and bend over just to breathe. Of course, Drusilla had jurisdiction over this also. If it wasn't done to her specifications and will, Angela would get beat. She would be called back to the house, barely able to walk or breathe; so dehydrated that even the sweat had dried up, her ears plugged up, face and heart pounding. Many times when she came into the house she got beat, because Drusilla said that she did not run fast enough, or because she had stopped to bend over and catch her breath.

    About a year after Angela had been running the track, Drusilla sent Crystal out to join her. Rules given; they were not allowed to run together nor close to one another. They were to continue running until Drusilla called them home. She would never call them home together. Most times Crystal would be last to arrive and first to leave. Angela had built up more endurance, and the expectation was that she maintain this endurance. Angela did not have 'runners' knees. Instead, they were 'knocking knees' and big clumsy feet. Her knees ached as she ran on the hard clay beneath the sun-scorched grass. There were times that she would trip and kiss the ground with her lips driving teeth through them, but expectation was to get back up and to run. As she ran without water for long periods of time, her mucous membranes would dry up making it difficult to breathe or to swallow, and her ears would plug up. The more tired she grew, her body felt like it would slip into auto and her legs would just keep running. When she was called home, each step seemed awkward. Her face deep red.

    One day, Angela was much further out front of Crystal on the tack when she heard Crystal scream. Looking behind her for her sister, she saw a man holding Crystal in his arms, trying to drag her with him in the opposite direction. Crystal was fighting! Angela screamed out as she turned to charge the man in her sister's defense. Running up to him she was kicking him and punching him, until he finally let go of her sister and took off. Crystal was crying. The neighbors had come out of their houses and were watching, but no one came to help them. Angela was shaking pretty hard. Fear hadn't set in until after it all happened. Crystal cried as Angela tried to reassure her that everything was going to be all right.

Angela looked up in time to see Drusilla climbing over the fence and coming toward them. Anger burned on her face, evident that she had not seen what had just transpired. She was ready to grab Angela's arm, as Angela blurted out, "Crystal just got attacked by a man!" "He tried to kidnap her!" Astonished, Drusilla looked at Crystal, then at Angela, and then notice that the neighbors were watching them. She told the girls to get home. Crystal still had tears falling down her face and Drusilla was demanding that she "stop the self-pity party." Angela still shook from the fright the incident caused her. Their daddy came out to meet them as they walked up the driveway. They told him or their ordeal. Crystal was sent inside and Angela was told to go out back and do her chores.

A few days later, Angela was told to return to the track and to run it. She was scared to death, but obeyed Drusilla's orders. She ran much faster and kept watch of her surroundings, praying that Drusilla would not make her stay out long. When called to return home, she high-tailed it home. She did not want any man grabbing her. Drusilla apparently enjoyed watching the frightened reaction of her stepdaughter when told to "go run the track", because she continued to give that order, even when it was dark out.

****

Graduation day was a day that most eighth grade graduates aim for. To most it is a day of celebration and joy, as they are now transitioning into High School. It's a step from puberty into 'young adulthood'. The excitement of finally making it to High School means, for most teens, more independence and privileges. As they go through High School they prepare for college, careers, and starting families of their own, equipped and ready for an aspiring future. Graduation day, is a day when parents and families can come together and share in the celebration to an end of elementary school and the unfolding of the last few years before many leave the 'nest' to pursue futures on their own. Their babies were no longer babies. They were becoming young adults, venturing into the last journey of finding out about life and making life decisions for themselves.

Angela ran home from school to meet her five-minute curfew on the last day of her eighth grade year. Her heart pounded as she anticipated the ceremonies of the coming evening. She would get her chores done immediately, so that Drusilla would not have any reason to keep her from the graduation ceremony. The rest of her graduating class was headed to Disneyland afterward, but Angela knew that Drusilla would never allow her to attend that function. So the official graduation ceremony would have to be enough.

Each chore was finished to perfection by the time that Drusilla arrived home from work. She had even gone through the house and redone her morning chores of vacuuming and bathroom cleaning. Nothing would mess up the possibility of her attending her graduation ceremony.

Drusilla was moody when she arrived home, so Angela walked on pins and needles. Everything extra demanded by Drusilla of her, was done quickly and to perfection. As the time grew near for her to get ready for the graduation ceremony, Drusilla had still not mentioned anything about Angela attending. Therefore, Angela brought up the topic herself.

"Mommy, am I going to my graduation?" She asked cautiously and politely.

"What graduation?" Drusilla was a school bus driver and knew what was going on in the school district. She was playing a fool's advocate; nonetheless, Angela played the fool. "My graduation ceremony is at 6:30 tonight."

"Why should you go?" Drusilla inflicted.

Holding a stiff upper lip, taking a deep breath, pretending that Drusilla's question didn't affect her she let her opinion be known in the friendliest and most cordial manner. "I would like to receive my certificate with the rest of my class." "Graduating means a lot to me." "I told the teachers that I would be there, and they are expecting me."

"Who gave you permission to make the choice?" "Did I say that you could go and participate?" Drusilla was challenging her stepdaughter.

Angela was close to tears. "I am sorry, but Crystal got to go to her eighth grade graduation, so I thought you would let me." "I knew you would approve of the trip to Disneyland with my class afterward, so I declined that." "I really thought you would let me go to the ceremony."

"You're damned right I won't let you go to Disneyland, and what right do you have to make decisions without my permission?"

"I…I…I am sorry, I…I…just thought…," Angela stammered and was interrupted by Drusilla.

"Well, you thought wrong!"

At that, Angela exited the house and ran to the backfield where the sobs spilled out and the tears fell. Drusilla had stolen all her joy and excitement for her graduation day from her. Angela was hurt and angry all at the same time. She had worked harder than her entire class, putting up with the life that competed with her schooling. Her life had been miserable throughout her elementary school years as she fought to stay alive and get good grades despite the antics of her stepmother; she deserved to go to the graduation. She fell to the ground ripping the weeds out by the handfuls, sobbing. Doing her chores to perfection in preparation of attending had all been in vain.

Angela was called to the house and reminded by Drusilla she had her chores to do. "I've done them before you got home."

"Why the hell so early?" Drusilla asked smirked knowing full well why her stepdaughter had completed the chores early. She just wanted to dig the knife in deeper.

Angela knew this, nonetheless, responded. "I did them because I thought you were allowing me to attend my graduation ceremony."

"Well, you thought wrong." Drusilla grinned an evil grin, as she turned to go, leaving Angela standing and staring at her back.

"What's this about a graduation?" Her daddy had arrived home and walked in at the tail end of their conversation.

"It is my eighth grade graduation today." Angela said turning to walk away.

"When…what time?" Her daddy was inquiring.

Angela turned back and answered him. "Six-thirty tonight."

"Well, what the heck are you standing out there for?" "You should be in here getting ready." Daddy was grinning.

Angela hung her head and looked down at her feet. "Mom won't let me go."

Just then, Drusilla flew out the back door and her hand met Angela's mouth. SLAP! SLAP!

"You bitch!" "Don't be lying about me!" Drusilla had not expected her daddy home so early, and now she was covering up her previous episode of the mean stepmother.

"Go get ready." Daddy told her, giving Drusilla a look of warning that could pierce your insides.

Angela did not have to be told twice. Wiping the tears from her eyes and face, she ran to her bedroom. She did not have much to wear but took her best dress out of the closet and quickly put it on. Running a comb through her hair, she went to tell her daddy that she was ready to go.

Drusilla and her daddy were still arguing, so she waited for as long as she could and then interrupted them. "Daddy, I'm ready to go." "It is after six o'clock, I need to leave."

"Sure honey, go on, we will be there before your name is called."

Happily, Angela ran out the front door and all the way to school. The graduation ceremony was being held outside on the basketball court. Parent sat in lawn chairs, while others stood waiting for the ceremony to start. Angela took her place in the back row as was rehearsed during school hours that day. She was in the back row up on the rafters, grinning from ear to ear as she searched the audience for her daddy's face. He hadn't yet arrived. Maybe he would come a bit late. She kept looking over in the direction of her house, hoping to see him coming. No one came out of her house.

The ceremony started and speeches were given. Then it was time to announce the graduating class and call them up one at a time to receive their diplomas. Still no daddy. Her name was toward the end of the alphabet, so there was still time for her daddy to come see her graduate. Her heart was set on seeing her daddy's familiar face, smiling at her when she went up to receive her diploma. Angela's thoughts drowned out the person speaking from the microphone. Having her daddy there to see her graduate meant a lot to her, but he had not yet arrived. She kept glancing back at their house and looking in all directions, hoping and scanning every face there. He didn't come. Her classmate at her side nudged her to let her know that her row was now moving forward and down the bleachers to the front to receive their diplomas. Angela held back the tears as she thanked the principal who handed her, her diploma and congratulated her. Heading back up the bleachers and to her spot, the tears fell. She wiped them on her bare arm and looked down at her shoes hoping no one noticed.

The ceremony ended as each student left the bleachers to seek out family members, most saying goodbye as they headed to the waiting buses to take them to an all-night celebration of fun at Disneyland. Angela took one last look around her and headed for home. Her heart ached and the tears flowed down her cheeks. She looked behind her at the school she had just graduated from; a lump growing in her throat as she recalled all the memories it held of her years there. All the work, effort, and her struggle to stay alive while attending Wallowing Junior High. No one knew, no one cared and no one showed up to celebrate her survival.

She looked up at the house she now approached. It was the place she called home, but she didn't like it and it wasn't a home. Crystal met her at the door a camera in hand to take a few 'graduation' pictures to send to her grandma. Grandma … grandma …that name that brought back memories of being happy, loved and accepted. Safe. Grandma would have come to my graduation, Angela thought to herself. She would have been proud of me. Angela wiped the tears from her eyes and came up with a fake smile, being that she was aching on the inside. Maybe if Grandma looked at the pictures carefully, she could read the secrets Angela had to keep hidden within her. Maybe Grandma could come and rescue the children again….

Daddy and Drusilla had already gone to bed to settle their differences, instead of coming out to celebrate Angela's graduation. Angela looked back at the school as buses, limousines, and cars paraded by their house, carrying families, friends and graduates to their celebratory destinations for the evening. Proud parents hugged their children as they walked by. Laughter filled the air outside her house. Angela ran to her room, threw herself on her bed, buried her face in her arms and cried. She did not care if anyone heard her. The pain became unbearable. Happy graduation, 1972.

18

The Uncommitted Detective

Where he came from, only Drusilla and her daddy knew, and why he was allowed into Drusilla's "extra curricular" marital activities, dumbfounded the children. Apparently, Drusilla was having a romantic interlude with an East Dover Detective, that went on for many years. How had Detective David Lariat come into Drusilla's life and why did their daddy have to put up with it?

Detective David Lariat and Drusilla's affair became common knowledge in their household when a fight between Drusilla and Angela's daddy broke out one night. Daddy had witnessed something that made him point the finger at Drusilla, and the argument flew into a "name-calling" screaming match. Drusilla did not deny the affair, instead, continued to challenge her daddy's manhood on "What did he expect?" She had "to do what she did, or they both would be in jail."

Confused, Angela listened from her bedroom. How could Drusilla do this to her daddy? This wasn't the first time in the marriage, but how could she be doing it again? What did Drusilla mean, "If she didn't have the affair they'd both be in jail?" Would Drusilla really leave her daddy? Deep down inside she hoped that this would happen, but then again, it would hurt her daddy. Putting aside her own thoughts for survival, she listened to her daddy's words and knew that he would be hurt if Drusilla left with Dennis. He still thought that Dennis was his, and had been his daddy since he was born. Since she was having an affair at the time he was conceived, Angela really didn't know if Dennis was her daddy's. Daddy never knew about that affair. Drusilla had frightened her to secrecy.

Suddenly Dennis let out a scream, which brought Angela back from her deep thoughts. She ran down the hallway to the livingroom doorway to see what was going on. Drusilla and her daddy were playing tug-o-war with Dennis as the argument ensued. Drusilla was threatening to leave and to take Dennis. Her daddy was holding one of Dennis' arms and Drusilla had the other one trying to get out the door. Crystal, Christopher and Angela watched horrified on seeing Dennis being stretched out between their parents. He was crying in terror as the two continued to argue. Daddy's three children felt sorry for Dennis, but had very mixed feelings on whether or not Drusilla would be missed if she chose to walk out the door with Dennis. They weren't that close to Dennis, Drusilla had made sure of it, and they were definitely not close to Drusilla. Her leaving would end their pain and suffering. They would no longer have to fight to survive every day.

On seeing his other children's faces from witnessing the fight, her daddy turned and asked them to go to their bedrooms. "Why should they?" Drusilla inquired sarcastically. "Why should they miss seeing how you treat Dennis and me?" Drusilla was all for an audience.

The children obeyed their daddy and headed to their bedrooms. Christopher was crying for Dennis. Crystal had tears in her eyes for him also. Crystal had always had the mother-figure instinct, and when Angela saw the look on Crystals face, she knew that Crystal was concerned for Dennis, and probably wanted to rush in and rescue him. Drusilla was using Dennis as an object to get what she wanted from her husband.

Angela walked back into her room, not really knowing what feelings to have. No, she did not like to see them fighting and definitely not with Dennis being the object to "get even" with each other. However, something inside, did not care if there was a split up between her daddy and Drusilla. Drusilla had never liked Angela and had let her know it throughout the years. Angela had almost died at the hands of the Amazon more than a few times. Because she really did not know Dennis all that well, she was not attached to him, so did not know how she felt about him leaving when Drusilla left. Drusilla would take great care of him as she always had. Therefore, Drusilla leaving daddy would not be heart breaking and at this moment, Angela was wishing she would leave.

The argument lasted late into the night. Dennis had been let go of and sent crying into Crystal's arms. Crystal comforted him and rocked him to sleep, just as Drusilla began throwing things at their daddy. Angela felt her body stiffen. She did not want Drusilla hurting her daddy. She could not see what was going on, but heard her daddy asking Drusilla to 'quit throwing things' as glass was heard breaking and there were several thuds on the walls and floor. Fear that she would hurt their daddy kept them awake in their beds listening to the fight. If Drusilla did something to their daddy, they would be next on her list. They shivered from the thought.

Who was this detective who had come into their lives and why was Drusilla giving him more than just the time of day? What had Drusilla meant when she told daddy she 'had' to sleep with him? What were they all covering up? Angela would have a mess to clean up in the morning; Drusilla was making sure of that as she continued breaking things as she threw them at their daddy from across the room.

"Let me go…let me go…let me go." Drusilla was pleading with their daddy as he struggled to restrain her from throwing and breaking anything else in the house.

"I'll let you go when you settle down." He told her.

All of a sudden, daddy yelled out, and the children heard what came next. Drusilla had kicked their daddy in the groin. "You bitch!" her daddy yelled, and then they heard a thud on the floor. Several more things were thrown at their daddy and then Drusilla's voice was heard.

"You bastard! That'll teach you to play around on me!' Drusilla was stronger than their daddy was, or else he was too much of a gentleman to really give her what she deserved all these years of abusing his children. More choice name-callings expelled from their mouths, and then Drusilla started to laugh. It was tear down daddy time for Drusilla. Her mouth was worse than that of a long haul trucker. She had been raised with brothers, had an alcoholic father and a mother who worked hard to keep the family in business, until she herself gave up and fell prey to alcohol and its devastating oppressions.

"Dan is more a man than you are, anyway." "It may be a relationship of convenience for me, but I do enjoy the danger in it." "With you, I have no feelings." "You are a wasted old man!" Drusilla dug the knife into daddy's manhood.

No rebuttal was offered from daddy, it would not be worth the effort to refute what was coming out of Drusilla's mouth. It would only be met with unfounded disagreement and all she was doing was trying to hurt Angela's daddy. The words cut deep. Drusilla was now apparently satisfied with her verbal inflictions of pain. Her husbands' only reaction was the hurt shown on his face, as she turned to go into her bedroom, slamming the door behind her. She had physically hurt him by kicking him in the groin, but also emotionally by cutting down his manhood. Her husband was only six years older than she was, and to his children he was not an 'old man.'

Angela listened intently, wondering if daddy would get up. She heard him grunt in pain as the attempt was made. Unsteady deep breathing could be heard as she heard him get up and sit down on the faux leather couch. There were a few more grunts as she heard him lay down. He sniffled a few times. Was her daddy crying? Drusilla hurt him in more ways than one, and got away with it.

By the time Angela awoke in the morning, her daddy had already left for work, and Drusilla was on her way out to drive the big yellow school bus, her socially acceptable cover-up to the cruel mean person she was. Angela came out to the livingroom to survey the previous night's battleground. It was worse than she had imagined, and she was not being given extra time to clean it up before having to leave for school. It was a disaster and the expectation would be that she had to clean it up on top of all her other chores. There would not be any breakfast for Angela this morning.

The children worked in silence as they cleaned up the house. Crystal and Christopher sat down to breakfast, as Angela headed out into the backyard to tend to her outside chores. She worked quickly as the time for her to leave for school was just moments away. Her stomach growled as usual this morning, but she didn't' let it bother her as much today. She had last nights brawl between her daddy and Drusilla on her mind. Drusilla was cheating on her daddy, and did not think that her daddy should care, because she claimed it had to do with keeping the two of them out of jail. What did that mean? What had they done and why was this detective in the picture? What would the detective do if Drusilla didn't sleep with him? What would he find out? Was Drusilla lying to her daddy? Or perhaps, did this have something to do with the possibility of the State of Wisconsin finding out where these children were at?

If Drusilla wanted to be with the detective, why didn't she just leave their daddy and go live with the detective? Was he married? On the other hand, would his department frown upon a commitment with a woman he had been sent out to investigate? Instead, was the detective getting the best from both sides of the fence? So many questions to ponder for this little girl, who, in the long run, did not want her daddy hurt. Angela wished that Drusilla would 'make good' on her threats to leave their daddy. This would give his children the opportunity to live in a safe environment and not have to fear losing their lives by the hands of an Amazon.

The house remained a war zone, in and around the issue of Drusilla's infidelity with this detective. She even brought his jeep home to put salt into the would of daddy's broken heart. There were nights that she did not come home until the wee hours of the morning. To the rest of the children, it meant a break for them. Their daddy was home with them and for the first time in years, they were able to spend some time with him without the fear of Drusilla hovering over them to stay away from him. Their daddy was home for them, though they could feel that he was not happy with Drusilla's rendezvous with Detective David. Even if she had to do what she had to do, she did not have to flaunt it in front of her husband and in the eyes of her children. They were not dumb. They saw. They knew. Moreover, like most children, what affected their parents affected them. Daddy was still their daddy. A little absent, neglectful and a bit in denial, but nonetheless, their daddy. What did this detective have 'on them' that would involve this kind of relationship to go on?

There was a time that they all got invited to a wedding, and the detective was there. Drusilla and Detective David sat next to one another, while Angela's daddy sat with his children in seats behind them. If the relationship was to be one that was discreet, this was not the case that day. Many on-lookers took notice. The detective and Drusilla even danced together while her husband and the children watched. Talk about subtle. Drusilla carried on until Angela's daddy could take no more and told his children to 'go to the car.' After giving his best to the bride and groom he joined his children for the ride home, leaving Detective David and Drusilla at the wedding to dance the night away.

The children had walked to the car not saying a word to one another until they got there. Crystal was first to speak, "Daddy is right, she is a whore." Crystal knowing the definition of the word, made it known to the other children.

"Yeah, how could she do this to daddy?" "Why did Detective David have to come?" All they did was embarrass our daddy." Crystal was just about to answer her, when they both saw their daddy approaching the car. He had tears in his eyes as he climbed into the car. They all drove home in silence, not saying a word. His children felt sorry for him, but did not know how to tell him. To them it was easy, just get rid of the one who was causing him and his children all the pain. Divorce sounded pretty good to his children. They were sure that there were other better women in the world that could make them and their daddy happy. Problem was, their daddy had buried himself deep into this nightmare and could not find a way to rise up out of it. Too many things held them 'partners in crime' instead of partners in a marriage.

The months that followed, daddy started coming home later and later. Drusilla would get home late herself, and her jealousy would hit the roof if their daddy was not home when she arrived home. "Why is he late?" "Has he called?" "What is the excuse tonight?" "Why aren't the chores all done?" Of course, Drusilla had to blame his absence on his children, as she turned the tables and began flinging out accusations and false charges. The swinging of the belt upon their bodies seemed to even the score between there daddy and Drusilla. Angela was drug out of bed many nights in a row to clean the oven or vacuum again, when her daddy didn't get home by Drusilla's' designated time. Drusilla was miserable and Angela and the other children would be her target of revenge against his actions. Home life could not get any worse.

What right did Drusilla have to accuse their daddy of having affairs when she herself was involved in one that everyone knew about? An affair with an officer of the law, who was 'taking restitution out in trade', or so Drusilla had indicated. The only difference between Drusilla's affair and their daddy's was that he would not take his revenge out on his children. He did it in a manner in which attacked only the guilty party, and that was the one who was having an affair against him. Two wrongs did not make a right, but clear thinking did not placed at the forefront of the conflict.

Life was becoming a real mess. Neither Drusilla, nor their daddy could trust one another which put the whole household in an uproar. Drusilla's attacks upon the children were at an all time high. Daddy's three children did not know what to think or do. Drusilla was extremely unpredictable as to when she would attack them. Every moment she spent alone with them, was a moment they repeatedly lived to regret, as they had to defend their own lives from her vicious attacks.

Drusilla beat up Crystal and then started shoving food down her throat again. Christopher was beat with the belt and punched in the stomach all the time. Angela couldn't even walk passed Drusilla without being punched, shoved into walls, kicked or beat with the belt or with anything else Drusilla could get her hands on. It wasn't even safe to go out into the field to get away from her stepmother any longer, she would be on her heels, or call her back before Angela could even head out to the field for safety. There was always work Drusilla was finding for Angela to do.

All Drusilla would have to do these days was open her mouth to the three children and they would start shaking in their shoes. At one point, Drusilla spent more time at home, than out with the detective. Perhaps they had broken up; the reason for the extreme torment she was dishing out at home. Who knew? The children could not help but wish that all this brutality toward them would cease and desist immediately.

Drusilla had begun drugging the girls with Ritalin again, and yet expected them to be alert and functional for every command she had on order for them to do. They fought the affects of the drug to try to keep up with her every command, yet the 'daze' caused by the Ritalin would not release its stronghold on their physical and mental well being. Drusilla would knock their heads into the cement walls for not responding to her as quickly as was appropriate in Drusilla's terms. Drusilla was aware that the drug was debilitating to her stepdaughters, but it gave her reason to torture and torment them further, when they couldn't perform the duties she commanded in the timeframe given or to the extent, which she desired.

One day she lined up the three children in the boys room. She was tired of them in her life and she wanted them to realize just how tired. It was almost as if each one was standing and facing the firing squad. Drusilla went down the line and punched each one in the gut and as they bent over in reaction to the gut-punch, she punched them in the face, which brought their heads back, slamming their heads into the wall. Crystal yelled out, just before everything around Angela went black. She passed out.

She woke up in her bed sometime later; her head hurt so badly. The light coming from down the hall brought a sharp piercing pain to her eyes and head. Angela was on her back dazed, unable to move much. The house was quiet; the night sky stared back at her from outside her open window. It had been quite a while since she had been placed in her bed. The beating had taken place in the late morning, early afternoon hour. Now it was pitch black out. She remembered what had happened to her.

All she didn't know, was who had put her to bed and how long had she been there? The pain in her head hurt. She was nauseous. Dark shadows danced around her as she closed her eyes again and passed out.

Waking up the next morning, Angela's head throbbed. The pain was unbearable. The brightness of the morning daylight sent piercing pain throughout her head and neck. She could not keep her eyes open to see. The pain made her sick. A big lump protruded from the back of her head. Angela wasn't moving very fast and at this pace, would not be able to get her chores done, yet even started. She was miserable to say the least. Drusilla was at work and she did not know if her daddy had even come home last night. Crystal wanted her to do her chores, but she just couldn't. Tears ran down her face as the pain took over every movement. Seeing her sister in this much pain and knowing the reason why, Crystal asked Angela if there was anything she could do for her. "No, I just hurt so bad, please don't make me do my chores," Angela cried.

Angela didn't see the mess Drusilla had made of Crystal's face, because her eyes had been closed, but as Crystal gave Angela a hug, Angela opened her eyes and saw the bruising that peered out from under 'caked' on foundation make-up. Her sisters face was swollen so bad that all the make-up in the world couldn't cover the mess Drusilla inflicted on Crystal's face. Her face looked deformed. Why had Drusilla done this to them? How much more of this mutilation could they take?

"What happened after I passed out?" Angela asked her sister.

"When Drusilla knocked you out, I couldn't take standing there any more letting her beat you, so I tried to come to your rescue." "I didn't care if I lived or died." "I thought she had killed you." "She then beat the crap out of me." "Afterward, she just left you laying on the floor where you dropped, so I put you to bed." "I thought you were going to die." Tears flowed down both their faces as their brother showed up in the doorway. He too, had bruising on his body. When he saw his sisters crying, he joined their side. They wanted Drusilla to leave their daddy so much. She was so mean to all of them. Being beat up by someone who never loved nor cared for, or accepted them, no matter how hard they tried to win her love, made life the worse nightmare, they thought they would never wake up from.

Crystal sent Christopher to go find out what time it was. She knew it was getting near time for them to leave for school. Angela did not want to move. Her head was pounding which made all of her feel like it hurt. The punches to the gut left some bruising, but her head pain was far worse. Crystal and Christopher quickly did Angela's chores for her while she continued to lay on her bed wishing that the pain would quit. She could not open her eyes; it only made the pain in her head hurt all the more. Angela did not want to be home when Drusilla returned home, and knew that the only answer to this was to go to school. The safe haven of her life. It was the only place she could go to get away from Drusilla and all the pain and hurt she brutally imposed upon her, physically, emotionally and mentally. Getting to school today would be a real miracle. Crystal and Christopher finished both their and Angela's chores. Not having time to eat breakfast themselves, Crystal made them all butter and sugar breads to take with them as they hurried to school.

    Angela moved slowly, for with each step, excruciating pain burst within her head. They were only given a ten minute time limit for a twenty to thirty minute distance. Normally, they would have to run it. Not wanting to be late herself, Crystal left her sister's side and ran on to school, leaving Angela to walk like a zombie, one careful step after the next. Angela held her heads with her hands as she tried to pick up the pace. She was not allowed to be late for school, for if Drusilla found out, she would surely beat her. The tears fell as she squinted from the pain to see where she was walking. The pain made her feel like she was going to pass out again, but she fought it.

    Angela hoped that Drusilla wouldn't drive the 'acceptable school route' on her way home to see if the children had made it to school on time. Today would not be a good day for her if she did. Angela was already late for school, and if Drusilla saw her like this, she would take advantage of this opportunity and add more brutality to an already serious situation.

    Arriving at school, Angela had to report to the office to pick up a pass to class for being late. The woman behind the counter asked for the 'purpose of her tardiness', and Angela said that she wasn't feeling very well. Looking up at Angela, the woman asked if she should call her mother to come pick her up.

    The question in itself brought Angela to a terrified awareness. "NO!" she blurted out, almost yelling back at the woman. Then realizing that she had given the woman a fright, she awkwardly smiled and responded, "No, I'll be alright."

The woman handed her a pass to class. Angela took the pass and trying to act like she would be alright, she proceeded to class. Her head still hurt and she was so dizzy from all the pain. All she really wanted to do was lay down and get over it, but at school there was no place to lie down without bringing concerned responses to her aid. This of course would be detrimental to her well being if she got sent home. Each step toward class brought agony beyond measure. Couldn't the classroom be closer?

Once arriving at her classroom and finally to her seat, the pounding in her head made her close her eyes tightly. The teacher asked if she was going to be alright. Angela nodded, and tried not to draw any more attention to herself. Angela was shaking now as she fought the pain and the feeling of nausea that was creeping up on her. Passing out would be a way out if but for a moments rest from the pain. The teacher was saying something up at the front of the classroom, but Angela could not concentrate on what he was saying. She stared blankly at him from squinted eyes. Everything was a blur, the sweat poured down as the pain failed to surrender its affliction on her. Let this class end. She wanted to die. There was no doing any assignments, she could not see or concentrate to work on them. Going from one class to the next, having to get up and move made her sick to her stomach. Her body shook uncontrollably. What was the matter with her? Why wouldn't this headache go away?

Meeting her sister at lunch, came the question on 'how she felt.'

"I feel like I am dying," Angela answered, tears falling down her face. Crystal gave her a hug, and tried to convince her that she 'would be okay.' They both knew that Angela could not go home. Drusilla would make her work, and she could not go to the office to lie down, because Drusilla would be notified. It was a no-win situation.

Angela went out to the fence just on the other side of the school's pool to spend the lunch hour as required by Drusilla, so that when Drusilla drove by her high school in the school bus, she could see her there. This too was the ritual even when Angela got to high school. There would never be any friends in Angela's life that way, for her to confide in. Sitting down against the fence and closing her eyes she tried to get passed the pain and agony. There would be no standing up watching for Drusilla to drive by to 'check up' on her. She wanted to fall asleep and never wake up. Her head pounded against her battered skull and the pain ricocheted all around her head. She wanted to die to ease the pain of this Drusilla inflicted headache, and to ease the pain of life.

Just as she was relaxed enough to get a grip on all the agony she was in, a large horn honked at her as it drove on by. Looking up through squinted eyes, Angela saw Drusilla drive by in her big yellow school bus. As it drove off, she closed her eyes once again. "Let this be a bad dream," she wished to herself. "Please let this be a bad dream."

The school bell rang in the distance. She wanted to stay right where she was at, from now until the pain ceased. In this position, she could control the pain to a dull roar in her head, than what it was when she moved about. Then again, Drusilla would be first to find out that she ditched her afternoon classes, and she would finish her off. Angela would die at the hands of the Amazon. Drusilla already had her inside source notifying her of what her stepdaughters did in school. Who this was, they never found out. Nevertheless, for everything they did, no matter how mediocre, Drusilla would find out and present them to the girls when she got home. Drusilla's spy who helped make their lives a living nightmare while they were in high school. Of course, Drusilla would take whatever information she was given and blow it way out of proportion to give her more reason to abuse her stepdaughters. It wouldn't surprise Drusilla that she had already been informed that Angela showed up at school stating she didn't feel well.

Angela headed slowly back to class, trying to make it back across the field to her locker before the tardy bell rang. With every step taken, the pain echoed in her head. She even tried walking with her eyes closed. Needing to stop at the bathrooms she instinctively knew that she would be late for class. Getting her books from her locker and then on to the bathroom. It felt great to not have to get permission to relieve herself while at school. As Angela went into one of the stalls, she glanced back at the mirror before closing the door. She couldn't see her reflection clearly, but what she saw wasn't encouraging. After closing the door she sat down to relieve herself. Her head pounded ferociously as she sat holding her head in her hands. Suddenly, she felt very sick to her stomach. She stood up and threw up. The feeling hit her with a vengeance! Involuntarily she let out a scream from the severe pain that exploded in her head as she bent over to throw up again.

Darkness was all around her as she tried desperately to hold herself up. It was no use. Angela lost her balance and fell to the dirty floor beneath her. She was breathing hard as she fought t keep consciousness on her side. She could not see, everything seemed to be growing darker by the moment. Her head was in her hands being squeezed tightly, as she tried to stop the pain. She wished that Crystal would come to her, hoping that no one else would see her, because if Drusilla found out that she was 'putting on a scene at school' to draw attention to herself she would be beat. A threat that continually hung as a severe warning over her life, day in and day out.

Angela sat down on the floor for what seemed a long time. She heard a few girls come in, relieve themselves and then go out. Someone had asked if she was okay, "Yes, I am," she said trying to sound convincing.

"Are you sure?" Another inquiry from another concerned person.

"Yes," Angela weakly responded trying to be reassuring.

They left the bathroom. Angela knew that she would really have to get up now. What if the girls went back to tell someone about her sitting on the floor in one of the stalls? She would be in deep trouble with Drusilla. Afterall, she also wasn't in class where she belonged right now.

Angela flushed the toilet and wiped up the mess that didn't quite make it where it should have. Going back over to the sink she splashed cold water on her face. Bending over hurt. Standing up hurt. There was nothing that would lessen the pain. Looking into the mirror, she noticed that her pupils were different sixes. One was so wide open and the other was only a pinpoint. The added pressure from having thrown up made her head pound. She held onto the sink trying to keep her balance. Angela really needed to get out of there and into her next class. It was quite late. But which class? She felt a sting of fear go up her spine. Angela could not remember what class she was supposed to be in right now. Looking down at the book on the edge of the sink, she hoped that that one was the class as she now headed out of the bathroom. After taking a few wrong turns, because for some reason she had forgotten the way, she finally arrived at the right room. The teacher and her classmates looked up as she came in. She had never been late before.

"Where have you been Angela?" asked her teacher with a slight smile on his face.

"Um...I didn't feel very well. I was in the bathroom." Angela responded truthfully. If she were going to get in trouble for being to class late, she would not compound the 'trouble' by lying.

Taking one look at her, her teacher let her stay for the remaining seven minutes of class, and wished her well, to return on time the next day.

She gave him a slight smile, as she headed out the door. There was no way she wanted to attend Phy. Ed. It was her last class of the day and normally she loved participating. Angela loved sports and could play well, nevertheless, today she was too sick and in too much pain to do anything but sit this one out today.

Approaching the teacher, Angela did not have to say a word. The teacher took on look at her and told her to get suited up, but that she would be allowed to sit at the sidelines today. Angela thanked her and headed slowly into the locker room to get dressed. She felt chilly with her little Phy Ed shorts and blouse on, but did as she was told. She felt like she was walking in a tunnel as she headed out doors to join the rest of her class. The teacher looked up as she approached and asked Angela if she had a sweater or sweatshirt she could put on. The teacher had noticed the goosebumps on Angela's bare arms and legs.

Angela shook her head 'no', so the teacher asked if there was someone in the class who would lend Angela there sweatshirt. After a slight hesitation by her classmates before one of the girls stepped forward and handed her, her sweatshirt. Angela was then instructed to go sit down by the gymnasium wall and did as she was told to do. Closing her eyes with her head slightly turned to protect the bump on the back of her head and leaning back against the wall Angela fell asleep.

It didn't seem long before she was being awakened by her teacher. "You better go home, you don't look well." "Maybe it's a touch of the flu bug."

Angela nodded and went to get dressed. It was now time to find her way home with this pounding headache. Fear gripped her body as she thought about what type of mood Drusilla might be in tonight. She knew that she had chores waiting for her at home and that Crystal had her own that needed to be done before Drusilla arrived home, so Angela would have to do them herself.

Her body shook as she walked home trying to keep her head from pounding any harder than it already was. She was just about home when she felt the urge to vomit again. She tried to swallow it down because there were other children around her, so this was not the time to get sick. Unfortunately, she lost the fight and out it came.

"O-o-h gross, look what that girl just did," came a little boys' voice from behind her. "O-o-h's and ishes" echoed from around her, as many children on there way home passed her by. Her peers from her high school just made faces of disgust at her as she looked up at them. Angela already dressed dorky, and now what would they be teasing her about at school tomorrow? Angela wanted to cry, but even that made her head hurt too much. The tears ran down her face as she found her way home.

Crystal had beaten her home. Drusilla was not yet home, but it would be a matter of moments before she pulled into the drive. "How are you?" "You are kind of late and I have to tell Mom; you know that."

It was true. Because if Crystal did not tell Drusilla and Drusilla found out "through the grapevine", both girls would be beat up. Tears streamed down Angela's face as she looked into her sisters' face. She knew that telling Drusilla would be difficult for her sister to do, but this too was a no-win situation. In this home, they were taught the CYOA theory. It was the "Cover Your Own Ass" theory. They all feared Drusilla and the damage she could do to all of them had just been demonstrated the morning previously. The reason Angela's head hurt and Crystal's face was swollen today. Therefore, if one acted against Drusilla's rules the other told on the person, or both would be beaten if one covered for that person. This was not a family of love; it was a family of protecting your own butt. The rules of survival in this family were established the day Drusilla walked into their lives.

Angela hung her head as she walked to her bedroom to change from her school clothes into her work clothes. The sobs came as she surrendered to the pain in her head and in her heart. Drusilla had yet another reason to beat her up again. Angela headed out to do her chores, still crying and miserable. Her head pounding so badly she couldn't think straight.

"Angela," Drusilla was calling her from the back door.

"Coming," the obedient response learned years ago, as Angela headed for the house. Her body shaking severely now as the fear jumped to the ultimate level inside of her. She wished she could run away from home, but where would she go. She knew of nowhere that would be a safe haven for her. School was out.

As Angela approached, Drusilla's eyebrow cocked as it always did when she was in a bad mood. Angela stood back from her, just out of arms reach to her as Drusilla questioned her about her late arrival home. "Were you late getting home this afternoon?" Drusilla already knew the answer to this question. She didn't ask why, because it didn't matter to Drusilla. To her, there was just no excuse for any type of disobedience to her rules. No exceptions. Being late was a severe violation that came with a severe penalty, and like always Drusilla was known to deliver the severe penalties without fail.

"Yes," responded Angela closing her eyes thinking that at that point Drusilla was going to knock her around and beat her up again.

Instead, Drusilla's tone changed from anger to inquiry. "What the hell is wrong with you?"

Angela did not know where that question was coming form or how to answer it, so she said, "nothing."

"What's wrong with your eyes?"

Angela didn't answer, as Drusilla came closer trying to get a better look at her. Instinctively, Angela backed up in response to Drusilla's approach because she didn't want to be hit at such a close proximity. One slap to her head and she knew that she'd be out for the count.

Drusilla now stared into her eyes, holding Angela's face up toward her own. "What's wrong with you anyway?"

"I don't feel well." "My head hurts from yesterday and I've been throwing up."

Drusilla's face went sullen. A glimpse of fear went through her as she told Angela to 'get into bed.'

The words took Angela by surprise, but she headed for her bedroom immediately. She got her nighty on and laid down on her bed. Her body shook. The pain in her head made the air seem so much cooler. She closed her eyes from the pain and wished that she could stop shaking so that sleep would take over.

Drusilla came in, gave her an aspirin, and covered Angela with a blanket. Another shock to her system, yet a very welcome one at that. Maybe the hostile Amazon did have a decent bone in her body, or was it that she did not want to have to take Angela to a doctor or hospital, because she was the reason her stepdaughter was in the pain she was. Angela fell into a light sleep, still feeling the throbbing pain in her head.

Getting through the night was difficult. Angela would wake up with stabbing bursts of horrific pain on top of the constant aching aspirin. Her body would shake and then settle as the stabbing pain subsided. She was tired, but couldn't get passed a light sleep into a deep one. Crying silently to herself only filled up her sinuses, which made the pain hurt even more. She shifted from the 'approved position" into other positions, hoping to find one comfortable enough to help alleviate the pain. The affects of the aspirin had worn off and the nausea was returning. Midway through the night, she rushed to the bathroom to vomit into the porcelain throne, and then had to drag her body back to bed on her knees. She was in so weak from being in so much pain all day. Angela wished that she could just pass out, as least by doing so, she wouldn't feel any more pain.

Morning came and with it sunlight. Angela was tired and her head still ached. Crystal came into her room and gave her a bowl of oatmeal. She tried to sit up to eat her breakfast in bed. This had never happened before. Breakfast in bed. "What's going on?"

"You are staying home today and Drusilla asked me to bring this to you in bed."

A few days ago, Drusilla had tried to kill her by shoving her head repeatedly into the hard plaster wall in the boys' bedroom and now for the first time in her life while living with Drusilla, Angela was receiving breakfast in bed and allowed to stay home and in bed 'sick.' She didn't know if she fancied the thought of staying at home with Drusilla in between her breaks from her bus runs, but the bowl of oatmeal in bed was a nice gesture.

Crystal helped Angela sit up in bed. She had no pillow to rest up against the wall with to protect the bump on the back of her head, so she tried to sit all the way up. Wrong move. The pain in her head started throbbing again, which made her nauseous, which now took away her appetite. Pushing the bowl away, she asked Crystal to help her lay back down. She wanted to try getting some more sleep. As she laid down, she realized she needed to go to the bathroom, so very slowly she sat up again. Dizziness filled her senses, so much so, that she had to crawl to the bathroom. Pulling herself up on the toilet, she emptied her bladder, giving herself some sense of relief. Grabbing onto the sink, she pulled herself up to wash her hands and look into the mirror. Her eyes were still unevenly dilated. The tears flowed as visions of the beating returned to her. Angela dried her hands and went back to bed. If only she had curtains on her window and was allowed to close them. The light still hurt her eyes. Angela crawled back into bed, covered up with the blanket and closed her eyes. Crystal came into her room and hugged her goodbye. Angela smiled weakly as she dozed off to sleep.

There was a bang of a door closing in the distance. Angela ignored it. The pain had made her so tired, that even the house could burn down and she wouldn't have cared if she went with it. Angela was in so much pain and agony, Drusilla could have come in and finished her off, and it wouldn't have mattered. She did hear footsteps approaching her room but she did not move even a muscle. Angela felt like she was asleep, yet then again, she could hear what was going on around her. The footsteps stopped outside of her door, hesitated, and then as quickly as they arrived, they seemed to drift off into the distance. A sign let go in the silence of her bedroom as she fell into a deep sleep.

It was late evening before Angela woke up. Her daddy was sitting on the edge of her bed looking down at her. "I heard you have a case of the flu."

Puzzled, she went to sit up to see him better, but the pain in her head was still very real and she fell back down to her mattress holding her head. Drusilla had lied to her daddy about her condition, but this was not the first time. Angela did not know where Drusilla was at this moment, so she just stared at her daddy through squinted eyes and did not say a word to him regarding the diagnosis he had been given on her.

"How do you feel now?" Daddy was concerned.

"It still hurts badly," came her answer.

"What still hurts badly, your tummy?" He questioned her.

She had been talking about her head, but her tummy did ache a bit also. So, she nodded.

Suddenly her daddy's face was right into her face as he took a closer look into his daughters' eyes. She now knew that he had seen her pupils. "What's wrong with you?"

Angela asked him where 'mom' was. Upon finding out that, Drusilla was still on her bus runs, Angela told him what Drusilla had done to her and to Crystal and Christopher. Her daddy turned his head and stared out the window without saying a word. Shaking his head, he got up and left her bedside, giving her hand a squeeze, and then walked out of her room. Angela knew that Drusilla would not appreciate the fact that she had filled her daddy in on how she had deliberately and repeatedly shoved their heads into the plaster wall, but her daddy had to know the truth as to why she was not feeling well.

Angela listened as she heard Christopher give his rendition on what happened to them, and as the bookshelf was being moved away from the wall to show her daddy the holes in the plaster from their heads being shoved into it. Her daddy was then heard leaving the boys room and walking into the kitchen to get Crystals' version of the story. Crystal filled him in on her version and then the office door was heard being slammed shut. This was another night that Angela wished for Drusilla not to come home.

The telephone rang. A few minutes later daddy was yelling at Drusilla over the phone. "You told me that it was the flu!" "You lying bitch!" "You're lucky she's not dead!" "It's a bad concussion!" "Don't bother coming home!" "Go see your dumb-ass boyfriend, see if I care!" Their daddy was angry. He slammed down the phone.

Angela now knew that she would again be on Drusilla's mud list when she arrived home. The stress made the pain in her head ache even more. Why did things work out this way? She was drained emotionally and physically. Tonight she wanted to go to sleep and never wake up again. Having to face Drusilla after her daddy's last phone call with her, was a nightmare that had already started.

Drusilla did not come home until the wee hours of the next morning. She had been with Detective David most of the night. Of course, she made it all her husband's fault. Angela heard her come through the front door. Her body shook in the dark as she listened for Drusilla's footsteps approaching. They stopped at her bedroom door …hesitated…then proceeded into the bathroom. Drusilla would wait until morning, after her daddy left for work, to make Angela pay for her big mouth. Drusilla took a shower and headed off to the other side of the house to go to bed.

Sure enough, after their daddy left for work, Drusilla entered Angela's room. The look on her face told Angela that she wasn't playing any games. "You fucken bitch!" "Can't keep your fucken mouth shut!" "The next time, you won't be so lucky as to live to tell your daddy bad things about me." Smack! Drusilla hit Angela in the face.

Angela cried out in pain. Smack! Smack! Drusilla was 'going to town' on Angela's face. This just added more stabbing pain to Angela's headache.

"Now get your fucken ass out of that bed and get dressed!" "You're well enough to run your mouth, you are well enough to get to work!"

Angela choked on the mucous that was in her throat as she cried from the pain. Obediently she got dressed in her work clothes and was shoved out the back door by Drusilla. Angela missed the steps and fell flat on her face on the sidewalk leading to the shed. Her hands slapped the sidewalk so hard and she tried to break her fall. Angela got up before Drusilla got to her again and she headed to go clean the stall.

This was not going to be a good day. Her body shook from the pain and intense fear embraced her body. Angela heard Drusilla leave for work. Sitting down on a tree stump outside the horse stall, she put her head into her hands and cried aloud. Something she would have never done if Drusilla had been home. Crying was not allowed. It may have been a pity party, but her life was miserable.

Crystal called out to her that she was leaving for school. Angela looked up, fear in her eyes. "What time was it?" "She didn't want to stay home with Drusilla all by herself. She wanted to go to school where she would be safe, even as sick as she felt.

"Mom said that you are going to be staying home." Crystal instructed.

"No! I don't want to!" "She will kill me, I know it." "Help me finish my chores so I can go to school too," Angela begged of her sister.

"I've got to leave; I'm going to be late." Crystal replied.

Angela was sobbing uncontrollably. Tears and snot ran down her face. "Please Crystal, please." She begged.

"I've got to leave," Crystal stated and then turned and left for school leaving Angela behind.

Angela tried to move quickly through her chores to get them completed and then she would get dressed and run to school. If she could work at home for Drusilla, she could go to school. Her chores were finished to the best of her aching ability and then she dressed for school. She left the house headed for school when suddenly she saw a very familiar vehicle approaching her from the opposite direction. Angela felt the tears rise up and spill over onto her cheeks as Drusilla's car came toward her. The car stopped at the curb along side of her.

"Get your ass in this car, now!"

"I'm going to school," Angela argued back. It was the first time she had ever argued with Drusilla. But fear and determination; maybe a little stupidity also, to get away from Drusilla, combined with the throbbing pain of her aching head made her take the chance at making a point.

Drusilla was not impressed. "I said, get your fucken ass in this car right now, or I will come after you!"

Angela knew that Drusilla could outrun her any time, and that Drusilla's threats were promises she would carry out. Angela got into her car just in time to have Drusilla's fist slam into her mouth. Angela's head swung backwards and her teeth went through her lip. The blood trickled down. Angela passed out.

19

A Friend and a Gift

After Angela's last beating, Drusilla made it mandatory that Angela be kept home for a few days. Drusilla called the school, informed them that she was sick, and would not be returning to school until "after she was well." Angela did her chores regardless, and was then forced to scrub the hardwood floors of every room in the house. This would keep her busy while the bruising vanished from her face and while Drusilla was out on her bus routes.

If something was not finished within a 'Drusilla given' time-period, the usual beating would still occur, setting back the day that she could return to school. Angela was never sick as far as influenza, or coughs from colds were concerned. The only time she missed from school was after one of Drusilla's severe beatings, because when Angela was legitimately sick, Drusilla would send her to school. Drusilla would make the "I'm keeping my daughter home from school" call after beating up her stepdaughter, and then Angela would be sentenced to heavy labor until she healed. This would make sure that there would be no inquiries by school authorities. Drusilla had already gone through one scrutinizing inquiry that almost cost her, her freedom back in Wisconsin. Keeping Angela home to heal, kept all the evidence under one roof.

It was not until her sophomore year in high school that a girl by the name of Ellen-Jane Ryman befriended Angela. The girl herself had a bit of a childhood story. A beautiful couple had adopted her. She was a bit overweight, so her peer group also shunned her. Ellen-Jane had long beautiful brown hair and a round face with a cheery smile. Angela met her in one of her classes as they worked on a project together. Between classes, they would talk, and at times Ellen would join Angela out by the fence at lunchtime. Angela grew to trust her new friend and began relating some of the tough time she was having at home to Ellen. Her friend could not really comprehend everything Angela told her because the tragedies happening in her life were beyond acceptance.

When one lives with a family that loves, cares and adores you, you would have difficulty grasping the details of what Angela had to endure in her life. Nonetheless, Ellen listened intently while Angela talked, tears flowing down both girls' cheeks as Angela gave account of her home life ordeals. This was the first friend Angela ever had. Ellen listened intently and then shared her story about how she came to be adopted by a wonderful couple who were childless, making her their only child. They gave Ellen more than just love and a wonderful loving home throughout her years with them. She was blessed in ways that only Angela could dream about.

Ellen extended her parents invitation to go home with her one of these afternoons to meet her parents. Angela knew that this would never be a possibility during her lifetime. Drusilla no sooner allowed her to have friends, let alone spend time after school with them. She had already given warning to her stepdaughter the first time she saw Angela standing with her friend at the fence.

"You are not to say a word about your home life to anyone, or your friend will not be allowed to be at the fence with you; do I make myself clear?" Drusilla threatened. Angela knew she meant business, but was not going to volunteer that she had already filled her friend in to many things. Angela understood the threat, but she had come to a point in her life that she could not keep it in any longer. She needed someone she could confide in to let off the steam that had been building for years and as a teenager now, she needed some release. Therefore, when Ellen came along, she had confidence, and trust in her, so Angela spilled the whole story. Having a friend was new to Angela and sharing life's secrets was also a new venture. Trusting someone with her life's secrets was also new. They grew close as the months went by. The popular crowd was rejecting each girl. They were both feeling like outsiders when their friendship began, and talking it out, relieved some of the stresses from the rejection.

Angela looked forward to seeing Ellen at school every day. They accepted one another for who each other was. They had gotten through the topical epidermis of the relationship into the deep inner beauty of who and what they were. They did their homework out at the fence everyday, giving them opportunity to finish it before school ended. Angela was still not being allowed to do homework at home, so this time spent together with her friend out at the fence helped her grades. Their friendship was so special and only grew every time they saw one another.

Many times, Ellen had told Angela that she felt Angela should go to the Police or to her school counselor about her home life. Angela would shake her head 'no' in fear that if Drusilla found out; and she always did, she would kill her. Drusilla's threats were lethal. The State of Wisconsin could not help them get away from her; certainly, California would be no different. Angela could not trust any adult with her life secrets. How would they react? Ninety-nine percent sure that they would contact Drusilla herself, instead of turning to an agency who could do the proper investigation to help get them out without letting Drusilla know first, what was going on. Even when she tried to confide how Drusilla was treating her to her daddy, he turned immediately to Drusilla, and then when he was at work, she would brutally beat Angela up for talking to her own daddy. No, talking to authorities who would not first provide a safe environment for her, was not on the agenda of 'to do's.' She would not live long enough for anyone to do an investigation of the home while she was still in it.

Drusilla also had a way of acting that things were just wonderful, when in fact they were not. She could turn on and off the charm like a light switch. How many times had the next-door neighbor come over to tell Drusilla that she was concerned about the screaming she had heard from the children, and Drusilla said that there was nothing wrong with the children. "They were arguing and fighting, but I've got them under control", when in fact, she had been beating them. The children were not allowed to communicate to one another while she was around, so how could she use the excuse that the children were having a sibling spat? When the neighbor left, she would go around the house closing all the windows, only to return to her brutality upon the children, threatening if they made a noise, they would get it worse.

Her explanation to the neighbor was totally absurd. The children lived in the same house all these years, and yet barely knew one another. Their communication skills between one another, or anyone else for that matter, lacked the depth needed to establish relationships. Eye contact was the only form of communication that was completely developed. They could read one another's reactions and thoughts by looking into one another's eyes.

Ellen-Jane's friendship helped to get Angela through the first couple of years of High School. Having someone to talk to and someone to trust and depend upon, was the shock absorber for her life. They could sit and talk for hours if given the chance. For now, it had to be taken in one-hour increments out at the fence at lunchtime. Drusilla was adamant that she did not want Angela having any friends. No after school visiting. No life where someone might find out what and who she really was.

Drusilla and her daddy were still at odds with each other. When and if they were home, they would spend a lot of time in their bedroom with one another. At other times, it seemed as if daddy had given up on his 'late hour' life, and now spent more time at home with his children. Drusilla was happy about this arrangement. She knew where her husband was, so now she could go out on the town with her detective boyfriend.

The children would get their chores done as quickly as they could after school so they could spend more time with their daddy. Crystal was in her last year of high school, while Angela was in her sophomore year at the same high school. Christopher was still back at Wallowing Wood Jr. High School in the Educational Handicapped program for educationally slow learners.

****

Life had made its impact on Christopher also. Yet every school official thought that it was just a 'toss of the dice' on how one sibling out of a family can end up slower. "Some children have got it and some don't. His two sisters were bright, while he was held back. It could not possibly have had anything to do with the fact that Drusilla had entered his young life at a very influential underdeveloped time-period, now could it. Drusilla's lack of step-mothering skills, combined with the brutal cruelty she inflicted on him in his developmental years, ages one through six had great influence on him. No, instead the school chalked it off to 'slow learner' and placed him accordingly. They did not do any home environmental studies, or counseling, to perhaps give greater detail on what was interfering with his educational development and social abilities. Placing Christopher on Ritalin was not answering the necessary questions to the cause. Also allowing the Amazon to administer the prescription to him in doses above what was prescribed without taking notice that she was using much more than the doctor knew he was prescribed. She using the excuse that he was acting up, or that she had lost the bottle of prescription. Drusilla was also giving his two sisters doses of his Ritalin that were not prescribed to them. No one took notice.

Inexperience holds everyone faultless. How were the authorities to know? Drusilla was one of a kind, and society has its venue. The 'common practices of parenthood' were the norm, and that which statistics are based upon for most all situations. Very few cases differ from the 'norm', and very few social service programs will seek out or fund each case for its individuality. Most are handled in the same manner and according to the 'book'. The clever criminals of child abuse pass the given criterion. Would Christopher have been placed into an Educationally Handicapped class if they had investigated his home environment? Yes, probably. Drusilla had done a lot of damage to him before they caught on to the fact that he needed some help educationally. The oversight was that he needed to be transferred to a 'safe environment', thereby increasing his opportunity to advance and adjust well educationally. The damage was already done before he began his elementary years. The time they had said that Christopher was "too immature to pass kindergarten", should have been a first piece of the puzzle to find out why. He flunked his kindergarten year. He was not social. Did not seem to understand what was being said to him. Christopher was never a hyperactive child. Quite the contrary. He was a child who sat and watched a lot. Was timid and unsure of himself. Cried a lot. Why the Ritalin and how did Drusilla convince the doctor to prescribe it? Had she lied about her stepson's character to obtain it? Pretty likely. She was a great liar.

A home investigation would have turned up another investigation, leading them all the way back to the State of Wisconsin. Are there enough funds in a department to save a child's life? There should be. Because if an investigation had been done at any point throughout these years, the three children would have never remained in their daddy's home as long as Drusilla resided there. They had a grandmother who would have taken on the responsibility the moment they called her in. So many questions without answers. The lives of three children were in the hands of an Amazon. The children were judged by their behavior, and not by what was causing their behavior. The damage was done and growing worse by the day.

****

Angela rushed home from school one day very excited. Her friend Ellen-Jane had encouraged her to sign up for the 'Talent Exhibition' at school that would be held in a couple of weeks. Her High Schools' student council was conducting a talent contest, and this was the first student activity she had ever taken part in because it was being held during school hours where Drusilla had no control of saying whether she could participate or not. Excitement brewed within her as she did her chores. She thought about the events that had taken place earlier in the day, when her friend convinced her to 'go for it.'

At first, Angela had been hesitant and thought that her friend was daft, but after days of working on her and encouraging her and saying that, she believed that Angela had a singing voice, she finally signed up. Angela could hardly believe that she had taken the step. Since Ellen-Jane had come into her life, Angela gained some confidence to explore the unknown.

Angela would sing to herself a lot. Wherever she was, wherever she went, she could sing. Any song that came to her heart. One's she knew, others she made up. Each song meant something to her. Singing helped to deal with the cloudy days that filled so much of her life up since Drusilla walked in. There were also times for the crying songs, the type that fit what she was going through and she sang them in full expression of what she was feeling. Ellen-Jane said that Angela had a talent that needed to be shared. Then after much persuasion, Angela took the pen and signed her name as a participant. They giggled as they walked away from the table. Ellen-Jane was a great friend.

Now Angela was home, finishing off her last chore, as she heard one of her parents' cars arrive in the driveway. Peering out through the gate from the backyard, she looked to see which one it was. It was Drusilla. She quickly took one last look around to make sure all her chores were finished and headed out to the backfield to pull weeds. Angela really did not want to approach Drusilla, let alone have Drusilla approach her this evening, so she placed some distance between them by heading to the backfield. Another break for her came when their neighbor asked Angela if she would like to clean her horse stalls for her. "Yes, of course!" she would. Grabbing her wheelbarrow, pitchfork, and shovel, she headed next door to clean the stalls.

Angela finished cleaning the neighbor's stalls when she heard her daddy's car pull into the driveway. Her heart leaped for joy. She wanted to share her exciting news with him. Afterall, it had been her daddy that had gotten her to singing way back when they had lived with grandma. Daddy loved singing and could sing like Johnny Cash. She would be the only child he had to join in, and together they would make harmony. It was fun once, a fun that ended when Drusilla came into their lives. There were times that her daddy still belted out some of the good old songs while shaving or showering. Angela was not allowed to join in now. Instead, she would wait until she was out of earshot of Drusilla to bring back the melody and lyrics of one of her daddy's favorite songs.

Drusilla was calling Angela in for dinner. Looking up she hurried back to the house not wanting to be late. Nothing could spoil the evening's announcement she had for her daddy. She would save the news for after dinner. That way, she would be able to tell him all about how Ellen-Jane had gotten her to sign up. The children were not allowed to talk at the dining room table, so this fact clinched her decision.

Drusilla was in a lousy mood, but the joy in Angela's heart seemed unmovable tonight. Even the pancakes on her plate did not slow her down, as she looked around and saw that she; once again, was the only one having to eat them. Everyone else had something better on their plates. Angela smiled to herself as she ate her meal, and as she did, she caught more than just her daddy's attention. Crystal and Christopher were looking oddly at her. Drusilla's eyebrow raised as it always did when she didn't approve of something. Her daddy was the only one that smiled back at her, which only made her eat all the faster, because she really wanted to tell him her news.

Angela finished her dinner and asked to be excused from the table. As her daddy nodded his approval, she got up, grabbed her plate and headed to the kitchen to place her dishes into the sink. Coming back down into the dining room she excitedly blurted her good news out to her daddy.

"I'm going to be singing in the talent show!" the words flew from Angela's mouth.

Daddy was just about to comment when Drusilla responded with uncontrollable laughter. "You're what?" "I thought I just heard you say that you were going to be singing in some talent show." The laughter penetrated Angela's soul. "Who said that you had any talent?" Drusilla's laughter and remarks cut like a knife.

Angela felt the sting of pain, so familiar to her after all these years of living with Drusilla. Tears started to well up in her eyes. Trying to ignore the rhetoric of hate coming from her stepmother's mouth, she turned to look directly at her daddy for his response.

Once again, her daddy tried to respond, but was interrupted by Drusilla. "Who told you, you could be in a talent show?" "You've got no talent anyway."

Angela turned to leave the room on Drusilla's last remark. She could no longer hold back the tears from the pain that now pierced her heart.

"Hey you, get back here." "You think you got talent to be in a talent show, then come here." "Get up on that step, and sing for us." "A good musician can sing without music." "Your claim to fame is that you are a good musician, good enough to be in a talent show…so let's hear it." Drusilla was sneering and clapping as if she was the audience welcoming a star. However, everything was done in sarcasm. A sarcasm that tore every confidence out of her stepdaughter. "I said, give us a song." Drusilla's critical side began to show. Her stepdaughter stood with tears in her eyes, but no song came from her mouth. "I sa-a-i-d SING!"

"No, that's okay; I'll not be in it." Angela said as she once again turned to leave.

Drusilla came up out of her chair, caught her stepdaughter by the arm and yanked her back onto the steps. She then called all the other children into the dining room and ordered Angela to sing.

Angela had tears running down her face. She looked at her daddy hoping he would intervene on her behalf. Instead, he sat there and let Drusilla had her vicious moment upon his daughter. At this point, Angela could not sing. Drusilla had wiped every last bit of confidence from her. Tears fell. She choked back the sobs that were rising up out of the hurt from Drusilla's intimidating display of venomous infliction upon her. She couldn't talk, let alone, sing. Her daddy just sat there and did nothing but watch what Drusilla was doing to his daughter. Angela was more hurt from her daddy's lack of intervention on her behalf, then the mockery coming from Drusilla's mouth.

"If you don't start singing NOW, maybe a belt to your ass will help you start." Drusilla was serious.

'Humiliated', could not even describe what Angela felt now. Knowing that Drusilla would carry out good on her threat, she began to sing one of her daddy's favorite Johnny Cash's songs. She had not even gotten halfway through the first verse and Drusilla started howling like a dog. She was motioning to the rest of the children to join in on her howling. Angela stopped singing.

"Come on, we want to hear you make a fool of yourself, like you would if given the opportunity to join in on some stupid talent show, so keep singing." Was there no end to the torment Drusilla had for Angela?

Angela did not want to be living in this moment. Drusilla had not only stolen all her joy, but was doing so much unrepairable damage to any self esteem she might have drawn from her friend, Ellen-Jane's encouragement.

Drusilla walked up, put her face right in Angela's face, and demanded that she "start singing or she would be wearing her stepmother's fist in her face."

Angela sang through sobs, while her stepmother picked up the tempo of making fun of her, ordering her siblings to join in with their howling. Her daddy got up and walked out the back door. Angela watched as he left. She finished her song, and started for the backdoor when Drusilla decided she had not done enough damage to her stepdaughter.

"Get back up on this step." "You don't leave until I tell you to." "You will be singing for us all night." "Get ready…Get set…Sing!"

Angela sang for hours, singing and re-singing song after song, after song her daddy had taught her, or she had picked up from listening to the country station her daddy listened to on the stereo in the livingroom. The songs she once loved, she now hated. Drusilla's teasing had killed the joy and love she had once felt for the songs. It was bad enough to be teased at school by her peers, but to have to live in a house where it was endless; coming from a person who was supposed to love and encourage her, brought in the feeling of wanting to die. Right then and right there.

It was late before her daddy came back into the house. Seeing his daughter still standing on the steps having to sing, he gave Drusilla a look, which finally ended her escapades of humiliation and abuse of her stepdaughter. Angela was released to go to bed.

Angela did not sleep well that night. Every time she closed her eyes, Drusilla's mocking face appeared before her. The "drilled in" laughter tormented her sleepless night. The laughter of her brothers and sister kept coming back to her, as she held her ears, wishing that it would all go away. She felt as if she would never want to sing again. Why hadn't her daddy come to her rescue when Drusilla's torment all started? Her daddy had always said that she had a great voice and that they harmonized well together and yet, last night; he did not defend her. Was he just trying to keep the peace with Drusilla, all the while hers was diminished?

The next day she went to school and when a rehearsal session was called, she did not go. Her teacher was called to send her down to the choir room, but Angela shook her head 'no' on his inquiry. Ellen-Jane turned around in her chair bewildered as to what happened and why was Angela not going. Tears filled Angela's eyes as she related to Ellen-Jane what had happened to her the night before in whispered sobs. "It was awful." "My stepmother was wicked." "She won't let me sing." "I just can't do it now."

"It is not Drusilla's choice; it is your choice." "You've got a great voice, I think you should do this," encouraged her friend.

"No, it's okay." "I don't think I can do this." "I haven't stopped shaking from last night." "I couldn't even get to sleep, it was horrible." "Drusilla's face and laughter tormented me all night." "Besides, if I did do it, my stepmother would find out and she would probably show up at the talent show and ridicule me." "I would die of embarrassment." "No, I won't do it." Angela was adamant. She had, had all she could take of Drusilla's torment and she would not give in to giving her another chance to inflict more pain on her. If Angela did not compete in the talent show, Drusilla would have no one to torment. Her presence would prove to be a waste of time.

"Oh come on, Angela…If not for anyone else, do it for yourself."

"Ellen-Jane, I'm sorry but I just can't." "After last night, I don't think I will ever sing again."

"Hey girls, do you think that we can get you two to settle your differences out side of the classroom?" "I get paid to teach here." "If there is something I can help the two of you with, see me after class." "Until then, Ellen-Jane, please turn around in your seat and look up here." Their teacher was half-smiling, so they knew that his request was direct, but that he was not mad at them. Mr. Kirk was patient, yet to the point. A point well received by both girls. He was a wonderful teacher, very understanding and they learned a lot from his lectures.

"Yes," came Ellen-Jane's reply as she turned back around in her chair to face the front of the classroom.

Angela whispered an apology to Ellen-Jane's back. Ellen just shook her head in acceptance.

Angela never again signed up for any talent expo of any kind throughout the rest of her school years, and it was a subject the two girls agreed, to never to bring up again.

That next evening Drusilla had her one last laugh as she asked if Angela was still considering 'embarrassing herself in the talent contest.'

Angela shook her head 'no' and left to do her chores.

After a few months, Angela found out that she could not give up totally on her singing. Singing brought life into her and without it, she felt pretty depressed. So when she was out of earshot of everyone, she sang softly to her hearts content. Singing brought out the best in her, even on the cloudiest of days. To her, it was the only thing she had, that no one could take from her. A sentimental gift. A remembrance of the time when she and her daddy had once been so close. They used to sing together to their hearts content. Him teaching her the words to the old songs he knew, and she learning them and harmonizing along side him. Those were the happier times in her life that seemed to carry her through the thickest of life's storms. An embraceable memory that would never die, or so she thought.

20

First Kiss

Daddy's three children were enjoying themselves in the early evenings after school, because daddy was arriving home before Drusilla on a pretty regular basis. After doing their chores, they were allowed to talk to daddy about the events of their day at school. When Drusilla drove up in the driveway later in the evenings, the children would scurry to get out of sight, as if cockroaches reacting to a switched on light. Their daddy knew his place and they all had theirs to go to when she arrived home.

The time spent together brought forth some deep discussions, many of which evolved around why he let Drusilla treat them the way she was treating them. His excuse was that "he couldn't afford to divorce her." "It would cost more to divorce her than to keep her." "Just hang in there, because they would eventually be of age and be able to move out on their own." "Lay low, do what she says, and things will work out for you." "Besides, where would their brother Dennis be without them?" There stepmother would "take Dennis with her and they would never see him again." The children knew that this last comment was more for their daddy's heart and peace of mind than for theirs, because, really, other than Christopher, the girls had not really spent any time with their half brother. The divorce would affect their daddy negatively, whereas, for his children, they would finally be freed from the oppression of pain and possible death. Angela's' daddy's feelings were more important to her than her own feelings. For now, she would bear with his life decisions.

'Laying low' around Drusilla was not an option. It was wishful thinking, and a definite impossibility around Drusilla. If she wanted to prey on them, all she had to do was call their names, and they would have to come running. They were damn if they did and damned if they didn't. Drusilla did not pose a threat to her own son, and had proved it from the day he was born. He was spoiled. He was Drusilla's son and she made sure that they understood that fact every chance that she could drill it into her stepchildren. Given whatever he wanted whenever he wanted, and none of the other children received anything. Dennis was the envy of her husband's children, and as he grew, he too took on the characteristics of Drusilla. Knowing that by yelling out, if one of the children walked passed him brought Drusilla to the rescue; he would do it just to see the other children disciplined. Like mother, like son. Dennis used this method of operation on Christopher so many times. Christopher was sent in to play or to baby-sit Dennis. If Dennis wanted his way, but Christopher was trying to teach him to play fair, Dennis would yell out and sure enough…Drusilla to the rescue. Christopher would be beat up without even a question asked. Christopher hated playing with Dennis. All the toys belonged to Dennis, and Dennis emphasized this. Christopher had to play by Dennis' rules, or Drusilla would be beckoned.

During the times when Drusilla was away, she put Crystal in charge of Dennis. No one was to hurt her child. Crystal grew close to Dennis as Drusilla spent more and more time away from the house. Christopher was allowed to play with him, but only if there was no fighting. Angela spent more time outside and away from the whole bunch of them, so she never really got to know him or see him much. Angela knew her daddy, and if her daddy wanted them all to continue living together as a 'family', who was she to ask any differently. It was her daddy's wishes, and because she loved him, she gave in to his plan and never mentioned the possibility of divorce again. Life would go on as always. She had just two more years to endure the brutality of Drusilla before she could legally leave this house.

Daddy eventually started changing. One day he would allow the children to spend time with him when he arrive home from work, and then suddenly, the day came when he would send Angela and Christopher out to pull weeds in the field when he got home. What happened with their daddy? Had Drusilla found out and instructed their daddy to do this to Angela and Christopher? They did not know and they really did not like it. Nevertheless, out to the backfield they went after their afternoon chores were done and when there daddy came home. When suppertime was called, they were allowed to come back to the house.

Whether Drusilla was home or not, an atmosphere thicker than molasses hung in the air. No one spoke to one another. Crystal always seemed to be upset and was having difficulty eating her meals. She seemed to be on edge and would flare out at her brother and sister when her parents were gone. Both Angela and Christopher would look at one another in dismay. What the heck had gotten into their sister? Was she trying to be like Drusilla? They not only had to walk on thin ice around

Drusilla, but now their own sister had joined her ranks. This was not good for them. Her change in attitude became a mystery to them and one they could not figure out. Crystal started 'making mountains out of mole hills' these days. Angela and Christopher could not breathe or say anything to her or she would tell them off. She started accusing them of doing things they did not do nor did they dare do for fear of her telling Drusilla. Had she gone off the deep end?

    The pressure at home was growing worse by the day. Angela and Christopher were made the object of Crystal's hidden torment, and it seemed like she had joined forces with their stepmother against them. Drusilla still had her moments of torment on Crystal's life, but for some reason, their stepmother was giving their sister privileges never given out before. It was true that she was in her senior year of high school, but for Drusilla to allow Crystal to wear panty hose and make-up was beyond belief to Angela. Daddy and Drusilla bought Crystal a record player and gave her all their old records. She now had a room filled with pretty clothes and make-up. She was allowed to have friends at school and one day, she even had a boy from school walk her home. That is when Angela and Christopher peered through the back gate at them, when they were kissing in the driveway. They laughed until Crystal entered the gate scolding them for their intrusive immaturity. Crystal then piled more and more chores on them to keep them away from the fence.

    Their daddy began spending more and more time with Crystal; and the more time they spent together the worse her attitude grew. Angela and Christopher thought there sister had become conceited because she was a senior getting ready to graduate from high school, and that this had all gone to her head.

    "You're conceited, you're conceited!" they yelled at her when they felt she was picking on them. This type of revenge-filled behavior did not last long. Crystal told Drusilla on them, and the both of them got to eat her fist. Neither of them liked the idea that their sister was no longer behind them. They felt as if she had abandoned them. Crystal was far off in the attitude department. Two Drusilla's were now chewing them up alive. Couldn't their sister see that Drusilla was not on her side and that she was only using Crystal to gain information to use against Angela and Christopher? Was this her option for saving her own life? If you can't beat the enemy, join em'? The problem with this is that the enemy was still turning tables on Crystal and getting in some brutal attacks on her regardless, the alliance.

Angela and Christopher were out in the weeds muttering under their breaths about their miserable home life and the situation they were living in, when Drusilla walked up from behind them. They had not heard her approaching. Angela flew head first into the weeds as Drusilla's foot slammed in between her legs from behind. She laid there gasping for breath as the pain from between her legs penetrated her insides. Drusilla was dragging her brother to the other side of the field by his ear as he was crying out in pain, trying to get to his feet to keep her from pulling his ear. She slammed him on the ground and left them as quickly as she had come upon them. Both children silently cried to themselves as they tried to gain an understanding of what had just happened to both of them.

"I hate her, I hate her, I hate her!" Christopher sobbed.

Angela felt the same way about Drusilla deep down in her heart, but cautiously tried to console and shush her brother. It was a matter of life and death for them. Drusilla would really come back to hurt him if she heard what he was saying now.

"I don't care, I hate her!" Christopher sobbed aloud in rebuttal to his sister's warning hushes.

'Listen," she called out to him. "I know that you hate her, but she will come back out here and do worse than she just did to you, if you don't shut up!" Angela was both angry at her brother's thick-headedness that would land him in worse trouble and angry at what Drusilla had just done to them and gotten away with. She was worried about the welfare of her brother, even though he was venting now and not too worried about it himself.

Her crotch still ached all the way up to her abdomen, but she ignored it. It was important to keep everything inside; both the pain and her feelings about the Amazon. Angela was hoping for her brother's sake that he would take her lead. It would mean the difference between another brutal attack from their stepmother or a chance to recover from this attack. There was no way to take the pain away from him. His ear hurt, his neck hurt, and he was allergic to dust and pollen, so being out in the field in the first place was detrimental to his health. Christopher was crying too hard, his sinus' full already than to take on more mucous from a reaction from all the pollen in the air. He began choking and coughing, almost asthmatic, but not quite.

There was nothing Angela could do for him from her side of the field. If Drusilla caught her over on his side trying to console him, they would both be beaten. Instead, she started to sing a song. Ever so quietly, her voice carried to his side of the field, and he began to settle down. After a moments time, and a few phrases Christopher joined in. He stood up, bent over and began pulling weeds, still singing. Together, they turned terror into melody.

By the time dinner was called, Christopher was feeling much better. He had a bit of a time trying to breathe clearly, but even that cleared up after using his inhaler before sitting down to dinner. Angela looked at him and smiled slightly to let him know that he would be all right. They both stared down at their plates. Crystal had already eaten, as well as for their daddy, Drusilla and Dennis. Given the go ahead, they both ate their pancakes and drank their water. It wasn't long before Drusilla came in to interrupt their eating. "I heard what the two of you were saying about how you feel about a few things and some people around here." "I hope now, you'll know better than to get together to share your thoughts." "Stay away from one another." "It's a standing order." "Do I make myself clear?" she inquired with her hands on her hips.

"Yes," they both answered in unison. They had been well aware of the rule, but now as they had grown older, they had taken the opportunity to confide in one another if for nothing else, than to help relieve the pent up stresses within. No one else would, let alone could understand what they were living through, because no one was allowed to come near them. No one to understand their fears, pain, anxieties and frustrations. Not one of their peers had a life like that which they had to live through. How could anyone understand what they were living through, they barely understood it themselves. Their lives were so much out of the 'normal', and they were not allowed to reveal their home life to anyone, so it was known to them only.

Their daddy looked at them as if to say, "What is this all about?" The looked at him and back down at their plates. Finishing their dinner in silence, they returned their dishes to the kitchen. Christopher was sent to get his PJ's on and Angela was sent to do all her outside chores, which included putting the farm animals away.

She did not hurry back into the house when she finished the chores. Instead, she went out to the backfield and sat down looking up at all the stars in the night sky, grabbing what peace she could for this moment. A dog barked in the distance, and the sound of a door closing somewhere off to the west of their property, followed by the sounds of nature on a farm at night. Crickets chirping, frogs croaking, fire flies blinking like tiny sparkles in the night. Angela chewed on a long stem of grass as she inhaled the clean fresh night air, folding her arms across her chest as if to give herself the big hug she had needed for so long.

Her mind thought about her life and then quickly ventured to Ellen-Jeans' life. Even Ellen was going through some tough times in life. It had all to do with finding out what life was all about. Peers can be so mean when they did not take the time to find out who a person was from the inside. Even if they did find out, the differences between them was enough to cause a thorn between them. Rejection is the worst type of feeling inside. It tears a person apart from the inside out. Ellen-Jane just received it from school; Angela got it from school and from home. When strangers dish out rejection it hurts, when those who are supposed to love and care for you, reject you; it mutilates your innermost being. Rejection left Angela with the feeling of being all alone in this great big harsh world.

On instinct, your body builds walls to protect your heart and your soul from receiving any further rejection. Walls that harden the senses and raises your defenses. Wall that cannot be broken down and penetrated by anyone or anything, as the sense of survival takes over every aspect. Struggling to beat the stronghold of devastation as long as you are alive. Some give into uncontrollable instincts and form the sense of denial. Though they know that things are happening, they still deny it. Christopher became the weaker vessel, and became numb. Crystal had both the sense of survival and the sense of denial, whereas Angela; took on the sense of survival. She began to fight the rejection with a heart of steal.

Ellen-Jane was Angela's best and only friend. She was going through some changes a normal teenager goes through, not wanting to be left out of her friend's life, she cautiously followed suit. Ellen-Jane ventured into extreme unexplored territory of the heart, getting involved with some senior guys just looking to have a 'good time.' Homely looking would describe their looks and character, but at the time when everyone else was experiencing 'love' relationships of popularity, two innocent girls who had not ventured became the targets of some desperate guys.

Angela did not want to be left out of her friend's life, so she tried to tag along as much as her limitations and family restrictions allowed her. Being with these guys made her very nervous. She did not feel safe, however, where Ellen-Jane went, she went when she could, during school hours. Having to spend time with these guys just so she could be with her one and only friend was worth the trade-off. She felt like a third heel to her friend Ellen-Jane's charades. Ellen-Jane was desperate to have a boyfriend to like and accept her, so settle for these guys she did.

On the day that Ellen-Jane announced to Angela that she was 'in love' with Jerry and they would be spending time alone together without her, broke Angela's heart. She felt all alone again, just as she had before Ellen-Jane came into her life. Since Angela could not keep up with Ellen-Jane and was not getting involved with Jerry's friend Ellen-Jane had said that she wanted for Angela not to hang with them. The fear of love, as well as the fear of being caught either by Drusilla or her sister kept Angela right where she was. Dumb, naïve and alive yet out of style, out of fashion, off the beaten track, and just out of it.

Angela watched as Ellen-Jane was held in the arms of her boyfriend. The embracing, the kisses, the laughter, it all seemed so perfect, yet so foreign to her. Ellen-Jane was wearing Jerry's class ring wrapped in angora yarn, sized to fit her finger, and brushed often to display her 'going steady' status. She had joined the 'in crowd' of girls who also had boyfriends and were in the 'fuzzy ring' phase. Angela looked on at a distance with envy. She was being left behind, which had been the ongoing story of her life.

Angela stared blankly at the pages of her geometry book, trying desperately to complete her homework without letting the absence of her friend bother her too much. She could not get Ellen-Jane out of her mind. She missed her and wished that they could go back to the days when they did their homework out at the fence and shared their deepest secrets. Ellen-Jane's school marks had dropped and she was cutting classes, so Angela did not even get to speak to her friend in class. She was not there. Ellen-Jane was 'in love' and so many things had changed about her. Angela couldn't imagine what her friend was going through; she had never walked in her friend's shoes. Everything had happened so fast it had suddenly dumped her back into the world of loneliness.

Weeks went by without Ellen-Jane so much as saying 'hi' to her. She would be in some of Angela's classes and then some Ellen-Jane would skip to go out somewhere with her boyfriend. Angela thought that she did not like the idea of 'falling in love' too much, because of what it was doing to her friend. Getting into trouble was not her idea of fun. Ellen-Jane's whole character had changed. She went from being a great friend and good student to never around to be a friend and ditching school.

Angela was walking to her locker one day, when she felt a hand on her shoulder. She jumped and gasped nervously as she did when anyone touched her. This, a reaction from the years of Drusilla attacking her repeatedly when least expected. In-grained fear, you might call it. Realizing that it was Ellen-Jane wanting to say something to her, she settled and turned to talk to her. Ellen-Jane wanted Angela to become a part of the group she was hanging with. Some guy by the name of Dan Petrolkin was inquiring on whom she was, so Ellen-Jane wanted to introduce Angela to him. She was saying that Dan thought she was cute.

Angela stood in disbelief, looking around her. "What?" "Me?" "You're joking, right?"

"No, I'm not joking." "I've never been more serious." Ellen-Jane verified, smiling up at her friend.

"Who is he and why would someone who doesn't even know me like me?" Angela wanted answers. A guy really liking her seemed to be unbelievable and also an imposition into her personal life that she did not feel like sharing with anyone she did not know.

"Come on, I'll introduce the two of you." "I think you will like him too." Said her friend Ellen-Jane leading her by the arm to a group of guys standing in front of the gymnasium. "Here she is Dan, the girl of your dreams."

Angela was taken back by the introductions but could not spend time on giving it much thought as a hand reached out to her. "Hi Angela, I'm Dan." He said smiling at her.

Angela back up as he and his hand approached her. Touching was out of the question. She smiled slightly looking into his eyes, trying to read his intentions.

Regaining his composure after being taken back with Angela's retreat with his approach, he stopped and put his hand down. "Okay, we can talk this way." He stood a distance away from her, leaving space between them.

Angela shyly said, "Hi."

Ellen-Jane put her arm through her boyfriends arm and said, "Now you two, get to know one another." "I told Dan all about you, when he told me he wanted to know who you were." "So the ice is broken."

Angela was stunned. Her friend had lost her mind. How dare she reveal things about her without her permission. What she had told her friend in confidence was just that, in confidence. Not for the world to know. If word got around about her life, Drusilla would find out and then she would never be able to go to school.

"I hope you don't mind that I inquired about you." "Your friend here filled me in and I still wanted to meet you." Dan was a senior. Kind of homely looking, but friendly.

Angela shook her head and gave her girlfriend a look that said 'they would talk later.'

Ellen-Jane caught on and began to laughed saying, "Don't worry Angela, everything will be okay." "Dan's a nice guy."

Angela stood with the group, uncomfortable at first, but then as the moments went by and they proved that she was one of them, she began to relax. She joined in the conversations and the laughter with Dan standing next to her all the while, which made her feel nervous at first, but then eventually, his presence almost made her feel protected. From time to time, their eyes met but no real direct conversation between them. Here was a group of people that the 'in-crowd rejected, but together as a group they accepted the unacceptables, and Angela was one of them. This was her first sense of feeling that she belonged somewhere in this lifetime.

There were a few times her sister would walk by and give her warning looks, but would never say a word. Angela found that she could make people laugh, she could tell her stories or do comical stand-ups and laughter ensued throughout the group. The only times she felt out of place in the group is when teachers who knew her walked by, looked at her and then at the group, and shook their heads.

The guys were not the best of students so that explained why Ellen-Jane was not going to class on a regular basis. They were not the best-looking people either. What drew Angela to the group was that they were the first people who had ever openly accepted her as she was. Dressed the way Drusilla sent her to school, and they also accepted having to go out to the fence from time to time for the 'appearance' Drusilla required of her. She was ugly, and by most peer votes, they were all ugly.

One day Angela remarked on 'how much the cigarettes smoke stunk.'

They responded that she 'shouldn't knock it until she tried it', and with that Dan gently shoved his cigarette into her mouth. Just as he put it into her mouth, her sister walked up. If looks could kill, Angela was dead meat when she arrived home. Handing the cigarette back to Dan, she went to try to explain to Crystal what had happened, and to plead with her not to tell her parents. It was no use. Crystal was ready to chalk up some brownie points with her parents these days, and informed Angela that there was no way out.

Sure enough, just as promised. Crystal went directly to Drusilla when she arrived home and told on her. Drusilla called Angela into the livingroom and after being told to grab her ankles, she was beat more than twenty times. However, the punishment did not stop there. When her daddy got home, he laid a pack of Camel non-filtered cigarettes on the table. Angela tried to explain to him that she did not really smoke and what had happened, but her explanation fell on dead ears. Her daddy lit the first one and handed it to her. Drusilla made sure that she inhaled the smoke and told her to blow it out her nose. Angela gagged on the first puff. She was told to swallow her throw-up and expected to repeat the process over and over again until the whole pack of cigarettes were smoked. She was sick. Tears flowed down her cheeks and her nose ran as she gagged over and over again. Because Drusilla made her blow it out through her nose, her nose eventually began to bleed. Angela was not a smoker, nor had she wanted to be a smoker.

When the pack was finished, Drusilla demanded that she eat a bar of Irish Spring soap. She threw-up right at Drusilla! Drusilla slugged her in the face.

"Don't you throw-up on me again, you little bitch!"

Angela was still gagging as Drusilla dragged her down the hallway into the bathroom, slamming her face into the toilet bowl. She brought Angela's face up again and forced a piece of Irish Spring soap into her mouth again. Angela threw-up again. The bloody snot in her nose was blowing bubbles. Drusilla drove her head back into the toilet bowl. Angela's face was in the throw-up. She was choking and suffocating. Blood was flowing out her mouth and nose and forehead. She was a mess!

Angela had never intended on smoking, and this was to make sure she never did it again. Both Drusilla and her daddy were heavy smokers and had done so for as long as Angela could remember. Double standard was applied to the maximum. "Don't do as we do, do as we say!"

Angela was sent to bed without supper or so much as even a drink of water. Drusilla wanted her to have that "lasting affect of soap." The bits of soap stuck in her teeth continued to make her gag. Her nose was swollen and dried blood caked at the base. Her tummy felt like it was on fire as it burned within her. She needed a drink of water, but she would have to wait until everyone went to sleep.

****

The house was still as she crept into the bathroom. She relieved herself and turned the water on ever so slightly. Using her hands, she cupped the water and brought it to her face. Rinsing out her mouth, she then began to drink the water. The soapy taste lingered as her tongue scraped it off her teeth. She spit the bits out and finished with a long cold drink of water, then headed for bed.

The floorboards squeaked beneath her feet. She was too exhausted to notice. Just as she got into bed, she heard Drusilla's footsteps coming toward the hallway. Angela closed her eyes as if she was asleep. Drusilla paused at her doorway and then went into the bathroom to relieve herself. Angela lay still in her bed hoping that she had not left any clues behind that would make Drusilla suspect that she had been up. The toilet flushed and Drusilla headed back down the hall. Angela let out a sigh of relief, still feeling 'green behind the gills' from the cigarettes and soap. Her lungs hurt, her stomach ached and the fresh scent of the green striped soap made her gag.

Angela went to school the next day. Ellen-Jane and the group met her coming onto campus. It was nice to see them all waiting for her to arrive. She had never had this happen to her before. Just as she said her hello's the bell rang. Drusilla never gave her any 'hang' time before school.

"Hey girl, tell us what happened to you last night." "We saw your sister earlier this morning and she seemed mad at us." Ellen-Jane and the group seemed concerned for her.

Angela related what had happened to her on the way to her locker, the group following closely behind and listening to every word she said. "I got beat badly, you should see the welts." She lifted her skirt to show them the bruising. "Then I had to smoke a whole pack of unfiltered cigarettes…I gagged, and blood came out my nose because she made me exhale through my nose." "My stepmother then made me eat a whole bar of that green striped soap…I had to chew it and swallow it." "I threw up on her, so she dunked my head in the toilet a few times, smashing my head against the inside," she said showing them her split forehead. Tears welled up in her eyes.

Dan came over to her, gave her a hug, and apologized. He had been the one who had stuck the cigarette into her mouth as a joke just as her sister had walked by. He felt responsible. Angela's body stiffened. All she needed was for her sister to see a guy hug her, and it would surely go home to her parents. If last night was any indication of what would happen to her, she feared for her safety. Looking around to see if Crystal was anywhere in sight, she asked Dan that he not touch her. The hug had felt great and sincere, but the walls had eyes, and she knew that having Ellen-Jane as a friend was being frowned upon by Drusilla; God help her if she found out about Dan and the group of friends.

Ellen-Jane kissed her boyfriend goodbye and Angela and she headed to class.

"Dan really likes you Angela, he told me today." "He thinks you're funny and cute rolled into one great person." Ellen-Jane insisted as they walked to class.

"Ellen-Jane, I don't want to get involved." "My life is a mess right now, and if my parents found out, I would not be allowed to attend school." "Drusilla would really carry through with killing me this time, if I did." "Dan seems to be a nice guy, but I don't think he would want a relationship that went nowhere." "He deserves better." "My life would be ended if my stepmother found out." Angela was not only trying to convince her girlfriend that she did not need a boyfriend, but herself also.

She had liked the attention that Dan gave her, and it would be easy to fall for him being the first guy who had ever given her the time of day, but getting involved with him could cost her life.

Ellen-Jane wasn't settling for a 'no' answer. She continued, "I think you need a change in your life." "I mean, letting someone who does care for you have a chance." "Look at me, I'm happy."

"Yes, but you have loving parents and anything you want in this world." "We are from two very different home environments." "You don't have to worry about being beat up or rejected by your parents." "When you step out of line, they ground you." "Yours are open to the fact that you are a Sophomore in High School and there are stages to healthy development." "Mine are slave masters who own me and I work for them, and when they get mad or have a bad day, they beat me up." "I don't have a life to offer a boyfriend." "Heck, I don't even have a life." "The only reason I am allowed to go to school is the fact that the neighbors would report my parents to the police department if they didn't let me go to school." "Then there would be an investigation and the two of them would probably end up in jail for taking me and my brother and sister out of the State of Wisconsin when it was investigating them for child abuse years ago." "No, if I want to stay alive until I can move out legally, and they can't do anything about it, then I had better wait on that boyfriend stuff." Angela sounded sure of herself, yet down inside, she was wishing she could be back in the hug that embraced her moments ago. Just to be held and comforted had felt wonderful; that time it had come from Dan.

Angela and Ellen-Jane arrived at their classroom and went in not saying another word to one another. Ellen-Jane took her seat, as did Angela. Midway through class Ellen-Jane passed Angela a note. It read, Dear Angela, I think you are so wrong about yourself. You have never had love, and hear comes a guy who has watched you from the sidelines for quite sometime. One who is willing to accept you for who you are and what you have to offer. Dan wants to get to know you better and is willing to do whatever it takes. Your rules. You deserve to be happy. Your friend, Ellen-Jane.

Angela looked up at the back of her friends' head, and back down at the note. What was love anyway? She didn't know and didn't think that she could deal with anything else on her plate of life. So she wrote a note back to Ellen-Jane. Dear Ellen-Jane. Thank you for being concerned for me, but I cannot handle anything more on my plate of life. I just want to be friends and have friends, nothing more, and nothing less. Please continue to be there for me, I do value our friendship. Tell Dan that this is the way I want to keep it. His friendship is good enough. Always, Angela.

Angela passed the noted back to Ellen-Jane. Ellen-Jane read it, turned and looked at her sadly, then jotted down; 'Angela, you do not know what you are missing', and passed the note back to her.

Angela read it. Maybe Ellen-Jane was right. Maybe she did not know what she was missing, but how could she miss anything if it had never happened before? Why would anyone care about her? Angela stared blankly at the assignment in front of her, then again at the note. This thing called 'love' does get in the way of schoolwork, she thought as she tried to put the note aside and do her assignment. Ever since Angela had joined the group, Ellen-Jane had been spending more time in classes with her. A welcome improvement. She finished the assignment and handed it in.

The bell rang and they both left the classroom together. Outside, Ellen-Jane's boyfriend waited for her, and right next to him stood Dan. Angela looked up into his eyes. A smile came to his lips as he watched her approach them with Ellen-Jane. Angela felt a bit embarrassed and went to walk by him to her locker until he reached out and took her by the arm. Startled, Angela looked up into his face and he kissed her right on the lips.

Fear penetrated her whole body. She pulled her arm away and ran to her locker. Tears welled up in her eyes. What if Crystal had seen it happen? On the other hand, it felt great! She was confused. Dan ran after her trying to apologize. "I'm sorry." "I wanted you to know that I still feel that it is my fault for getting you into trouble last night, and I just wanted you to know that I care about you a great deal." He seemed sincere, but was it sincerity, or just the right words to calm a fearful heart? So many people who should have cared for her and been sincere had let her down so many times, why would Dan be any different?

There were onlookers all around them, listening in on Dan's words to her. Angela was embarrassed and scared at this moment, and all she could do was turn the dial on her combination lock over and over again. Tears streaming down her face as she tried to remember the combination so she could get her books for her next class. She wanted to run away from him, she did not know what to say or how to respond to him. This kind of thing had never come up in her life, and not having loving parents, she could not discuss life's lessons with them.

Ellen-Jane saw that her friend was in deep distress and reached up did the combination for her and opened Angela's locker. Angela was shaking as she grabbed her textbook for class and then pushed her way passed Dan to get to class. Dan stood back bewildered, trying to apologize to Ellen-Jane for upsetting Angela.

"Don't worry, I'll talk with her", Ellen-Jane told him as she hurried to catch up with Angela.

Arriving in the classroom, Angela wiped her tears from her eyes and headed for her seat. Her peers turned and stared at her. She looked down at her desk as she opened up her textbook and tried to look as if she was studying. She dared not look up at them.

"Angela," it was Ellen-Jane's voice. "Dan is sorry for kissing you." "Please don't be mad at him." "He really likes you."

"I don't want him too!" Angela whispered angrily back to her friend. "Tell him to leave me alone and to not kiss me again."

"Now wait a minute." "You have always said that you wished you had someone in your life that would love and care about you, well Dan does and so do I." Ellen-Jane was bringing back the memoirs of their earlier conversations. "Here comes a guy that cares and wants to have you in his life, and you reject him." "I don't believe you." "Why?" Ellen-Jane wanted answers.

Angela was still confused. "I...I don't know why myself." "I'm scared." "Drusilla and my dad would beat me up if they ever found out that I even talked to a guy, let alone had one kiss me." What Angela was going through right now did not make sense to her either. Dan's kiss had caught her off-guard, but for some reason, just like his earlier hug, she almost craved having another one. There had been no past experiences, nor teachings on what 'love' really was. She did not know how to respond, and didn't know if she should respond.

The tardy bell rang and the class was called to order. Ellen-Jane was told to face front and so she did. Angela pondered the events of her day. 'The kiss' had just caught up with her. It was the first time a guy had ever kissed her. Thinking back on it, suddenly it didn't seem as threatening as it first was. Wow! Dan had kissed her. Was he really interested in her? She had never been kissed like that. Maybe he did like her. A smile came to her face.

"Angela, can you answer the question I just asked the class?" her teacher inquired of her.

Startled, she came back to reality and to her senses. "Uh...," looking at the board to see if she could figure out what the question had been, and then back down at her textbook, "no, I can't, because I didn't hear the question."

"Oh, I thought that the smile on your face just a moment ago meant that you knew the answer." Her Teacher stated.

Angela was so embarrassed. Her friend in front of her giggled. Ellen-Jane turned to look at her. "What were you thinking?" she whispered.

Angela smiled. "Don kissed me, didn't he?" she whispered back.

Ellen-Jane realized that her friend had finally come out of shock. "Of course he did, he likes you." Ellen-Jane smiled back just as the teacher caught them talking together.

"Could you two please share with the class the conversation you are having, so the rest of us will know what is more important than the topic I am teaching on?"

"No!" Angela responded abruptly, her face turning deep red. She did not want anyone to know what they had been talking about.

"Well, unless I was mistaken, I saw the two of you conversing instead of paying attention to what I had to say, so let us be the judge of whether my lecture is less important than what the two of you were sharing." He was not giving in.

Ellen-Jane gave in to his persistent inquiry, "Angela just received her first kiss before class."

Angela wanted to crawl beneath the desk. The response from the classroom was one filled with laughter and some applause. The teacher saw the expression on Angela's face and called the class back to order. There were whispers heard around the room. Angela's face was redder than an autumn sunset.

Ellen-Jane just looked back at Angela with a smile on her face and winked. Angela did not smile or wink back. Her friend had just shared a very personal situation with the entire class. How much further would this go, would it get back to Crystal, or perhaps even Drusilla?

Dan was nowhere to be seen as the girls left the classroom. Ellen-Jane's boyfriend again met her at the door. Angela looked around searching for Dan. When he didn't appear, she headed for her locker. Wondering where he was, she headed out to the fence, it was lunchtime and Drusilla would be driving by to check up on her. She was halfway to the fence when she heard Dan's voice calling after her. She stopped and turned around. Something inside of her was happy he was there, and yet this area was very visible from the roadway, and Drusilla would surely see her talking to him. Angela felt torn. Her loyalty was to her life where Drusilla was concerned, and yet, here was someone who had not only told her he cared for her, but had given her, her first kiss this very day.

Angela chose to go to Don. She needed to be cared for and accepted. She wanted to explore this unknown territory of human expression. Though they both knew that their being together could not be openly expressed, the time they did spend together was special. Dan was there for her as a friend who, he himself needed to be accepted and cared for. While Ellen-Jane carried on quite a physical relationship with her boyfriend, Angela and Dan expressed a true friendship. He too, wanted her to wear his class ring, but she refused. Not because she didn't want a commitment, it was because her parents and sister would not allow it.

Despite her refusal to accept his ring, he gave it to her anyway. It was to be symbolic of their close friendship. Dan said that he would wait until she was out of school and she was freed from her house, before becoming more seriously involved. For now, they would be best of friends. A kiss here and a kiss there. Nothing more until after she was out of High School.

One night, a few weeks before school let out for the summer, Drusilla drove Angela to school to do her regular evening locker inspection. She browsed through Angela's textbooks reading every scrap of paper, and just as she was going to close the locker door, Dan's ring hanging on the hook caught her eye. Grabbing it out of the locker, Drusilla slammed the locker closed and then took her stepdaughter by the arm, digging her fingernails into it, and walked back to the car. Angela had some explaining to do. After trying to reassure Drusilla that it was only given to her to seal a friendship, after arriving home, she beat Angela nearly to death, repeatedly calling her a slut and a whore.

When her daddy arrived home, Drusilla showed him the ring and then gave him her interpretation of what the ring meant and then he beat her, again, calling his daughter a slut and whore. She lay in a heap on the floor, unable to rise up from her double beatings. Darkness all around her, she could not even cry out. She heard Crystal being questioned about Angela's activities in school, and they were specifically told that she knew that Dan was just a friend. Drusilla and her daddy did not believe Crystal. They wanted to believe the worst. All the more reason to justify what they had both just done to Angela. Given that Angela was in every class and at school every moment, when could anything other than an innocent friendship take place? They had Crystal as their spy, and others neither girl knew who, but somehow things always got back to their parents. Crystal got beat that night also because they thought she was covering for Angela.

Angela was made to stay home from school for a week while the bruising disappeared. Crystal brought word home that the group was asking about her. Angela missed being with them, especially Ellen-Jane and Don. She had been home working while healing and continued to be referred to as a slut and a whore by both parents. She knew that she wasn't either, but in her parents minds perhaps by calling her the names, they were justifying the abuse she had endured that night.

She returned to school the next week and told her friends what had happened to her and that she was not to hang with them any more. Dan asked for his ring back, but Angela couldn't give him it back, because Drusilla still had it. Why she would not let her give it back was as unknown, as to why she was keeping it.

Less than two weeks after Angela was told to stay away from the group, they disappeared. Left school all together. A telephone call to Angela's parents by Ellen-Jane's parents, brought fear into Angela. They had all vanished without even a trace, or even so much as to say goodbye to her. Where did they go and why? It was unlike Ellen-Jane to leave her loving and wonderful parents. Ellen-Jane would have confided in Angela, she was sure. Yet nothing turned up. Her parents were heartbroken, and Angela couldn't go comfort them and help look for Ellen-Jane. Drusilla said that it was none of her business. The disappearance of her best friend was her business, but Drusilla would not allow it.

Rumors ran around the school. Some said that Jerry, Dan and she were found dead somewhere. Others said that she had gotten herself pregnant and left for the eastern states. Angela knew that Ellen-Jane's adoptive parents were extremely understanding and there was no way that they would not accept her condition and help to make it easier on her. So the running away to the eastern states was highly unlikely, yet the first thought of them being found dead somewhere makes one wonder, who dunnit? Could the answer come too close to home for Angela? It would not be beyond the imagination in her home.

Angela was alone at school once more, the way Drusilla liked it. She spent the rest of the school year grieving the loss of her friends. She was the 'leftover' outsider of a group who had disappeared off the face of the earth and for no good reason. She now had no friends. Angela was back at the fence at lunchtime doing her homework as a 'check in' point for Drusilla.

Crystal would be graduating this year, so next year she would really be in the high school all by herself. Where had her friends gone to and why had not anyone heard from them? She felt as if they all had died. She would never see them again. Angela cried for them for many weeks. Not knowing where they were and if they were alive, brought fear and tears all at the same time. They had all been friends. Misfits in society that had found love and acceptance in one another.

21

The Sting of a Lost Virtue

The earlier nightfall's indicated that autumn was quickly approaching. The summer had been a long and treacherous one, Drusilla still having her rendezvous with Detective David and their daddy coming home early after work to spend time with Crystal while her sister and brother were dept out of doors to work in the fields in the hot summer's heat.

Angela could not imagine going back to school in the coming week without either her sister being there or without her friend Ellen-Jane. Angela still mourned the loss of her friend, and summer had brought no comfort from her aching heart. Drusilla had increased her demands in the chore department and was back to depriving her of meals. There were many times she felt the blunt blows of Drusilla's fist in her mouth or somewhere else on her body. Angela's own backyard had been a prison to her for the entire summer.

Crystal was headed to Junior College at Mt. San Everest College. This was the furthest that Crystal had been allowed to venture since coming to California. She was eighteen and knew nowhere but home and school, and since Drusilla said that she did not want her staying home all by herself all day, everyday, was her excuse to enroll her into college. Drusilla dealt out the plan so as to continue control over her eldest stepdaughters eighteenth year. Actually, Crystal had no problem with the venture, because it gave her opportunity to be further from the grip of the oppression at this house, and also the opportunity to explore her new horizons to possible freedom.

Drusilla brought home the new school year 'specimens' from the Thrift store for Crystal to wear, while once again giving her 'last year clothes' to Angela. Since Crystal was larger in size, her hand-me-downs were oversized for Angela. Crystal did not know what missing a meal was, as did Angela. Angela had missed plenty of meals, regardless the harvest of vegetables she was taking from the garden to feed the hunger pangs from having to go without meals. Crystal's clothes looked even worse on Angela this year than they did in year's past.

Once again Crystal's little worn out saddle shoes were given to Angela, but this year her feet had grown and were much narrower than her older sister's feet. The shoes did not fit in the least. A whole inch of foot stuck out the back of the shoe by the time her toes hit the inside front of the shoes. Drusilla tried to shove Angela's foot into them, but it was no use, this year, Angela would be the one getting new shoes. Her first pair on new shoes since living with her grandmother years ago. This was an exciting first for her. Most children receive new clothing and shoes every year as a standard practice to starting school, year after year. However, for Angela, to have new shoes, was a first. What others took for granted, Angela was now thrilled about. She was sent out to the back garden to weed it, while Drusilla went to buy her son, Dennis a new wardrobe and shoes for school, and to pick up Angela's new shoes. Drusilla did not like the idea of having to buy new anything for Angela, let alone, new shoes for her. However, this year her feet had surpassed the maximum requirement of snugness, so Drusilla was forced into having to spend some of her precious money on her middle stepdaughter. The one she loathed with a venomous passion.

Angela worked long and hard under the hot end-of-summer sun while Drusilla was out. Yet even the heat could not steal Angela's excitement of getting a brand new pair of shoes. Crystal was made to keep her old saddle shoes from last year for this year and was not at all happy about it. She felt that since she had always gotten a new pair of shoes why couldn't she just get new one this year, especially since she was starting her first year of college? Crystal was upset with her sister and her big feet. Angela's big feet were really beyond her own control; nevertheless, Crystal made it out to be Angela's fault that she would not be given new shoes this year. Angela was the direct target for Crystal's moodiness for days to come into the new school year. Every time Angela was within earshot of Crystal when their parents were gone, she would take aim at Angela about the issue of her having to wear her old saddle shoes. It was stupid and senseless. How many years had Crystal been giving Angela her old saddle shoes as hand-me-downs? She didn't even bother to think that both her parents worked, why weren't they ever spending money on shoes for all their children and not just one in particular? Why couldn't they afford new shoes, or why had they chosen not to afford new shoes for all their children? Angela did not like being Crystals' bad mood target.

"You're always the one who gets the new shoes and I never get them." "Now you know what I've felt like year after year, having to wear your old shoes." "This year I get to have new ones." "My first year ever to have new shoes." Angela's words were not too sympathetic toward her sister. The injustices of life were now catching up, and since her sister Crystal was the only recipient of her own frustrations, Angela turned target on Crystal.

For both of them it would be useless to blame their own parents, because they had been taught that their parents are always right, and they were always wrong. They were not allowed to question anything their parents did, so they turned their frustrations on one another. At least with them, the competition could be won by who was the most vocal and could justify the conclusion better. It was a communication that went on when the parents were not home, for when they were; neither was to speak to one another. Drusilla had the complex that if the children talked amongst themselves they were speaking against her. So in their parents' presence the glares shared between them spoke volumes, and when their parents left the house, it was all out war. A war due to their parents neglect, and a frustration aimed at one another.

If they had looked at the whole situation from an unbiased perspective, they would have figured out who the blame should have been pinned on. A set of parents who were not providing for them in the manner that loving parents could and would. Living in a high stress family as they were, and can do nothing to change the situation, you turn your frustrations on those whom you can. The one's who will not kill you for doing so. They understand what you are going through because they are being put through the same situation. For Angela and Crystal, the whole ordeal was not just over who was getting new shoes this year; the emotions wrapped up in it included venting about their whole life situation that they were forced to remain in. This venting helped to relieve some of the anger and pains, yet on the other hand, the words spoken toward one another caused other pain and aggravations.

The lack of provision for the three children had nothing to do with their parents' inability to provide financially, because both worked in good jobs and they had been with the same jobs for quite some time. The rent on the house they lived in was dirt cheap, and in the beginning, there had been no rent charges because they were fixing the place up. Because their daddy had stolen most of the supplies to fix up the place and did not charge the property owner for the work and supplies, they agreed on a low continuous rent for the duration of their stay. There was no heating bills, the simple closing of the windows provided the warmth needed back then in California. The electrical bill was bare minimum. Only one light was allowed on in the house at one time, most times, and the only ones that watched TV were Drusilla, their daddy and Dennis. The three children received baths only once to twice per month. There were no doctor bills, except for the one time Christopher was diagnosed for asthma and behavioral disorders just so Drusilla could get him on medication, and then at refill time, she claimed that she was busy, could they just call it in. All shots for school had been administered at the school for free.

    They were not taken to a dentist except for one time as they reached the fifth grade, and at that time Drusilla found out that Angela had TMJ and needed braces to correct the problem, but she never did anything about it. There were no optician bills, none of the children needed glasses or so it was thought. None of the three children were allowed to participate in after school sports, so there were no school activities being financially supported by either parent. The clothing bills were from the thrift store and those were only if someone did not donate clothing to them. The only time they went to a hospital was when Crystal was taken out of the home in Wisconsin and prior to being placed in foster care, and when the girls were having to lift heavy eucalyptus tree logs and take them into the backyard out in California. A log slipped and rolled over on Crystal's two fingers and broke them.

    Judging by the diets fed to the three children since their daddy's marriage to Drusilla, the food served to the children cost their parents next to nothing. A continuous diet of oatmeal and pancakes with a sporadic treat of spaghetti or maybe hamburgers or hotdogs once per month, did not constitute a large food budget. They had a large garden and poultry sustaining the parents, so overall, even their food budget did not dwindle the paychecks or savings accounts. All work on the property and home was mainly accomplished by the three children being treated like 'white slaves', and if it was a tear down project that included electrical or fixing the automobiles, it was done by their daddy with the aid of Angela.

    The lack of provision and support leaned heavily on the one who called the shots for the family, and that was Drusilla. She was the one who set down the rules of provision for the children, but then again, what dad wouldn't want his children to have the best in life? Why didn't their daddy take a stand and make sure his children were clothed, shoed, fed, and provided with proper health care? They were his children, not his wife's. She never did adopt them and legally should have never been allowed to lay a finger on them. She tried to forge their birth certificates once, placing her name on them as if she was the mother of the children. They went throughout school, with the school thinking she was. She was good at lying and manipulating things to go her way. When you've got the looks and a fake friendly smile, you can get away with murder.

Drusilla made sure her son received everything he wanted and more. His interests came first and only. Dennis was the child the three other children were to treat as if a god. He got what he wanted when he wanted it, and none of the three other children was to respond negatively in any fashion or Drusilla would deal with them severely. Angela dealt with Dennis by staying as far away from him at all times. She would dodge his presence and avoid making any eye connections with him. Being sent out into the field to work was all right with her as long as she did not have to be around Drusilla's 'precious little god' child. Angela did not want to be accused of doing anything to him.

Crystal was in tears as she left for her first day at college with the dirty old saddle shoes on her feet. Angela felt sorry for her; because she herself knew what it was like to have to go to school year after year with a dirty old pair of hand-me-down shoes on her feet. It had been her sister's shoes from the year before, that she wore on every first day of school for the past 9 years or so. This year Drusilla could not find a pair of saddle shoes in her size, so this year, on her feet was a brand new pair of black buckle shoes.

Angela's dress was extremely unstylish, but the shoes on her feet were the best she had ever worn since leaving her grandmothers home. Every step that she took, she could not help but look down at her feet and smile. Angela hurried out the door and on her way to school, knowing that the school bell would be ringing the moment she stepped onto the school grounds.

The day seemed long, still wishing her friend Ellen-Jane would show up in one of her classes as confirmation that she was still alive, but it did not happen. Each class she attended had familiar faces in it, but none of whom would accept her for who she was. At lunchtime, she headed out to the fence for Drusilla's benefit. Here she was one year before graduation with Drusilla still in total control of her life's every movement. The only thing she was allowed to do was to breathe on her on, yet even that privilege had been taken from her many times when Drusilla punched her in the gut. If she was made to ask Drusilla for permission to breathe, she would have been dead a long time ago, and sometimes, she wished that she had been.

Tears welled up in her eyes as she remembered school life with Ellen-Jane. Angela had not had the opportunity to say her goodbyes. Where was Ellen-Jane now, what was she doing? If only she could come back for this year, they would be talking and catching up on what happened during the summer. Was Ellen-Jane alive? Angela instinctively knew that she would never see her friend again.

The rest of the day seemed to drag on and on. Being in school kept Drusilla at a distance from her for just over a six-hour period, five days per week. A safe haven without friends now, but safe nonetheless. After school, she was ordered to run home and do the chores. This year had not changed anything.

Crystal loved her new classes at the college. She seemed to be happy when she arrived home, but something in her attitude changed when their daddy got home. It would again be expressed in silence at the dinner table and last until the time she was to leave for the bus the next morning. Christopher and Angela did what they were supposed to do and tried to stay out of their sister's way.

One night as Christopher and Angela were called in to the supper table after Drusilla arrived home, Crystal was not at the table. Instead, they heard Drusilla beating the sister ferociously down the hall in her bedroom. They then heard her being choked as she tried to scream out for help. Angela and Christopher looked at one another in fear and then over at their daddy who seemed to be oblivious to what Drusilla was doing to their sister in the other room.

Angela could not sit there and listen to the cries coming from her sister, no matter how mean Crystal had treated her lately. Crystal was her sister and it sounded like Drusilla was trying to kill her! Looking at her daddy she yelled, "Do something!"

Her daddy just looked in the general direction of the sounds and told Angela "not to worry."

Angela was in tears. She stood up quite suddenly and involuntarily, which sent her chair into the wall behind her. "If you don't do something, I will!" "Drusilla is killing her!" Angela shook as she spoke. She was mad and feared for her sister's life at the same time. It was only after she took a stance that her daddy pushed his chair back and headed in the direction of Crystal's bedroom.

Drusilla and her daddy both returned to the dining room leaving Crystal in her room. Angela was shaking from fear and anger, as she heard her sister being tormented. Drusilla looked at her wryly, and Angela glared back at her. What had the Amazon done to her sister?

Drusilla's fist landed in Angela's mouth. Angela was dazed. She had never before been brave enough to show Drusilla her emotions, and this was Drusilla's feelings on how she felt about people who glared at her in anger. "Don't you ever look at me like that again, you bitch!" Drusilla was upon Angela knocking her off her chair and laying her out on the floor. Daddy pulled Drusilla off Angela, and told Angela to respect her mother.

Angela looked at him, astonished, but said nothing. Drusilla told her to leave the table. It was for the better because Angela could not have eaten after hearing her sister's choked screams of terror. She was shaking with fear from the thought that her sister might be dead. Drusilla had been choking her sister and she had screamed out, but now there was nothing, not a sound coming from her sister's room. Not even a whimper or a sniffle, just dead silence. Was Crystal alive, or was she dead? Angela was more afraid of Drusilla tonight, than she had ever been.

Angela had always thought it would be herself that would die at the hands of their Amazon stepmother. Tonight, it had sounded as if Drusilla had made Crystal her first real victim. Angela's body shook as tears fell from her eyes as she did her evening chores quickly. She wanted to go see if Crystal was alive. How could she get into Crystal's room to check on her without Drusilla finding out? Would she have to wait until her parents fell asleep before sneaking into Crystal's room? Then again, what if she was dead? Going into her sister's room in the dark and finding that she was dead, scared her.

Angela saw only a large dark still figure laying on Crystal's bed as she passed by her sister's room on the way to her own room, later that evening after Drusilla let her come back into the house. Angela wanted to call out to her sister to see if she was alive, but Drusilla was close at her heels, pushing Angela toward her own room. She undressed quickly and went through the nightly fashion show for Drusilla's approval of what she was to wear to school the next day. Then her stepmother gave her permission for Angela to relieve herself and brush her teeth, and then off to bed she was sent. In the darkness, Angela waited until the family all went to bed. In the meantime, she strained to see if she could hear her sister breathing in the next room. If only she could hear just a snore or intake of a deep breath, it would relieve some of the fear built up inside of her. Was Crystal still alive? No evidence came to her ears while she waited for her parents to retire into the far back bedroom on the other side of the house.

Tears flowed down her cheeks. Was her sister dead? If she were, what would Drusilla do with her body in the morning? How could Drusilla cover up what she had done to her eldest stepdaughter, or would anyone ever find out? If Drusilla had killed Crystal, what would life be like now? One down, two to go. Angela was wide-awake. Sleep was the last thing on her mind. If Drusilla had killed her sister, she would definitely be next. Would it be tonight? Her body shook in the cool night air. Images of terror played in her mind, tormenting her thoughts with uncontrollable fear.

Angela was startled when Drusilla walked into her room the next morning to get her up out of bed to do her chores. She must have drifted off to sleep sometime, not too long before Drusilla walked in. Drusilla kind of jumped back when Angela let out a grunt of surprise when Drusilla woke her up.

"What's wrong with you?"

Angela regained her composure and answered, "Nothing." Nevertheless, kept a safe distance between herself and Drusilla.

"Get dressed then, and get your chores done," demanded Drusilla as she turned and left Angela's room.

Drusilla got the boys up, then left the house and headed for work. Angela quickly dressed for school. She needed to go see if Crystal was alive. She had fallen asleep before everyone else had fallen asleep, so failed to check last night. This morning she could go see. Shoving her feet into her dirty 'barnyard' tennis, she headed to her sister's room.

There was her sister. She was sitting at the edge of her bed moving very slowly. Deep dark bruises and some blood red just beneath the skin all over her body. Her face deformed and swollen bruised handprints wrapped around her throat. Scrapes to her face, arms and chest. Lumps and bumps everywhere. Crystal was mutilated, but nonetheless, alive!

"You're alive!" Angela exclaimed with tears of joy and yet pain flowing down her face.

Crystal looked up at Angela with tears of pain and agony in her own eyes. Her sister could barely move. Getting up and walking was near an impossibility. Angela did not know how she could help Crystal, or what she could do to make her sister feel better. Even hugging her sister would hurt her. The two stood and cried, not saying a word. They both knew they had chores that needed doing, the question was, how? Crystal had helped Angela when she had gotten badly beat up by Drusilla. Angela had the most chores, so she would have to hustle through hers, come back, and help Crystal.

Suddenly Crystal told Angela to get out of her room and go do her chores. One minute they were consoling one another, and then next she was being abruptly sent out of her sister's room to do chores. Angela looked at her sister bewildered. All she wanted to do was to let her sister know she was ecstatic to find her alive and to let her know that she was concerned. Angela had been where her sister was this day on more than one occasion. If anyone knew how she was feeling it was Angela. She had spent most of the night worried sick about Crystal, and now she was pushing Angela away.

"Sorry for caring," Angela blurted as she headed out of the house to do her chores. What a quick change in attitude and very undeserving. Her feelings had been hurt by her sister's sudden rejection. Angela was tired from having been awake most of the night. Fear and stress had driven up the level of fatigue a few notches, so reaction to being rejected by her sister was also inflated. Anger set in, which blocked any further sympathy pangs for Crystal.

Angela did not say a word to Crystal as she sat down with her at the breakfast table. All she had wanted to do was to let Crystal know how concerned she was about her and how glad she was to know now, that she was alive. Crystal's actions were strange this morning. She seemed out of it and distant to Angela. Angela had never seen her act this way and figured that it was maybe a head injury or just her reaction to what had happened the evening before. Maybe silence and pushing her sister away was Crystals' way of handling the reality of it. Angela made up her mind to give her sister space and time. Perhaps, Crystal would be feeling better when she returned home from school this evening, and then they could talk about it and console one another.

Angela could not shake the fear that burned inside of her from last night's attack on her sister by Drusilla. She was very tired from being awake all night and could not concentrate in her classes at school. Crystal's choked screams from the night before, and her daddy's lack of going to her sister's aid played back in her head over and over again. The strange mood the whole situation left her sister in during their brief exchange this morning, kept Angela pondering its significance in her memory. Angela was having a difficult time trying to deal with everything about last evening and this morning, but knew that she could not talk to anyone about it so they could help her sort through it. She was not allowed to share the "family life secrets" with anyone, for if she did and Drusilla found out, Angela would die. Drusilla had promised her. After seeing what Drusilla had done to her sister last night and to herself on several occasions, Angela knew that Drusilla was capable of killing her.

The last bell of the school day rang. Angela gathered up her books and headed for her locker. Running all the way home as required by Drusilla, she noticed that Crystal had not arrived home from school yet. Crystal had the key to the door of the house, and because she was not yet home, Angela decided that she would get into the backyard and start her chores while waiting for her sister to arrive home. Drusilla would be home soon, and Angela did not want to get into trouble for not having her chores done before Drusilla arrived.

Christopher came home just as she was going into the backyard and joined her lead. Angela did her chores while Christopher sat on the back step waiting for their stepmother. Crystal was still not home when Angela finished doing her chores. Angela grew concerned. What if Drusilla arrived home before Crystal did, then what? Would there be an instant replay of the previous nights' beating; would she survive it as she had last evening? Fear crawled through her senses and her body shook. Please come home before Drusilla, please, Angela half wished, half thought for her sister.

Angela paced the backyard with nervous tension rising inside of her. Drusilla would pull up into the driveway at any moment. She and her brother were stuck outside in the backyard in their school clothes, but there was not much they could do about it now. Crystal had not come home to let them into the house to change or to do their inside afternoon chores.

Angela heard a car pull into the driveway. Peering through the gate and fence post, she looked to see who it was. The Pontiac signified that Drusilla had in fact beaten their daddy home. She shook with intense fear as she left the backyard to approach Drusilla.

"What the hell are you still doing in your school clothes?" Drusilla growled.

"We're locked out of the house," Angela calmly responded not returning her stepmothers firing squad of inquiry.

"Where's the key and your sister?"

"She's not home yet."

Panic crossed Drusilla's face, knowing full well that she had been in this situation one other time in her life. Back when she had beaten Crystal up and sent her to school in Wisconsin and the school had stepped in and taken her eldest stepdaughter away while they investigated her.

"Where the hell is your sister?!" Drusilla demanded the unknown from Angela. "I can't take that you don't know." "You are covering for her, aren't you?" Drusilla was growing more panicky by the moment. She knew that she had severely and brutally attacked Crystal last night, and was now facing the probability of her stepdaughter turning her in once more. "I should have never let her go to school this morning!" Drusilla was now trying to back track to where she had failed to realize this outcome of possibility that the authorities might show up and finally have the proof against her they needed years ago. "I want to know where your sister is and I want to know NOW!" Drusilla was frantic, accusing Angela of knowing yet not revealing her whereabouts.

"I don't know where Crystal is and I did not know that she wouldn't be coming home tonight." Angela wanted to clear herself of Drusilla's accusations. Inside, she was thinking that she wished Crystal had taken her with her when she left, and then the both of them would be missing from home tonight.

"You do know where she is!" Slap! Slap! Drusilla was digging for answers in her desperation to just get some sort of clue on where her daughter was and whether she had been turned into the authorities for abusing her severely again. Maybe by beating it out of Angela she would find out as she slapped her across the face.

"I don't know where she is, because if I did, I would have gone with her.!" Angela cried back.

SLAP! "You do know, I know you know…and you are going to tell me!" Anxiety rising in Drusilla's voice. She would obtain the needed information.

"I don't know that she wasn't coming home tonight, because if I had, I would have left with her!" I hate you!" Angela was caught up in the moment of panic and terror and the loss of her sister all at the same time.

Drusilla's eyebrow raised in surprise of her stepdaughters' gutsy reply as her fist met Angela's mouth. "You bitch!" "How dare you speak to me like that!" She drew back her fist and was going to hit her again, when Angela's daddy walked in the front door.

Seeing Drusilla on top of his daughter and the blood flowing from his daughter's nose, he asked, "What's up?"

"Crystal is gone, and she is not coming home." Drusilla was breathing hard as she explained the situation. Terror was in her eyes, the same terror that showed in her eyes years before when the phone call came in to say that they were taking her stepdaughter from her until further investigations into the alleged child abuse could take place.

Angela's daddy looked at Drusilla with fear in his eyes. Dejavu! It had happened again, or so they were thinking. He had sat at the table the night before and had allowed Drusilla to beat up his daughter. Now Crystal had not returned home. "Why did you let her go to school?" was his panicked inquiry. An argument broke out between the two of them on who was to blame and who wasn't to blame, not even taking into consideration the fact that they were both to blame for her leaving. Anxiety filled the room. Who would be going to jail if Crystal had turned them in to authorities? Neither of them thinking of Crystals' welfare and well-being. They were, like previously, more concerned on whether the authorities were going to show up or not. The argument eventually turned to plans on how they were going to cover what had actually happened to what they would want the authorities to believe. As they sought to create the 'story' on how Crystal came by her injuries, Angela walked out of the room, to her room changed her clothes and then walked out of the house shaking her head. Her lips were swollen and blood dripped down from her nose from the punch to the face Drusilla had given her. How would they explain her condition if the authorities did show up to question all partied in the house? Angela was getting fed up. She could see just how much they did not mean to their daddy.

"Angela, get back in here." "I need to talk to you." Her daddy was calling her back into the house to gain some kind of information that she did not have.

"Coming." She really had nothing to give him that could help. Crystal had been acting weird, but never indicated that she would be saying her last goodbyes. Her departure and now absence was a mystery to Angela. Could they blame Crystal for leaving? Absolutely not. Did they think for one moment that she would not take the first opportunity after starting college to leave? Moreover, after last nights' attack on her, the timing could not have been better, Angela thought to herself as she returned to the house. There is only one thing that Angela regretted that very moment, and that was; why hadn't Crystal invited her to go along with her? How dare she leave her behind in this hellhole called home. For her own sake, she hoped that Crystal had gotten up the nerve to contact the authorities and to tell them about their life.

Daddy led her to the table by the hand as she entered the house. Drusilla sat staring at her. Angela looked briefly at her and then back at her daddy.

"Angela, you need to think back to this morning…did Crystal do or say anything that would give you the impression that she was leaving home today?" Daddy was pretending to be concerned and patient.

Angela shook her head as she told him "No." "Crystal did not even talk to us this morning." "She didn't even say goodbye to me." Angela teared up as she spoke her last sentence. No, Crystal had not even said goodbye. "Daddy, she was hurting pretty bad, and looked really bad." She looked into his eyes hoping to see even one ounce of concern for Crystal; but instead, the look of terror of what was going to happen to himself if his daughter had gone to the authorities.

"Now tell your daddy what you said to me about leaving yourself." Drusilla joined in on the drill.

Looking back at Drusilla and knowing full well that she was panning for points with her daddy again, Angela hesitantly answered, "I told her that if I knew that Crystal was leaving this morning, I would have gone with her."

Her daddy did not seem too pleased with her last answer, but did not comment or offer any physical reaction. "You will let us know if you hear from Crystal, right?"

Angela took a moment to think on that one, and then shook her head 'yes.' She lied.

With that, her daddy excused her from the table and Drusilla told her to go back out and finish her chores. Drusilla wanted Angela out of the house so her daddy and she could discuss what they were going to do now.

Angela did not mind leaving the house. She needed to catch up on her thoughts and reactions to what her sister had done. She left home without even telling Angela that she was going to do it. Angela would have begged to go with. She didn't know the surrounding neighborhoods, but Crystal did, being that she had to travel by bus to get to the college. Crystal could have gotten them both out. Instead, here she remained, stuck in 'hell' with Drusilla's venomous afflictions. Would she ever get out alive? Angela did not really rely on the assumption that the authorities had been contacted, and even if they had, they had failed the three children the last time. What would make this time any different?

Nighttime and laying in bed brought in the silencing of her thoughts and the memoirs of life with her sister, Crystal. Tears streamed down her cheeks when the realization that she may never see her sister again sunk in. She quietly cried to herself, knowing that because Crystal was eighteen now, she would never be returning to this house. This morning had been her last moment here. Angela closed her eyes and envisioned her sister's face as she had closed the door this morning. She was not just leaving for school; she was leaving this house forever. Sobs broke as Angela buried her face in her pillow-less mattress. Why Crystal, didn't you take me with you? Angela sobbed in the darkness.

Angela remained depressed as she mourned her sister in the days that followed. She was very alone these days. Even school held nothing for her. She could no longer see into the future, so her subjects were useless to her. She had no one she could turn to, to confide in any more. No one who would believe what had been going on over the years, because it was all Drusilla's' protected life-threatening secrets. Crystal was the only person she could talk to when Drusilla was not around, about their life in this house. Without Crystal, there was now no one. Even Ellen-Jane had not returned to school, and was still a 'missing teenager.'

****

Daddy started to get home early again. Angela would be doing her chores and now those that Crystal had abandoned when she left home. Drusilla would still not take on any of the housekeeping responsibilities. Instead, she gave the added work to Angela and expected all to be done in the same given amount of time that she had before Crystal left and had fewer chores. As she did the chores after school, her daddy would stand around talking to her. She found his company pleasant and started looking forward to his company in the afternoons.

For the first time in many years, daddy seemed interested in building the relationship they used to have prior to Drusilla coming into their lives. Angela was enjoying her daddy and her relationship, and began sharing many of her thoughts and ideas she had in life. Careful not to mention Drusilla in her conversations, knowing that she could not trust him to keep their conversations confidential; she pretty much kept the conversations topical. The conversations would last until Drusilla's car would be heard arriving in the driveway, and then Angela's daddy would head into his bedroom leaving her to continue with her chores.

Daddy started getting friendlier toward the last few months of Angela's junior year of high school. Their conversations were laced with her daddy placing his arms around her, squeezing her, and trying to kiss her on the lips. She would turn her head away. Angela did not feel right inside. They had gone years without so much as even a kiss or a hug, and hear he was now holding her in her arms and trying to kiss her on the lips. Dan had been the only guy to kiss her on the lips, which had been for just a moment in time, and now it was over with. She did not like her daddy kissing her on the lips.

Angela did like being hugged, but even daddy's hugs these days made her uncomfortable. They always seemed to come from behind her when she was doing her chores and his hands seemed to always than on her breasts. She would wiggle out of his embraces, turning around to face him, trying to start up a conversation that would keep his mind off having to hug and kiss her. His hugs and kisses these days were an invasion of her space. Her daddy did not deserve to hug and kiss her. If he wanted to show her that he 'loved' her, he should start with trying to protect his children by getting rid of the Amazon. Instead, his actions felt dishonorable. They made her feel uncomfortable and strange. Angela wanted him to keep 'arms length' away from her. The feeling of 'invasion' made her shiver.

Eventually, his persistency on having to hug and kiss her, made Angela quite moody as she fought his advances. She had waited what seemed a lifetime for her daddy to pay attention to her, but this was not the attention she wanted. It seemed as if the moment Drusilla was gone her daddy would start pushing himself on to her. There were times she would wake up to find him laying on top of her in his underwear, rubbing himself back and forth on top of her. When he would realize that she was awake, he pretended to be playing airplane on top of her. Come on, now...she was a junior in high school. A bit too old to play airplane and a bit too old to have a daddy laying on top of her. Angela did not like this method of being woke up, nor did she want her daddy laying on top of her. There were no sunshines in her mornings on these days, as she would fight to roll him off her to avoid his kissing her on the lips and being touched on her breasts. Angela became moody, a feeling she could not fight.

She could tell him to get off her and stay off her, because she had been taught that her parents could do or say anything they wanted. Angela wished that he would leave her alone as he had in many years. She was now becoming afraid of her daddy. Angela shook from fear as she remembered how similar her daddy's actions were to those from the time she was a little girl in Wisconsin, when her daddy had, had some guy come in to baby-sit her and her brother. Angela was sixteen years old and her own daddy was now making her fear him.

"You're squishing me, I can't breathe," she begged.

Rising to his knees, he held her arms above her head and kissed her chest. Pausing, his lips at her nipples, she felt an unfamiliar twinge between her legs, which made her tremble as she tried desperately to get out from under him. Tears began to fall as she fought to get away. Her daddy came down on her rubbing her body into hers. She was stuck. She felt something wet on her tummy, as her daddy finally stopped rubbing himself on her. She lay there, trying to breathe beneath his weight, wishing he would get off her. Her daddy seemed to be tired now and fell asleep on top of her.

Angela stared at the sky outside her window. This 'underwear clad' man was not her friend, nor was he her daddy. Things had changed more than she realized at this moment. She did not understand what he was doing to her, or why he was doing it, but whatever it was, she did not like it. She started to cry, which woke him up.

"What is the matter with you?" he asked her as he rose up off her.

She couldn't find the words to tell him, because she could not explain it herself. All she could say to him was, "Get off me dad, you're too heavy."

Her dad got up off her and told her to get dressed, then headed to the bathroom to take a shower. Angela looked down at her stomach. There was a smelly white substance on her nighty that she didn't want on it. The smell made her nauseous. What was it? Where had it come from. Tears fell down her face. She would have to go out to the shed to wash up.

Angela got dressed and headed for the shed before her dad got out of the shower. Once in the shed, she found a rag in the dirty wash and began to wash her stomach off. The smell lingered, so she put some laundry detergent onto the rag she was using and washed off. Her belly was red when she finished scrubbing it, but at least the horrible smell was gone. She then took her nighty and wet it under the hot water tap, took the detergent and hand washed it too. She was angry at her dad. She did not understand all the mixed up feelings she was feeling at this moment, but she knew one thing, and that was, she did not want her dad around her.

Day in and day out, she tried to avoid him. Angela was a nervous wreck. Drusilla started giving her Ritalin again, so Angela was also having to fight its effects on her. She would be in zombie land trying to do all her chores at home, and to do her schoolwork. It took everything she had to overcome the hardship that the drug caused her. The drug fought against any clear thinking she had, it's affects increasing as the days went by. There was no doctor prescribing it to her; it was the latent abuse of her stepmother administering her brother's prescription to her.

Angela's dad's advancements were becoming more difficult for her to fight off and avoid, as Drusilla was spending more and more time away from the house. Angela would opt to go to bed early after all the work was done to sleep off the effects of the drug. She always fell fast asleep, oblivious to what went on around her for the rest of the night.

One Saturday morning she woke up with a stinging pain between her legs. There was blood on her sheet and between her legs. She hurt. Thinking that she had started her period, she pulled her nighty down and went to tell Drusilla she needed a menstrual napkin. Arriving at the office door that led to her parent's bedroom she knocked. They weren't yet awake.

"Mom, I need to tell you something."

A tired voice from Drusilla responded, "What the hell are you doing up?"

Angela shook. Yes, this had been a first. She was not supposed to get up before being told to do so, even at sixteen. She felt a cold shiver go up her spine. Nervously she called back to Drusilla. "I think I've started my period." She didn't really know if she had or not. All she knew is that there was blood between her legs. Her sister had started hers back in the fifth grade and here was Angela in her Junior year of High School. She had been late on practically everything. Her breasts were now past the stage of mere bumps, yet Drusilla had still not let her wear a bra.

Angela heard Drusilla coming to the door. Looking down at her stepdaughter, she handed her a pad and an elastic belt. Angela looked down at the contraption that now hung in her hand. She had never used one of these, and with the closing of the door in her face, she found that she was not going to get any lessons on how it worked. Angela was on her own.

Angela went into the bathroom and washed off the dried on blood between her legs. There was a sharp stinging feeling felt as the soap went up inside her. She wasn't sure she liked having periods if they made her sting down there. She failed at several attempted to work the belt-pad contraption. Frustration brought on the sweat as she twisted and turned to try to make sense out of it, like a cat chasing her tail. She let out a sigh of relief as she finally figured it out and got it on and headed back to bed.

Drusilla was the one who had the authority to tell her when she could or could not get up out of bed, even at the age of sixteen, so since the command had not been given, Angela was going to take this moment to think. She was wondering what was going on with her body. She felt a bit queasy and her vagina stung. Other than that, she was fine.

The morning hours went by before Drusilla came to her room to tell her to get up. Drusilla asked her to show her how she had gotten the pad and belt on, so Angela lifted up her nighty and showed her. Her stepmothers inquiring mind also wanted to see the blood, so Angela pulled down the pad. There was one tiny drop of blood on the pad. Drusilla asked if Angela was sure that she had started her period and Angela then showed her the blood on her bed sheet. Drusilla seemed puzzled as she walked into the bathroom and closed the door. Angela got dressed and started her chores.

All through the day, there was no more blood on the pad. Angela took off the pad and three it away. She didn't know much about periods, so she wasn't concerned that it only lasted for a brief moment. The stinging went away by the next day, so she though nothing of it.

From time to time after going to bed early when Drusilla was not yet home, because Angela felt sedated by the affects of the Ritalin, she'd get those same stinging feelings the following mornings, but never any more blood. Not even a month later. Her dad was still having major problems with his hands and his kisses and hugs. There weren't many more times of him getting on top of her in the mornings to 'wake her up.'

Drusilla asked her one morning why she wasn't having any more periods.

Angela looked up at her in surprise. Was she supposed to have more periods? She did not know, so she asked, "Am I supposed to have more periods?"

"More periods…more bleeding…it's supposed to happen every month." Drusilla explained.

Angela thought about what Drusilla had just explained. She didn't have any more answers than Drusilla did. What was wrong with her? Why did she only bleed one night, and hadn't since? Angela looked up at Drusilla and asked, "What's wrong with me?"

"I don't know, I was hoping you could tell me."

Angela looked at her dad, who at this moment seemed to be engulfed in his breakfast, as if he hadn't heard a word. He made no comments, but did seem a bit nervous.

Angela knew that something was wrong but could not put a finger on it. She feared falling to sleep now. She would hide the Ritalin pills back between her upper molars and cheek, spitting them out when Drusilla left the room. She would dump the morning drinks that Drusilla left out on the counter for her knowing they had the Ritalin in them. No more dull person. She wanted to find out the truth.

Her dad stayed home from work one day and seemed to be all over her. He was constantly in her way of allowing her to complete her chores, which aggravated her to no end. However, she could not say a word to him. Seeing that she had not finished her chores by the time she was supposed to leave for school, he told her that he would finish them for her, so Angela left for school.

Angela was totally frustrated by the time she got into class. She felt moody and could not concentrate on her studies, and did not know why. He dad was acting like some of the guys on campus did with their girlfriends, toward her, and it was pissing her off. She was becoming afraid of him. Why was he treating her this way?

Thinking on how she felt right now and the mood she was in, she suddenly remembered Crystal. Crystal had been very moody toward the end of the time she spent home with them. Christopher and herself had been sent out and locked out of the house every afternoon when their daddy got home. Things were starting to make sense. With herself, she had facts to base her synopsis; with her sister Crystal, she had only assumption to base her findings. Angela had more than just Drusilla to fear now. Her dad had joined the rank of 'fear inflictor'.

The biggest migraine headache came upon her from all the stress that now weighted down on her. She felt cold and shaky and the light bothered her as she tried to stare down at her studies. Angela had one more hour of class before she could go home. Home. What home? Her head pounded. The thought of being around her dad made her sick. What was she going to do? Where was her sister Crystal? Angela did not want to go home, but she had no choice. She had no one and nowhere to turn. Everyone posed a threat to her because she did not know whom she could trust with her terrible family secrets. The fear that Drusilla would find out that she had even shared a mite of her home life kept her silent for over another decade.

The bell rang and she headed for home. Angela could not run, her head hurt too bad. She knew there would be a beating waiting for her for being late home, when she arrived home, but today she did not care. She was giving up.

Angela arrived home late as she had expected. Her dad had stayed home and was waiting on the porch when she arrived. He looked at her and asked her, "What is wrong?"

"I don't feel well; I've got a massive headache."

"Well, I've already done your chores, so go ahead and get to bed."

What a break, Angela thought as she got undressed and climbed into her bed. Just what she had wished for. Sleep, wonderful sleep is all she wanted. Her head was pounding which made it difficult for her to sleep, but it did eventually catch up to her.

Angela was sound asleep. Peaceful uninterrupted sleep. An escape from the reality of her life. A muscle twinged here and there, but never broke the steady breathing of her sleeping body.

Late into the night, her body went to rotate from its position. Something heavy on top of her restricted her movement. Startled, she woke up. A hand came over her mouth. She felt something being shoved up inside of her vagina, over and over again. A stinging sensation from between her legs penetrated her senses. The dark form upon her body was that of her dad. Tears ran down her face in the darkness. She lay motionless as he finished and got off her. She listened as he headed down the hall, through the livingroom, and then the door to the office closed. Angela waited until the house was quiet and got up to go clean up. Her body shivered as the memory of the male babysitter from Wisconsin came back to her. She felt ashamed back then, now she felt like dirt. This time it had been her own dad. Angela never did get her periods for another year and a half.

The identity of the 'stinging sensation' between her legs had been solved. It was the sting of a lost virtue.

22

Winner of Her Trust

"A rock feels no pain, and an island never cries", Angela read the chorus part of the song. She now explained to the class the reason she had chosen this song as her favorite song and why it touched her heart and life the way it did. She related why the words of the song brought out the deepest of feelings within her, without really telling them about her life. Angela went on to tell her English-mini class of Musical Lyric Appreciation Studies, the purpose for choosing this song and her interpretation of what the song said to her. Every word of the song had impact on her life, maybe more than when the songwriter had expressed himself in their creation. Hearing the song sung from the record player in her sister Crystal's room back when she was still home, and made impact on her. The class stared back at her through teary eyes; as Angela went on to explain the songs' rhetoric.

A rock is hard; nothing can penetrate it, not even the pain of life's torments. A rock is formed one grain at a time, and hardens through the years. The same was with the way life had treated her. Angela could have let life get to her, grinding her as the dust of the sand on a beach, but instead she had developed the survival instinct from the fires of life's torment. She was arriving at a place in life where she would no long let it be her torment.

The island is alone out amidst the rolling sea. Angela had no friends. After losing her one and only friend Ellen-Jean, and having to live through all the pain losing her had caused her, she had decided that she did not want any friends. No one could touch her, and she would touch no one. Being alone by herself kept Angela from the suffering of another loss at the hands of love.

School had become her refuge from the torment of the home life, and she had found that hiding behind her studies at school, would block out the harassment form her peers. Do not talk of love; she had lived the love of a loveless family. Lost the love of her dearly departed best friend, and having had love torn from her as she was swept out of the loving and safe arms of her grandmother to live in hell with Drusilla and her daddy. Then yet another loss came; her sister brutally beaten had left home, not leaving word on where she was going. Months had gone by, and no word had come. Her only last confidant who knew what their home life was like and could share her pain had left her. Angela's first kiss from Dan, was yet another memory from a broken heart, love had left her with. Laughter came only from the mockery of all her peers at school, and then from her dad and stepmother as they told her repeatedly, she would never amount to anything. Moreover, by what they did to her, they were making sure of it. She hated love.

Her written poetry told the story of her life in parable. The words within every finished assignment described a sadness and torment of an aching heart. The darkness and treachery of life's horrified confinement, the sting of pain, and the wretchedness of her lacerated soul, all described Angela's life. This was the only way she could relieve the pent up stresses growing inside of her. She was not allowed to come directly out with the truth, so in each stanza written she described her life in parable. Many thought she was a good writer. Her words had a deep inner feeling felt by everyone who read them. How could she author the tragedies, unless she was living them, and knew them?

Angela had taken a few courses with Mr. Julian. He had a way of teaching that would embrace her soul. Music and lyric writing had attracted her. It became an outlet of expression for her. What she could not say to anyone verbally, spilled out on the pages of her writings. She loved her teacher. He taught band and mini English studies. Many times, he would make comments, leaving question sometimes as to the nature or inspirations of the contents of her assignments. There were the occasions that the two would sit down together and discuss the contents of one of her poems, or short stories, or lyrics to a song she had written.

"You are very talented," he'd say to her. "But what I felt when I read this, is that it isn't made up." "The feeling of the story you expressed is something that I feel you might be experiencing in real life." "Would you like to talk?"

After several times of giving Mr. Julian the brush off, she was finally feeling like giving in to him and spilling her heart out to him about her life. Fear crept up on her for a moment. She wanted to say something, but she still felt uneasy. Her school years here at the High School and her experience at having him for her favorite teacher stirred something inside of her, that finally urged her to open up to him. He had been the first and only teacher who had really been an encouragement in her life. One that was sensitive to the students he taught. Teaching was not just a job to him. His students loved him because he made them feel they could do anything. Mr. Julian believed in them. He was their friend. Someone who cared and showed it. Nothing about Mr. Julian was superficial. He did and said what he meant. He was genuine and a fantastic teacher.

Today, Mr. Julian sat asking the question that no other teacher had ever asked her in a manner that had long since won her trust. Angela looked at Mr. Julian and nodded. All her writing had been written based on what she was living through and was truly feeling down inside, and on the surface.

"I know", Mr. Julian assured her. "Is there anything I can help you with?"

"No", she answered quickly. It was one thing for him to perceive his findings, and then another thing to attempt to solve them for her. "I can't really tell you what I am living through, I'm afraid of what might happen to me if I did."

Looking into her eyes that were now filling with tears, he very gently said, "Angela, you can trust me." "What you say to me goes no further than me." "I just want to help you if I can help you." "I can feel your pain through your writings, and it's a mighty big burden you are carrying." "It doesn't have to be that way, if you will let me help."

Angela looked into his eyes and then back down at her feet. The tears from her eyes dripped down her face. She felt a shudder run up her spine for a brief moment and then she looked back at Mr. Julian. His eyes said that he really did care, but she just could not get the words out, and she didn't know where to start. It was overwhelming, like a volcanic eruption wanting to burst through the iron rock top of the mountain that had grown for years. Angela was not ready to talk just yet. She needed to make sure that he could help her after she told him her life story. If he couldn't, and Drusilla found out that she had talked, Angela would not be alive to see the next day.

"Angela, I'll be here when you are ready to talk, I promise. "I would really like to help if you would let me." "No one should be going through what you are going through, will you promise to come see me when you are ready to talk?" Mr. Julian was sincere. She felt it in her heart. His expression spoke clearer than his words. Mercy and kindness was being extended to her today. Something she had not felt in a long, long time. Not since grandma had taken the three children into her loving arms and given them a home.

"Okay, Mr. Julian," she replied in a whispered voice, drying her eyes on her sleeve. Angela gave him a bit of a smile and looked back down at her feet. Part of her wanted to run into his arms of safety, bursting out with the whole story, and the other part of her restrained the emotional outburst from fear if Drusilla found out that she had 'talked' even this much.

Mr. Julian seemed to understand, as he smiled back at her and wished her a good day. Angela almost tripped out of the 'practice room' as she headed for her next class. Feeling sill from her lack of coordination she smiled to herself, feeling better as she arrived at her next class. Life did not seem as dark today as it had been in the last several years. There was a bit of a light shining at the end of a long tunnel, for her now.

In the days that followed, Angela looked forward to Mr. Julian's class. Eye contact with him reassured her that his promise was still open. In his class, she felt safe from the ongoing torment of life at home and the harassment that her unpopularity caused her at school. Nothing had changed in either situation, but something within herself had changed. Knowing that there was someone in her life that cared for her well being, gave her new hope for a better tomorrow. She gave her all to her assignments in his class and to those she took elsewhere. Mr. Julian's guidance and encouragement somewhat eased the struggle in her life.

Trust had to be earned. Too many people had let her down and so this relationship between herself and Mr. Julian was one that went from being real fragile to one that was a friendship. It was not based on words. The eyes are the window to the soul as it is said, and their eyes communicated what needed to be said for now. Mr. Julian's actions were the turning point that gave way to the growing trust that built between them. Mr. Julian was patient and his words reassuring. Something that gave his credentials more value than any other teacher or person in Angela's life.

Angela's attitude became more positive and bubbly, especially around school. At home Drusilla began to notice and at every chance she got, challenged Angela's cheerfulness with her own tormenting ways. Angela began showing a more resilient attitude toward Drusilla's abusive negativity, and this would only give Drusilla more reason to increase her aggressive and demonstrative behavior toward Angela.

Until one day, when Angela decided that she could take no more abusive treatment from Drusilla. Drusilla had come home in one of her evil moods and was trying to suck out every last joy filled feeling Angela had inside. Nothing that Angela did that evening was good enough for Drusilla. Drusilla was slapping and punching Angela around, kicking her here and there, when suddenly, Angela felt a terrible feeling of anger rise up inside her. She was not going to be Drusilla's punching and kicking bag any longer! She was not going to take any more torment from her! She was not a 'good for nothing!' Drusilla may not have felt that Angela's chores met her inspection, but Angela knew that they had been done to the utmost of her own capabilities, and the way Drusilla had previously approved them. Drusilla was just looking for excuses to beat her up and her dad was allowing her to treat Angela this way, as he sat on his duff watching TV, pretending not to notice Drusilla mistreating his daughter with this unjustified cruelty. For Angela, she had had enough!

Drusilla had given her a five minute time period to get the oven cleaned with nothing but a dish-soapy rag again, and this would be the last time! The time limit was up and Drusilla came into the kitchen knowing full well that the oven would not meet her inspection. Well this time, Angela was NOT going to take the punches like an unresponding 'rag doll'. Angela stood up just as Drusilla came in to kick her in the butt. Angela caught Drusilla by surprise as she slugged Drusilla with all of her might. A look of shock came across Drusilla's face, but within a few seconds she had recovered and was punching Angela all over the kitchen. Angela fought back with everything she had within her. She did not care if she lived or died at this moment. All she knew is that she did not want to ever be the object of Drusilla's torment again.

Angela was losing the battle. This was her first fight ever, and Drusilla had had years of brutal practice on Angela throughout the years. Angela still fought against her with all of her might she had left. The back of her head had hit the refrigerator door handle over and over again. She was dazed, but her fists kept flying out as if in 'auto-pilot'. Drusilla was calling her names with each connecting blow to Angela's body. Blood dripped down from Angela's nose and lips, but Drusilla had barely even a scratch. Drusilla's brothers used to fight her, and that is where she learned her technique.

Angela was losing ground fast. Her might and grip on life was ending with each swing toward Drusilla. Angela was now down on the floor fighting for her life. Drusilla was literally on top of her, throwing her punches into Angela's face and gut. Angela's head was bouncing off the floor. Then Drusilla put both her hands around Angela's neck and squeezed them tightly around her throat. Angela could not breathe. She couldn't even lift another arm toward Drusilla. She thought that at this moment she was going to die. Who cared? She would know that at least she went out fighting.

Suddenly, Drusilla was being lifted of her. Dad must have been thinking the same thought Angela was, because now he was holding Drusilla off Angela with everything he had. Drusilla was stronger than he was, and at this moment, she was fighting him to let her continue her attack on Angela.

Breathing hard, with an evil smirk of victory written all over her face she growled at Angela, "That'll teach you bitch, you don't fucken hit me!" Dad was still holding Drusilla back as she sneered at Angela.

Her dad looked down at her and told her to "get up and go to her room."

Angela did not have to be told twice. She practically crawled all the way to her bedroom, coughing and shaking from the stranglehold Drusilla had had on her. Angela hurt all over. Blood dribbled down her throat and from her nose and lips. It tasted terrible. She could not swallow. Her neck hurt and the passageway for her windpipes seemed blocked for a while after Drusilla's brutal attack. Angela sat on her bed knowing that Drusilla would be coming back after her soon. Angela could not even cry. She was breathing heavily tying to get enough air into her to replace that which had been deprived from her with Drusilla strangled her. Her dad was saying something to Drusilla in the kitchen that she could not quite hear. It did not matter. He had come in, gotten Drusilla off her and given her a few more days of life.

Although Angela had lost this fight, she knew that she was not going to ever be giving to any more. She hated the beatings that Drusilla had given her throughout what seemed her whole lifetime. Beating that she did not deserve. She was tired of being Drusilla's target of torment and her white slave! Yes, she still feared Drusilla, but something inside of her had changed. This was a turning point in her life. One that was not going to let Drusilla continue. There were no more tears. Angela was not going to tolerate or accept any more of Drusilla's abusive attacks toward her. She would even risk losing her life if it came down to it. What did she have to live for in this family anyway? Absolutely nothing!

Angela was right. It was not long before Drusilla headed down the hall toward her room. Without even saying a word to Angela, she knocked Angela off her bed, sending her flying on the floor. She grabbed Angela's mattress of the bed and threw it into the hallway. She then went over to Angela's drawers and closet and emptied them, throwing all her clothes out the window into the backyard.

Angela watched in horror! This woman had gone berserk! Angela tried to get off the floor, when Drusilla came up and knocked her right back down. Kneeling down next to her with her long fingernail piercing her lip she growled her whispered threat, "You are not going to be alive much longer…You are going to die!"

Terror rose up in Angela as Drusilla left her bedroom, dragging the mattress back up the hall and out the backdoor. Angela's ears were humming, as she looked around herself. Her body trembled uncontrollably now. Drusilla's threat scared her more than any threat she had given Angela. Her heart pounded hard in her chest. Angela was gasping for air now, trying desperately to keep from passing out. She was dizzy. What could she do to save her own life?

Angela was not called to supper and no one came to her room to tell her to get to bed. She looked at the springs of her bed frame that was now her bed. She opted for the floor instead and laid down on it. Angela was just about ready to fall asleep when a dark figure walked into her room and lifted her body off the floor. Drusilla tossed her onto the springs as if she was a piece of trash, and walked out slamming the door behind her.

The springs pinched and cut into her flesh. Angela laid there, not moving a muscle. She had the feeling that although the door was shut, Drusilla was not too far away, listening to see if she moved off the springs. The springs hurt her bruised body, but she did not move. Angela could not sleep now; she feared for her life.

The next morning no one came to get her up. The daylight filled her room. Angela did not know what time it was. She listened, but there were no noises in the house. It was a school day so she got up to look at the clock in the livingroom. It was late and she needed to get her butt to school. Her chores would not be done this morning. She quickly got dressed in the only dress Drusilla had left her in her closet, and that was because it had fallen to the floor of her closet.

Instead of going to her first class, she went directly to Mr. Julian's room. She wad decided to take a chance on telling him the whole story of her life. She did not care if Drusilla found out. Drusilla had threatened to kill her, anyway.

Mr. Julian was in the middle of his class, but when he saw her come into the band room, he ushered the class into the practice rooms, then led her into his office and closed the door behind them. "What's up," he asked her.

Angela was still out of breath from running all the way to school, but began to tell him bits and pieces about her life, what had just occurred the night before and Drusilla's threat that now hung over her life now. His eyebrows rose a few times but Mr. Julian listened intently. Angela was shaking badly as she blurted out everything she could, to give him an understanding of what her life was like and what she was having to go through, and how much she feared going home now.

Mr. Julian was without words, when she finished. Astonished, maybe. Not really knowing what to do next. Yes. After what seemed like a long while to Angela, the class bell rang indication that class was over with. She had missed her first class all together. Mr. Julian got up out of his chair and asked her to remain behind while he went to excuse his class. Angela felt uncomfortable and as if she was in his way. Mr. Julian had another class coming into his room, so Angela got up to leave. Seeing her get up, he called out to her, "Are you going to be all right?"

She nodded, as he approached her.

"Thank you for telling me." "I need to think on this awhile.' "By the time we see one another this afternoon, I will try to think what it is that I can do to assist you." "You need to get out of that home." Mr. Julian was out of answers, but was willing to go to the limits to help Angela with her situation. He was willing to become involved, which set him above any teacher she had ever known."

Angela walked nervously to her class. Something inside of her made her feel a bit better, giving her reassurance that she was in the right hands. The hands of someone who really cared and acted on his gut instincts to save one of his students.

By the afternoon, Angela headed eagerly to Mr. Julian's class. What could he do for her? How could he help her get away from Drusilla and the threat she had over her life?

Mr. Julian asked the class to take their seats. Academics first, talk later. He briefly filled her classmates in on their assignment and then beckoned Angela into his office. Closing the door behind her, she asked if "there was any family members, or anyone that she could seek refuge with today?"

She thought hard, but she did not know any. Shaking her head 'no', she looked up at him. This was not the answer he was hoping for.

"Are you sure?" "Think hard." "Where's your sister, Crystal?" he asked her.

Knowing that the two of them were sisters, because Mr. Julian had had either in his classes at one time or in another. He had known that Crystal had graduated and was going to college.

The mention of Crystal's name made Angela perk up. "She ran away from home earlier this year, and I haven't seen her since."

"Do you know where she is at?" He asked.

Angela shook her head and looked down at her feet.

"Any idea at all?" Mr. Julian was persistent. He really wanted to help.

"She might be at her college," Angela answered him.

"Are you sure?" he questioned.

"No, but it is where she was when she ran away.

"Okay, let's try reaching her." "Do you think that she will be able to come and get you?"

Angela shrugged her shoulders. It had been months since her sister had left, and she did not know anything about Crystal now.

"Well, I think it will be worth a try." Mr. Julian was not going to give up on finding his student a safe-haven. He was going above and beyond the letter of his duties and was now being moved by compassion for his duties. His students' lives mattered to him. Anything that stood in the way from them achieving all they could achieve was his battle, and not just theirs.

Angela looked up at Mr. Julian with a hopeful smile. He was going the distance for her. She could not put into words how much this meant to her. He was really something special. A stranger that was willing to walk a mile in her shoes to save her life and to give her life by giving her hope. Mr. Julian cared enough not to give up or give in. Reassuring her that he hoped everything worked out, he would get in touch with her sister's college.

Angela headed to her next class. She trusted Mr. Julian. There was only one more day before school let out for the summer. She knew she would not be able to live through the summer, let alone the next twenty-four hours if she was sent home after school. Her mind was stayed on her home situation and what was transpiring between Mr. Julian and herself.

The bell rang and she rushed back to Mr. Julian's class. When he saw her he was smiling. "Your sister is still registered at the college as a student there and they promise to get in touch with her." "I explained to them that this was an emergency, so we should be hearing from them tomorrow."

'Tomorrow', the word itself sounded awful. How would she get through one more night at home? Would she make it? Mr. Julian's news was good, and then again, for survival reasons, it sounded terrible.

"Now I know what else we can do to settle things for you." "You do have a counselor you can speak to if you'd like to."

"No", she shook her head. Drusilla would really find out, if she did. Angela could not trust any of the 'office staff' at the school. She did not know them, and with the history of how often Drusilla had obtained information on Angela's behavior at school, no one could be trusted. Angela looked up at Mr. Julian. "Can we keep this between ourselves?"

"Well, I've already told a few people about this, in order to get some information and some advice."

Angela knew that it was probably policy and procedure, but if Drusilla found out, she may not live through tonight. The thought made her shiver.

"Do you have a place to stay for tonight?" Mr. Julian asked.

"I guess, I'm going to have to go home." "I don't know where else I could go, I don't know anywhere except school and home."

There were no guarantees that her sister would be responding to the S.O.S. call her teacher had made for her. So uncertainty tied her to going home and facing whatever lay ahead. Angela left the school grounds knowing that she was already going to be in trouble for not doing her chores this morning, so she ran home with all her might, hoping to arrive home before Drusilla did to do them.

The few breaks she had gotten in life, struck once more. Drusilla had not been home all day. Angela dressed into her work clothes and headed out the backdoor to do them. Finishing the outside chores, she raced in to do her inside chores. Supper was placed into the oven, and then she set the table. A car drove up into the driveway. Goose bumps lifted on her whole body as she began to tremble. Her legs felt like rubber now as she placed the last utensil next to her dad's place setting. There was nowhere she could go to hide; it would do any good if she could.

The front door opened and then closed behind the person who had entered. Angela shook with fright, feeling herself grow weak. If this was Drusilla, would this be her last moment of life? She froze, as she listened.

"Hello, any body home?" It was her dad! She let out a sigh, almost dropping to her knees from the relief.

"I...I...g-g-o-t my chores done," she stammered.

"Good, is supper ready?"

"No...I...I just put it into the oven." Angela answered him.

Her dad glanced at the table and headed into his bedroom, closing the door behind him. There was a distance between them tonight. She wanted to tell him that Drusilla had threatened her life, but the way her dad was acting toward her tonight, he would probably think that she had it coming. Afterall, Angela had tried to defend herself yesterday. But how it probably looked to him was the way Drusilla had stated it to him..."the little bitch attacked her."

Angela headed to her bedroom to wait for dinner to finish cooking. She was hungry. She had been without food for over thirty hours. Tonight she had made meatloaf; it was all she could find to make. There wasn't much else in the house. Drusilla had not done grocery shopping, so tonight, she might even be joining the rest of the family in having meatloaf.

Drusilla arrived home, just as Angela was taking the dinner out of the oven. Drusilla called the boys to the table and her dad came out of his bedroom. Angela placed the meal on the table and went to take her seat when Drusilla told her to "go to her room." "A bitch like you doesn't deserve to eat."

Angela looked at Drusilla with surprise. "I am hungry.'

Drusilla rose up from her chair. Angela did not need an engraved invitation to leave the room. She got up and walked passed Drusilla to go to her room. Drusilla shoved her as Angela walked by, which caused Angela to trip going up the steps from the dining room into the livingroom. She slammed her hands against the doorway as she tried to break her fall.

"Remember that promise I made to you last night." "I was not kidding." Drusilla reminded in a tone that let Angela know she was not joking. Revenge would be hers. It was Drusilla's intention to kill her.

Angela shook as she walked to her room. If only she could make it through this night, there would be hope of 'getting out' tomorrow. Her heart pounded and her chest ached. She had just to get through the night. She was tired because not only was this a stressful situation, but also because she had only slept a couple hours the night before.

Her family finished their meal and she was sent in to do the dishes and clean the kitchen. Being around Drusilla was pure unadulterated terror for her. Her body shook with fear as Drusilla's continued presence intimidated her. Pots and pans were slammed into the back of her head as Drusilla told her that they were not clean enough. Angela held her breath, squeezing her fists tightly together, hoping that she would not lose it. Any 'replays' of the previous night would most definitely prove lethal for her. Drusilla was coaxing her on, every moment, trying to push her to the brink, giving her every excuse to kill Angela, and claim it self-defense.

Angela held on. There was no way she would give the Amazon the ticket she needed to kill her and get away with it. Tomorrow would be her last chance for freedom, and right now, that hope, meant everything to her.

23

Escape to Freedom

The warm fresh air of the pre-summer morning brought about an awakening of promise for Angela today. She had made it through the night, upon her bed of springs. She had even suppressed the tension Drusilla inflicted in her little attacks of cruelty to challenge her with last evening. Hope for a final escape from this tormented life, gave strength to her weary and beaten body now.

Angela quickly dressed in the dress she had worn the previous day, as Drusilla had not returned any of her clothes to her. The house was cleaned and the outside chores done for what she now hoped would be her last time. Giving all the animals a hug and a squeeze or a pat as if to say her goodbyes, she headed through the house and out the front door.

The wind blew through her hair as she raced to school to see if Mr. Julian had heard anything from her sister yet. Arriving at his classroom, she saw him in his office with another student. Angela turned to leave when he saw her and asked her to wait. She set down her things on a chair and paced eagerly between the classroom door and his office. The bell rang, which ushered his first period students through the door and into his classroom. Finally his office door opened and he greeted her.

"Good morning Angela," came his friendly greeting. His warm smile embraced her with the confidence she needed to respond.

"Hi," she said as he ushered her into his office. "Did my sister call?" she anxiously asked.

Mr. Julian turned and smiled. "Yes, she did call, and she will be calling back this morning." "I thought that I could contact you when her call comes back in." "Can I have a list of your classes, so I know where to get you when she calls?"

Angela gave him her schedule for the day. Her insides were jumping for joy!" Crystal was going to call her back! Crystal knew what life was for her, and there would be no way she would not come and get her out, especially if she knew that Drusilla had threatened to really kill her. Tears of happiness and excitement ran down her face after all the plans were made to get in touch with Angela as soon as her sister's call came in.

This was the last day of school and there would not be any other chances for her to get out of her abusive family home. She had to leave today, or she may not be alive to ever leave it. Drusilla had said that she would not be living much longer, and Angela meant business; she had restated her threat just last night. Angela feared for her life, but at this moment, it looked as if she might not have to ever face Drusilla again. She hoped that today would give her, her ticket to freedom.

This, being the last day of school, there was no real class work being assigned. It was a day of receiving test scores back, asking questions about the test results and in most of her classes, her peers were discussing what they were doing for the summer. Her mind was thinking about her sister coming to rescue her. What if she couldn't show? A shiver went through her spine. There was no way that she could go home tonight. She felt fear enter her body at the thought of not being rescued. Worry set in. She would have to block out the doubt, it was putting her into a panic. She would just have to trust that Crystal would come to get her.

Midway through class, Angela was called out. Mr. Julian had beckoned her to come back to his class. She quickly ran back to the band room. As she entered his office, he handed her the telephone. Putting the receiver up to her head, she heard a familiar voice that she had not heard in months.

"Angela, is that you?" "What's the matter?" Crystal asked.

Angela choked up and sobs poured out. Tears streaming down her face as she tried to tell Crystal everything about the last two nights and Drusilla's threat of death to her. Her body shook with fear. "Drusilla's going to kill me." "She's taken all my clothes and my mattress off my bed." "I...I...fought back when she tried to beat me...I couldn't take it any longer...and now she wants to kill me." Angela sobbed hysterically, letting years of torment pour out of her soul.

"Angela, I need to know what happened." "Talk slower." Crystal wanted the whole story.

"Crystal, please just come and get me." "I'm scared of dying." "Please, just come and get me." Angela begged with everything in her.

Crystal explained that it would have to be 'the end of the day before she came to get her'.

Angela listened intently as Crystal told her where to meet her directly after school. Angela's heart pounded. She was afraid to have to wait all day, there was no telling if Drusilla would show up to pick her up or if someone in the office would notify Drusilla before Crystal got there after school. This was the only way Angela could get to freedom. She would have to wait to meet Crystal.

The rest of the day was a complete blur. Nothing, but the thought of freedom passed through her mind. She thought about every instruction her sister had given her. She would be there immediately after the bell rang, because her sister said that she would not wait long. Angela would have to pop down in the back seat until they got out of town. Crystal would be taking her back to the place she was staying, but she would not say where it was on the telephone. Crystal still feared Drusilla and did not want to get caught in town by her.

In between now and the time the last school bell rang, Angela hoped that nothing would interfere with her escape from the tormented life of agony she had lived since Drusilla came into their lives. She also hoped that the inside office informants Drusilla had regular contact with had not received or sent any information to Drusilla, or it might be Drusilla meeting her after school and not Crystal. A shudder went through her body on that last thought. No, please no Drusilla, Angela thought. Let this day get over and let Crystal come and get her. This was her last hope on life.

****

Time almost seemed to come to a stand still as she waited for the last hour of the school day to end. One minute to go. There was empty chatter all around her, but nothing mattered or could redirect her attention from the second hand on the clock. Everyone seemed to have plans for the entire summer. Right now, all Angela could concentrate on was being able to get where she was supposed to meet her sister on time, and hoping nothing fouled up any of the plans for her rescue and freedom.

Her heart pounded. What lay ahead was a scary step in itself and then dealing with the unknown of what tomorrow held for her. She was only sixteen, and if caught, could legally be sent back to live with Drusilla until she was eighteen. The thought made her tremble in fear. Drusilla meant what she said, and now Angela had gotten authorities involved and there was no going back. She would not live to see her senior year of high school, let alone next week if she returned home. Drusilla had already been investigated in Wisconsin for child abuse and had left the state before the verdict on the investigation was in. Their move to California made them fugitives. The paperwork never caught up.

The last bell of the school year sounded. Angela jumped out of her seat and was more than halfway down the hallway before the others even got out the door. She ran straight toward the parking lot. Mr. Julian was standing just outside his classroom doorway wishing her well as she ran passed him. She yelled back a thank you as she reached the parking lot.

There were cars all over waiting for other students, but none she could see that held her sister. Panic and fear embraced her. Angela surveyed the parking lot repeatedly. Where was Crystal? She was shaking and having a hard time breathing from the panic and anxiety.

Suddenly a horn honked at her as it pulled into the parking lot. Angela ran nervously toward it as her sister waved at her to hurry and get in. She held the rear passenger door open as Angela climbed in. A blanket was thrown over her, Crystal climbed back into the front passenger seat, and they were off. As quickly as they had pulled into the parking lot, they left it, hurrying to get out of the city.

Beneath the blanket, it was hot, but Angela knew the consequences of getting out from under it before they got out of the city. With all the big yellow school buses driving by them, they did not know if one of them would be Drusilla's. Crystal talked to her as her boyfriend drove the car.

"Now explain to me what made Drusilla threaten to kill you this time."

"Try to, she was going to." "I didn't want to get beat up any more, it got worse after you left, and I was tired of it." "So I defended myself." Angela explained from beneath the blankets.

"You what?" Crystal asked astonished. "She could have killed you right then and there!"

"I know, she tried, but dad got her off of me." "I was tired of getting beat up." "Maybe I just wanted to die, I don't know." "She went crazy on me." "She didn't kill me then but she wanted to, I know it.

However, she wouldn't do it with him in the house." "Dad got her off of me and sent me to my bedroom before she could totally waste me." "That's when she came and took all my stuff away; including my mattress, and then told me she was going to kill me." Angela continued to relate the turn of events that lead to her request to be rescued. "She even reminded me of the threat last night, while she was trying to get me mad last night." "Hitting me in the head with pots and pans and anything she could find." "You should feel the bumps on my head." "Last night I held it in, because I knew if I didn't, she would have killed me right then, saying she was defending herself." "The woman is a psycho." "I wouldn't be here if I had given in to her challenges." Angela was sweating beneath the blanket.

"How is Christopher?" Crystal asked her sister

I feel sorry for him now, but I don't think he ever had it as bad as us girls did." "I think he might survive." Angela thought about the words that had just come from her mouth. How would her brother get by now? Getting out herself was a huge miracle in itself, but what would life be life for him now? Angela pondered the thoughts that were now racing through her head. What would happen to her brother?

The atmosphere inside the car was quiet. They were out on the highway headed for an unknown destination. Angela could feel a slight breeze as it blew up under the blanket giving her somewhat of a relief from the heat. Fear had not totally left her. She was under age and leaving hell the place, she had called home for so many years, very lucky to be alive. She did not know what normal life was. She did not know what to expect. She was afraid of everything, feeling like a fish out of water.

Family services were called in, but the investigation stopped before it got started. Drusilla had not lost her ability to lie, nor her dad to charm them. They did not even get beyond a first stage interview or do an investigation that would lead them back to the records in Wisconsin. Their brother had to remain in the hell home, while Angela was allowed to remain with the woman who had taken her sister in, previously. Both her dad and Drusilla knew where she was, for on her eighteenth birthday she received a birthday card from them.

****

After leaving the hell she had called home for many years, Angela finished high school early and went on to graduate from both College and

University. Throughout her years, she had learned to survive. She knew that if she wanted something, she would have to work at it. No one stood ready to come to her aid and hand her a better life. She had been rescued twice, and set on her feet. Once by her grandmother, and once by a wonderful teacher who 'got involved' and did more than just teach his students; he cared for them. Angela was not to become a statistic in society. She knew how to fight for her life, and knew the odds that stood against her. Determined to prove her dad and Drusilla wrong, that 'she'd never amount to anything', Angela kept her promise to her teacher; that she would become all she could be. She would believe in herself and not in her circumstance. A circumstance that many times almost cost her, her life.

Life is better at handing out critics than it is at handing out encouragers and motivators. If you want to get somewhere in life, do not let the past hold you back. Let go and move forward, because no one listens to excuses, and there are not many who care. Today is a new day. Let your experience be turned into today's blessings to others. Others are more impressed when they find out later, on what has made you who you are today. Angela has a great compassion for the lost and hurting. She has counseled many and given them the encouragement and motivation to move on. She is alive today, because someone cared and took a risk for her freedom. In return, she risked taking the new journeys and giving everything she had to rise above what yesterday tried to do to hold her back.

****

She is watching the reflection on her sunroom window, as the Canadian Geese make their return to the Midwest after a long winter's blast of dark and dreary scorn. The sun is shining now and the robins have returned. The essence of lilac fills her senses as she stirs her morning tea, smiling quietly to herself, knowing there is a Savior.

Angela's life was not easy after leaving her childhood home. Being faced with new realities unfamiliar to her, led her in directions uncommon to most people. Travel further into Angela's life in

K. Belle Draper's next Novel ~ Based on a True Story in "Life's Journey ~ A Search for Love."

*K. Belle Draper's next Novel, "Life's Journeys-Looking For Love", will be out late 2004.

To receive updates on published materials or a copy of the monthly newsletter, please write: Belle Enterprise
          1011 Washington Street
        Pekin, Illinois 61554
                Email: bellentrprzs@bitwisesystems.com

My Fate Broken
By K. Belle Draper
...©K. Belle Draper 1997

I was bruised, battered, rejected and torn growing up as a child,
Entered adulthood with self destructive baggage,
Guaranteed to torment and beckon me to eternal hell fires,
The world as I knew it was so cruel and so savage.

The darkness of this world's pleasures groped my life,
From one turmoil to the next I crawled,
Gut wrenching society plagues of torment and strife,
Self-gratification, loveless, empty and outlawed.

I cried out in the darkness, at the gates of hell,
Heart torn abuse had stolen my soul.
The grave awaited my tormented body, and hell awaited my soul when I fell.
No rest, no peace from Satan's fiery chamber below.

Silence surrounded me; no answers from the darkness came,
Taunted by the shadows in the dark dim night.
Given up to surrender it all, no one to take the blame,
No one to care, no one was there, nothing inside me left to fight.

Down to my knees I fell,
Ready to give up, and use my free ticket to hell.
Tears streamed down my cheeks as always before,
One last cry out in the darkness, could not take any more.

Slumped over, waiting for life to pass, and declaring the end,
Suddenly a gentle soothing voice called out my name,
I lifted my head to the call,
Looking to see from whence it came.

His gentle voice melted my heart like never before,

Pouring out love filled with compassion from the window of Heaven's golden door.
Embracing my torn and battered life with the greatest promises of His Word.
Reaching up, I said 'yes', like a child, His love assured.

Love healed me and cleansed me from life's wrenching past,
Saved me from the torment of hate and rejection, at last.
Bringing joy and rejoicing, a song to my heart.
Salvation, newness; a brand new start.

He will never leave me, nor forsake me like all the rest,
Could not ask for more, He has given me His best.

BIOGRAPHICAL SKETCH

K. Belle Draper is a graduate of Almeda College and University, Iowa, with the degree, rank and academic status of Bachelor of Science, with a major in Business Administration-Distinction. She also has her Associates in Administration of Justice/Law Enforcement from Mt. San Antonio College, California.

She is the mother of one son. She has had editorials, short stories, poems and recipes published in the past with various publications, however; this is her first Novel ~ based on a true story, which is first in a three-part series.

K. Belle Draper writes using full graphical description, so that you, the audience can feel, experience, and be moved, with compassion to join her in her fight against child abuse and child neglect in this nation. The foul language used, was that of the individuals who were the abusers in this Novel ~ based on a true story. The story is told the way it happened. Reality is fact. Be prepared to suffer with the child whose story this is. Names and places have been changed to protect the innocent. This Novel was written to be the voice of the innocent child.

The statistics are astounding! Nearly one million children are the victims of abuse and neglect each year, and yet child abuse seems to be a growing epidemic in the United States and throughout the world.

Portions of the proceeds from the sales of this Novel will be sent to such organizations that provide "safe houses" for abused children and those organizations that help 'social service departments' locate children who have been absconded by parental fugitives.

Educational programs should be enhanced to train those people who work with children on how to identify child abuse and what steps to take in protecting a child you are aware or suspect is being abused. Turning a blind eye can and will cost a child his/her life. Give an abused child a chance at life and be a hero. Turn in child abuse, but first make sure the child is safe. Contact your local authorities to report child abuse. Get involved. Do not give up until the child is safe.

If you are a child who is being abused by parents or anyone else, please call 911, tell a school counselor or teacher, go to a 'safe house' and call social services. Or call 1-800-555-1212 and ask for the child abuse hotline in your area.

- Discounts for this Novel are given on multiple orders exceeding 100 (one hundred) count.

100 count = 10% discount
1000 count = 25% discount
500 count = 15% discount
5000 count = 30% discount

All Companies or Educational institutions must include tax exempt numbers with your orders if not paying tax.
No refunds given.
- For _single_ orders of 25 count, a free book is given.

All orders must be 'paid for' in advance.
Illinois residents add 8% tax.
Individual copy orders are $13.97
Tax for Illinois residents $ 1.12
Total cost $15.09
Add $4.00 per book S&H on single book orders.
Call for S & H prices for caseload.

You may copy or tear out this page and send with your payment on individual orders.
Larger orders must be called in, emailed or faxed in.

A. The Tears and Fears of a Childhood ____
B. Life's Journey ~ A Search for Love ____

Name & Address	Phone Number	Quantity Ordered	Estimated Total Cost

Please send orders to: Belle Enterprises, 1011 Washington Street
                                            Pekin, Illinois 61554
bellentrprzs@bitwisesystems.com   (309)353-4768
For those requesting a public speaking engagement by the author, or for a 'book signing', please call or write with request and we will mail you the 'Speaking/Book Signing' packet to fill out and return.